PRAISE FOR *MIRROR IMAGE* AND
#1 *NEW YORK TIMES* BESTSELLING AUTHOR
SANDRA BROWN

"Sandra Brown is a master at weaving a story of suspense into a tight web that catches and holds the reader from the first page to the last."　　　　　*—Library Journal*

"A master storyteller."　　　*—Newport News Daily Press*

"Author Sandra Brown proves herself top-notch."
　　　　　　　　　　　　　　　—Associated Press

"She knows how to keep the tension high and the plot twisting and turning."　　　　　　*—Fresno Bee*

"Brown's storytelling gift [is] surprisingly rare, even among crowd-pleasers."　　　　　　*—Toronto Sun*

"A novelist who can't write them fast enough."
　　　　　　　　　　　—San Antonio Express-News

"Sandra Brown is known for her memorable storytelling."
　　　　　　　　　　　　　　　—Tulsa World

"Plotting and pacing are Brown's considerable strengths."
　　　　　　　　　　　—San Jose Mercury News

SANDRA BROWN

MIRROR IMAGE

GRAND CENTRAL
PUBLISHING

NEW YORK   BOSTON

Grand Central Publishing
Hachette Book Group
1290 Avenue of the Americas
New York, NY 10104
Visit our website at www.HachetteBookGroup.com

Grand Central Publishing is a division of Hachette Book Group, Inc. The Grand Central Publishing name and logo is a trademark of Hachette Book Group, Inc.

The Hachette Speakers Bureau provides a wide range of authors for speaking events. To find out more, go to www.hachettespeakersbureau.com or call (866) 376-6591.

The publisher is not responsible for websites (or their content) that are not owned by the publisher.

Printed in the United States of America

First printing: June 1990
Reissued: July 1995, September 2001, October 2003, October 2011

43 42 41 40

PROLOGUE

The hell of it was that it couldn't have been a better day for flying. The January sky was cloudless and so blue it was almost painful to look at. Visibility was unlimited. There was a cool, harmless breeze out of the north.

Airport traffic was moderate to heavy at that time of day, but efficient ground crews were keeping to schedules. No planes were circling, awaiting permission to land, and there were only a couple of aircraft in line to take off.

It was an ordinary Friday morning at the San Antonio International Airport. The only thing the passengers of AireAmerica's Flight 398 had found troublesome was getting into the airport itself. Road construction on 410 West, the major freeway artery in front of the airport, had caused bumper-to-bumper traffic for nearly a mile.

Yet ninety-seven passengers had boarded on schedule, stowing carryon baggage in overhead compartments, buckling up, settling into their seats with books, magazines, newspapers. The cockpit crew routinely went through the preflight check. Flight attendants joked among themselves as they loaded up drink dollies and brewed coffee that would never be poured. A final head count was taken and anxious standby passengers were allowed to board. The jetway was withdrawn. The plane taxied to the end of the runway.

The captain's friendly drawl came over the speakers and informed his passengers that they were next in line on the runway. After he reported that the current weather conditions in their destination city of Dallas were perfect, he instructed the attendants to prepare for takeoff.

Neither he nor anyone on board guessed that Flight 398 would be airborne less than thirty seconds.

"Irish!"

"Hmm?"

"A plane just went down at the airport."

Irish McCabe's head snapped up. "Crashed?"

"And burning. It's a hell of a fire at the end of the runway."

The news director dropped the latest Nielsen ratings onto his messy desk. Moving with admirable agility for a man of his age and untended physical condition, Irish rounded the corner of his desk and barreled through the door of his private glass cubicle, almost mowing down the reporter who had brought him the bulletin from the newsroom.

"Taking off or landing?" he asked over his shoulder.

"Unconfirmed."

"Survivors?"

"Unconfirmed."

"Airline or private craft?"

"Unconfirmed."

"Hell, are you sure there's even been a crash?"

A somber group of reporters, photographers, secretaries, and gofers had already collected at the bank of police radios. Irish elbowed them aside and reached for a volume knob.

". . . runway. No sign of survivors at this time. Airport firefighting equipment is rushing toward the site. Smoke and flames are evident. Choppers are airborne. Ambulances are—"

Irish began barking orders louder than the radios, which were squawking noisily. "You," he said, pointing toward the male reporter who had barged into his office only seconds earlier, "take a live remote unit and get the hell out there on the double.'' The reporter and a video cameraman peeled away from the group and raced for the exit. ''Who called this in?'' Irish wanted to know.

''Martinez. He was driving to work and got caught up in traffic on 410.''

''Is he standing by?''

''He's still there, talking on his car phone.''

''Tell him to get as close to the wreckage as he can, and shoot as much video as possible until the mobile unit arrives. Let's get a chopper in the air, too. Somebody get on the phone and chase down the pilot. Meet him at the heliport.''

He scanned the faces, looking for one in particular. ''Ike still around?'' he asked, referring to the morning news anchorman.

''He's in the john taking a crap.''

''Go get him. Tell him to get on the studio set. We'll do a break-in bulletin. I want a statement from somebody in the tower, from the airport officials, the airline, police—*something* to go on the air with before the NTSB boys put a gag on everybody. Get on it, Hal. Somebody else call Avery at home. Tell her—''

''Can't. She's going to Dallas today, remember?''

''Shit. I forgot. No, wait,'' Irish said, snapping his fingers and looking hopeful. ''She might still be at the airport. If she is, she'll be there ahead of everyone else. If she can get into the AireAmerica terminal, she can cover the story from the human interest angle. When she calls in, I want to be notified immediately.''

Eager for an update, he turned back to the radios. Adrenaline rushed through his system. This would mean he would have no weekend. It meant overtime and headaches, cold meals and stale coffee, but Irish was in his element. There was nothing like a good plane crash to round out a news week and boost ratings.

Tate Rutledge stopped his car in front of the house. He waved to the ranch foreman who was pulling out of the driveway in his pickup. A mongrel, mostly collie, bounded up and tackled him around the knees.

"Hey, Shep." Tate reached down and petted the dog's shaggy head. The dog looked up at him with unabashed hero worship.

Tens of thousands of people regarded Tate Rutledge with that same kind of reverent devotion. There was a lot about the man to admire. From the crown of his tousled brown hair to the toes of his scuffed boots, he was a man's man and a woman's fantasy.

But for every ardent admirer, he had an equally ardent enemy.

Instructing Shep to stay outdoors, he entered the wide foyer of the house and peeled off his sunglasses. His boot heels echoed on the quarry tile flooring as he headed toward the kitchen, where he could smell coffee brewing. His stomach rumbled, reminding him that he hadn't eaten before making the early round trip to San Antonio. He fantasized about a breakfast steak, grilled to perfection; a pile of fluffy scrambled eggs; and a few slices of hot, buttered toast. His stomach growled more aggressively.

His parents were in the kitchen, seated at the round oak table that had been there for as long as Tate could remember. As he walked in, his mother turned toward him, a stricken expression on her face. She was alarmingly pale. Nelson Rutledge, his father, immediately left his place at the table and moved toward him, arms outstretched.

"Tate."

"What's going on?" he asked, puzzled. "To look at the two of you, you'd think somebody just died."

Nelson winced. "Weren't you listening to your car radio?"

"No. Tapes. Why?" The first stirring of panic seized his heart. "What the hell's happened?" His eyes flickered to the portable television on the tile countertop. It had been the focus of his parents' attention when he walked in.

"Tate," Nelson said in an emotionally ragged voice, "Channel Two just broke into 'Wheel of Fortune' with a news bulletin. A plane crashed on takeoff a few minutes ago at the airport." Tate's chest rose and fell on a quick, soundless gasp.

"It's still unconfirmed exactly which flight number it

was, but they think—'' Nelson stopped and shook his head mournfully. At the table, Zee crammed a damp Kleenex to her compressed lips.

"Carole's plane?" Tate asked hoarsely.

Nelson nodded.

Sandra Brown

"How long . . . to respond?"

". . . patience . . . trauma like this injures more . . . the body."

"What will . . . look like when . . . is finished"

". . . surgeon tomorrow. He'll . . . procedure with you."

"When?"

". . . no longer danger . . . infection."

"Will . . . effects on the fetus?"

"Fetus? Your wife wasn't pregnant."

The words were meaningless. They hurtled toward her like meteors out of a dark void. She wanted to dodge them, because they intruded on the peaceful nothingness. She craved the bliss of knowing and feeling absolutely nothing, so she tuned out the voices and sank once again into the cushiony pillows of forgetfulness.

"Mrs. Rutledge? Can you hear me?"

Reflexively, she responded, and a low moan escaped her sore chest. She tried to lift her eyelids, but she couldn't do it. One was prized open and a beam of light painfully pierced her skull. At last the hateful light was extinguished.

"She's coming out of it. Notify her husband immediately," the disembodied voice said. She tried turning her head in its direction, but found it impossible to move. "Have you got the number of their hotel handy?"

"Yes, Doctor. Mr. Rutledge gave it to all of us in case she came to while he wasn't here."

Lingering tendrils of the gray mist evaporated. Words she couldn't previously decipher now linked up with recognizable definitions in her brain. She understood the words, and yet they made no sense.

"I know you're experiencing a great deal of discomfort, Mrs. Rutledge. We're doing everything possible to alleviate that. You won't be able to speak, so don't try. Just relax. Your family will be here shortly."

Her rapid pulse reverberated through her head. She wanted to breathe, but she couldn't. A machine was breathing for her. Through a tube in her mouth, air was being pumped directly into her lungs.

Experimentally she tried opening her eyes again. One was coaxed into opening partially. Through the slit, she could see fuzzy light. It hurt to focus, but she concentrated on doing so until indistinct forms began to take shape.

Yes, she was in a hospital. That much she had known.

But how? Why? It had something to do with the nightmare she had left behind in the mist. She didn't want to remember it now, so she left it alone and dwelled on the present.

She was immobile. Her arms and legs wouldn't move no matter how hard she concentrated. Nor could she move her head. She felt like she was sealed inside a stiff cocoon. The paralysis terrified her. Was it permanent?

Her heart started beating more furiously. Almost immediately a presence materialized at her side. "Mrs. Rutledge, there's no need to be afraid. You're going to be fine."

"Her heart rate is too high," a second presence remarked from the other side of her bed.

"She's just scared, I think." She recognized the first voice. "She's disoriented—doesn't know what to make of all this."

A form clothed in white bent over her. "Everything's going to be all right. We've called Mr. Rutledge and he's on his way. You'll be glad to see him, won't you? He's so relieved that you've regained consciousness."

"Poor thing. Can you imagine waking up and having this to cope with?"

"I can't imagine living through a plane crash."

An unvoiced scream echoed loudly through her head.

She remembered!

Screaming metal. Screaming people. Smoke, dense and black. Then flames, and stark terror.

She had automatically performed the emergency instructions drilled into her by hundreds of flight attendants on as many flights.

Once she had escaped the burning fuselage, she began running blindly through a world bathed in red blood and black smoke. Even though it was agonizing to run, she did so, clutching—

Clutching what? She remembered it was something precious—something she had to carry to safety.

She remembered falling. As she had gone down, she had

taken what she had then believed to be her last look at the world. She hadn't even felt the pain of colliding with the hard ground. By then she had been enveloped by oblivion, which until now had protected her from the agony of remembering.

"Doctor!"

"What is it?"

"Her heartbeat has escalated dramatically."

"Okay, let's take her down a bit. Mrs. Rutledge," the doctor said imperiously, "calm down. Everything is all right. There is nothing to worry about."

"Dr. Martin, Mr. Rutledge just arrived."

"Keep him outside until we've stabilized her."

"What's the matter?" The new voice seemed to come from miles away, but carried a ring of authority.

"Mr. Rutledge, please give us a few—"

"Carole?"

She was suddenly aware of him. He was very close, bending over her, speaking to her with soft reassurance. "You're going to be fine. I know you're frightened and worried, but you're going to be all right. So is Mandy, thank God. She has a few broken bones and some superficial burns on her arms. Mom's staying in the hospital room with her. She's going to be fine. Hear me, Carole? You and Mandy survived, and that's what's important now."

There was a bright fluorescent light directly behind his head, so his features were indistinct, but she could piece together enough strong features to form a vague impression of what he looked like. She clung to each comforting word he spoke. And because he spoke them with such conviction, she believed them.

She reached for his hand—or rather, tried to. He must have sensed her silent plea for human contact because he placed his hand lightly upon her shoulder.

Her anxiety began to wane at his touch, or perhaps because the powerful sedative that had been injected into her IV began to take effect. She allowed herself to be lured, feeling safer somehow by having this stranger with the compelling voice beside her, within reach.

"She's drifting off. You can leave now, Mr. Rutledge."

"I'm staying."

She closed her eye, blotting out his blurred image. The drug was seductive. It gently rocked her like a small boat, lulling her into the safe harbor of uncaring.

Who is Mandy? she wondered.

Was she supposed to know this man who referred to her as Carole?

Why did everyone keep calling her Mrs. Rutledge?

Did everybody think she was married to him?

They were wrong, of course.

She didn't even know him.

He was there when she woke up again. Minutes, hours, days could have elapsed for all she knew. Since time had no relevance in an intensive care unit, her disorientation was augmented further.

The moment she opened her eye, he leaned over her and said, "Hi."

It was nerve-racking, not being able to see him clearly. Only one of her eyes would open. She realized now that her head was swathed in bandages and that's why she couldn't move it. As the doctor had warned her, she couldn't speak. The lower portion of her face seemed to have solidified.

"Can you understand me, Carole? Do you know where you are? Blink if you can understand me."

She blinked.

He made a motion with his hand. She thought he raked it through his hair, but she couldn't be certain. "Good," he said with a sigh. "They said you shouldn't be upset by anything, but knowing you, you'll want all the facts. Am I right?"

She blinked.

"Do you remember boarding the airplane? It was the day before yesterday. You and Mandy were going to shop in Dallas for a few days. Do you remember the crash?"

She tried desperately to convey to him that she wasn't Carole and didn't know who Mandy was, but she blinked in response to his question about the crash.

"Only fourteen of you survived."

She didn't realize that her eye was shedding tears until he

used a tissue to blot them away. His touch was gentle for a
man with such strong-looking hands.

"Somehow—God knows how—you were able to get out
of the burning wreckage with Mandy. Do you remember
that?"

She didn't blink.

"Well, it doesn't matter. However you managed it, you
saved her life. She's upset and frightened, naturally. I'm
afraid her injuries are more emotional than physical, and
therefore harder to deal with. Her broken arm has been set.
No permanent damage was done. She won't even need skin
grafts for the burns. You," and here he gave her a penetrating stare, "you protected her with your own body."

She didn't comprehend his stare, but it was almost as
though he doubted the facts as he knew them. He was the
first to break the stare and continue with his explanation.

"The NTSB's investigating. They found the black recorder box. Everything seemed normal, then one of the
engines just blew up. That ignited the fuel. The plane
became a fireball. But before the fuselage was completely
engulfed in flames, you managed to get out through an
emergency exit onto the wing, carrying Mandy with you.

"One of the other survivors said he saw you struggling to
unlatch her seat belt. He said the three of you found your
way to the door through the smoke. Your face was already
covered with blood, he said, so the injuries to it must have
happened on impact."

She remembered none of these details. All she recalled
was the terror of thinking she was going to die the suffocat-
ing death of smoke inhalation, if she didn't burn to death
first. He was giving her credit for operating courageously
during a disaster. All she had done was react to every living
creature's survival instinct.

Perhaps the memories of the tragedy would unfold gradually.
Perhaps they never would. She wasn't certain she wanted to
remember. Reliving those terrifying minutes following the
crash would be like experiencing hell again.

If only fourteen passengers had survived, then scores had
died. That she had survived perplexed her. By a twist of

fate, she had been selected to live, and she would never know why.

Her vision grew blurry and she realized that she was crying again. Wordlessly, he applied the tissue to her exposed eye. "They tested your blood for gases and decided to put you on a respirator. You've got a concussion, but there was no serious head injury. You broke your right tibia when you jumped from the wing.

"Your hands are bandaged and in splints because of burns. Thank God, though, that all your injuries, except for the smoke inhalation, were external.

"I know you're concerned about your face," he said uneasily. "I won't bullshit you, Carole. I know you don't want me to."

She blinked. He paused, gazing down at her with uncertainty. "Your face sustained serious damage. I've retained the best plastic surgeon in the state. He specializes in reconstructive surgery on accident and trauma victims just like you."

Her eye was blinking furiously now, not with understanding, but with anxiety. Feminine vanity had asserted itself, even though she was lying flat on her back in a hospital ICU, lucky to be alive. She wanted to know just how badly her face had been damaged. Reconstructive surgery sounded ominous.

"Your nose was broken. So was one cheekbone. The other cheekbone was pulverized. That's why your eye is bandaged. There's nothing there to support it."

She made a small sound of pure terror. "No, you didn't lose your eye. That's a blessing. Your upper jawbone was also broken. But this surgeon can repair it—all of it. Your hair will grow back. You'll have dental implants that will look exactly like your front teeth."

She had no teeth and no hair.

"We've brought him pictures of you—recent pictures, taken from every angle. He'll be able to reconstruct your features perfectly. The burns on your face affected only the outer skin, so you won't have to have grafts. When the skin peels, it will be like taking off ten years, the doctor said. You should appreciate that."

The subtle inflections in his speech slipped past her comprehension while she focused on key words. The message that had come through loud and clear was that beneath the bandages, she looked like a monster.

Panic welled up inside her. It must have communicated itself to him because he laid his hand on her shoulder again. "Carole, I didn't tell you the extent of your injuries to upset you. I know that you're worried about it. I thought it best to be frank so you could mentally prepare yourself for the ordeal ahead of you.

"It won't be easy, but everybody in the family is behind you one hundred percent." He paused and lowered his voice. "For the time being, I'm laying personal considerations aside and concentrating on putting you back together again. I'll stick by you until you are completely satisfied with the surgeon's results. I promise you that. I owe it to you for saving Mandy's life."

She tried to shake her head in denial of everything he was saying, but it was no use. She couldn't move. Making an effort to speak around the tube in her throat caused pain to her chemically scorched esophagus.

Her frustration increased until a nurse came in and ordered him to leave. When he lifted his hand off her shoulder, she felt forsaken and alone.

The nurse administered a dose of narcotic. It stole through her veins, but she fought its anesthetizing effects. It was stronger than she, however, and gave her no choice but to submit.

"Carole, can you hear me?"

Roused, she moaned pitiably. The medication made her feel weighted down and lifeless, as though the only living cells in her entire body resided in her brain and the rest of her was dead.

"Carole?" the voice hissed close to her bandaged ear.

It wasn't the man named Rutledge. She would have recognized his voice. She couldn't remember if he had left her. She didn't know who was speaking to her now. She wanted to shrink from this voice. It wasn't soothing, like Mr. Rutledge's.

"You're still in bad shape and might succumb yet. But if you feel that you're fixing to die, don't make any deathbed confessions, even if you're able to."

She wondered if she was dreaming. Frightened, she opened her eye. As usual, the room was brightly lit. Her respirator hissed rhythmically. The person speaking to her was standing outside her peripheral vision. She could sense him there, but she couldn't see him.

"We're still in this together, you and I. And you're in too deep to get out now, so don't even consider it."

To no avail, she tried to blink away her grogginess and disorientation. The person remained only a presence, without form or distinction—a disembodied, sinister voice.

"Tate will never live to take office. This plane crash has been an inconvenience, but we can work it to our advantage if you don't panic. Hear me? If you come out of this, we'll pick up where we left off. There'll never be a Senator Tate Rutledge. He'll die first."

She squeezed her eye closed in an attempt to stave off her mounting panic.

"I know you can hear me, Carole. Don't pretend you can't."

After several moments, she reopened her eye and rolled it as far back as she could. She still couldn't see anybody, but she sensed her visitor had left.

Several minutes more ticked by, measured by the maddening cycle of the respirator. She hovered between sleep and wakefulness, valiantly fighting the effects of drugs, panic, and the disorientation inherent to an ICU.

Shortly afterward, a nurse came, checked her IV bottle, and took her blood pressure. She behaved routinely. Surely if someone were in her room, or had been there recently, the nurse would have acknowledged it. Satisfied with her patient's condition, she left.

By the time she fell asleep again, she had convinced herself that she had only had a bad dream.

TWO

Tate Rutledge stood at the window of his hotel room, gazing down at the traffic moving along the freeway. Taillights and headlights were reflected on the wet pavement, leaving watery streaks of red and white.

When he heard the door opening behind him, he turned on the heels of his boots and nodded a greeting to his brother. "I called your room a few minutes ago," he said. "Where have you been?"

"Drinking a beer down in the bar. The Spurs are playing the Lakers."

"I'd forgotten. Who's winning?"

His brother's derisive frown indicated the silliness of that question. "Dad's not back yet?"

Tate shook his head, let the drape fall back into place, and moved away from the window.

"I'm starving," Jack said. "You hungry?"

"I guess so. I hadn't thought about it." Tate dropped into the easy chair and rubbed his eyes.

"You're not going to do Carole or Mandy any good if you don't take care of yourself through this, Tate. You look like shit."

"Thanks."

"I mean it."

"I know you do," Tate said, lowering his hands and giving his older brother a wry smile. "You're all candor and no tact. That's why I'm a politician and you're not."

"Politician is a bad word, remember? Eddy's coached you not to use it."

"Even among friends and family?"

"You might develop a bad habit of it. Best not to use it at all."

"Jeez, don't you ever let up?"

"I'm only trying to help."

Tate lowered his head, ashamed of his ill-tempered outburst. "I'm sorry." He toyed with the TV's remote control, punching through the channels soundlessly. "I told Carole about her face."

"You did?"

Lowering himself to the edge of the bed, Jack Rutledge leaned forward, propping his elbows on his knees. Unlike his brother, he was clad in suit slacks, a white dress shirt, and a necktie. This late in the day, however, he looked rumpled. The starched shirt had wilted, the tie had been loosened, and his sleeves were rolled back. The slacks were wrinkled across his lap because he'd been sitting most of the day.

"How did she react when you told her?"

"How the hell do I know?" Tate muttered. "You can't see anything except her right eye. Tears came out of it, so I know she was crying. Knowing her, how vain she is, I would imagine she's hysterical underneath all those bandages. If she could move at all, she would probably be running up and down the corridors of the hospital screaming. Wouldn't you be?"

Jack hung his head and studied his hands, as though trying to imagine what it would feel like to have them burned and bandaged. "Do you think she remembers the crash?"

"She indicated that she did, although I'm not sure how much she remembers. I left out the grisly details and only told her that she and Mandy and twelve others had survived."

"They said on the news tonight that they're still trying to match up charred pieces and parts of bodies and identify them."

Tate had read the accounts in the newspaper. According to the report, it was a scene straight out of hell. Hollywood couldn't have created a slasher picture more gruesome than the grim reality that faced the coroner and his army of assistants.

Whenever Tate remembered that Carole and Mandy could have been among those victims, his stomach became queasy. He couldn't sleep nights for thinking about it. Each casualty had a story, a reason for being on that particular flight. Each obituary was poignant.

In his imagination, Tate added Carole's and Mandy's names to the list of casualties: *The wife and three-year-old daughter of senatorial candidate Tate Rutledge were among the victims of Flight 398.*

But fate had dictated otherwise. They hadn't died. Because of Carole's surprising bravery, they had come out of it alive.

"Good Lord, it's coming down in buckets out there." Nelson's voice boomed through the silence as he came in, balancing a large, square pizza box on his shoulder and shaking out a dripping umbrella with his other hand.

"We're famished," Jack said.

"I got back as soon as I could."

"Smells great, Dad. What'll you have to drink?" Tate asked as he moved toward the small, built-in refrigerator that his mother had stocked for him his first night there. "Beer or something soft?"

"With pizza? Beer."

"Jack?"

"Beer."

"How were things at the hospital?"

"He told Carole about her injuries," Jack said before Tate had a chance to answer.

"Oh?" Nelson lifted a wedge of steaming pizza to his mouth and took a bite. Around it, he mumbled, "Are you sure that was wise?"

"No. But if I were where she is, I'd want to know what the hell was going on, wouldn't you?"

"I suppose." Nelson took a sip of the beer Tate had brought him. "How was your mother when you left?"

"Worn out. I begged her to come back here and let me stay with Mandy tonight, but she said they were into their routine now, and for Mandy's sake, she didn't want to break it."

"That's what she told you," Nelson said. "But she probably took one look at you and decided that you needed a good night's sleep more than she does. You're the one who's worn out."

"That's what I told him," Jack said.

"Well, maybe the pizza will help revive me." Tate tried to inject some humor into his voice.

"Don't make light of our advice, Tate," Nelson warned sternly. "You can't let your own health deteriorate."

"I don't intend to." He saluted them with his can of beer, drank from it, then solemnly added, "Now that Carole's regained consciousness and knows what's ahead of her, I'll rest better."

"It's going to be a long haul. For everybody," Jack remarked.

"I'm glad you brought that up, Jack." Tate blotted his mouth with a paper napkin and mentally braced himself. He was about to test their mettle. "Maybe I should wait another six years to run for office."

For the beat of several seconds, there was an air of suspended animation around the table, then Nelson and Jack spoke simultaneously, each trying to make himself heard over the other.

"You can't make a decision like that until you see how her operation goes."

"What about all the work we've put in?"

"Too many folks are counting on you."

"Don't even think of quitting now, little brother. This election is the one."

Tate held up his hands for silence. "You know how badly I want it. Jesus, all I've ever wanted to be was a legislator. But I can't sacrifice the welfare of my family to anything, even my political career."

"Carole doesn't deserve that kind of consideration from you."

Tate's razor-sharp gray eyes found his brother's. "She's my *wife*," he enunciated.

Another taut silence ensued. Clearing his throat, Nelson said, "Of course, you must be at Carole's side as much as possible during the ordeal she's facing. It's admirable of you to think of her first and your political career second. I would expect that kind of unselfishness from you."

To emphasize his next point, Nelson leaned across the ravaged pizza that had been opened over the small, round table. "But remember how much Carole herself encouraged you to throw your hat into the ring. I think she would be terribly upset if you withdrew from the race on her account. Terribly upset,'' he said, jabbing the space between them with his blunt index finger.

"And looking at it from a very cold and crass viewpoint,'' he went on, "this unfortunate accident might be turned to our advantage. It'll generate free publicity.''

Disgusted by the observation, Tate tossed down his wadded napkin and left his chair. For several moments he prowled aimlessly around the room. "Did you confer with Eddy on this? Because he said virtually the same thing when I called him earlier to discuss it.''

"He's your campaign manager.'' Jack had turned pale and speechless at the thought that his brother might give up before his campaign even got off the ground. "He's paid to give you good advice.''

"Harp on me, you mean.''

"Eddy wants to see Tate Rutledge become a United States senator, just like all the rest of us, and his desire for that has nothing to do with the salary he draws.'' Smiling broadly, Nelson got up and slapped Tate on the back. "You'll run in the November election. Carole would be the first in line to encourage you to.''

"All right then,'' Tate said evenly. "I had to know that I could depend on your unqualified support. The demands placed on me in the coming months will be all I can handle, and then some.''

"You've got our support, Tate,'' Nelson said staunchly.

"Will I have your patience and understanding when I can't be two places at once?'' Tate divided his inquiring look between them. "I'll do my best not to sacrifice one responsibility to the other, but I'm only one person.''

Nelson assured him, "We'll take up the slack for you.''

"What else did Eddy say?'' Jack asked, greatly relieved that the crisis had passed.

"He has volunteers stuffing questionnaires into envelopes to be mailed later this week.''

"What about public appearances? Has he scheduled any more?''

"A tentative speech to a high school in the valley. I told him to decline."

"Why?" Jack asked.

"High school kids don't vote," Tate said reasonably.

"But their parents do. And we need those Mexicans in the valley on our side."

"We've got them on our side."

"Don't take anything for granted."

"I don't," Tate said, "but this is one of those instances where I have to weigh my priorities. Carole and Mandy are going to require a lot of my time. I'll have to be more selective about where I go and when. Each speech will have to count, and I don't think a high school audience would be that beneficial."

"You're probably right," Nelson said, diplomatically intervening.

Tate realized that his father was humoring him, but he didn't care. He was tired, worried, and wanted to go to bed and at least try to sleep. As tactfully as possible, he conveyed that to his brother and father.

As he saw them out, Jack turned and gave him an awkward hug. "Sorry I badgered you tonight. I know you've got a lot on your mind."

"If you didn't, I'd get fat and lazy in no time. I rely on you to badger me." Tate flashed him the engaging smile that was destined to appear on campaign posters.

"If it's okay with y'all, I think I'll go home tomorrow morning," Jack said. "Somebody needs to check on things at the house, and see how everybody is making out."

"How is everything there?" Nelson asked.

"Okay."

"It didn't look okay the last time I was home. Your daughter Francine hadn't been heard from in days, and your wife . . . well, you know the state she was in." He shook his finger at his elder son. "Things have come to a sad pass when a man doesn't exercise any more influence over his family than you do." He glanced at Tate. "Or you, either, for that matter. Both of you have let your wives do as they damn well please."

Addressing Jack again, he said, "You should see to getting help for Dorothy Rae before it's too late."

"Maybe after the election," he mumbled. Looking at his brother, he added, "I'll only be an hour's drive away if you need me."

"Thanks, Jack. I'll call as developments warrant."

"Did the doctor give you any indication when they'd do the surgery?"

"Not until the risk of infection goes down," Tate told them. "The smoke inhalation damaged her lungs, so he might have to wait as long as two weeks. For him it's a real dilemma, because if he waits too long, the bones of her face will start to heal the way they are."

"Jesus," Jack said. Then, on a falsely cheerful note, he said, "Well, give her my regards. Dorothy Rae's and Fancy's, too."

"I will."

Jack went down the hall toward his own room. Nelson lingered. "I talked to Zee this morning. While Mandy was asleep, she slipped down to the ICU. Zee said Carole was a sight to behold."

Tate's wide shoulders drooped slightly. "She is. I hope to God that surgeon knows what he's talking about."

Nelson laid a hand on Tate's arm in a silent gesture of reassurance. For a moment, Tate covered his father's hand with his own. "Dr. Sawyer, the surgeon, did the video imaging today. He electronically painted Carole's face onto a TV screen, going by the pictures we'd given him. It was remarkable."

"And he thinks he can reproduce this video image during surgery?"

"That's what he says. He told me there might be some slight differences, but most of them will be in her favor." Tate laughed dryly. "Which she should like."

"Before this is over, she might believe that every woman in America should be so lucky," Nelson said with his characteristic optimism.

But Tate was thinking about that single eye, bloodshot and swollen, yet still the same dark coffee brown, looking up at him with fear. He wondered if she was afraid of dying. Or of living without the striking face that she had used to every advantage.

Nelson said good night and retired to his own room. Deep in thought, Tate turned off the TV and the lights, stripped, and slid into bed.

Lightning flashes penetrated the drapes, momentarily illuminating the room. Thunder crashed near the building, rattling panes of glass. He stared at the flickering patterns with dry, gritty eyes.

They hadn't even kissed good-bye.

Because of their recent, vicious argument, there had been a lot of tension between them that morning. Carole had been anxious to be off for a few days of shopping in Dallas, but they'd arrived at the airport in time to have a cup of coffee in the restaurant.

Mandy had accidentally dribbled orange juice on her dress. Naturally, Carole had overreacted. As they left the coffee shop, she blotted at the stained, ruffled pinafore and scolded Mandy for being so careless.

"For crissake, Carole, you can't even see the spot," he had said.

"*I* can see it."

"Then don't look at it."

She had shot her husband that drop-dead look that no longer fazed him. He carried Mandy through the terminal, chatting with her about all the exciting things she would see and do in Dallas. At the gate, he knelt and gave her a hug. "Have fun, sweetheart. Will you bring me back a present?"

"Can I, Mommy?"

"Sure," Carole replied distractedly.

"Sure," Mandy told him with a big smile.

"I'll look forward to that." He drew her to him for one last good-bye hug.

Straightening up, he asked Carole if she wanted him to wait until their plane left the gate. "There's no reason for you to."

He hadn't argued, but only made certain they had all their carryon luggage. "Well, see you on Tuesday then."

"Don't be late picking us up," Carole called as she pulled Mandy toward the jetway, where an airline attendant was waiting to take their boarding passes. "I hate hanging around airports."

Just before they entered the passageway, Mandy turned and waved at him. Carole hadn't even looked back. Self-confident and assured, she had walked purposefully forward.

Maybe that's why that single eye was filled with such anxiety now. The foundation of Carole's confidence—her looks—had been stolen by fate. She despised ugliness. Perhaps her tears hadn't been for those who had died in the crash, as he had originally thought. Perhaps they had been for herself. She might wish that she had died instead of being disfigured, even temporarily.

Knowing Carole, he wouldn't be surprised.

In the pecking order of assistants to the Bexar County coroner, Grayson was on the lowest rung. That's why he checked and rechecked the information before approaching his immediate supervisor with his puzzling findings.

"Got a minute?"

An exhausted, querulous man wearing a rubber apron and gloves gave him a quelling glance over his shoulder. "What'd you have in mind—a round of golf?"

"No, this."

"What?" The supervisor turned back to his work on the charred heap of matter that had once been a human body.

"The dental records of Avery Daniels," Grayson said. "Casualty number eighty-seven."

"She's already been IDed and autopsied." The supervisor consulted the chart on the wall, just to make certain. A red line had been drawn through her name. "Yep."

"I know, but—"

"She had no living relatives. A close family friend IDed her this afternoon."

"But these records—"

"Look, pal," the supervisor said with asperity, "I got bodies with no heads, hands without arms, feet without legs. And they're on my ass to finish this tonight. So if somebody's been positively IDed, autopsied, and sealed shut, don't bother me with records, okay?"

Grayson stuffed the dental X-rays back into the manila

envelope they had arrived in and sailed it toward a trash barrel. "Okay. Fine. And in the meantime, fuck you."

"Sure, sure—any time. As soon as we get all these stiffs IDed."

Grayson shrugged. They weren't paying him to be Dick Tracy. If nobody else gave a damn about a mysterious inconsistency, why should he? He went back to matching up dental records with the corpses as yet to be identified.

THREE

The weather seemed to be in mourning, too.

It rained the day of Avery Daniels's funeral. The night before, thunderstorms had rumbled through the Texas hill country. This morning, all that was left of them was a miserable, cold, gray rain.

Bareheaded, impervious to the inclement weather, Irish McCabe stood beside the casket. He had insisted on a spray of yellow roses, knowing they had been her favorite. Vivid and flamboyant, they seemed to be mocking death. He took comfort in that.

Tears rolled down his ruddy cheeks. His fleshy, veined nose was redder than usual, although he hadn't been drinking so much lately. Avery nagged him about it, saying an excessive amount of alcohol wasn't good for his liver, his blood pressure, or his expanding midsection.

She nagged Van Lovejoy about his chemical abuses, too, but he had showed up at her funeral high on cheap Scotch and the joint he had smoked on the drive to the chapel. The outmoded necktie around his ill-fitting collar was a concession to the solemnity of the occasion and attested to the fact that he held Avery in higher regard than he did most members of the human family.

Other people regarded Van Lovejoy no more favorably than he did them. Avery had numbered among the very few who could tolerate him. When the reporter assigned to cover the story of her tragic death for KTEX's news asked Van if he would shoot the video, the photographer had glared at him with contempt, shot him the finger, and slunk out of the newsroom without a word. This rude mode of self-expression was typical of Van, and just one of the reasons for his alienation from mankind.

At the conclusion of the brief interment service, the mourners began making their way down the gravel path toward the row of cars parked in the lane, leaving only Irish and Van at the grave. At a discreet distance, cemetery employees were waiting to finish up so they could retreat indoors, where it was warm and dry.

Van was fortyish and string-bean thin. His belly was concave and there was a pronounced stoop to his bony shoulders. His thin hair hung straight down from a central part, reaching almost to his shoulders and framing a thin, narrow face. He was an aging hippie who had never evolved from the sixties.

By contrast, Irish was short and robust. While Van looked like he could be carried off by a strong gust of wind, Irish looked like he could stand forever if he firmly planted his feet on solid ground. As different as they were physically, today their postures and bleak expressions were reflections of each other. Of the two, however, Irish's suffering was the more severe.

In a rare display of compassion, Van laid a skinny, pale hand on Irish's shoulder. "Let's go get shit-faced."

Irish nodded absently. He stepped forward and plucked one of the yellow rosebuds off the spray, then turned and let Van precede him from beneath the temporary tent and down the path. Raindrops splashed against his face and on the shoulders of his overcoat, but he didn't increase his stolid pace.

"I, uh, rode here in the limousine," he said, as though just remembering that when he reached it.

"Wanna go back that way?"

Irish looked toward Van's battered heap of a van. "I'll go

with you." He dismissed the funeral home driver with a wave of his hand and climbed inside the van. The interior was worse than the exterior. The ripped upholstery was covered with a ratty beach towel, and the maroon carpet lining the walls reeked of stale marijuana smoke.

Van climbed into the driver's seat and started the motor. While it was reluctantly warming up, he lit a cigarette with long, nicotine-stained fingers and passed it to Irish.

"No thanks." Then, after a seconds' reconsideration, Irish took the cigarette and inhaled deeply. Avery had gotten him to quit smoking. It had been months since he'd had a cigarette. Now, the tobacco smoke stung his mouth and throat. "God, that's good," he sighed as he inhaled again.

"Where to?" Van asked around the cigarette he was lighting for himself.

"Any place where we're not known. I'm likely to make a spectacle of myself."

"I'm known in all of them." Left unsaid was that Van frequently made a spectacle of himself, and, in the places he patronized, it didn't matter. He engaged the protesting gears.

Several minutes later Van ushered Irish through the tufted red vinyl door of a lounge located on the seedy outskirts of downtown. "Are we going to get rolled in here?" Irish asked.

"They check you for weapons as you go in."

"And if you don't have one, they issue you one," Irish said, picking up the tired joke.

The atmosphere was murky. The booth they slid into was secluded and dark. The midmorning customers were as morose as the tinsel that had been strung from the dim, overhead lights several Christmases ago. Spiders had made permanent residences of it. A naked señorita smiled beguilingly from the field of black velvet on which she had been painted. In stark contrast to the dismal ambience, lively mariachi music blared from the jukebox.

Van called for a bottle of scotch. "I really should eat something," Irish mumbled without much conviction.

When the bartender unceremoniously set down the bottle

and two glasses, Van ordered Irish some food. "You didn't have to," Irish objected.

The video photographer shrugged as he filled both glasses. "His old lady'll cook if you ask her to."

"You eat here often?"

"Sometimes," Van replied with another laconic shrug.

The food arrived, but after taking only a few bites, Irish decided he wasn't hungry after all. He pushed aside the chipped plate and reached for his glass of whiskey. The first swallow played like a flamethrower in his stomach. Tears filled his eyes. He sucked in a wheezing breath.

But with the expertise of a professional drinker, he recovered quickly and took another swig. The tears, however, remained in his eyes. "I'm going to miss her like hell." Idly, he twirled his glass on the greasy tabletop.

"Yeah, me, too. She could be a pain in the ass, but not nearly as much as most."

The brassy song currently playing on the jukebox ended. No one made another selection, which came as a relief to Irish. The music intruded on his bereavement.

"She was like my own kid, you know?" he asked rhetorically. Van continued smoking, lighting another cigarette from the tip of the last. "I remember the day she was born. I was there at the hospital, sweating it out with her father. Waiting. Pacing. Now I'll have to remember the day she died."

He slammed back a shot of whiskey and refilled his glass. "You know, it never occurred to me that it was her plane that went down. I was only thinking about the story, the goddamn news story. It was such a piss-ant story that I didn't even send a photographer along. She was going to borrow one from a station in Dallas."

"Hey, man, don't blame yourself for doing your job. You couldn't have known."

Irish stared into the amber contents of his glass. "Ever had to identify a body, Van?" He didn't wait for a reply. "They had them all lined up, like . . ." He released an unsteady sigh. "Hell, I don't know. I never had to go to war, but it must have been like that.

"She was zipped up in a black plastic bag. She didn't

have any hair left," he said, his voice cracking. "It was all burned off. And her skin . . . oh, Jesus." He covered his eyes with his stubby fingers. Tears leaked through them. "If it weren't for me, she wouldn't have been on that plane."

"Hey, man." Those two words exhausted Van's repertoire of commiserating phrases. He refreshed Irish's drink, lit another cigarette, and silently passed it to the grieving man. For himself, he switched to marijuana.

Irish drew on his cigarette. "Thank God her mother didn't have to see her like that. If she hadn't been clutching her locket in her hand, I wouldn't even have known the corpse was Avery." His stomach almost rebelled when he recalled what the crash had done to her.

"I never thought I'd say this, but I'm glad Rosemary Daniels isn't alive. A mother should never have to see her child in that condition."

Irish nursed his drink for several minutes before lifting his tearful eyes to his companion. "I loved her—Rosemary, I mean. Avery's mother. Hell, I couldn't help it. Cliff, her father, was gone nearly all the time, away in some remote hellhole of the world. Every time he left he asked me to keep an eye on them. He was my best friend, but more than once I wanted to kill him for that."

He sipped his drink. "Rosemary knew, I'm sure, but there was never a word about it spoken between us. She loved Cliff. I knew that."

Irish had been a surrogate parent to Avery since her seventeenth year. Cliff Daniels, a renowned photojournalist, had been killed in a battle over an insignificant, unpronounceable village in Central America. With very little fuss, Rosemary had ended her own life only a few weeks after her husband's death, leaving Avery bereft and without anyone to turn to except Irish, a steadfast family friend.

"I'm as much Avery's daddy as Cliff was. Maybe more. When her folks died, it was me she turned to. I was the one she came running to last year after she got herself in that mess up in D.C."

"She might have fucked up real bad that one time, but she was still a good reporter," Van commented through a cloud of sweet, pungent smoke.

"It's just so tragic that she died with that screwup on her conscience." He drank from his glass. "See, Avery had this hang-up about failing. That's what she feared most. Cliff wasn't around much when she was a kid, so she was still trying to win his approval, live up to his legacy.

"We never discussed it," he continued morosely. "I just know. That's why that snafu in D.C. was so devastating to her. She wanted to make up for it, win back her credibility and self-esteem. Time ran out before she got a chance. Goddammit, she died thinking of herself as a failure."

The older man's misery struck a rare, responsive chord in Van. He gave the task of consoling Irish his best shot. "About that other—you know, how you felt about her mother? Well, Avery knew."

Irish's red, weepy eyes focused on him. "How do you know?"

"She told me once," Van said. "I asked her just how long you two had known each other. She said you were in her memory as far back as it went. She had guessed that you secretly loved her mother."

"Did she seem to care?" Irish asked anxiously. "I mean, did it seem to bother her?"

Van shook his long, stringy hair.

Irish withdrew the wilting rose from the breast pocket of his dark suit and rubbed his pudgy fingers over the fragile petals. "Good. I'm glad. I loved them both."

His heavy shoulders began to shake. He curled his fingers into a tight fist around the rose. "Oh, hell," he groaned, "I'm going to miss her."

He lowered his head to the table and sobbed brokenly while Van sat across from him, nursing his own grief in his own way.

ONE

She clawed her way up through the gray mist.

The clearing beyond it must exist, she reassured herself, even if she couldn't see it yet. For a minute, she thought that reaching it couldn't possibly be worth the struggle, but something behind her was so terrifying it propelled her ever forward.

She was steeped in pain. With increasing frequency she emerged from blessed oblivion into a glaring awareness that was accompanied by pain so intense, so encompassing, she couldn't localize it. It was everywhere—inside her, on the surface. It was a saturating pain. Then, just when she didn't think she could stand it an instant longer, she would be flooded with a warm rush of numbness—a magic elixir that washed through her veins. Soon after, the prayed-for oblivion would embrace her again.

Her conscious moments became extended, however. Muffled sounds reached her despite her muzziness. By concentrating very hard, she began to identify them: the incessant whooshing of a respirator, the constant bleeping of electronic machinery, rubber soles squeaking on tile floors, ringing telephones.

Once when she surfaced from unconsciousness, she overheard a hushed conversation taking place nearby.

". . . incredibly lucky. . . with that much fuel splashed on her. . . burns, but they're mostly superficial."

FOUR

Avery woke up knowing who she was.

She had never exactly forgotten. It was just that her medication, along with her concussion, had left her confused.

Yesterday—or at least she guessed it had been yesterday, since everyone who had recently come within her range of vision had greeted her with a "good morning"—she had been disoriented, which was understandable. Waking after having been comatose for several days to find that she couldn't move, couldn't speak, and couldn't see beyond a very limited range would confound anyone. She was rarely ill, certainly not seriously, so being this injured was shocking.

The ICU, with its constant light and activity, was enough to hamper anyone's mental process. But what really had Avery puzzled was that everyone was addressing her incorrectly. How had she come to be mistaken for a woman named Carole Rutledge? Even Mr. Rutledge seemed convinced that he was speaking to his wife.

Somehow, she must communicate this mistake to them. But she didn't know how, and that frightened her.

Her name was Avery Daniels. It was clearly printed on her driver's license, her press pass, and all the other forms of identification in her wallet. They had probably been destroyed in the crash, she thought.

Memories of the crash tended to panic her still, so she determinedly put them aside to be dealt with later, when she was stronger and had this temporary mix-up straightened out.

Where was Irish? Why hadn't he come to her rescue?

The obvious answer startled her unexpectedly. Her whole body reacted as though it had been electrically charged. It was unthinkable, untenable, yet it was glaringly apparent. If she had been mistaken for Mrs. Rutledge, and Mrs. Rutledge was believed alive, then Avery Daniels was believed dead.

She imagined the anguish Irish must be going through. Her "death" would hit him hard. For the present, however, she was helpless to alleviate his suffering. No! As long as she was alive, she wasn't helpless. She must think. She must concentrate.

"Good morning."

She recognized his voice immediately. The swelling in her eye must have gone down some because she could see him more clearly. His previously blurred features were now distinct.

His heavy, well-shaped brows almost met above the bridge of a long, straight nose. He had a strong, stubborn jawline and chin, yet it fell short of being pugnacious, despite the vertical cleft at the edge of it. His lips were firm, wide, and thin, the lower one slightly fuller than the upper.

He was smiling, but not with his eyes, she noted. He didn't really feel the smile. It didn't come from his soul. Avery wondered why not.

"They said you had a restful night. Still no sign of pulmonary infection. That's terrific news."

She knew this face, this voice. Not from yesterday. It was before that, but she couldn't recall when she had met this man.

"Mom left Mandy's room long enough to come say hello to you." He turned his head and signaled someone to move closer. "You have to stand here, Mom, or she can't see you."

An exceptionally pretty, middle-aged face materialized in Avery's patch of vision. The woman's soft, dark hair had a very flattering silver streak that waved up and away from her smooth, unlined forehead.

"Hello, Carole. We're all very relieved that you're doing so well. Tate said the doctors are pleased with your progress."

Tate Rutledge! Of course.

"Tell her about Mandy, Mom."

Dutifully, the stranger reported on another stranger. "Mandy ate most of her breakfast this morning. They sedated her last night so she would sleep better. The cast on her arm bothers her, but that's to be expected, I suppose. She's the sweetheart of the pediatric wing, and has the entire staff wrapped around her little finger.'' Tears formed in her eyes and she blotted at them with a tissue. ''When I think of what . . .''

Tate Rutledge placed his arm across his mother's shoulders. ''But it didn't happen. Thank God it didn't.''

Avery realized then that it must have been Mandy Rutledge she had carried from the plane. She remembered hearing the child's screams and frantically trying to unfasten her jammed seat belt. When it came free, she had gathered the terrified child against her and, with the assistance of another passenger, had plunged through the dense, acrid smoke toward an emergency exit.

Because she had had the child, they had assumed she was Mrs. Carole Rutledge. But that wasn't all—they had been in each other's seats.

Her mind clumsily pieced together a puzzle of which only she was aware. She recalled that her boarding pass had designated the window seat, but when she had arrived, a woman was already sitting there. She hadn't pointed out the error, but had taken the seat on the aisle instead. The child had been sitting in the seat between them.

The woman had worn her dark hair shoulder length, much like Avery wore hers. She also had dark eyes. They bore a resemblance to each other. In fact, the flight attendant, who had made a fuss over the little girl, had asked who was the mother and who was the aunt, implying that Avery and Carole Rutledge were sisters.

Her face had been smashed beyond recognition. Mrs. Rutledge had probably been burned beyond recognition. They had misidentified her on the basis of the child and a seating rearrangement that no one knew about. My God, she had to tell them!

''You'd better go back now before Mandy becomes anxious, Mom,'' Tate was saying. ''Tell her I'll be there shortly.''

''Good-bye for now, Carole,'' the woman said to her. ''I'm sure when Dr. Sawyer's done, you'll be as pretty as ever.''

Her eyes don't smile either, Avery thought as the woman moved away.

''Before I forget it,'' Tate said, stepping close to the bed so that she could see him again, "Eddy, Dad, and Jack send their regards. I think Dad's coming to the meeting with the plastic surgeon this afternoon, so you'll see him then.

"Jack went home this morning." Tate continued talking, not knowing he wasn't speaking to his wife. "I'm sure he's worried about Dorothy Rae. God only knows what Fancy is up to without any supervision, although Eddy has got her working as a volunteer at the headquarters. None of them will be allowed to see you until you're moved to a private room, but I don't think you'll miss them, will you?"

He assumed that she knew who and what he was talking about. How could she convey that she hadn't the foggiest idea? These people were unknown to her. Their comings and goings were no concern of hers. She must contact Irish. She must let this man know that he was a widower.

"Listen, Carole, about the campaign." By the motion his shoulders made, she thought he had probably slid his hands into his hip pockets. He bowed his head for a moment, almost resting his chin on his chest, before looking at her again. "I'm going ahead with it as planned. Dad, Jack, and Eddy agree. They've pledged their support. It was going to be a tough fight before, but nothing I was afraid to tackle. Now, with this, it's going to be even tougher. Still, I'm committed."

Tate Rutledge had been making news recently. That's why his name and face were familiar to her, though she had never met him personally. He was hoping to win the primary election in May and then go up against an incumbent senator in the November election.

"I won't shirk any of my responsibilities to you and Mandy while you're recovering, but going to Congress is what I've been preparing for all my life. I don't want to wait another six years to run or I'll lose the momentum I've built. I need to do it now."

After consulting his wristwatch, he said, "I'd better get back to Mandy. I promised to feed her some ice cream. With her arms bandaged and all, well," he added, glancing toward her bandaged hands, resting in their splints, "you can understand. The psychologist has the first session with her today. Nothing to worry about," he rushed to say.

"More precautionary than anything. I don't want her to be permanently traumatized."

He paused, looking down at her meaningfully. "That's why I don't think she should see you just yet. I know that sounds cruel, but these bandages would scare her half to death, Carole. Once the surgeon rebuilds your face and you start looking like yourself, I'll bring her in for short visits. Besides, I'm sure you don't feel up to seeing her now, either."

Avery struggled to speak, but her mouth had the breathing tube taped inside it. She had overheard a nurse say that smoke inhalation had rendered her vocal cords temporarily inoperable. She couldn't move her jaw anyway. She batted her eye to convey her distress.

Misconstruing the reason for it, he laid a consoling hand on her shoulder. "I promise that your disfigurement is temporary, Carole. Dr. Sawyer says it looks much worse to us than it actually is. He'll be in later today to explain the procedure to you. He knows what you looked like before and guarantees that you'll look the same when he gets finished."

She tried to shake her head no. Tears of panic and fear overflowed her eye. A nurse came in and edged him aside. "I think you'd better let her rest now, Mr. Rutledge. I've got to change her bandages anyway."

"I'll be with my daughter."

"We'll call if you're needed," the nurse told him kindly. "Oh, and while I'm thinking of it, they called from downstairs to remind you that Mrs. Rutledge's jewelry is in the hospital safe. They took it off her when she arrived in the emergency room."

"Thanks. I'll get it later."

Now! Get it now, Avery's mind screamed. It wouldn't be Carole Rutledge's jewelry in the hospital safe—it would be hers. Once they saw it, they would realize that a horrible mistake had been made. Mr. Rutledge would learn that his wife was dead. It would come as a blow to him, but it would be better that he discover the error now rather than later. She would lament the Rutledges' tragic loss, but Irish would be overjoyed. Dear Irish. His bereavement would end.

But what if Mr. Rutledge failed to retrieve his wife's jewelry before the plastic surgeon began to change her face into Carole Rutledge's?

That was her last conscious thought before the pain-relieving medication claimed her once again.

Tate will never live to take office.

She was reliving the nightmare again. She tried desperately to ward it off. Again, she couldn't see him, but she could feel his sinister presence hovering above her, just beyond her field of vision. His breath fanned across her exposed eye. It was like being taunted in the dark with a sheer veil—unseen but felt, ghostly.

There will never be a Senator Tate Rutledge. Tate will never live. Senator Tate Rutledge will die first. There'll never be . . . Never live . . .

Avery woke up screaming. It was a silent scream, of course, but it reverberated through her skull. She opened her eye and recognized the lights overhead, the medicinal smell she associated with hospitals, the hissing sound of her respirator. She had been asleep, so this time it had been a nightmare.

But last night it had been real. Last night she hadn't even known Mr. Rutledge's first name! She couldn't have dreamed it if she hadn't known it, but she distinctly remembered hearing that menacing, faceless voice contemptuously whispering it into her ear.

Was her mind playing games with her, or was Tate Rutledge in real danger? Surely she was becoming panicked prematurely. After all, she had been heavily sedated and disoriented. Maybe she wasn't keeping the chronology straight. Was she getting events out of order? Who could possibly want him dead?

God, these were staggering questions. She had to know the answers to them. But her powers of deductive reasoning seemed to have deserted her, along with her other faculties. She couldn't think logically.

The threat to Tate Rutledge's life had far-reaching and

enormous ramifications, but she was helpless to do anything about it. She was too woozy to formulate an explanation or solution. Her mind was operating sluggishly. It wouldn't, couldn't function properly, even though a man's life was at stake.

Avery almost resented this intrusion into her own problem. Didn't she already have enough to cope with without worrying about a senatorial candidate's safety?

She was incapable of motion, yet on the inside she was roiling with frustration. It was exhausting. Eventually, it was no match for the void that continued to remain at the fringes of her consciousness. She combated it, but finally gave up the struggle and was sucked into its peacefulness again.

FIVE

"I'm not at all surprised by her reaction. It's to be expected in accident victims." Dr. Sawyer, the esteemed plastic surgeon, smiled placidly. "Imagine how you would feel if your handsome face had been pulverized."

"Thanks for the compliment," Tate said tightly.

At that moment, he would have liked to crush the surgeon's complacent face. Despite his sterling reputation, the man seemed to have ice water flowing through his veins.

He had done fine-tuning on some of the most celebrated faces in the state, including debutantes who possessed as much money as vanity, corporate executives who wanted to stay ahead of the aging process, models, and TV stars. Although his credentials were impressive, Tate didn't like the cocky way he dismissed Carole's apprehensions.

"I've tried to put myself in Carole's place," he explained.

"Under the circumstances, I think she's bearing up very well—better than I would ever have guessed she could."

"You're contradicting yourself, Tate," Nelson remarked. He was sitting beside Zee on a sofa in the ICU waiting room. "You just told Dr. Sawyer that Carole seemed terribly upset at the mention of the surgery."

"I know it sounds contradictory. What I mean is that she seemed to take the news about Mandy and the crash itself very well. But when I began telling her about the surgery on her face, she started crying. Jesus," he said, raking a hand through his hair. "You can't imagine how pitiful she looks when she cries out of that one eye. It's like something out of 'The Twilight Zone.'"

"Your wife was a beautiful woman, Mr. Rutledge," the doctor said. "The damage to her face panics her. Naturally, she's afraid of looking like a monster for the rest of her life. Part of my job is to assure her that her face can be reconstructed, even improved upon."

Sawyer paused to make eye contact with each of them. "I sense hesitation and reluctance from you. I can't have that. I must have your cooperation and wholehearted confidence in my ability."

"If you didn't have my confidence, I wouldn't have retained your services," Tate said bluntly. "I don't think you're lacking in skill, just sympathy."

"I save my bedside manner for my patients. I don't waste time or energy bullshitting their families, Mr. Rutledge. I leave that to politicians. Like you."

Tate and the surgeon stared each other down. Eventually Tate smiled, then laughed dryly. "I don't bullshit either, Dr. Sawyer. You're necessary. That's why you're here. You're also the most pompous son of a bitch I've ever run across, but by all accounts, you're the best. So I'll cooperate with you in order to see Carole returned to normal."

"Okay, then," the surgeon said, unaffected by the insult, "let's go see the patient."

When they entered the ICU, Tate moved ahead, arriving first at her bedside. "Carole? Are you awake?"

She responded immediately by opening her eye. As best

he could tell, she was lucid. "Hi. Mom and Dad are here."
He moved aside. They approached the bed.

"Hello again, Carole," Zee said. "Mandy said to tell
you she loves you."

Tate had forgotten to caution his mother against telling
Carole about Mandy's initial session with the child psychologist. It hadn't gone well, but thankfully, Zee was sensitive
enough not to mention it. She moved aside and let Nelson
take her place.

"Hi, Carole. You gave us all a fright. Can't tell you how
pleased we are that you're going to be okay."

He relinquished his position to Tate. "The surgeon's
here, Carole."

Tate exchanged places with Dr. Sawyer, who smiled
down at his patient. "We've already met, Carole. You just
don't remember it. At the request of your family, I came in
to examine you on your second day here. The staff plastic
surgeon had done all the preliminary treatment in the emergency room when you arrived. I'll take over from here."

She registered alarm. Tate was gratified to see that Sawyer had noticed it. He patted her shoulder. "The bone
structure of your face was seriously damaged. I'm sure
you're aware of that. I know your husband has already told
you that it will be fully restored, but I want you to hear it
from me. I'll make you look like a better Carole Rutledge
than you were before."

Beneath the bandages, her body tensed. She tried to
shake her head vigorously, and she began to make desperate
guttural sounds.

"What the hell is she trying to say?" Tate asked the
doctor.

"That she doesn't believe me," he calmly replied. "She's
frightened. That's customary." He leaned over her. "Most
of the pain you're experiencing is from the burns, but
they're superficial. The burn specialist here at the hospital is
treating them with antibiotics. I'm going to delay surgery
until the risk of infection both to your skin and your lungs is
minimal.

"It will be a week or two before you can move your

hands. You'll start physical therapy then. The damage isn't permanent, I assure you."

He bent down closer. "Now, let's talk about your face. X-rays were taken while you were still unconscious. I've studied them. I know what must be done. I have a staff of excellent surgeons who will assist me during the operation."

He touched her face with the tip of his ballpoint pen, as though tracing over the bandages. "We'll rebuild your nose and cheekbones by using bone grafts. Your jaw will be put back into place with pins, screws, and wires. I've got a whole bag of tricks.

"You'll have an invisible scar across the top of your head from temple to temple. We'll also make incisions beneath each eye at the lash line. They're invisible, too. Some of the work on your nose will be done from inside, so there will be no scars at all there.

"After the surgery you'll be swollen and bruised and you'll generally look like hell. Be prepared for that. It will take a few weeks before you're a raving beauty again."

"What about her hair, Dr. Sawyer?" Zee asked.

"I'll have to shave off a patch because I'll be taking a graft from her skull to use as part of her new nose. But if you're asking if the hair that was burned off will grow back, the burn specialist says yes. That's the least of our problems," he said, smiling down into the bandaged face.

"You won't be eating solid foods for a while, I'm afraid. A prosthodontist will take out the roots of your teeth during the surgery and install implants. Two or three weeks later, you'll get your new teeth, which he'll make to look exactly like the ones you lost. Until you get the replacements, you'll be fed through a tube from your mouth to your stomach, then progress to a soft diet."

Tate noticed, even if the surgeon failed to acknowledge it, that Carole's eye was roving as though looking for a friend among them, or possibly a means of escape. He kept telling himself that Sawyer knew what he was doing. The surgeon might be accustomed to anxiety like this among his patients, but it was as disturbing as hell to Tate.

Sawyer extracted a glossy eight-by-ten color photograph from the folder he had carried in with him. "I want you to look at this, Mrs. Rutledge." It was a picture of Carole. She was smiling the beguiling smile that had caused Tate to fall in love with her. Her eyes were shining and mischievous. Glossy dark hair framed her face.

"It'll be an all day, bring-your lunch operation," he told her, "but my staff and I will fix you up. Give us eight to ten weeks from the day of your surgery and this is what you'll look like, only younger and prettier, and with shorter hair. Who could ask for more than that?"

Apparently Carole could. Tate noticed that, rather than assuaging her fears, the surgeon's visit had seemed to heighten them.

Avery tried moving her extremities and coaxing motion out of her fingers and toes, but her limbs still felt too heavy to lift. She couldn't move her head at all. Meanwhile, each passing minute brought her closer to a disaster she seemed incapable of preventing.

For days—it was difficult to calculate exactly how many, but she guessed around ten—she had tried to figure out a means of letting everyone else in on the truth that only she knew. Thus far, she hadn't arrived at a solution. As the days passed and her body healed, her anxiety increased. Everyone thought it was caused by the delay of her reconstructive operation.

Finally, Tate announced one evening that her surgery had been scheduled for the next day. "All the doctors involved consulted this afternoon. They agreed that you're out of the danger zone. Sawyer issued the go-ahead. I came as soon as I was notified."

She had until tomorrow to let him know that a dreadful mistake had been made. It was strange but, even though he was partially responsible for this tragic chain of events, she didn't blame him. Indeed, she had come to anticipate his visits. She felt safer somehow when he was with her.

"I guess it's all right to tell you now that I didn't like Sawyer at first," he said, sitting gingerly on the edge of her bed. "Hell, I still don't like him, but I trust him. You know that he wouldn't be doing the operation if I didn't think he would do the best job."

She believed that, so she blinked.

"Are you afraid?"

She blinked again.

"Can't say that I blame you," he said grimly. "The next few weeks are going to be tough, Carole, but you'll get through them." His smile stiffened slightly. "You always land on your feet."

"Mr. Rutledge?"

When he turned his head toward the feminine voice who had spoken to him from the doorway, he provided Avery a rare view of his profile. Carole Rutledge had been a lucky woman.

"You asked me to remind you about Mrs. Rutledge's jewelry," the nurse said. "It's still in the safe."

Avery's mind quickened. She had envisioned him entering her room and dumping her jewelry onto the bed. "These aren't Carole's things," he would say. "Who are you?" But that scenario hadn't occurred. Maybe there was hope yet.

"I keep forgetting to stop by the office and pick it up," he told the nurse with chagrin. "Could you possibly send somebody down to get it for me?"

"I'll call down and check."

"I'd appreciate that. Thank you."

Avery's heart began to pound. She offered up a silent prayer of thanksgiving. Here, at the eleventh hour, she would be saved from disaster. Reconstructive surgery would have to be done to her face, but she would come out of it looking like Avery Daniels, and not someone else.

"The jewelry won't do you much good in the operating room," Tate was saying, "but I know you'll feel better once your things are in my possession."

In her mind, she was smiling hugely. It was going to be all right. The mistake would be discovered in plenty of time, and she could leave the emotional roller-coaster she had been riding behind.

"Mr. Rutledge, I'm afraid it's against hospital regulations for anyone except the patient himself or next of kin to retrieve possessions from the safe. I can't send anyone down for it. I'm sorry."

"No problem. I'll try to get down there sometime tomorrow."

Avery's spirits plummeted. Tomorrow would be too late. She asked herself why God was doing this to her. Hadn't she been punished enough for her mistake? Would the rest of her life be an endless and futile endeavor to make up for one failure? She had already lost her credibility as a journalist, the esteem of her colleagues, her career status. Must she give up her identity, too?

"There's something else, Mr. Rutledge," the nurse said hesitantly. "There are two reporters down the hall who want to speak with you."

"Reporters?"

"From one of the TV stations."

"Here? Now? Did Eddy Paschal send them?"

"No. That's the first thing I asked them. They're after a scoop. Apparently word has leaked out about Mrs. Rutledge's surgery tomorrow. They want to talk to you about the effect of the crash on your family and senatorial race. What should I tell them?"

"Tell them to go to hell."

"Mr. Rutledge, I can't."

"No, you can't. If you did, Eddy would kill me," he muttered to himself. "Tell them that I'm not making any statements until my wife and daughter are drastically improved. Then, if they don't leave, call hospital security. And tell them for me that if they go anywhere near the pediatric wing and try to see my mother or daughter, I'll sue their asses for all they've got."

"I'm sorry to have bothered you with—"

"It's not your fault. If they give you any trouble, come get me."

When his head came back around, Avery noticed through her tears that his face was lined with worry and exhaustion. "Media vultures. Yesterday the newspaper took a statement I had made about the shrimping business along the coast and printed it out of context. This morning my phone rang incessantly until Eddy could issue a counterstatement and demand a retraction." He shook his head with disgust over the unfairness.

Avery sympathized. She had spent enough time in Washington to know that the only politicians who didn't suffer were the unscrupulous ones. Men with integrity, as Tate Rutledge seemed to be, had a much more difficult time of it.

It was little wonder that he appeared so tired. He was not only burdened with running for public office, but he had to cope with an emotionally traumatized child and a wife facing her own ordeal.

Only she wasn't his wife. She was a stranger. She couldn't tell him that he was confiding in an outsider. She couldn't protect him from media assaults or help him through Mandy's difficulties. She couldn't even warn him that someone might be planning to kill him.

He stayed with her through the night. Each time she awakened, he instantly materialized at her bedside. The character lines in his face became more pronounced by the hour as fatigue settled in. The whites of his eyes grew rosy with sleeplessness. Once, Avery was aware of a nurse urging him to leave and get some rest, but he refused.

"I can't run out on her now," he said. "She's scared."

Inside she was crying, *No, please don't go. Don't leave me. I need someone.*

It must have been dawn when another nurse brought him a cup of fresh coffee. It smelled delicious; Avery craved a sip.

Technicians came in to adjust her respirator. She was gradually being weaned from it as her lungs recovered from their injury. The machine's job had been drastically scaled down from what it had originally done for her, but she would need it a few days more.

Orderlies prepped her for surgery. Nurses monitored her blood pressure. She tried to catch someone's eye and alert them to the mix-up, but no one paid any attention to the mummified patient.

Tate stepped out for a while, and when he returned, Dr. Sawyer was with him. The surgeon was brisk and buoyant. "How are you, Carole? Mr. Rutledge told me you spent some anxious hours last night, but this is your big day."

He methodically perused her chart. Much of what he said

was by rote, she realized. As a human being, she didn't like him any better than Tate did.

Satisfied with her vital signs, he shut the metal file and passed it to a nurse. "Physically, you're doing fine. In a few hours, you'll have the framework of a new face and be on your way to a full recovery."

She put all her strength into the guttural sounds she made, trying to convey the wrongness of what they were about to do. They misinterpreted her distress. The surgeon thought she was arguing with him. "It can be done. I promise. In about half an hour we'll be underway."

Again, she protested, using the only means available to her, her single eye. She batted it furiously.

"Give her a pre-op sedative to calm her down," he ordered the nurse before bustling out.

Avery screamed inside her head.

Tate stepped forward and pressed her shoulder. "Carole, it's going to be all right."

The nurse injected a syringe of narcotic into the IV in her arm. Avery felt the slight tug on the needle in the bend of her elbow. Seconds later, the now-familiar warmth began stealing through her, until even the pads of her toes tingled. It was the nirvana that junkies would kill for—a delicious jolt of numbness. Almost instantly she became weightless and transparent. Tate's features began to blur and become distorted.

"You're going to be all right. I swear it, Carole."

I'm not Carole.

She struggled to keep her eye open, but it closed and became too heavy to reopen.

". . . waiting for you, Carole," he said gently.

I'm Avery. I'm Avery. I'm not Carole.

But when she came out of the operating room, she would be.

SIX

"I don't understand what you're so upset about."

Tate spun around and angrily confronted his campaign manager. Eddy Paschal suffered the glare with equanimity. Experience had taught him that Tate's temper was short, but just as short-lived.

As Eddy expected, the fire in Tate's eyes downgraded to a hot glow. He lowered his hands from his hips, making his stance less antagonistic.

"Eddy, for crissake, my wife had just come out of a delicate operation that had lasted for hours."

"I understand."

"But you can't understand why I was upset when hordes of reporters surrounded me, asking questions?" Tate shook his head, incredulous. "Let me spell it out for you. I was in no mood for a press conference."

"Granted, they were out of line."

"Way out of line."

"But you got forty seconds of airtime on the six and ten o'clock newscasts—all three networks. I taped them and played them back later. You appeared testy, but that's to be expected, considering the circumstances. All in all, I think it went in our favor. You look like a victim of the insensitive media. Voters will sympathize. That's definitely a plus."

Tate laughed mirthlessly as he slumped into a chair. "You're as bad as Jack. You never stop campaigning, measuring which way this or that went—in our favor, against us." He dragged his hands down his face. "Christ, I'm tired."

"Have a beer." Eddy handed him a cold can he'd taken

46

from the compact refrigerator. Taking one for himself, he sat down on the edge of Tate's hotel room bed. For a moment they drank in silence. Finally, Eddy asked, "What's her prognosis, Tate?"

Tate sighed. "Sawyer was braying like a jackass when he came out of the operating room. Said he was perfectly satisfied with the results—that it was the finest work his team had ever done."

"Was that P.R. bullshit or the truth?"

"I hope to God it's the truth."

"When will you be able to see for yourself?"

"She doesn't look like much now. But in a few weeks . . ."

He made a vague gesture and slouched down deeper into the chair, stretching his long legs out in front of him. His boots almost came even with Eddy's polished dress shoes. The jeans Tate had on were at the opposite end of the wardrobe scale from Eddy's creased and pressed navy flannel slacks.

For the present, Eddy didn't badger his candidate about his casual attire. The political platform they were building was one that common folk—hardworking middle-class Texans—would adhere to. Tate Rutledge was going to be the champion of the downtrodden. He dressed the part—not as a political maneuver, but because that's the way he had dressed since the early seventies, when Eddy had met him at the University of Texas.

"One of the crash survivors died today," Tate informed him in a quiet voice. "A man my age, with a wife and four kids. He had a lot of internal injuries, but they had patched him up and they thought he was going to make it. He died of infection. God," he said, shaking his head, "can you imagine making it that far and then dying from *infection*?"

Eddy could see that his friend was sinking into a pit of melancholia. That was bad for Tate personally and for the campaign. Jack had expressed his concern for Tate's mental attitude. So had Nelson. An important part of Eddy's job was to boost Tate's morale when it flagged.

"How's Mandy?" he asked, making his voice sound bright. "All the volunteers miss her."

"We hung that get well banner they had all signed on her bedroom wall today. Be sure to thank them for me."

"Everyone wanted to do something special to commemorate her release from the hospital. I'll warn you that tomorrow she's going to receive a teddy bear that's bigger than you are. She's the princess of this election, you know."

Eddy was rewarded with a wan smile. "The doctors tell me that her broken bones will heal. The burns won't leave any scars. She'll be able to play tennis, cheerlead, dance—anything she wants."

Tate got up and went for another two beers. When he was once again relaxing in the chair, he said, "Physically, she'll recover. Emotionally, I'm not so sure."

"Give the kid a chance. Adults have a hard time coping with this kind of trauma. That's why the airline has counselors trained to deal with people who survive crashes and with the families of those who don't."

"I know, but Mandy was shy to begin with. Now she seems completely withdrawn, suppressed. Oh, I can get a smile out of her if I try hard enough, but I think she does it just to please me. She has no animation, no vitality. She just lies there and stares into space. Mom says she cries in her sleep and wakes up screaming from nightmares."

"What does the psychologist say?"

"That dyke," Tate said, cursing impatiently. "She says it'll take time and patience, and that I shouldn't expect too much from Mandy."

"I say ditto."

"I'm not angry with Mandy for not performing on command," he snapped irritably. "That's what the psychologist implied, and it made me mad as hell. But my little girl sits and stares like she's got the weight of the world on her shoulders, and that's just not normal behavior for a three-year-old."

"Neither is living through a plane crash," Eddy pointed out reasonably. "Her emotional wounds aren't going to heal overnight, any more than her physical ones will."

"I know. It's just . . . hell, Eddy, I don't know if I can be what Carole and Mandy and the voting public need, all at the same time."

Eddy's greatest fear was that Tate would second-guess his decision to remain in the race. When Jack had told him that there were rumors in journalistic circles of Tate withdrawing from the race, he'd wanted to hunt down the gossiping reporters and kill them single-handedly. Luckily, Tate hadn't heard the rumors. Eddy had to keep the candidate's fighting spirit high.

Sitting forward, he said, "You remember the time you played in that fraternity tennis tournament and won it for us our sophomore year?"

Tate regarded him blankly. "Vaguely."

"Vaguely," Eddy scoffed. "The reason the recollection is dim is because you had such a hangover. You'd forgotten all about the tournament and had spent the previous night drinking beer and banging a Delta Gamma. I had to rout you out of her bed, get you into a cold shower and onto the court by nine o'clock to keep us from getting a forfeit."

Tate was chuckling with self-derision. "Is this story going somewhere? Does it have a point?"

"The point is," Eddy said, scooting farther forward so that his hips were barely on the edge of the bed, "that you came through, under the worst possible conditions, because you knew you had to. You were the only chance we had of winning that tournament and you knew it. You won it for us, even though minutes before your first match you were massaging your blue balls and puking up two six-packs of beer."

"This is different from a college tennis tournament."

"But you," Eddy said, aiming an index finger at him, "are exactly the same. Since I've known you, you've never failed to rise to the occasion. Through those two years we spent together at UT, through flight training, through Nam, when you were carrying me out of that goddamn jungle, when have you ever failed to be a fucking hero?"

"I don't want to be a hero. I just want to be an effective congressman for the people of Texas."

"And you will be."

Slapping his knees as though an important decision had been reached, Eddy stood up and set his empty beer can on the dresser. Tate stood up, too, and he happened to catch a glimpse of his reflection in the mirror.

"Good God." He ran his hand over the heavy stubble on

his jaw. "Who'd vote for *that*? Why didn't you tell me I looked so bad?"

"I didn't have the heart." Eddy slapped him lightly between the shoulder blades. "All you need is some rest. And I recommend a close shave in the morning."

"I'll be leaving for the hospital early. They told me that Carole will be taken out of the recovery room about six and moved into a private room. I want to be there."

Eddy studied the shiny toes of his shoes for a moment before raising his eyes to his slightly taller friend. "The way you're sticking so close to her through this—well, uh, I think it's damned admirable."

Tate bobbed his head once, tersely. "Thanks."

Eddy started to say more, thought better of it, and gave Tate's arm a companionable slap. Tate wouldn't welcome marriage counseling from anyone, but especially not from a bachelor.

"I'll leave and let you get to bed. Stay in touch tomorrow. We'll be standing by for word on Carole's condition."

"How are things at home?"

"Status quo."

"Jack said you'd put Fancy to work at headquarters."

Eddy laughed and, knowing that Tate wouldn't take offense at an off-color comment about his niece, added, "By day I've got her stuffing envelopes. By night, God only knows who's stuffing her."

Francine Angela Rutledge crossed the cattle guard doing seventy-five miles per hour in a year-old car that she'd inflicted with five years' worth of abuse. Because she didn't like safety belts, she was jounced out of her seat a good six inches. When she landed, she was laughing. She loved feeling the wind tear through her long, blond hair, even in wintertime. Driving fast, with flagrant disregard for traffic laws, was just one of Fancy's passions.

Another was Eddy Paschal.

Her desire for him was recent and, so far, unfulfilled and unreciprocated. She had all the confidence in the world that he would eventually come around.

In the meantime, she was occupying herself with a

bellhop at the Holiday Inn in Kerrville. She'd met him at a twenty-four-hour truck stop several weeks earlier. She had stopped there after a late movie, since it was one of the few places in town that stayed open after ten o'clock and it was on her way home.

At the truck stop Buck and Fancy made smoldering eye contact over the orange vinyl booths while she nursed a vanilla Coke through a large straw. Buck gobbled down a bacon cheeseburger. The way his mouth savagely gnawed at the greasy sandwich aroused her, just as intended. So on her way past his booth, she had slowed down as though to speak, then went on by. She settled her tab quickly, wasting no time to chat with the cashier as she usually did, and went directly to her convertible parked outside.

Sliding beneath the steering wheel, she smiled smugly. It was only a matter of time now. Watching through the wide windows of the café, she saw the young man stuff the last few bites of the cheeseburger into his mouth and toss enough currency to cover his bill onto the table before charging for the door in hot pursuit.

After exchanging names and innuendos, Buck had suggested that they meet there the following night, same time, for dinner. Fancy had an even better idea—breakfast at the motel.

Buck said that suited him just fine since he had access to all the unoccupied rooms at the Holiday Inn. The illicit and risky arrangement appealed to Fancy enormously. Her lips had formed the practiced smile that she knew was crotch-teasing. It promised a wicked good time.

"I'll be there at seven o'clock sharp," she had said in her huskiest drawl. "I'll bring the doughnuts, you bring the rubbers." While she exercised no more morals than an alley cat, she was too smart and too selfish to risk catching a fatal disease for a mere roll in the hay.

Buck hadn't been a disappointment. What he lacked in finesse he made up for with stamina. He'd been so potent and eager to please that she'd pretended not to notice the pimples on his ass. Overall, he had a pretty good body. That's why she'd slept with him six times since that first morning.

They'd spent tonight, his night off, in the tacky apartment he was so proud of, eating bad Mexican TV dinners, drinking cheap wine, smoking expensive grass—Fancy's contribution to the evening's entertainment—and screwing on the carpet because it had looked marginally cleaner to her than the sheets on the bed.

Buck was sweet. He was earnest. He was horny. He told her often that he loved her. He was okay. Nobody was perfect.

Except Eddy.

She sighed now, expanding the cotton sweater across her braless breasts. Much to the disapproval of her grandmother, Zee, Fancy didn't believe in the restraints imposed by brassieres any more than those imposed by seat belts.

Eddy was beautiful. He was always perfectly groomed, and he dressed like a man, not a boy. The local louts, mostly shit-kickers and rednecks, wore cowboy clothes. God! Western wear was okay in its place. Hadn't she worn the gaudiest outfit she could find the year she was rodeo queen? But it belonged exclusively in the rodeo arena, as far as she was concerned.

Eddy wore dark three-piece suits and silk shirts and Italian leather shoes. He always smelled like he'd just stepped out of the shower. Thinking about him in the shower made her cream. She lived for the day she could touch his naked body, kiss it, lick him all over. She just knew he would taste good.

She squirmed with pleasure at the thought, but a frown of consternation soon replaced her expression of bliss. First she had to cure him of his hang-up over the gap in their ages. Then she'd have to help him get over the fact that she was his best friend's niece. Eddy hadn't come right out and said that's why he was resistant, but Fancy couldn't think of any other reason he would avoid the blatant invitation in her eyes every time she looked at him.

Everybody in the family had been tickled to death when she had volunteered to work at campaign headquarters. Grandpa had given her a hug that had nearly wrung the breath out of her. Grandma had smiled that vapid, ladylike smile Fancy detested and said in her soft, tepid voice, "How wonderful, dear." Daddy had stammered his surprised approval. Mama had even sobered up long enough to tell her she was glad she was doing something useful for a change.

Fancy had hoped Eddy's response would be equally as enthusiastic, but he had only appeared amused. All he had said was, "We need all the help down there we can get. By the way, can you type?"

Screw you, she had wanted to say. She didn't because her grandparents would have gone into cardiac arrest and because Eddy probably knew that's exactly what she was dying to say and she wouldn't give him the satisfaction of seeing her rattled.

So she had looked up at him with proper respect and said earnestly, "I do my best at whatever I undertake, Eddy."

The high-performance Mustang convertible sent up a cloud of dust as she wheeled up to the front door of the ranch house and cut the engine. She had hoped to get to the wing she shared with her parents without encountering anyone, but no such luck. As soon as she closed the door, her grandfather called out from the living room. "Who's that?"

"It's me, Grandpa."

He intercepted her in the hallway. "Hi, baby." He bent down to kiss her cheek. Fancy knew that he was sneakily checking her breath for alcohol. In preparation for that, she had consumed three breath mints on the way home to cover the smell of the cheap wine and strong pot.

He pulled away, satisfied. "Where'd you go tonight?"

"To the movies," she lied blithely. "How's Aunt Carole? Did the surgery go okay?"

"The doctor says it went fine. It'll be hard to tell for a week or so."

"God, it's just awful what happened to her face, isn't it?" Fancy pulled her own lovely face into a suitably sad frown. When she wanted to, she could bat her long lashes over her big blue eyes and look positively angelic. "I hope it turns out okay."

"I'm sure it will."

She could tell by his gentle smile that her concern had touched him. "Well, I'm tired. The movie was so boring, I nearly fell asleep in it. 'Night, Grandpa." She went up on tiptoe to kiss his cheek and mentally cringed. He would horsewhip her if he knew how her lips had been occupied barely an hour ago.

She moved along the central hallway and turned left into another. Through wide double doors at the end of it, she entered the wing of the house that she shared with her mother and father. She had her hand on the door to her room and was about to open it when Jack poked his head through his bedroom door.

"Fancy?"

"Hi, Daddy," she said with a sweet smile.

"Hi."

He didn't ask where she'd been because he didn't really want to know. That's why she told him. "I was at a . . . friend's." Her pause was deliberate, strategic, and rewarded by a pinched look that came to her father's mouth and eyes. "Where's Mama?"

He glanced over his shoulder into the room. "Sleeping."

Even from where she stood, Fancy could hear her mother's resonant snores. She wasn't just "sleeping," she was sleeping it off.

"Well, good night," Fancy said, edging into her bedroom.

He detained her. "How's it going down at headquarters?"

"Fine."

"You enjoying the work?"

"It's okay. Something to do."

"You could go back to college."

"Fuck that."

He winced but didn't chide. She had known he wouldn't. "Well, good night, Fancy."

" 'Night," she replied flippantly and soundly closed her bedroom door behind her.

SEVEN

"I might bring Mandy to see you tomorrow." Tate regarded her closely. "Since the swelling's gone down some, she'll be able to recognize you."

Avery gazed back at him. Even though he smiled encouragingly every time he looked at her face, she knew it was still frightful. There were no bandages to hide behind. As Irish would say, she could make a buzzard puke.

However, in the week since her operation, Tate had never avoided looking at her. She appreciated that charitable quality in him. As soon as her hands were capable of holding a pencil, she would write him a note and tell him so.

The bandages had been removed from her hands several days ago. She had been dismayed at the sight of the red, raw, hairless skin. Her nails had been clipped short, making her hands look different, ugly. Each day she did physical therapy with a rubber ball, squeezing it in her weak fists, but she hadn't quite graduated to grasping a pencil and controlling it well enough to write. As soon as she could, there was much she had to tell Tate Rutledge.

She had finally been weaned from the despised respirator. To her mortification, she hadn't been able to make a single sound—a traumatizing occurrence for a broadcast journalist who was already insecure in her career.

However, the doctors had cautioned her against becoming alarmed with the assurance that her voice would be restored gradually. They told her that the first few times she tried to speak she probably wouldn't be able to make herself understood, but that this was normal, considering the damage done to her vocal cords by the smoke she had inhaled.

Beyond that, she was virtually hairless, toothless, and taking liquid nourishment through a straw. Overall, she was still a mess.

"What do you think about that?" Tate asked her. "Do you feel up to having a visit with Mandy?"

He smiled, but Avery could tell his heart wasn't in it. She pitied him. He tried so valiantly to be cheerful and optimistic. Her earliest postoperative recollections were of him speaking soft words of encouragement. He had told her then and continued to tell her daily that the surgery had gone splendidly. Dr. Sawyer and all the nurses on the floor continued to commend her on her rapid progress and good disposition.

In her situation, what other kind of disposition could one have? She could cope with a broken leg if her hands could handle crutches, which they couldn't. She was still a prisoner to the hospital bed. Good disposition be damned. How did they know that she wasn't raging on the inside? She wasn't, but only because it wouldn't do any good. The damage had already been done. Avery Daniels' face had been replaced by someone else's. That recurring thought brought scalding tears to her eyes.

Tate misinterpreted them. "I promise not to keep Mandy here long, but I believe even a short visit with you would do her good. She's home now, you know. Everybody's pampering her, even Fancy. But she's still having a tough go of it at night. Seeing you might reassure her. Maybe she thinks we're lying to her when we say that you're coming back. Maybe she thinks you're really dead. She hasn't said so, but then, she doesn't say much of anything."

Dejectedly, he bent his head down and studied his hands. Avery stared at the crown of his head. His hair grew around a whorl that was slightly off-center. She enjoyed looking at him. More than her gifted surgeon, or the hospital's capable nursing staff, Tate Rutledge had become the center of her small universe.

As promised, sight in her left eye had been restored once the shelf to support her eyeball had been rebuilt. Three days following her surgery, the sutures on her eyelids had been taken out. She'd been promised that the packs inside her nose and the splint covering it would be removed tomorrow.

Tate had had fresh flowers delivered to her private room every day, as though to mark each tiny step toward full restoration. He was always smiling when he came in. He never failed to dispense a small bit of flattery.

Avery felt sorry for him. Though he tried to pretend otherwise, she could tell that these visits to her room were taxing. Yet if he stopped coming to see her, she thought she would die.

There were no mirrors in the room—nothing in fact that would reflect an image. She was sure that was by design. She longed to know what she looked like. Was her ghastly appearance the reason for the aversion that Tate tried so hard to conceal?

Like anyone with a physical disability, her senses had become keener. She had developed an acute perception into what people were thinking and feeling. Tate was being kind and considerate to his "wife." Common decency demanded it. There was, however, a discernible distance between them that Avery didn't understand.

"Should I bring her or not?"

He was sitting on the edge of her bed, being careful of her broken leg, which was elevated. It must be a cold day out, she reasoned, because he was wearing a suede jacket over his casual shirt. But the sun was shining. He'd been wearing sunglasses when he had come in. He had taken them off and slipped them into his breast pocket. His eyes were gray-green, straightforward, disarming. He was an extremely attractive man, she thought, mustering what objectivity she could.

How could she refuse to grant his request? He'd been so kind to her. Even though the little girl wasn't her daughter, if it would make Tate happier, she would pretend to be Mandy's mother just this once.

She nodded yes, something she'd been able to do since her surgery.

"Good." His sudden bright smile was sincere. "I checked with the head nurse and she said you could start wearing your own things if you wanted to. I took the liberty of packing some nightgowns and robes. It might be better for Mandy if you're wearing something familiar."

Again Avery nodded.

Motion at the door drew her eyes toward it. She recognized the man and woman as Tate's parents. Nelson and Zinnia, or Zee, as everybody called her.

"Well, looky here." Nelson crossed the room ahead of his wife and came to stand at the foot of Avery's bed. "You're looking fine, just fine, isn't she, Zee?"

Zee's eyes connected with Avery's. Kindly she replied, "Much better than yesterday even."

"Maybe that doctor is worth his fancy fee after all," Nelson remarked, laughing. "I never put much stock in plastic surgery. Always thought it was something vain, rich women threw away their husbands' money on. But this," he said, lifting his hand and indicating Avery's face, "this is going to be worth every penny."

Avery resented their hearty compliments when she knew she still looked every bit the victim of a plane crash.

Apparently Tate sensed that she was uncomfortable because he changed the subject. "She's agreed to let Mandy come see her tomorrow."

Zee's head snapped toward her son. Her hands met at her waist, where she clasped them tightly. "Are you sure that's wise, Tate? For Carole's sake, as well as Mandy's?"

"No, I'm not sure. I'm flying by the seat of my pants."

"What does Mandy's psychologist say?"

"Who the hell cares what she says?" Nelson asked crossly. "How could a shrink know more what's good for a kid than the kid's own daddy?" He clapped Tate on the shoulder. "I believe you're right. I think it'll do Mandy a world of good to see her mother."

"I hope you're right."

Zee didn't sound convinced, Avery noticed. She shared Zee's concern, but was powerless to express it. She only hoped that the benevolent gesture she was making for Tate's sake wouldn't backfire and do his emotionally fragile daughter more harm than good.

Zee went around the bright room watering the plants and flowers Avery had received, not only from Tate, but from people she didn't even know. Since no mention had ever been made of Carole's family, she deduced that she didn't have one. Her in-laws were her family.

Nelson and Tate were discussing the campaign, a topic that seemed never to be far from their minds. When they referred to Eddy, she mentally matched the name with a smooth-shaven face and impeccable clothing. He had come to see her on two occasions, accompanied by Tate each time. He seemed a pleasant chap, sort of the cheerleader of the group.

Tate's brother was named Jack. He was older and had a much more nervous nature than Tate. Or perhaps it just seemed so since during most of the time he'd been in her room, he had stammered apologies because his wife and daughter hadn't come to see her along with him.

Avery had gathered that Dorothy Rae, Jack's wife, was permanently indisposed by some sort of malady, though no one had referred to a debilitating illness. Fancy was obviously a bone of contention to everyone in the family. Avery had pieced together from their remarks that she was old enough to drive, but not old enough to live alone. They all lived together somewhere within an hour's drive of San Antonio. She vaguely recalled references to a ranch in the news stories about Tate. The family evidently had money and the prestige and power that accompanied it.

They were all friendly and cheerful when speaking to her. They chose their words carefully, so as not to alarm or distress her. What they didn't say interested her more than what they did.

She studied their expressions, which were generally guarded. Their smiles were tentative or strained. Tate's family treated his wife courteously, but there were undercurrents of dislike.

"This is a lovely gown," Zee said, drawing Avery's thoughts back into the room. She was unpacking the things that Tate had brought from home and hanging them in the narrow closet. "Maybe you should wear this tomorrow for Mandy's visit."

Avery gave her a slight nod.

"Are you about finished there, Mom? I think she's getting tired." Tate moved closer to the bed and looked deeply into her eyes. "You'll have a full day tomorrow. We'd better let you get some rest."

"Don't worry about a thing," Nelson said to her. "You're

getting along fine, just like we knew you would. Come on, Zee, let's give them a minute alone.''

"Good-bye, Carole," Zee said.

They slipped out. Tate lowered himself to the edge of her bed again. He looked weary. She wished she had the courage to reach out and touch him, but she didn't. He'd never touched her with anything except consolation—certainly not affection.

"We'll come in the middle of the afternoon, after Mandy's nap." He paused inquiringly; she nodded. "Look for us around three o'clock. I think it would be best if Mandy and I came alone—without anybody else."

He glanced away, and drew a hesitant breath. "I have no idea how she'll respond, Carole, but take into account all that she's been through. I know you've been through a lot, too—a hell of a lot—but you're an adult. You've got more power to cope than she does."

He met her eyes again. "She's just a little girl. Remember that." Then he straightened and smiled briefly. "But, hey, I'm sure the visit will go well."

He stood to go. As usual when he was about to leave, Avery experienced a flurry of panic. He was the only link she had with the world. He was her only reality. When he left, he took her courage with him, leaving her to feel alone, afraid, and alienated.

"Have a restful evening and get a good night's sleep. I'll see you tomorrow."

In farewell, he brushed her fingertips with his own, but he didn't kiss her. He never kissed her. There wasn't too much of her that was accessible to kiss, but Avery thought that a husband would have found a way to kiss his wife if he had really wanted to.

She watched his retreating back until it disappeared through the door of her room. Loneliness crept in from all sides to smother her. The only way she could combat it was to think. She spent her waking hours planning how she was going to tell Tate Rutledge the heartbreaking news that she wasn't who he thought she was. His Carole was no doubt buried in a grave marked Avery Daniels. How would she tell him that?

How could she tell him that somebody close to him wanted him dead?

At least a thousand times during the past week, she had tried convincing herself that her ghostly visitor had been a nightmare. Any one of a number of contributing factors could have made her hallucinate. It was easier to believe that the speaker of those malevolent words had been a delusion.

But she knew better. He had been real. In her mind, his words were as clear as a tropical lagoon. She had memorized them. The sinister tone and inflection were indelibly recorded on her brain. He had meant what he had said. There was no mistaking that.

He had to have been someone in the Rutledge family because only immediate family was allowed in the intensive care unit. But who? None seemed to show any malice toward Tate; quite the contrary, everyone seemed to adore him.

She considered each of them: His father? Unthinkable. It was evident that both parents doted on him. Jack? He didn't appear to harbor any grudges toward his younger brother. Though Eddy wasn't a blood relation, he was treated like a member of the family, and the camaraderie between Tate and his best friend was plain to see. She had yet to hear Dorothy Rae or Fancy speak, but she was fairly certain the voice she had heard had been masculine.

None of the voices she had heard recently belonged to her visitor. But how could a stranger have sneaked into her room? The man had been no stranger to Carole; he had spoken to her as a confidante and coconspirator.

Did Tate realize that his wife was conspiring to have him killed? Did he guess she meant him harm? Was that why he administered comfort and encouragement from behind an invisible barrier? Avery knew he gave her what he was expected to give, but nothing more.

Lord, she wished she could sit down with Irish and lay out all the components of this tangle, as she often did before tackling a complex story. They would try to piece together the missing elements. Irish possessed almost supernatural insight into human behavior, and she valued his opinion above all others.

Thinking about the Rutledges had given Avery a splitting headache, so she welcomed the sedative that was injected into her IV that evening to help her sleep. Unlike the constant brilliance of the ICU, only one small night-light was left burning in her room every night.

Wavering between sleep and consciousness, Avery allowed herself to wonder what would happen if she assumed the role of Carole Rutledge indefinitely. It would postpone Tate's becoming a widower. Mandy would have a mother's support during her emotional recuperation. Avery Daniels could perhaps expose an attempted assassin and be hailed a heroine.

In her mind, she laughed. Irish would think she had gone crazy for sure. He would rant and rave and probably threaten to bend her over his knee and spank her for even thinking up such a preposterous idea.

Still, it was a provocative one. What a story she would have when the charade was over—politics, human relationships, and intrigue.

The fantasy lulled her to sleep.

EIGHT

She was more nervous than she had been before her first television audition at that dumpy little TV station in Arkansas eight years earlier. With damp palms and a dry throat, she had stood ankle deep in mud and swill, gripping the microphone with bloodless fingers and bluffing her way through an on-location story about a parasite currently affecting swine farmers. Afterward, the news director had drolly reminded her that the disease was affecting the swine, not the farmers. But he had given her the job of field reporter anyway.

This was an audition, too. Would Mandy detect what no one else had been able to—that the woman behind the battered face was not Carole Rutledge?

During the day, while the caring, talkative nurses had bathed and dressed her, while the physical therapist had gone through her exercises with her, a haunting question persisted: Did she want the truth to be revealed?

She had arrived at no definite answer. For the time being, what difference did it make who they perceived her to be? She couldn't alter fate. She was alive and Carole Rutledge was dead. Some cosmic force had deemed the outcome of that plane crash, not she.

She had tried desperately, with her severely limited capabilities, to alert everyone to their error, but without success. There was nothing she could do about the consequences of it now. Until she could use a tablet and pencil to communicate, she must remain Carole. While playing that role, she could do some undercover research into a bizarre news story and repay Tate Rutledge for his kindness. If he believed that Mandy would benefit from seeing her "mother," then Avery would temporarily go along with that. She thought the child might be better off by knowing the truth of her mother's death right away, but she wasn't in a position to tell her. Hopefully, her appearance wouldn't frighten the child so badly that she regressed.

The nurse adjusted the scarf covering her head, where her hair was still no more than an inch long. "There. Not bad at all," she said, appraising her handiwork. "In a couple more weeks, that handsome husband of yours won't be able to take his eyes off you. You know, of course, that all the single nurses, as well as a few married ones," she amended dryly, "are wildly in love with him."

She was moving around the bed, straightening the sheets and fussing with the flowers, pinching off blooms that had already peaked and were withering.

"You don't mind, do you?" she asked. "Surely you're used to other women lusting after him by now. How long have y'all been married? Four years, I believe he said when one of the nurses asked.'' She patted Avery's shoulder. "Dr. Sawyer works miracles. Wait and see. Y'all will be the best-looking couple in Washington."

"You're taking a lot for granted, aren't you?"

At the sound of his voice, Avery's heart fluttered. She looked toward the door to find him filling it. As he came farther into the room, he said to the nurse, "I'm convinced that Dr. Sawyer can work miracles. But are you that sure I'll win the election?"

"You've got my vote."

His laugh was deep and rich and as comfortable as an old, worn blanket. "Good. I'll need all the votes I can get."

"Where's your little girl?"

"I left her at the nurses' station. I'll get her in a few minutes."

Taking his subtle cue for what it was, the nurse smiled down at Avery and winked. "Good luck."

As soon as they were alone, Tate moved to Avery's side. "Hi. You look nice." He expelled a deep breath. "Well, she's here. I'm not sure how it'll go. Don't be disappointed if she—"

He broke off as his eyes flickered across her breasts. She didn't adequately fill the bodice of Carole's nightgown, modest as it was. Avery saw the puzzlement register on his face and her heart began to pound.

"Carole?" he said huskily.

He knew!

"My God."

How could she explain?

"You've lost so much weight," he whispered. Gently, he pressed his hand against the side of her breast. He looked over her body. Avery's blood flowed toward the contact of his hand. A small, helpless sound issued out of her throat.

"I don't mean to imply that you look bad—just...different. Stands to reason, I guess, that you would lose several pounds." Their eyes met and held for a moment, then he withdrew his hand. "I'll go get Mandy."

Avery took a deep breath to steady her jangled nerves. Until now she hadn't realized how unnerving the discovery of the truth was going to be to both of them. Nor had she realized how far her feelings for him had extended. His touch had left her insides as weak as her extremities.

But she didn't have the luxury of letting her emotions crumble now. She braced herself for what was to come. She even closed her eyes, dreading the horror she would see on the child's face when she first looked at her disfigured "mother." She heard them enter and approach the bed. "Carole?"

Slowly, Avery opened her eyes. Tate was carrying Mandy against his chest. She was dressed in a white pinafore with a navy blue and white print dress beneath it. Her legs were encased in white stockings and she had on navy leather shoes. There was a cast on her left arm.

Her hair was dark and glossy. It was very thick and heavy, but not as long as Avery remembered it. As though reading her mind, Tate explained, "We had to cut her hair because some of it was singed." It was bobbed to chin length. She wore straight bangs above solemn brown eyes as large and round as quarters and as resigned as a doe's caught in cross hairs.

She was a beautiful child, yet she was unnaturally impassive. Instead of registering repulsion or fear or curiosity, which would have been the expected reactions, she registered nothing.

"Give Mommy the present you brought her," Tate prompted.

With her right fist she was strangling the stems of a bouquet of daisies. She timidly extended them toward Avery. When Avery's fingers failed to grasp them, Tate took them from Mandy and gently laid them on Avery's chest.

"I'm going to set you here on the bed while I find some water to put the flowers in." Tate eased Mandy down on the edge of the bed, but when he moved away, she whimpered and fearfully clutched the lapels of his sports jacket.

"Okay," he said, "guess not." He shot Avery a wry smile and gingerly sat down behind Mandy, barely supporting his hip on the edge of the mattress.

"She colored this for you today," he said, addressing Avery over Mandy's head. From the breast pocket of his jacket, he withdrew a folded piece of manila paper and shook it out. "Tell her what it is, Mandy."

The multicolored scribbles didn't look like anything, but Mandy whispered, "Horses."

"Grandpa's horses," Tate said. "He took her riding yesterday, so this morning I suggested that she color you a picture of the horses while I was working."

Avery lifted her hand and signaled for him to hold the picture in front of her. She studied it at length before Tate laid it on her chest, along with the bouquet of daisies.

"I think Mommy likes your picture." Tate continued looking at Avery with that odd expression.

The child wasn't much interested in whether or not her artwork was appreciated. She pointed at the splint on Avery's nose. "What that?"

"That's part of the bandages Grandma and I told you about, remember?" To Avery he said, "I thought it was coming off today."

She rolled her hand from a palm down position to palm up.

"Tomorrow?" he asked.

She nodded.

"What's it doing?" Mandy asked, still intrigued by the splint.

"It's sort of like your cast. It's protecting Mommy's face until it gets well, like the cast is protecting your arm while the bone inside grows back together."

Mandy listened to the explanation, then turned her solemn stare back onto Avery. "Mommy's crying."

"I think it's because she's very glad to see you."

Avery nodded, closed her eyes, held them closed for several seconds, then opened them. In that way she hoped to convey an emphatic yes. She was glad to see the child, who could so easily have died a fiery death. The crash had left emotional scars, but Mandy had survived and she would live to overcome her residual fear and timidity. Avery was also assailed by guilt and sorrow that she wasn't who they thought she was.

In one of those sudden, unexpected moves that only a child can execute, Mandy thrust out her hand, ready to touch Avery's bruised cheek. Tate reached around her and caught her hand just before it made contact. Then, thinking better of it, he guided her hand down.

"You can touch it very gently. Don't hurt Mommy."

Tears welled up in the child's eyes. "Mommy's hurt." Her lower lip began to tremble and she inclined toward Avery.

Avery couldn't bear to witness Mandy's anguish. Responding to a spontaneous maternal urge, she reached up and cradled Mandy's head with her scarred hand. Applying only as much pressure as her strength and pain would afford, she guided Mandy's head down to her breasts. Mandy came willingly, curling her small body against Avery's side. Avery smoothed her hand over Mandy's head and crooned to her wordlessly.

That inarticulate reassurance communicated itself to the child. In a few moments she stopped crying, sat up, and meekly announced, "I didn't spill my milk, Mommy."

Avery's heart melted. She want to take the child in her arms and hold her tight. She wanted to tell her that spilled milk didn't matter a damn because they had both survived a disaster. Instead, she watched Tate stand and pull Mandy back up into his arms.

"We don't want to wear out our welcome," he said. "Blow Mommy a kiss, Mandy." She didn't. Instead, she shyly wrapped her arms around his neck and turned her face into his collar. "Some other time," he told Avery with an apologetic shrug. "I'll be right back."

He was gone for a few minutes and returned alone. "I left her at the nurses' station. They gave her a Dixie cup of ice cream."

He lowered himself to the edge of the bed and sat with his hands between his knees. Rather than look at her, he stared at his hands. "Since it went so well, I may bring her back later in the week. At least *I* felt like it went well. Did you?" He glanced over his shoulder for her answer. She nodded.

He diverted his attention back to his hands. "I'm not sure how Mandy felt about it. It's hard to tell how she feels about anything. We can't seem to get through, Carole." The despair in his voice tore at Avery's heart. "A trip to

McDonald's used to make her do cartwheels. Now, nothing." His elbows settled on his knees and he dropped his head into his waiting palms. "I've tried everything I know of to reach her. Nothing works. I don't know what else to do."

Avery lifted her arm and smoothed back the hair that grew away from his temple.

He flinched and whipped his head around, almost knocking her hand away. She snatched it back so quickly and reflexively that it sent a pain shooting up her arm. She moaned.

"I'm sorry," he said, instantly coming to his feet. "Are you all right? Should I call somebody?"

She made a negative motion with her head, then self-consciously repositioned the slipping scarf. More than ever before, she felt exposed and naked. She wished she could conceal her ugliness from him.

When he was convinced she was no longer in pain, he said, "Don't worry about Mandy. Given time, I'm sure she'll be fine. I shouldn't have brought it up. I'm just tired. The campaign is escalating and . . . never mind. Those are my concerns, not yours. I've got to be going. I know our visit has been hard on you. Good-bye, Carole."

This time, he didn't even brush her fingertips in farewell.

NINE

"Are we boring you, Tate?"

Guiltily, he glanced up at his campaign manager. "Sorry."

Tate, acknowledging that Eddy had every right to be perturbed with him, cleared his throat and sat up straighter in the leather easy chair. He stopped mindlessly twirling a pencil between his fingers.

They were spending the day at home, holding a powwow

to outline campaign strategy for these last few weeks before the primary.

"Exactly where did you drift off?"

"Somewhere between El Paso and Sweetwater," Tate answered. "Look, Eddy, are you sure that sweep through West Texas is essential?"

"Absolutely essential," Jack chimed in. "With the price of Texas crude where it is, those folks out there need all the pep talks you can give them."

"I'll tell it like it is. You know how I feel about false hopes and empty promises."

"We understand your position completely, Tate," Nelson said. "But Senator Dekker is partly responsible for the fix the oil business is in. He favored that trade agreement with the Arabs. Those unemployed roughnecks need to be reminded of that."

Tate tossed the pencil onto the conference table and stood up. Sliding his hands into the hip pockets of his jeans, he went to stand in front of the window.

It was a spectacular day. Spring was still a fledgling chick, but redbud trees and daffodils were blooming. Grass in the pastures was gradually turning green.

"You don't agree with Nelson's observation?" Eddy asked.

"I agree wholeheartedly," Tate replied, keeping his back to them. "I know I need to be out there citing Dekker's bad judgment and doling out optimism, but I also need to be here."

"With Carole."

"Yes. And with Mandy."

"I thought Mandy's shrink said all she needed was time, and that after Carole returned home, Mandy would naturally improve," Jack said.

"She did."

"So, whether you're here or not won't matter a whole hell of a lot to Mandy. There's not a thing you can do for Carole, either."

"I can be with her," Tate said impatiently. Feeling defensive, he turned to face them.

"Doing what? Just standing there and staring at those two

big, bruised eyes,'' Jack said. ''Jesus, they give me the
creeps.'' Tate's face grew taut with anger over his brother's
insensitive remark.

''Shut up, Jack,'' Nelson snapped.

Tate said crisply, ''Just standing there staring might be all
I can do for her, Jack, but it's still my responsibility to do
it. Didn't I make that clear to you weeks ago?''

With a long-suffering sigh, Eddy lowered himself into a
chair. ''I thought we had all agreed that Carole was better
off in that private clinic than here at home.''

''We did.''

''She's treated like royalty there—better than she was in
the hospital,'' Jack observed. ''She's looking better every
day. I was just kidding about her eyes. Once the redness
goes away and her hair grows back, she'll look great. So
what's the problem?''

''The problem is that she's still recovering from trauma
and serious physical injury,'' Tate said testily.

''No one is arguing that point,'' Nelson said. ''But
you've got to seize every opportunity, Tate. You've got a
responsibility to your campaign that can't be neglected any
more than you can neglect your wife.''

''Don't you think I realize that?'' he asked the three of
them.

''You realize it,'' Eddy said. ''And so does Carole.''

''Maybe. But she doesn't do as well when I'm away. Dr.
Sawyer told me she becomes very depressed.''

''How the hell does he know whether she's depressed or
laughing her head off? She still can't say a goddamned—''

''Jack!'' Nelson spoke in the tone he had frequently used
during the course of his military career to reduce cocky
airmen to groveling penitents. Every inch the retired air
force colonel, he glared at his older son.

He had rarely spanked his children when they were
growing up, resorting to corporal punishment only when he
felt it was absolutely necessary. Usually a single, quelling
look and that harsh tone of voice would whip them back
into line. ''Have a little consideration for your brother's
predicament, please.''

Parental respect silenced Jack, but he flopped back in his chair with obvious exasperation.

"Carole would be the first to tell you to go on this trip," Nelson said to Tate in a quieter voice. "I wouldn't say that if I didn't believe it."

"I agree with Nelson," Eddy said.

"And I agree with both of you. Before the accident, she would have been packing right along with me." Tate rubbed the back of his neck, trying to work out some of the tension and fatigue.

"Now when I tell her I'm leaving, I see panic in her eyes. It haunts me. She's still so pathetic. I feel guilty. Before I leave for any extended time, I have to take into account how she's going to respond to my being away."

He took a silent inventory of their reactions. On each of their faces was an argument wanting to be spoken. Out of consideration, they were keeping their opposing opinions to themselves.

He expelled a deep breath. "Shit. I'm going out for a while."

He stamped from the room and left the house. In under five minutes, he was mounted on horseback and galloping across one of the ranch's pastures, skirting herds of lazily grazing hybrid beef cattle. No particular destination was on his mind; he just needed the privacy and peace that the open air afforded.

These days, he was rarely by himself, but he had never felt more alone in his entire life. His father, Eddy, and Jack could all advise him on political issues, but personal decisions were just that—personal. Only he could make them.

He kept thinking about the way Carole had touched him. He wondered what it meant.

In the two weeks since it had happened, he had reviewed and analyzed it to death and still couldn't get it off his mind. Because of his stunned reaction to it, it hadn't lasted more than a split second—just long enough for her fingertips to rake gently through the hair at his temples. But he considered it the most important caress he and Carole had ever shared—more important than their first kiss, than the first

time they had made love ... than the last time they had
made love.

He reined in and dismounted beside a spring-fed stream
that trickled down from the limestone hills. Scrub oak,
cedar, and mesquite trees dotted the rocky ground. The
wind was strong, out of the north. It stung his cheeks and
made his eyes water. He'd left without a jacket, but the sun
was warm.

That touch had surprised the hell out of him because it
was such an uncharacteristic thing for her to do. She knew
how to touch a man, all right. Even now, after all that had
happened between them, memories of their earlier days
together could make him hard with desire. Very skillfully,
Carole had used touching to communicate when she wanted
him. Whether she chose to be teasing, subtle, or downright
dirty, she knew how to convey her desires.

This one had been different. He had felt the difference. It
had been a touch of concern and caring and compassion. It
had been untutored—spawned by a guileless heart, not a calculating mind. Unselfish, not the reverse.

Very unlike Carole.

The sound of a horse approaching brought his head
around. Nelson reined in and dismounted with almost as
much agility as Tate had minutes before. "Thought I'd ride
out, too. Good day for it." He tilted his head back and
gazed at the cloudless, cerulean sky.

"Bullshit. You came to aid and abet."

Nelson chuckled and indicated with a nod that they
should sit on one of the bleached white boulders. "Zee
spotted you taking off. She suggested it was time to call a
break in the meeting. She served sandwiches to the others
and sent me after you. Said you looked upset."

"I am."

"Well, get over it," Nelson ordered.

"It's not that easy."

"We knew from the beginning that this campaign was
going to be a bitch, Tate. What did you expect?"

"It's not the campaign. I'm ready for that," he said with
a determined jut of his cleft chin.

"Then it's this business with Carole. You knew that wasn't going to be a picnic, either."

Tate swiveled his head around and asked bluntly, "Have you noticed the changes in her?"

"The doctor warned you that there would be some slight alterations in her appearance, but they're hardly noticeable."

"Not physical changes. I'm talking about the way she reacts to things."

"Can't say that I have. Like what?"

Tate cited several instances when Carole's eyes had registered uncertainty, insecurity, fear.

Nelson listened to every word, then ruminated for a long time before saying anything. "I'd say her anxiety was natural, wouldn't you? Her face was torn up to a fare-thee-well. That would make any woman uncertain, but a woman who looked like Carole—well, the thought of losing her beauty would be enough to shake her confidence."

"I suppose you're right," Tate muttered, "but I would expect rage from her before fear. I really can't explain it. It's just something I feel." Absently, he recounted Mandy's first visit to Carole. "I've taken her back three times, and during each visit Carole cries and holds Mandy against her."

"She's thinking how easily she could have lost her."

"It's more than that, Dad. One day while she was still at the hospital, when we stepped off the elevator, she was sitting there in the hall in a wheelchair, waiting for our arrival. It was before her teeth were replaced. Her head was wrapped in a scarf. Her leg was propped up in that cast." Perplexed, he shook his head. "She looked like hell, but there she was, bold as brass. Now, is that something Carole would do?"

"She was eager to see you, to show off her ability to get out of bed."

Tate considered that for a moment, but it still didn't gel. When had Carole ever put herself out to please someone else? He could have sworn that despite her inability to smile, she was beaming at the sight of Mandy and him when the elevator doors opened. "So you think it's all an act?"

"No," Nelson said hesitantly. "I just think it's—"

"Temporary."

"Yes," he said flatly. "I face facts, Tate. You know that. I don't mean to butt into your personal life. Zee and I want you and Jack and your families to stay here on the ranch with us. And because we do, we've made it a point never to interfere with your private business. If I did what I felt inclined to, I'd see to it that Dorothy Rae got professional help for her problem and I'd blister Fancy's butt for all the times it should have been blistered and wasn't."

He paused before continuing. "Maybe I should have said something before now, but I was hoping that you would take the initiative to set your marriage straight. I know that you and Carole have sort of grown apart over the last couple of years." He held up both hands. "You don't have to tell me why. I don't need to know. It's just something that I've sensed, you know?

"Hell, every marriage goes through rough spots now and then. Zee and I hope that you and Carole will iron out your differences, have another baby, go to Washington, and live to grow old together. Maybe this tragedy will patch up the problems you had and bring you closer together.

"But," he said, "don't expect Carole to change entirely as a result of what's happened to her. If anything, it'll take more patience to get along with her than it has up till now."

Tate edited his father's speech, picking out the pertinent points and reading between the lines. "You're telling me that I'm looking for something that isn't there, is that it?"

"I'm saying it's a possibility," the older man stressed. "Usually when someone has a close brush with death, he goes through a period of smelling the roses. I've seen it happen with pilots who ditched their planes and lived to tell about it.

"You know, they contemplate all that could have been taken from them in the blink of an eye, feel guilty for not appreciating their loved ones, and promise to make amends, improve their general attitude toward life, become a better person—that kind of thing." He rested his hand on Tate's knee. "I think that's what you're seeing in Carole.

"I don't want you to start hoping that this incident has rid her of all her faults and left her a paragon of what a wife should be. Dr. Sawyer guaranteed to remove some of the imperfections in her face, but he never said a word about her soul," he added with a smile.

"I guess you're right," Tate said tautly. "I *know* you're right. That's exactly what I was doing, looking for improvements that aren't really there."

Nelson used Tate's shoulder as a prop as he stood up. "Don't be so hard on yourself or on her. Time and patience are indispensable investments. Anything worth having is worth waiting for, no matter how long it takes—even a lifetime."

They mounted and turned the horses toward the house. On the way back, they said very little. As they drew up in front of the stable, Tate leaned on his saddle horn and turned to address his father.

"About that trip to West Texas."

"Yeah?" Nelson threw his right leg over and stepped to the ground.

"I'll compromise. One week. I can't be gone any longer than that."

Nelson slapped Tate's thigh with the reins he was holding, then handed them to Tate. "I figured you'd come around. I'll tell Eddy and Jack." He headed for the house.

"Dad?" Nelson stopped and turned. "Thanks," Tate said.

Nelson waved off the gratitude. "Put those horses up properly."

Tate walked his horse into the stable, pulling Nelson's along behind. He dismounted and began the rubdown procedure he'd been taught to do as early as he'd been taught to ride.

But after several minutes, his hands fell idle on the horse's rump and he stared into space.

He had needed her compassion and tenderness that night. He had wanted to trust the motives behind her touch. For the sake of their marriage and Mandy, he had hoped these changes in her would be permanent.

Only time would tell, but his father was probably right. It was wishful thinking to believe that Carole had changed, when her previous actions had shown her to be faithless and untrustworthy. He couldn't give her the benefit of the doubt without everybody, chiefly himself, thinking he was a fool for trusting her even that far.

"Damn."

TEN

"After that, we intend to send him up to the panhandle for a speech at Texas Tech." As Jack detailed Tate's itinerary to his sister-in-law, a fresh thought occurred to him. "You know, Tate, there are a lot of cotton farmers in that region. I wonder if Eddy's considered having you speak to a co-op or something?"

"If he hasn't, he should. I definitely want to."

"I'll make a mental note to have him schedule something."

From her bed, Avery observed the two brothers. There was enough resemblance to place them in the same family, but enough difference to make them drastically unlike each other.

Jack appeared more than three years older than Tate. His hair, several shades darker than Tate's, was thinning on top. He wasn't exactly paunchy, but his physique wasn't well honed, as Tate's was.

Of the two, Tate was much better looking. Although there was nothing offensive about Jack's appearance, there wasn't anything distinguishing about it, either. He faded into the woodwork. Tate couldn't if he tried.

"Forgive us for taking him away from you for so long, Carole." She noticed that Jack never looked directly at her when speaking to her. He would always address some other area of her body besides her face—her chest, her hand, the cast on her leg. "We wouldn't if we didn't feel it was important to the campaign."

Her fingers closed around the oversized pencil in her hand and she scrawled "okay" on the tablet. Jack tilted his head, read what she'd written, shot her a weak smile, and nodded curtly. There were unpleasant undercurrents between Jack and his sister-in-law. Avery wondered what they were.

"Tate said you managed to say some words today," he said. "That's great news. We'll all be glad to hear what you've got to say once you can talk again."

Avery knew Tate wouldn't be glad to hear what she had to say. He would want to know why she hadn't written down her name, why she had let him go on believing that she was his wife, even after she'd regained enough coordination in her hand to use the pencil on the tablet.

She wanted to know that herself.

Anxiety over it brought tears to her eyes. Jack immediately stood and began backing toward the door. "Well, it's getting late, and I'm facing that long drive home. Good luck, Carole. You coming, Tate?"

"Not quite yet, but I'll walk you to the lobby." After telling her that he would be back in a few minutes, he accompanied his brother from the room.

"I think I upset her by talking about your trip," Jack remarked.

"She's been touchy the last few days."

"You'd think she'd be glad she was getting her voice back, wouldn't you?"

"I guess it's frustrating to try and speak plainly when you can't." Tate moved to the tinted glass doors of the exclusive clinic and pulled one open.

"Uh, Tate, have you noticed something weird when she writes?"

"Weird?"

He moved aside to admit a pair of nurses into the lobby, followed by a man carrying an arrangement of copper chrysanthemums. Jack stepped outside, but used his hand to prevent the door from closing behind him.

"Carole's right-handed, isn't she?"

"Yeah."

"So why is she writing with her left hand?" As soon as Jack posed the puzzling question, he shrugged. "I just thought it was odd." His hand fell to his side and the hydraulic door began to close. "See you at home, Tate."

"Drive carefully."

Tate stood staring after his brother until someone else approached the door and looked at him inquiringly. He pivoted on his heels and thoughtfully retraced his steps toward Carole's room.

While Tate was gone, Avery thought about how he had changed. She had sensed a difference in his attitude more than a week ago. He still paid her regular visits, but they were no longer on a daily basis. At first she had excused this, knowing that his campaign was in full swing.

Whenever he came, he still brought flowers and magazines. Now that she could eat solid foods, he brought her junk food to augment the hospital's excellent, but boring cuisine. He'd even had a VCR installed and had supplied her with a variety of movies to help entertain her. But he was often withdrawn and moody, guarded in what he said to her. He never stayed for very long.

As Carole's face became more distinct, Tate became more distant.

He hadn't brought Mandy to see her, either. She had printed Mandy's name, followed by a question mark, on the tablet and held it up to him. He had shrugged. "I thought the visits were probably doing her more harm than good. You'll have plenty of time to spend with her once you're back home."

The insensitive words had wounded her. Mandy's visits had become highlights in her monotonous existence. On the other hand, it was probably better that he had suspended them. She was growing too attached to the child and wanted desperately to help see her through this crisis in her young life. Since she wouldn't have that opportunity, it was wise to sever any emotional bonds now.

The attachment she had developed for Tate was more complex and would be considerably harder to sever when she moved out of his world and back into her own.

At least she would be taking something back with her: the ingredients of a juicy inside story on the man running for the U.S. Senate whom someone wanted murdered.

Avery's journalistic curiosity ran rampant. What had been amiss in the Rutledges' marriage? Why had Carole wanted her husband dead? She wanted to exhaust all the possibilities until she arrived at the truth. Telling that truth might lift her out of the muck she'd made of her professional life. Yet it left a bad taste in her mouth to think about broadcasting that truth.

Tate Rutledge's problems belonged to her now just as much as they did to him. She hadn't asked for them; they'd been imposed on her. But she couldn't just turn her back on them. For some bizarre reason that defied explanation, she felt compelled to make up for Carole's shortcomings.

The one time she had extended a compassionate hand to him, he had emphatically rebuffed her, but the strife between Tate and Carole went beyond the normal marriage in trouble. There was another almost malevolent dimension to it. He treated her as one might a caged wild beast. He saw to all her needs, but from a careful distance. His approach was mistrustful, as though her behavior couldn't be depended on.

As Avery knew, Tate's wariness of his wife was well-founded. Carole, along with another individual, had plotted to kill him. How and why were the questions that haunted her more than any others.

The troubling thoughts were temporarily shelved when he returned from escorting Jack out. However, her welcoming smile wavered as he approached her chair. He was scowling.

"Why are you writing with your left hand?"

Avery froze. So, this was to be the moment of truth. She had hoped to choose the time herself, but it had been chosen for her. How stupid she'd been to make such a blunder! Percentages were strongly against Carole Rutledge being left-handed.

She looked up at him with appeal and managed to speak a guttural version of his name.

God help me, she prayed as she fumbled for the pencil with her left hand. As soon as she revealed her identity, she must warn him of the planned assassination. The only time limit placed on it was that he would never live to take office. It could happen tomorrow, tonight. It might not happen until next November, but he had to be warned immediately.

Who in his family would she accuse? She hadn't revealed herself as soon as she could control a pencil because she didn't have enough facts. She had vainly hoped that each new day would provide her with some.

Once she had outlined the meager facts she knew, would he believe her?

Why should he?

Why should he even listen to a woman who had, for almost two months, passed herself off as his wife? He would think she was an unconscionable opportunist, which could be uncomfortably close to the truth if she weren't genuinely concerned for his and Mandy's welfare.

The pencil moved beneath the painstaking coaxing of her fingers. She drew the letter *h*. Her hand was shaking so badly, she dropped the pencil. It rolled downward, slid across her lap, and finally became lodged between her hip and the seat of the upholstered chair.

Tate went after it. His strong fingers nudged her flesh. He replaced the pencil in her hand and guided it back onto the tablet. "*H* what?"

Beseechingly, she looked up at him, silently asking for his forgiveness. Then she finished the word she had begun. When she had printed it, she turned the tablet toward him.

"Hurts," he read. "It hurts to use your right hand?"

Immersed in guilt, Avery nodded her head. "It hurts," she croaked, and raised her right hand where the skin was still sensitive.

Her lie was justified, she assured herself. She couldn't tell him the truth until she could explain everything in detail. A scrawled message, a few key words without any elaboration, would only pitch him into a frenzy of anger and confusion. In that kind of mental state, he would never believe that someone wanted to kill him.

He gave a soft, short laugh. "You had Jack spooked. I

can't believe I didn't notice it myself. I guess I've had too much on my mind to sweat the details.''

He placed his hands in the small of his back and arched it, stretching luxuriantly. ''Well, I've got that drive ahead of me, and it's getting late. I understand your cast comes off tomorrow. That's good. You'll be able to move around better.''

Avery's eyes clouded with tears. This man, who had been so kind to her, was going to hate her when he discovered the truth. Through the weeks of her recuperation, he had unwittingly become her lifeline. Whether he was aware of it or not, she had depended on him for physical and emotional healing.

Now, she must repay his kindness by telling him three ugly truths: his wife was dead; in her place was a broadcast journalist who was privy to aspects of his personal life; and someone was going to try to assassinate him.

Rather than eliciting his pity, her tears provoked him. He glanced away in irritation, and as he did, he noticed the newspapers stacked on the deep windowsill. She had requested them from the deferential staff. They were back issues, containing accounts of the plane crash. Tate gestured toward them.

''I don't understand your tears, Carole. Your face looks great. You could have died, for crissake. So could Mandy. Can't you consider yourself lucky to be alive?''

After that outburst, he drew himself up and took a deep breath, controlling his temper by an act of will. ''Look, I'm sorry. I didn't mean to lash out like that. I know you've suffered a lot. It's just that you could have suffered a hell of a lot more. We all could have.''

He reached for the sports jacket he frequently wore with his jeans and pulled it on. ''I'll see you later.''

With no more than that, he left her.

Avery stared at the empty doorway for a long while. A nurse came in and helped her prepare for sleep. She had graduated from a wheelchair to crutches for her broken leg, but was still awkward on them. Gripping them hurt her hands. By the time she was settled and left alone, she was exhausted.

Her mind was as tired as her body, and yet she couldn't sleep. She tried to envision the expression that would break across Tate's face when he discovered the truth. His life would undergo another upheaval, and at a time when he was most vulnerable.

The instant the word vulnerable formed in her mind, Avery was struck by a new and terrifying thought. As soon as she was exposed, she, too, would be vulnerable to whoever planned to kill Tate!

Why hadn't she thought of that before? When Avery Daniels, a television news reporter, was revealed, the culprit would realize his grave error and be forced to do something about it. She would be as susceptible to attack as Tate. Judging by the deadly calculation she had heard in his voice, the would-be assassin wouldn't hesitate to murder both of them.

She sat up and peered into the shadows of the room, as if expecting her faceless, nameless nemesis to leap out at her. Her rapid heartbeats echoed loudly against her eardrums.

Lord, what could she do? How could she protect herself? How could she protect Tate? If only she really were Carole, she—

Before the idea was even fully developed, her mind began hurling objections, both conscientious and practical. It couldn't be done. Tate would know. The assassin would know.

But if she could keep playing the role long enough to determine who Tate's secret enemy was, she could save his life.

Yet it was inconceivable to step into another woman's life. And what about her own? Officially, Avery Daniels no longer existed. No one would be missing her. She had no husband, no children, no family.

Her career was in a shambles. Because of one mistake—one gross error in judgment—she was deemed a failure by anyone's standards. Not only had she failed to live up to her father's sterling reputation, she'd taken the glint off it. Working at KTEX in San Antonio was like being sentenced to years of hard labor. While the station had a solid reputation for a market its size, and while she would be eternally grateful to Irish for giving her a job when no one else would even grant her an interview, employment there was tantamount to banishment in Siberia. She was alienated from journalistic circles that really counted. KTEX was a long step down from a network job and a Washington, D.C., beat.

But now, a sensational story had been dropped into her lap. If she became Mrs. Tate Rutledge, she could document a senatorial campaign and an attempted murder from an insider's point of view. She wouldn't just be covering the story, she would be living it.

What better vehicle to launch herself back to the top echelon of broadcast news? How many reporters had ever been given an opportunity like this? She knew scores who would give their right arm for it.

She smiled wanly. Her right arm hadn't been required of her, but she had given her face, her name, and her own identity already. Saving a man's life and getting a career boost would be repayment enough for such an indignity. And when the truth finally came out, no one could accuse her of exploitation. She hadn't asked for this chance; it had been forced on her. She wouldn't be exploiting Tate, either. Even above her desire to restore her professional credibility, she wanted to preserve his life, which had become precious to her.

The risks involved were astronomical, but she couldn't name a single ace reporter who hadn't stuck his neck out to get where he was. Her father had taken daily risks in the pursuit of his profession. His courage had paid off with a Pulitzer prize. If he was willing to risk everything for his stories, could less be expected of her?

However, she realized that this had to be a rational business decision. She must approach it pragmatically, not emotionally. She would be assuming the role of Tate's wife and all that the relationship implied and entailed. She would be living with his family, constantly observed by people who knew Carole intimately.

The enormity of the challenge was intimidating, but it was also irresistible. The consequences could be severe, but the rewards would be worth any price.

She would make a million mistakes, like writing with the wrong hand. But she'd always had a knack for thinking on her feet. She would talk her way out of mistakes.

Could it work? Could she do it? *Dare* she try?

She threw off the covers, propped herself on her crutches, and hobbled into the bathroom. Beneath the glaring, merciless fluorescent lighting, she stared at the face in the mirror and compared it to the photograph of Carole that had been taped to the wall for encouragement.

The skin looked new, as pink and smooth as a baby's butt, just as Dr. Sawyer had promised. She peeled her lips back and studied the dental prostheses that were duplicates of Carole Rutledge's front teeth. She ran her hand over the close cap of dark hair. No scars were discernible, unless one looked very closely. In time, all traces would fade into invisibility.

She didn't allow herself the luxury of sadness, though regret and homesickness for her own familiar image tugged at her heart. This was her destiny now. She had a new face. It could be her ticket to a new life.

Tomorrow, she would assume the identity of Carole Rutledge.

Avery Daniels had nothing else to lose.

ELEVEN

The nurse gave her a satisfied once-over. "You've got wonderful hair, Mrs. Rutledge."

"Thanks," Avery said ruefully. "What there is of it."

During the seven days that Tate had been away, she had fully regained her voice. He was due to arrive at any moment, and she was nervous.

"No," the nurse was saying, "that's my point. Not

everybody can wear such a short style. On you, it's a knockout.''

Avery glanced into the hand mirror, plucked at the spiky bangs on her forehead, and said dubiously, ''I hope so.''

She was seated in a chair with her right leg elevated on a footstool. A cane was propped against the chair. Her hands were folded together in her lap.

The nurses were as aflutter as she over Tate's imminent arrival after being out of town for more than a week. They had primped her like a bride waiting for her groom.

''He's here,'' one of them announced in a stage whisper, poking her head around the door. The nurse with Avery squeezed her shoulder. ''You look terrific. He's going to be bowled over.''

He wasn't exactly bowled over, but he was momentarily stunned. She watched his eyes widen marginally when he spotted her sitting in the chair, wearing street clothes— Carole's street clothes—which Zee had brought her several days earlier.

''Hello, Tate.''

At the sound of her voice, he registered even more surprise.

Her heart lurched. *He knew!*

Had she made another blunder? Did Carole have a pet name she always addressed him by? She held her breath, waiting for him to point an accusing finger at her and shout, ''You lying impostor!''

Instead, he cleared his throat uneasily and returned her greeting. ''Hello, Carole.''

Through her finely fashioned nose, she exhaled thin little wisps of air, not wanting to give away her relief by expelling the deep breath she'd been holding for so long it had made her chest ache.

He came farther into the room, and absently laid a bunch of flowers and a package on the nightstand. ''You look great.''

''Thank you.''

''You can talk,'' he said with an awkward laugh.

''Yes. Finally.''

''Your voice sounds different.''

"We were warned of that, remember?" she said quickly.

"Yeah, but I didn't expect the . . ." He made a motion with his fingers across his throat. "The hoarseness."

"It might eventually fade."

"I like it."

He couldn't take his eyes off her. If things between them had been what they should have been, he would be kneeling in front of her, skimming her new face with his fingertips like a blind man, marveling over its smoothness, and telegraphing his love. To her disappointment, he maintained a careful distance.

As usual, he was wearing jeans. They were pressed and creased, but old and soft enough to glove his lower body. Avery didn't want to be trapped by her own feminine curiosity, so she resolutely kept her eyes above the lapel of his sports jacket.

The view from there was very good, too. Her gaze was almost as penetrating as his.

She nervously raised her hand to her chest. "You're staring."

His head dropped forward, but only for a split second before he raised it again. "I'm sorry. I guess I really didn't expect you to ever look like yourself again. And . . . and you do. Except for the hair."

She gave a little shiver of joy because her ruse had worked.

"Are you cold?"

"What? Cold? No." She recklessly groped for something to divert him. "What's that?"

He followed her nod to the package he had carried in with him. "Oh, it's your jewelry."

"Jewelry?" Her bubble of happiness burst. She swallowed with difficulty.

"What you were wearing the day of the plane crash. The hospital called the law office today to remind me it was still in their safe. I stopped there on my way here to pick it up. I kept forgetting about it." He extended the envelope to her. Avery stared at it as though it were a poisonous snake and was just as loath to touch it. Seeing no way to avoid it, however, she took it from him. "I didn't take the time to inventory the contents,'' he said, ''but maybe you should now.''

She laid the envelope in her lap. ''I will later.''

''I thought you'd want your things back.''

''Oh, I do. It's just not very comfortable to wear jewelry right now.'' She formed a fist, then slowly opened it, extending her fingers. ''My hands are almost back to normal, but they still get sore. I think I'd have trouble slipping my rings on and off.''

''That would be a first, wouldn't it? For your wedding ring, anyway.''

The harsh words took her aback. He wasn't wearing a wedding ring, either, she noted, and was tempted to point that out in Carole's defense, but she curbed the impulse. If Carole had removed her wedding ring for illicit purposes, as he'd insinuated, the subject was best avoided—for now.

Tate sat down on the edge of the bed. The hostile silence stretched out. Avery was the first to break it. ''Did the trip go as well as you had hoped?''

''Yeah, it was fine. Tiring as hell.''

''I saw you on television nearly every night. The crowds seemed enthusiastic.''

''Everybody was pleased with the response I got.''

''All the political analysts are predicting that you'll win the primary by a landslide.''

''I hope so.''

They lapsed into another silence while each tried, without much success, to keep from staring at the other.

''How is Mandy?''

He gave a dismissive shrug. ''She's fine.''

Avery frowned doubtfully.

''Okay, not so fine.'' He stood again and began pacing the length of the bed, his boot heels making crescent impressions in the carpeting. ''Mom says she's still having nightmares. She wakes up screaming nearly every night, sometimes even during her nap. She moves around the house like a little ghost.'' He extended his hands as though reaching for something, then closed them around nothingness. ''Not quite there, you know? Nobody's getting through— not me, not the psychologist.''

"I asked Zee to bring her to see me. She said you had told her not to."

"That's right."

"Why?"

"I didn't think it would be a good idea for her to come when I wasn't here."

She didn't press her luck by asking why. It might spark another argument she wasn't yet equipped to handle. "I miss her. Once I'm at home, she'll do better."

His skepticism was plain. "Maybe."

"Does she ever ask for me?"

"No."

Avery lowered her gaze to her lap. "I see."

"Well, what do you expect, Carole? You only get back what you give."

For a moment their eyes clashed, then her hand came up to her forehead. Tears filled her eyes. She cried for the child who hadn't had enough of her mother's love. Poor little Mandy. Avery knew how it felt to be deprived of a parent's attention. That's why she justified pretending to be Mandy's mother when, initially, she had felt Mandy would profit from being told of Carole's demise immediately.

"Aw, shit," Tate said beneath his breath. He crossed the room and lightly rested his hand on the top of her head. His fingers worked their way through her stubby hair until the pads were gently massaging her scalp. "I'm sorry. I didn't mean to make you cry. Mandy's going to get better—much better." After a moment, he said, "Maybe I should go."

"No!" Her head snapped up. Tears still drenched her eyes. "I wish you wouldn't."

"It's time I did."

"Please stay a while longer."

"I'm tired and cranky from the trip—not good company."

"I don't mind."

He shook his head.

Valiantly, she masked her immense disappointment. "I'll see you out then."

She reached for her cane and placed her weight on it as she stood up. But her nervously perspiring hand slipped on the crook and caused her to lose her balance.

"Christ, be careful."

Tate's arms went around her. The manila envelope fell from her lap onto the floor, but neither noticed. His arm supported her back, and his strong fingers aligned with her ribs beneath the soft weight of her breast.

As he inched her toward the bed, Avery clung to him, curling her fingers into the cloth of his jacket. She deeply inhaled his scent—clean but outdoorsy, fragrant but masculine, with a trace of citrus. His strength permeated her and she imbibed it like an elixir.

She acknowledged then what she had avoided acknowledging during the long, torturous days he had been away. She wanted to become Mrs. Rutledge so she could be close to Tate. Based on the misery she'd felt during his absence and the joy she'd experienced when he had entered her room, that was no less valid a reason than the others. At least, it was just as strong.

He eased her onto the side of the bed, and gingerly touched the thigh of her injured leg. "That was a multiple fracture. The bone's still not as strong as you'd like to think."

"I guess not."

"We were right to decide you should stay here until after the primary. All that activity would be too much for you."

"Probably."

Her reply was qualified, because when Zee had told her that had been the decision reached without her consent or consultation, she had felt abandoned, like a family embarrassment that had been hidden away, out of the public eye.

"I can't wait to come home, Tate."

Their heads were close. She could see her new face reflected in the pupils of his eyes. His breath wafted over it. She wanted to be held. She wanted to hold him.

Touch me, Tate. Hold me. Kiss me, she wanted to say.

For several heartbeats he seemed to be considering it, then he pulled back.

"I'll go now," he said gruffly, "so you can rest."

She reached for his hand and clasped it as tightly as she was able to. "Thank you."

"For what?"

"For . . . for the flowers and . . . and for helping me back to bed."

"That's nothing," he said dismissively, pulling his hand free.

She made a wounded sound. "Why do you always refuse my thanks?"

"Don't play dumb, Carole," he whispered testily. "Your thanks don't mean anything to me and you know why." He said a curt good-bye and left.

Avery was crushed. She had hoped for so much more out of their reunion. Her fantasies of it hadn't been anything like the grim reality. But what could she expect from a husband who obviously didn't care a great deal about his wife?

At least he hadn't detected her lie. From a professional standpoint, she was still on firm ground.

She returned to the chair and picked up the envelope, pried open the metal brad, lifted the flap, and shook the contents into her hand. Her wristwatch was no longer ticking—the crystal had been shattered. A gold earring was missing, but it was no great loss. The item that was most important to her wasn't there. Where was her locket?

Then she remembered. She hadn't been wearing her locket when the accident had occurred. Carole Rutledge had had it.

Avery slumped against the chair, lamenting the loss of that treasured piece of jewelry, but she roused herself immediately. She would mourn the loss later. Right now, she had to act.

A few minutes later, a nurse at the central station glanced up from the keyboard of her computer terminal. "Good evening, Mrs. Rutledge. Did you enjoy your visit with your husband?"

"Very much, thank you." She handed the nurse the envelope. "I have a favor to ask. Would you please mail this for me tomorrow?" The nurse read the address Avery had printed on it. "Please," Avery pressed, before the nurse could ask any questions.

"I'd be glad to," she said, though she obviously found it a strange request. "It'll go out in the morning's mail."

"I would rather you not mention this to anyone. My husband accuses me of being too sentimental as it is."

"All right."

Avery handed her several folded bills, pilfered from the generous allowance Tate had left with her before his trip. "That's enough money to cover the postage, I believe. Thank you."

That represented another severance with Avery Daniels. She returned to the room assigned to Mrs. Carole Rutledge.

TWELVE

In stocking feet, Irish McCabe went to his refrigerator for another beer. He pulled off the tab and, as he sipped the malty foam from the top of the can, inspected his freezer for dinner possibilities. Finding nothing there that was a better option than hunger, he decided to do without food and fill up on beer.

On his way back into the living room, he picked up the stack of mail he'd dropped on the table when he had come in earlier. While idly watching a TV game show, he sorted through the correspondence, culling junk mail and setting aside bills.

"Humph." A puzzled frown pulled together salt-and-pepper eyebrows when he came across the manila envelope. There was no return address, but it bore a local postmark. He unfastened the brad and wedged his index finger beneath the flap. He upended the envelope and dumped the contents into his lap.

He sucked in a quick breath and recoiled, as though something foul had landed on him. He stared at the damaged jewelry while his lungs struggled for air and his heart labored in his chest.

It was several moments before he calmed down enough to reach out and touch the shattered wristwatch. He had immediately recognized it as Avery's. Gingerly he picked it up and tentatively investigated the gold earring he'd last seen decorating Avery's ear.

Quickly coming to his feet, he rushed across the room to a desk that he rarely used, except as a catchall. He pulled open the lap drawer and took out the envelope he'd been given at the morgue the day he had identified Avery's body. ''Her things,'' the forensic assistant had told him apologetically.

He remembered dropping her locket into the envelope without even looking inside. Up till now he hadn't had the heart to open it and touch her personal effects. He was superstitious. To paw through Avery's belongings would be as distasteful to him as grave robbing.

He'd had to empty her apartment because her landlady had insisted on it. He hadn't kept a single thing, except a few photographs. Her clothes and all other usable items had been donated to various charities.

The only thing that Irish had deemed worth keeping was the locket that had identified her body. Her daddy had given it to her when she was just a kid, and Irish had never seen Avery without it.

He opened the envelope that had been in his desk all this time and dumped the contents onto the desk's littered surface. Along with Avery's locket, there was a pair of diamond earrings, a gold bracelet watch, two bangle bracelets, and three rings, two of which comprised a wedding set. The third ring was a cluster of sapphires and diamonds. Together it added up to a hell of a lot more than Avery's jewelry, but it wasn't worth a plug nickel to Irish McCabe.

Obviously, the pieces belonged to one of the other crash victims, possibly to one of the survivors. Was somebody grieving its misplacement? Or had it even been missed?

He would have to check on that and try to get it back to the rightful owner. Now, all he could think about was Avery's jewelry—the watch and earring that had been delivered today to his post office box. Who had sent them? Why now? Where had they been all this time?

He studied the envelope, searching for possible clues as

to its sender. There were none. It didn't look like it had come from a municipal office. The printed lettering was rickety and uneven, almost childish.

"Who the hell?" he asked his empty apartment.

The pain of his grief over Avery should have been blunted by now, but it wasn't. He dropped heavily into his easy chair and stared at the locket with misty eyes. He rubbed it between his finger and thumb like a talisman that might make her miraculously materialize.

Later, he would try to solve the mystery of how her jewelry had become switched with that of another crash victim. For the present, however, he only wanted to wallow in the morass of his bereavement.

"I don't see why not."

"I told you why not."

"What would be wrong with me going down to Corpus Christi with you when you go later this week?"

"It's a business trip. I'll be busy setting up rallies for Tate."

Fancy's mouth drew into a petulant pout. "You could let me tag along if you really wanted to."

Eddy Paschal looked at her from the corner of his eye. "Guess that gives you your answer."

He switched out the lights at campaign headquarters. The property was located in a shopping center and had previously been a pet store. The rent was cheap. It was a central location, easily accessible to just about any point in the city. About its only drawback was the remnant odor of caged pets.

"Why are you so mean to me, Eddy?" Fancy whined as he used his key to secure the dead bolt.

"Why are you such a pest?"

Together they walked across the parking lot to his parked car, a serviceable Ford sedan that she privately scorned. He unlocked the passenger door and opened it for her. As she got in, she brushed the front of her body against his.

As he rounded the hood on his way to the driver's side, she noticed that he'd recently gotten a haircut. The barber had clipped his hair too short. Topping her list of Eddy "redos" was his car. Second was his barber.

He slid in behind the wheel and turned on the ignition. The air conditioner came on automatically and began filling the interior with hot, humid air. Eddy made a concession to his fresh-out-of-the-bandbox appearance by loosening his tie and unbuttoning his collar button.

Fancy went considerably further than that in her quest for comfort. She unbuttoned her blouse to her waist, then fanned it open and shut, providing Eddy with an excellent view of her breasts if he chose to take it, which she was peeved to note that he didn't. He was maneuvering the car through the intersection and up the entrance ramp to the freeway.

"Are you gay, or what?" she demanded crossly.

He burst out laughing. "Why do you ask?"

"Because if I gave away to other guys half of what I give away to you, I'd spend all my time on my back."

"To hear you tell it, you do anyhow." He glanced at her. "Or is that just so much talk?"

Fancy's blue eyes fairly smoked, but she was too clever to lose her temper. Instead, she curled up into the car seat with the sinuous laziness of a cat and asked slyly, "Why don't you find out for yourself, Mr. Paschal?"

He shook his head. "You're an incorrigible brat, Fancy, know that?"

"I should," she said breezily, pulling her fingers through her mass of dark-blond curls. "That's what everybody tells me." She leaned toward the air-conditioning vent, which was blowing out frigid air now. She held her hair up off her neck and let the air blow against her skin, which was dewy with perspiration. "Well, are you?"

"Am I what?"

"Gay."

"No, I'm not."

She sat up and angled her body toward him. Her hands were still holding her hair up off her neck—a pose that emphasized her breasts. The cold air had made her nipples hard. They jutted against the cloth of her shirt. "Then, how can you resist me?"

Congested freeway traffic had been left behind and they were now heading northwest toward the ranch. Eddy's gaze roved over her slowly, taking in all the alluring details. It gave her satisfaction to watch his Adam's apple slide up and down as he swallowed with difficulty.

"You're a beautiful child, Fancy." His eyes rested briefly on her breasts, where the dark impressions of their pert centers could be seen beneath her shirt. "A beautiful *woman*."

Gradually she lowered her arms, letting her hair fall loosely around her face and onto her shoulders. "Well, then?"

"You're my best friend's niece."

"So?"

"So to me that means you're off limits."

"How prudish!" she exclaimed. "You're a Victorian, Eddy, that's what you are. A throwback. A stuffy prude. Ridiculous."

"It wouldn't be ridiculous to your Uncle Tate. Or to your grandfather or father. If I laid a hand on you, any one or all three of them would come after me with a shotgun."

She reached across the seat and ran her finger up his thigh, whispering, "Now, wouldn't that be exciting?"

He removed her hand and pushed it back across the car. "Not if you're the target."

She flopped back in her seat, annoyed, and turned her head to gaze at the passing scenery. That morning she had deliberately left her car at the ranch and hitched a ride into San Antonio with her father, planning all along to stay late and finagle a ride home with Eddy. Months of subtle invitation had gotten her nowhere. Since patience had never been one of her virtues, she had decided to step up the pace of her pursuit.

Buck, the bellhop, had lasted less than a month before he had become possessive and jealous. Then the man who had come to spray the house for cockroaches had ended up in her bed. That affair had lasted until she had discovered he was married. It wasn't his marital status that bothered her so much as his postcoital guilt, which he morosely discussed with her. Remorse took all the fun out of fucking.

Since the exterminator there had been an assortment of partners, but all had simply been diversions to occupy her until Eddy surrendered. She was getting tired of waiting.

Indeed, she was getting tired of everything. The last three months had put a real strain on her generally good disposition. There had even been times when she had envied her Aunt Carole all the attention she was getting.

While Fancy was spending interminable hours stuffing envelopes and taking telephone polls in that noisy, crowded, stinky, tacky campaign headquarters, with people who could get off on a ten-dollar contribution, Carole was being waited on hand and foot in that posh private clinic.

Mandy was another thorn in her side. As if the little brat hadn't always been spoiled rotten, it was even worse now since the plane crash. Just last week Fancy had been sternly reprimanded by her grandmother when she had yelled at her young cousin for eating all the Oreos.

In Fancy's opinion, the kid was off her beam. Her hollow, vacant eyes were damn spooky. She was turning into a zombie and, in the meantime, everybody kissed her ass.

Her daddy had gone positively ape shit when she had gotten her most recent speeding ticket, and he had threatened to take away her car if she got another. He even warned that she would have to pay the fine out of money she earned herself. Of course her daddy's threats never panned out, but his shouting had really gotten on her nerves.

She couldn't believe the fuss everyone made over that primary election. You would have thought her uncle was running for fuckin' president the way everybody had carried on about it. He had won by a landslide, which had come as no surprise to her. She couldn't understand why they had paid a political analyst big bucks to predict the outcome a week before the election, when she could have given it to them months ago for free. Her uncle's smile made women cream their jeans. It didn't matter what his speeches were about; women would vote for him on the basis of his looks. But had anyone asked her? No. Nobody asked her opinion about anything.

Things were looking up, however. Now that the primary election was out of the way, Eddy wouldn't have so many distractions. His mind would be freer to think about her. She had been optimistic of a successful seduction when she had first launched the project. Now she wasn't so sure. He'd eluded her charms more adroitly than she would have guessed it was possible for a man to do. As far as she could tell, he wasn't even close to the breaking point.

She swiveled her head to glare at him. On the surface, at least, he looked as cool as a cucumber. She could have been as ugly as a warthog's ass for all the attention he was paying her. Maybe it was time she threw caution to the wind, stopped pussyfooting around, and, if nothing else, shocked the shit out of Mr. Clean.

"How 'bout a blow job?"

Moving with studied casualness, Eddy draped his right arm along the seat backs. "Come to think of it, that would feel real good about now."

Heat rushed to her face. She gritted her teeth. "Don't you dare patronize me, you son of a bitch."

"Then stop throwing yourself at me like a cheap street-walker. Dirty talk doesn't turn me on, any more than a ringside view of your chest. I'm not interested, Fancy, and this juvenile game of yours is getting tiresome."

"You *are* a fag."

He snorted. "Believe that if you want to, if it salves your ego."

"Then you're bound to be getting it from somebody, because it's just not normal for a man to go without." She scooted closer to him and clutched his sleeve. "Who are you sleeping with, Eddy—somebody who works at head-quarters?"

"Fancy—"

"That redhead with the skinny butt? I'll bet it's her! She's divorced, I hear, and probably real hot." She clutched his sleeve tighter. "Why would you want to screw some-body old like her when you could have me?"

He brought the car to a stop in the circular drive in front of the house. He caught her by both shoulders and shook her hard. "Because I don't screw children—especially one who opens her thighs to every stiff dick that comes along."

His anger only fanned her desire. Passion of any kind

aroused and excited her. Eyes alight, she reached down and pressed his crotch with the palm of her hand. Her lips curved into a smug smile. "Why, Eddy, darlin'!" she exclaimed in a sultry whisper. "Yours is stiff."

Cursing, he pushed her away and got out of the car. "As far as you're concerned, that's how it'll stay."

Fancy took time to rebutton her blouse and compose herself before following him into the house. The contest had resulted in a tie. He hadn't dragged her off to bed, but he had wanted to. That was progress she could live with for a while . . . but not indefinitely.

As she reached the door leading to her wing, her mother emerged. Dorothy Rae was walking straight, but her eyes were glazed with the effects of several drinks.

"Hello, Fancy."

"I'm going to Corpus Christi for a few days," she announced. If Eddy refused to take her, she'd just surprise him in the coastal city. "I'm leaving in the morning. Give me some money."

"You can't leave town right now."

Fancy's fist found a prop on her shapely hip. Her eyes narrowed the way they were wont to do when she didn't immediately get her way. "Why the hell not?"

"Nelson said everybody had to be here," her mother said. "Carole's coming home tomorrow."

"Oh, piss," Fancy muttered. "Just what I need."

THIRTEEN

She saw him in the mirror.

Seated at the small dressing table in her room at the clinic, Avery made eye contact with Tate as he came in. They held their stare as she gradually lowered the powder puff to the mirrored surface of the table, then swiveled on the stool and met him face-to-face.

He tossed his coat and several department store shopping bags onto the bed while his eyes remained on her. Tightly clasping her hands in her lap, Avery laughed nervously. "The suspense is killing me."

"You look beautiful."

She moistened her lips, which were already shiny with carefully applied gloss. "The resident cosmetologist came today and gave me a makeup lesson. I've been using cosmetics for years, but I figured I needed a refresher course. Besides, the consultation comes with the room." Again she gave him a nervous little smile.

Actually, she had wanted an excuse to improve Carole's mode of makeup, which, in Avery's opinion, had been applied with too heavy a hand. "I tried a new technique. Do you think it looks all right?"

She offered her face up for his review. In spite of his reluctance to come any closer, he did. Placing his hands on his knees, he bent from the waist and gave her uplifted face a thorough inspection. "Can't even see the scars. Nothing. It's incredible."

"Thank you." She gave him a smile a woman gives her loving husband.

Except Tate wasn't her husband and he wasn't loving. He straightened up and turned his back on her. Avery closed her eyes momentarily, tamping down her discouragement. He didn't have a forgiving nature, she'd learned. Carole had shattered his trust in her. It was going to be difficult to win him back.

"Are you accustomed to my new look yet?"

"It's growing on me."

"There are differences," she remarked in an unsure voice.

"You look younger." He shot her a glance over his shoulder, then added beneath his breath, "Prettier."

Avery left the dressing table and moved toward him. She laid her hand on his arm and drew him around. "Really? Prettier?"

"Yeah."

"Prettier how? In what way?"

Just as she had learned the extent of his inability to forgive, she had also learned the extent of his ability to control his temper. She was waving a red flag at it now. Lightning was flashing in his eyes, but she didn't back down. She felt compelled to know the discernible differences he saw between her and his wife. Research, she assured herself.

He swore impatiently, raking a hand through his hair. "I don't know. You're just different. Maybe it's the makeup, the hair—I don't know. You look good, okay? Can we leave it at that? You look . . ." His eyes lowered to take in more than her face. They swept down her body, moved up again, looked away. "You look good."

He dug into his shirt pocket and produced a handwritten list. "Mom and I got the things you asked for." Nodding toward the shopping bags, he read off the items. "Ysatis spray perfume. They were out of the bath stuff you wanted."

"I'll get it later."

"Panty hose. Is that the color you had in mind? You said light beige."

"It's fine." She rummaged in the bags, locating the items as he named them. She withdrew the boxed bottle of fragrance from the sack. Uncapping it, she misted her wrist with the atomizer. "Hmm. Smell."

She laid her wrist against his cheek, so that he had to turn his head toward it in order to sniff. When he did, his lips brushed her inner arm. Their eyes met instantly.

"Nice," he said and turned his head away before Avery lowered her arm. "A nightgown with sleeves." Again he questioned her. "Since when have you started sleeping in anything, but especially something with sleeves?"

Avery, tired of being put on the defensive, fired back, "Since I lived through a plane crash and got second-degree burns on my arms."

His mouth, open and ready to make a quick comeback, clicked shut. Returning to the last item on the list, he read, "Bra, 34-B."

"I'm sorry about that." Taking the garment from the sack, she removed the tags and refolded it. The bras that had been brought to her from Carole's drawers at home had been way too large.

"About what?"

"Coming down a full size."

"What possible difference could that make to me?"

The scorn in his expression made her look away. "None, I guess."

She emptied the shopping bags, adding the items to the things she had laid out to wear home the following day. The clothes Zee and Tate had brought her from Carole's closet had fit fairly well. They were only a trifle large. Carole's breasts and hips had been fuller, curvier, but Avery had explained that away by the liquid diet she had been on for so long. Even Carole's shoes fit her.

Whenever possible she kept her arms and legs covered, preferring pants to skirts. She was afraid that the shape of her calves and ankles would give her away. So far, no one had made a comparison. To the Rutledges, she was Carole. They were convinced.

Or were they?

Why hadn't Carole's coconspirator spoken to her again?

That worry was as persistent as a gnat that continually buzzed through Avery's head. Dwelling on it made her ill with fear, so she concentrated more on Carole's personality in an effort to avoid making mistakes that would give her away.

As far as she could tell, she'd been lucky. She wasn't aware of having made any major blunders.

Now that departure was imminent, she was nervous. Being under the same roof with the Rutledges, especially with Tate, would increase the opportunities for making errors.

In addition, she would resurface as a congressional candidate's wife and be called upon to cope with the problems associated with that.

"What's going to happen in the morning, Tate?"

"Eddy told me to prepare you. Sit down."

"This sounds serious," she teased once they were facing each other in matching chairs.

"It is."

"Are you afraid I'll commit a faux pas in front of the press?"

"No," he replied, "but I can damn well guarantee that they'll commit some social taboos."

Because he was criticizing her profession, she took umbrage. "Like what?"

"They'll ask you hundreds of personal questions. They'll study your face, looking for scars, that kind of thing. You'll probably have your picture taken more times tomorrow than at any other time during the campaign."

"I'm not camera shy."

He laughed dryly. "I know that. But tomorrow when you leave here, you'll be swarmed. Eddy's going to try to keep it orderly, but these things have a way of getting out of hand."

He fished into his breast pocket again, produced another piece of paper, and passed it to her. "Familiarize yourself with this tonight. It's a brief statement Eddy wrote for you to read. He'll have a microphone set—What's the matter?"

"This," she said, shaking the paper at him. "If I read this, I'll sound like a moron."

He sighed and rubbed his temples. "Eddy was afraid you'd think that."

"Anybody hearing this would think the crash had damaged my brain more than my face. Everyone would assume you had locked me away in this private hospital until I regained my sanity, like something out of *Jane Eyre*. Keep the mentally disturbed wife—"

"*Jane Eyre*? You've certainly gotten literary."

She was taken aback for a moment, but retorted quickly, "I saw the movie. Anyway, I don't want people to think I'm mentally dysfunctional and must have everything I say written out for me beforehand."

"Just don't let your mouth overload your ass, okay?"

"I know how to speak the English language, Tate," she snapped. "I can put more than three words together at any given time, and I know how to conduct myself in public." She ripped the prepared statement in half and tossed it to the floor.

"Apparently, you've forgotten that incident in Austin. We can't afford mistakes like that, Carole."

Since she didn't know what mistake Carole had made in Austin, she could neither defend herself nor apologize. One thing she must remember, however, was that Avery Daniels had experience speaking before television cameras. She was media sophisticated. Carole Rutledge obviously had not been.

In a calmer voice, she said, "I know how important every public appearance is from now until November. I'll try to conduct myself properly and watch what I say." She smiled ruefully and bent to pick up the torn paper. "I'll even memorize this vapid little speech. I want to do what's best for you."

"Don't put yourself out trying to please me. If it were up to me, you wouldn't even be making a statement. Eddy feels that you should, to alleviate the public's curiosity. Jack and Dad go along with his opinion. So you've got to please them, not me."

He stood to go. Avery rose quickly. "How's Mandy?"

"The same."

"Did you tell her I was coming home tomorrow?"

"She listened, but it's hard to tell what she was thinking."

Distressed that there had been no measurable improvement in the child's condition, Avery raised her hand to the base of her throat and rubbed it absently.

Tate touched the back of her hand. "That reminds me." He went for his jacket, which was still lying across the foot of her bed, and removed something from the pocket. "Since the hospital screwed up and lost your jewelry after all, Eddy thought I should replace your wedding ring. He said voters would expect you to be wearing one."

She hadn't exactly lied to him. When he had inquired about her jewelry, she had told him that when she had opened the envelope taken from the hospital safe, it had contained someone else's jewelry, not Carole Rutledge's. "I gave it to one of the nurses here to handle."

"Then where is yours?" he had asked at the time.

"God knows. Just one of those mix-ups that can't be explained, I guess. Take it up with the insurance company."

Tate was now removing a simple, wide gold band from the gray velvet lining of the ring box. "It's not as fancy as your other one, but it'll do."

"I like this one," she said as he slid the ring onto her third finger. When he tried to withdraw his hand, she noticed that he was wearing a matching band. She clutched his hand and called his name on a quick intake of breath.

She bowed her head over their clasped hands, holding them between their chests. Bending her head down farther, she softly kissed the ridge of his knuckles.

"Carole," he said, trying to pull his hand free. "Don't."

"Please, Tate. I want to thank you for all you've done. Please let me."

She implored him to accept her gratitude. "There were so many times—even from the very beginning, when I first regained consciousness—that I wanted to die. I probably would have willed myself to if it hadn't been for your unflagging encouragement. You've been . . ." She choked up and made no attempt to stem the tears that ran down her flawless cheeks. "You've been a wonderful source of strength through all this. Thank you."

She spoke from her heart. Each word was the truth. Responding to the prompting of her emotions, she came up on tiptoe and touched his lips with hers.

He yanked his head back. She heard the swift, surprised breath he took. She sensed his hesitation as his eyes roved over her face. Then he lowered his head. His lips made contact with hers briefly, airily, barely glancing them.

She inclined her body closer to his, reached higher for his lips with her own, and murmured, "Tate, kiss me, please."

With a low moan, his mouth pressed down on hers. His arm went around her waist and pulled her against him. He unraveled their clasped fingers and curved his hand around her throat, stroking it with his thumb while his tongue played at getting between her lips.

Once it had, he sent it deep.

He instantly broke off the kiss and raised his head. "What the—"

He peered deeply into her eyes while his chest soughed against hers. Though he wrestled against it, his eyes were drawn back to her mouth. He closed his eyes and shook his head in denial of something he couldn't explain before covering her mouth with his own.

Avery returned his kiss, releasing all the yearning she had secretly nurtured for months. Their mouths melded together with hunger and heat. The more he got of hers, the more he wanted and the more she wanted to give.

With his hand on her hips, he tilted her forward against his erection. Arching into it, she raised her hands to the back of his neck and drew his head down, loving the blend of textures encountered by her fingertips—his hair, his clothing, his skin.

And then it stopped.

He shoved her away, putting several feet between them. She watched with anguish as he drew the back of his fist across his mouth, wiping off her kiss. She emitted a small, pained noise.

"It won't work, Carole," he said tightly. "I'm unfamiliar with this new game you're playing, but until I learn the rules, I refuse to participate. I feel sorry for what happened to you. Since you're my legal wife, I did what duty demanded of me. But it has no bearing on my feelings. They haven't changed. Got that? Nothing's changed."

He snatched up his sports coat, slung it over his shoulder, and sauntered from the room without looking back.

Eddy stepped out into the courtyard. The May sunshine had brought out the blooming plants. Oleander bushes bloomed in pottery urns bordering the deck around the swimming pool. Moss rose carpeted the flower beds.

It was dark now, however, and the blossoms had closed for the night. The courtyard was illumined by spotlights placed in the ground among the plants. They cast tall, spindly shadows upon the white stucco walls of the house.

"What are you doing out here?" Eddy asked.

The loner, slouched in a patio lounger, answered curtly. "Thinking."

He was thinking about Carole—about how her face had looked reflected in the mirror when he had entered her room. It had been incandescent. Her dark eyes had glowed as though his arrival signified something special to her. He decided it was quite an act. For an insane moment or two, he'd even fallen for it. What an idiot.

If he had just walked out, never touched her, never tasted her, never wished that things were different, he wouldn't be snarling at his friend now, nursing a bottle of scotch and fighting a losing battle with an erection that wouldn't subside. Aggravated with himself, he reached for the bottle of Chivas Regal again and splashed some over the melting ice in the bottom of his tumbler.

Eddy sat down in a lounge chair close to Tate's and eyed him with concern. Tate, catching his friend's candidly critical gaze, said, "If you don't like what you see, look at something else."

"My, my. Cranky, aren't we?"

He was horny and lusting for an unfaithful wife. The unfaithfulness he *might* forgive, eventually, but not the other. Never the other.

"Did you see Carole?" Eddy asked, guessing the source of Tate's dark mood.

"Yes."

"Did you give her the statement to read?"

"Yes. Know what she did?"

"Told you to shove it?"

"Essentially. She tore it in half."

"I wrote it for her own good."

"Tell that to her yourself."

"The last time I told her something for her own good, she called me an asshole."

"She fell just short of spelling that out tonight."

"Whether she believes it or not, meeting the press for the first time since the crash is going to be a bitch, even on somebody as tough as Carole. Their curiosity alone will have them whipped into a frenzy."

"I told her that, but she resents getting unasked-for advice and having words put in her mouth."

"Well," Eddy said, rubbing his neck tiredly, "don't worry about it until you have to. She'll probably do fine."

"She seems confident that she will." Tate took a sip of his drink, then rolled the tumbler between his palms as he watched a moth making suicidal dives toward one of the spotlights in the shrubbery. "She's . . ."

Eddy leaned forward. "She's what?"

"Hell, I don't know." Tate sighed. "Different."

"How so?"

For starters, she tasted different, but he didn't tell his friend that. "She's more subdued. Congenial."

"Congenial? Sounds to me like she pitched a temper tantrum tonight."

"Yeah, but this is the first one. The crash and everything she's been through since then have sobered her up, I think. She looks younger, but she acts more mature."

"I've noticed that. Understandable, though, isn't it? Carole's suddenly realized that she's mortal." Eddy stared at the terrazzo tiles between his widespread feet. "How, uh, how are personal things between the two of you?" Tate shot him a hot, fierce glance. "If it's none of my business, just say so."

"It's none of your business."

"I know what happened in Fort Worth last week."

"I don't know what the hell you're talking about."

"The woman, Tate."

"There were a lot of women around."

"But only one invited you to her house after the rally. At least, only one that I know of."

Tate rubbed his forehead. "Jesus, doesn't anything escape your attention?"

"Not where you're concerned. Not until you're elected senator."

"Well, rest easy. I didn't go."

"I know that."

"So what's the point of bringing it up?"

"Maybe you should have."

Tate barked a short laugh of surprise.

"Did you want to?"

"Maybe."

"You did," Eddy said, answering for him. "You're human. Your wife's been incapacitated for months, and even before then—"

"You're out of line, Eddy."

"Everybody in the family knows that the two of you weren't getting along. I'm only stating the obvious. Let's be frank."

"You be frank. I'm going to bed."

Eddy caught his arm before he could stand up. "For God's sake, don't get mad at me and go off half-cocked. I'm trying to do you a favor here." He waited for several moments, giving Tate time to contain his anger.

"All I'm saying is that you've been doing without for a long time," Eddy said calmly. "The deprivation has got you uptight and edgy, and that's no good for anybody. If all it takes to get you happy again is a roll in the hay, let me know."

"And you'll do what?" Tate asked dangerously. "Pimp?"

Eddy looked disappointed in him. "There are ways to arrange it discreetly."

"Tell that to Gary Hart."

"He wasn't smart."

"And you are?"

"Damn right I am."

"Do you know what Dad would think if he heard you making me this offer?"

"He's an idealist," Eddy said dismissively. "Nelson really believes in motherhood and apple pie. Morality is his middle name. I, on the other hand, am a realist. We clean up pretty, but underneath our affectations, man is still an animal.

"If you need to get laid and your wife isn't accommodating, you get laid by somebody else." After his crude summation, Eddy gave an eloquent shrug. "In your situation, Tate, a little marital infidelity would be healthy."

"What makes you so sure I'm in desperate need of getting laid?"

Eddy smiled as he came to his feet. "I've watched you in action, remember? You've got that tension around your mouth that says you haven't gotten off lately. I recognize the black scowl. You might be running for public office, but you're still Tate Rutledge. Your cock doesn't know that it's expected to be a good little boy until you get elected."

"I'm investing my future in this election, Eddy. You

know that. I'm about to realize my ambition to go to Washington as a senator. Do you think I'd risk that dream on twenty minutes of marital infidelity?''

''No, I guess not,'' Eddy said with a rueful sigh. ''I was only trying to help you out.''

Tate stood and offered a crooked smile. ''The next thing you're going to say is, what are friends for?''

Eddy chuckled. ''Something that trite? Are you kidding?''

They headed toward the door leading into the main part of the house. Tate companionably rested his arm across Eddy's shoulders. ''You're a good friend.''

''Thanks.''

''But Carole was right about one thing.''

''What's that?''

''You are an asshole.''

Laughing together, they entered the house.

FOURTEEN

Avery slid on a pair of sunglasses.

''I think it would be better not to wear them,'' Eddy told her. ''We don't want it to look like we're hiding something unsightly.''

''All right.'' She removed the sunglasses and pocketed them in the raw silk jacket, which matched her pleated trousers. ''Do I look okay?'' she nervously asked Tate and Eddy.

Eddy gave her a thumbs-up sign. ''Smashing.''

''Lousy pun,'' Tate remarked with a grin.

Avery ran her hand over the short hair at the back of her skull. ''Does my hair . . . ?''

''Very chic,'' Eddy said. Then he clapped his hands

together and rubbed them vigorously. ''Well, we've kept the baited hounds at bay long enough. Let's go.''

Together, the three of them left her room for the last time and walked down the hallway toward the lobby. Good-byes to the staff had already been said, but good-luck wishes were called out to them as they passed the nurses' station.

''A limo?'' Avery asked when they reached the tinted glass facade of the building. The horde of reporters couldn't yet see them, but she could see outside. A black Cadillac limousine was parked at the curb with a uniformed chauffeur standing by.

''So both of us would be free to protect you,'' Eddy explained.

''From what?''

''The crush. The driver's already stowed your things in the trunk. Go to the mike, say your piece, politely decline to field any questions, then head for the car.''

He looked at her a moment, as though wanting to make certain his instructions had sunk in, then turned to Tate. ''You can take a couple of questions if you want to. Gauge how friendly they are. As long as it's comfortable, milk it for all it's worth. If it gets sticky, use Carole as your excuse to cut it short. Ready?''

He went ahead to open the door. Avery looked up at Tate. ''How do you abide his bossiness?''

''That's what he's being paid for.''

She made a mental note not to criticize Eddy. In Tate's estimation, his campaign manager was above reproach.

Eddy was holding the door for them. Tate encircled her elbow and nudged her forward. The reporters and photographers had been a clamoring, squirming mass moments before. Now an expectant hush fell over them as they waited for the senatorial candidate's wife to emerge after months of seclusion.

Avery cleared the doorway and moved to the microphone as Eddy had instructed her to. She looked like Carole Rutledge. She knew that. It was remarkable to her that the charade hadn't been detected by those closest to Carole, even her husband. Of course, none had reason to doubt that she was who she was supposed to be. They weren't looking for an impostor, and therefore, they didn't see one.

But as she approached the microphone, Avery was afraid that strangers might discern what intimates hadn't. Someone might rise above the crowd, aim an accusatory finger at her, and shout, "Impostor!"

Therefore, the spontaneous burst of applause astonished her. It took her, Tate, and even Eddy, who was always composed, by complete surprise. Her footsteps faltered. She glanced up at Tate with uncertainty. He smiled that dazzling, all-American hero smile at her and it was worth all the pain and anguish she had suffered since the crash. It boosted her confidence tremendously.

She graciously signaled for the applause to cease. As it tapered off, she said a timid thank-you. Then, clearing her throat, giving a slight toss of her head, and moistening her lips with her tongue, she began reciting her brief, prepared speech.

"Thank you, ladies and gentleman, for being here to welcome me back after my long hospitalization. I wish to publicly extend my sympathy to those who lost loved ones in the dreadful crash of AireAmerica Flight 398. It's still incredible to me that my daughter and I survived such a tragic and costly accident. I probably wouldn't have, had it not been for the constant support and encouragement of my husband."

The last line had been her addition to Eddy's prepared speech. Boldly, she slipped her hand into Tate's. After a moment's hesitation, which only she was aware of, he gave her hand a gentle squeeze.

"Mrs. Rutledge, do you hold AireAmerica responsible for the crash?"

"We can't comment until the investigation is completed and the results have been announced by the NTSB," Tate said.

"Mrs. Rutledge, do you plan to sue for damages?"

"We have no plans to pursue litigation at this time." Again, Tate answered for her.

"Mrs. Rutledge, do you remember saving your daughter from the burning wreckage?"

"I do now," she said before Tate could speak. "But I didn't at first. I responded to survival instinct. I don't remember making a conscious decision."

"Mrs. Rutledge, at any point during the reconstructive procedure on your face, did you doubt it could be done?"

"I had every confidence in the surgeon my husband selected."

Tate leaned into the mike to make himself heard above the din. "As you might guess, Carole is anxious to get home. If you'll excuse us, please."

He ushered her forward, but the crowd surged toward them. "Mr. Rutledge, will Mrs. Rutledge be going with you on the campaign trail?" A particularly pushy reporter blocked their path and shoved a microphone into Tate's face.

"A few trips for Carole have been scheduled. But there will be many times when she'll feel it's best to stay at home with our daughter."

"How is your daughter, Mr. Rutledge?"

"She's well, thank you. Now, if we could—"

"Is she suffering any aftereffects of the crash?"

"What does your daughter think of the slight alterations in your appearance, Mrs. Rutledge?"

"No more questions now, please."

With Eddy clearing a path for them, they made their way through the obstinate crowd. It was friendly, for the most part, but even so, being surrounded by so many people gave Avery a sense of suffocation.

Up till now, she'd always been on the other side, a reporter poking a microphone at someone in the throes of a personal crisis. The reporter's job was to get the story, get the sound bite that no one else got, take whatever measures were deemed necessary. Little consideration was ever given to what it was like on the other side of the mircophone. She'd never enjoyed that aspect of the job. Her fatal mistake in broadcasting hadn't arisen from having too little sensitivity, but from having too much.

From the corner of her eye she spotted the KTEX logo stenciled on the side of a Betacam. Instinctively, she turned her head in that direction. It was Van!

For a split second she forgot that he was supposed to be a

stranger to her. She came close to calling out his name and waving eagerly. His pale, thin face and lanky ponytail looked wonderfully familiar and dear! She longed to throw herself against his bony chest and hug him hard.

Thankfully, her face remained impassive. She turned away, giving no sign of recognition. Tate ushered her into the limo. Once inside the backseat and screened by the tinted glass, she looked out the rear window. Van, like all the others, was shoving his way through the throng, video camera riding atop his shoulder, his eye glued to the viewfinder.

How she missed the newsroom, with its ever-present pall of tobacco smoke, jangling telephones, squawking police radios, and clacking teletypes. The constant ebb and flow of reporters, cameramen and gofers seemed to Avery to be light-years in the past.

As the limo pulled away from the address that had been her refuge for weeks, she experienced an overwhelming homesickness for Avery Daniels' life. What had happened to her apartment, her things? Had they been boxed up and parceled out to strangers? Who was wearing her clothes, sleeping on her sheets, using her towels? She suddenly felt as though she'd been stripped and violated. But she had made an irrevocable decision to leave Avery Daniels indefinitely dead. Not only her career, but her life, and Tate's, were at stake.

Beside her, Tate adjusted himself into the seat. His leg brushed hers. His elbow grazed her breast. His hip settled reassuringly against hers.

For the time being, she was where she wanted to be.

Eddy, sitting on the fold-down seat in front of her, patted her knee. "You did great, even on the ad libs. Nice touch, reaching for Tate's hand that way. What'd you think, Tate?"

Tate was loosening his tie and unbuttoning his collar. "She did fine." He wagged his finger at Eddy. "But I don't like those questions about Mandy. What possible bearing does she have on the campaign issues or the election?"

"None. People are just curious."

"Screw curious. She's my daughter. I want her protected."

"Maybe she's too protected." Avery's husky voice sharply drew Tate's eyes to her.

"Meaning?"

"Now that they've seen me," she said, "they'll stop pestering you with questions about me and concentrate on the important issues."

During her convalescence, she had kept close tabs on his campaign by reading every newspaper available and watching television news. He had blitzed the primary election, but the real battle was still ahead of him. His opponent in November would be the incumbent senior senator, Rory Dekker.

Dekker was an institution in Texas politics. For as long as Avery remembered, he had been a senator. It was going to be a David-and-Goliath contest. The incredible odds in Dekker's favor, coupled with Tate's audacious courage against such an impressive foe, had sparked more interest in this election than any in recent memory.

On nearly every newscast there was at least a fifteen-second mention of the senate race, and, as Avery well knew, even fifteen seconds was an enviable amount of time. But while Dekker wisely used his time to state his platform, Tate's allotment had been squandered on questions regarding Carole's medical progress.

"If we don't keep Mandy under such lock and key," she said carefully, "their curiosity over her will soon abate. Hopefully, they'll get curious about something else, like your relief plan for the farmers who have been foreclosed on."

"She might have a point, Tate." Eddy eyed her suspiciously, but with grudging respect.

Tate's expression bordered between anger and indecision. "I'll think about it," was all he said before turning his head to stare out the window.

They rode in silence until they reached campaign headquarters. Eddy said, "Everybody's anxious to see you, Carole. I've asked them not to gape, but I can't guarantee that they won't," he warned her as she alighted with the chauffeur's assistance. "I think the goodwill would go a long way if you could stick around for a while."

''She will.'' Giving her no choice, Tate took her arm and steered her toward the door.

His chauvinism raised the hair on the back of her neck, but she was curious to see his campaign headquarters, so she went peaceably. As they approached the door, however, her stomach grew queasy with fear. Each new situation was a testing ground, a mine field that she must navigate gingerly, holding her breath against making a wrong move.

The doors admitted them into a place of absolute chaos. The volunteer workers were taking calls, making calls, sealing envelopes, opening envelopes, stapling, unstapling, standing up, sitting down. Everyone was in motion. After the silence and serenity of the clinic, Avery felt as though she had just been thrust into an ape house.

Tate removed his jacket and rolled up the sleeves of his shirt. Once he was spotted, each volunteer stopped his particular chore in favor of speaking to him. It was apparent to Avery that everyone in the room looked to him as a hero and was dedicated to helping him win the election.

It also became clear to her that Eddy Paschal's word was considered law, because while the volunteers looked at her askance and spoke polite hellos, she wasn't subjected to avidly curious stares. Feeling awkward and uncertain over what was expected of her, she tagged along behind Tate as he moved through the room. In his element, he emanated contagious confidence.

''Hello, Mrs. Rutledge,'' one young man said to her. ''You're looking extremely well.''

''Thank you.''

''Tate, this morning the governor issued a statement congratulating Mrs. Rutledge on her full recovery. He commended her courage, but he called you, and I paraphrase, a bleeding-heart liberal that Texans should be wary of. He cautioned the voting public not to let sympathy for Mrs. Rutledge influence their votes in November. How do you want to respond?''

''I don't. Not right away. The pompous son of a bitch wants to provoke me and make me look like a fire-breathing dragon. I won't give him the satisfaction. Oh, and that 'pompous son of a bitch' is off the record.''

The young man laughed and scurried toward a word processor to compose his press release.

"What does the current poll show?" Tate asked the room at large.

"We aren't paying attention to the polls," Eddy said smoothly, moving toward them. Somewhere along the way, he had picked up Fancy. She was eyeing Carole with her usual recalcitrance.

"The hell you're not," Tate said, countering Eddy's glib response. "How many points am I behind?"

"Fourteen."

"Up one from last week. I've been saying all along there's nothing to sweat." Everyone laughed at his optimistic analysis.

"Hi, Uncle Tate. Hi, Aunt Carole."

"Hello, Fancy."

The girl's face broke into an angelic smile, but there was malice behind it that Avery found unsettling. The one time Fancy had come to see her in the hospital, she had snickered at her scars, which had still been visible. The girl's insensitivity had angered Nelson so much that he'd sent her from the room and banished her from returning. She hadn't seemed to mind.

Just to look at her, one could tell that she was a calculating, selfish little bitch. If Fancy were ten years younger, Avery would think a hard spanking would be in order. Her regard for Carole, however, seemed to go beyond teenage sullenness. She seemed to hold a deep and abiding grudge against her.

"Is that your new wedding ring?" Fancy asked now, nodding down at Avery's left hand.

"Yes. Tate gave it to me last night."

She lifted Avery's hand by the fingertips and scornfully assessed the ring. "He wouldn't spring for more diamonds, huh?"

"I have a job for you," Eddy said tersely. "Back here." Taking Fancy's elbow, he spun her around and gave her a push in the opposite direction.

"Such a sweet child," Avery said from the corner of her mouth.

"She could stand a good paddling."

"I agree."

"Hello, Mrs. Rutledge." A middle-aged woman approached them and shook Avery's hand.

"Hello. It's nice to see you again, Mrs. Baker," she said after surreptitiously consulting the name tag pinned to the woman's breast pocket.

Mrs. Baker's smile faltered. She nervously glanced at Tate. "Eddy said you should read over these press releases, Tate. They're scheduled to be sent out tomorrow."

"Thanks. I'll do it tonight and send them back with Eddy tomorrow."

"That'll be fine. There's no rush."

"I made a mistake, didn't I?" Avery asked him as the woman moved away.

"We'd better go."

He called out a good-bye that encompassed everybody. Eddy waved to him from across the room but continued speaking into the telephone receiver he had cradled between his ear and shoulder. From her perch on the corner of his desk, Fancy gave them a negligent wave.

Tate escorted Avery outside and toward a parked silver sedan. "No limo this time?"

"We're just plain folks now."

Avery drank up the sights and sounds of the city as they slogged their way through noon traffic. It had been so long since her world had consisted of more than only a few sterile walls. The hectic pace at which everything moved, the racket, color, and light, were intimidating after her months of isolation. They were also thrilling. Everything was fondly familiar yet excitingly new, as spring must be to an animal emerging from hibernation.

When they passed the airport and she saw the jets taking off, chill bumps broke out over her arms and her insides tensed to the point of pain.

"Are you okay?"

Quickly, she averted her eyes from the airfield and caught Tate watching her closely. "Sure. I'm fine."

"Will you ever be able to fly again?"

"I don't know. I suppose. The first time is sure to be the toughest."

"I don't know if we'll ever get Mandy on a plane again."

"She might overcome her fear easier than I will. Children are often more resilient than adults."

"Maybe."

"I'm so anxious to see her. It's been weeks."

"She's growing."

"Is she?"

A smile broke across his face. "The other day I pulled her into my lap and noticed that the top of her head almost reaches my chin now."

They shared a smile for several seconds. Then his eyes dimmed, his smile relaxed, and he returned his attention to the traffic. Feeling shut out, Avery asked, "What about Mrs. Baker? What did I do wrong?"

"She only started working for us two weeks ago. You've never met her."

Avery's heart fluttered. This was bound to happen. She would make these little mistakes that she had to rapidly think up excuses for.

She lowered her head and rubbed her temples with her middle finger and thumb. "I'm sorry, Tate. I must have looked and sounded very phony."

"You did."

"Have patience with me. The truth is, I have lapses of memory. Sometimes the sequence of events confuses me. I can't remember people or places clearly."

"I noticed that weeks ago. Things you said didn't make any sense."

"Why didn't you say something when you first noticed?"

"I didn't want to worry you, so I asked the neurologist about it. He said your concussion probably erased part of your memory."

"Forever?"

He shrugged. "He couldn't say. Things might gradually come back to you, or they might be irretrievable."

Secretly, Avery was glad to hear the neurologist's prognosis. If she committed a faux pas, she could use a lapse of memory as her excuse.

Reaching across the car, she covered Tate's hand with her own. "I'm sorry if I embarrassed you."

"I'm sure she'll understand when I explain."

He slid his hand from beneath hers and placed both on the steering wheel to take an exit ramp off the divided highway. Avery paid close attention to the route they were taking. She would have to know how to find her way home, wouldn't she?

She had been born in Denton, a college town in north central Texas, and spent most of her childhood in Dallas, the base from which Cliff Daniels had worked as a freelance photojournalist.

Like most native Texans, regional pride had been bred into her. Though she'd spent hundreds of dollars on speech teachers in an effort to eradicate her accent, at heart she was all Texan. The hill country had always been one of her favorite areas of the state. The gently rolling hills and underground, spring-fed streams were beautiful any season of the year.

The bluebonnets were in full bloom now, covering the ground like a sapphire rash. More brilliantly colored wildflowers were splashed across the natural canvas, and the borders of color blurred to resemble a Monet painting. Giant boulders jutted out of the earth like crooked molars, saving the landscape from being merely pastoral.

Passion teemed in this countryside where Spanish *dons* had established empires, Comanche warriors had chased mustang herds, and colonists had shed blood to win autonomy. The land seemed to pulse with the ghosts of those indomitable peoples who had domesticated but never tamed it. Their fiercely independent spirits lurked there, like the wildcats that lived in the natural caves of the area, unseen but real.

Hawks on the lookout for prey spiraled on motionless wings. Rust-colored Herefords grazed on the sparse grass growing between cedar bushes. Like benevolent overseers, occasional live oaks spread their massive branches over the rocky ground, providing shade for cattle, deer, elk, and smaller game. Cypress trees grew along the rushing river-beds; the swollen banks of the Guadalupe were densely lined with their ropy trunks, knobby knees, and feathery branches.

It was a land rich in contrasts and folklore. Avery loved it.

So, apparently, did Tate. While driving, he gazed at the scenery with the appreciation of one seeing it for the first time. He turned into a road bracketed by two native stone pillars. Suspended between them was a sign made of wrought iron that spelled out "Rocking R Ranch."

From the articles about the Rutledges that she had secretly read during her convalescence, Avery had learned that the Rocking R covered more than five thousand acres and was home to an impressive herd of prime beef cattle. Two tributaries from the Guadalupe River and one from the Blanco supplied it with coveted water.

Nelson had inherited the land from his father. Since his retirement from the air force, he had devoted his time to building the ranch into a profitable enterprise, traveling to other parts of the country to study breeds of cattle and ways to improve the Rocking R's stock.

An article in *Texas Monthly* had carried an accompanying picture of the house, but Avery couldn't tell much about it from the photograph.

Now, as they topped a rise, she could see it in the distance. It was built of white adobe like a Spanish *hacienda*, with three wings that formed a horseshoe around a central courtyard. From the center, one had a spectacular view of the valley and the river beyond. The expansive house had a red tile roof that was currently reflecting the noon sun.

The driveway arced, forming a half circle in front of the main entrance. A majestic live oak shaded the entire front of the house, with curly gray moss dripping from its branches. Geraniums, scarlet and profuse, were blooming in terracotta pots on either side of the front door, which Tate guided her toward once she had alighted from the car.

It was quintessential Texana, breathtakingly beautiful, and, Avery suddenly realized, home.

FIFTEEN

The entire house was furnished with a taste and style one would expect from Zee. The decor was traditional, very cozy, and comfortable. All the rooms were spacious, with high, beamed ceilings and wide windows. Zee had made a good home for her family.

Lunch was waiting for them in the courtyard. It was served at a round redwood picnic table with a bright yellow umbrella shading it. After Avery had been embraced by Nelson and Zee, she approached Mandy and knelt down.

"Hi, Mandy. It's so good to see you."

Mandy stared at the ground. "I've been good."

"Of course you have. Daddy's been telling me. And you look so pretty." She smoothed her hand over Mandy's glossy page boy. "Your hair's growing out and you've got your cast off."

"Can I have my lunch now? Grandma said I could when you got here."

Her indifference broke Avery's heart. She should have been bursting with exciting things to tell her mother after such a lengthy separation.

As they took their places around the table, a maid carried a tray of food out from the kitchen and welcomed her home.

"Thank you. It's good to be back." A vapid, but safe response, Avery thought.

"Get Carole some iced tea, Mona," Nelson said, providing Avery with the housekeeper's name. "And remember to add real sugar."

The family unwittingly supplied her with clues like that. From them she gleaned Carole's habits, likes and dislikes.

She remained constantly alert for the clues she might be unwittingly giving away, as well, although only Tate's parents and Mandy were present.

Just when she was congratulating herself on her excellent performance, a large, shaggy dog loped into the courtyard. He came to within a few feet of Avery before realizing she was a stranger. All four of his legs stiffened, then he crouched down and began to growl deep in his throat.

A dog—the family pet! Why hadn't she thought of that? Rather than waiting for the others to react, she seized the initiative.

"What's wrong with him? Am I that changed? Doesn't he recognize me?"

Tate threw one leg over to straddle the bench of the picnic table and patted his thigh. "Come here, Shep, and stop that growling."

Keeping a wary eye on Avery, the dog crept forward and laid his chin on Tate's thigh. Tate scratched him behind the ears. Tentatively, Avery extended her hand and petted the dog's muzzle. "Hey, Shep. It's me."

He sniffed her hand suspiciously. Finally satisfied that she posed no danger, he gave her palm a warm, wet stroke with his tongue. "That's better." Laughing, she looked up at Tate, who was regarding her strangely.

"Since when have you wanted to become friends with my dog?"

Avery glanced around helplessly. Nelson and Zee also seemed baffled by her behavior. "Since . . . since I came so close to dying. I feel a bond with all living creatures, I guess."

The awkward moment passed and lunch continued without further mishap. Once it was over, however, Avery was ready to retire to their room and use the bathroom—only she didn't know where, within the sprawling house, their room was located.

"Tate," she asked, "have my bags been brought in yet?"

"I don't think so. Why, do you need them?"

"Yes, please."

Leaving Mandy in her grandparents' care, Avery followed him from the courtyard and back to the car still parked out front. She carried the smaller bag; he took the larger.

"I could have gotten both," he told her over his shoulder as he reentered the house.

"It's all right." She lagged behind so she could follow him. Wide double doors opened into a long corridor. One wall of the hallway was made of windows overlooking the courtyard. Several rooms gave off from the other side. Tate entered one of them and set her suitcase down in front of a louvered closet door.

"Mona will help you unpack."

Avery nodded an acknowledgment, but she was distracted by the bedroom. It was spacious and light, with a saffron-colored carpet and blond wood furniture. The bedspread and drapes were made of a floral print chintz. It was a little too flowery for Avery's taste, but obviously expensive and well made.

She took in every detail at a glance, from the digital alarm clock on the nightstand to the silver framed photo of Mandy on the dresser.

Tate said, "I'm going to the office for a while. You probably ought to take it easy this afternoon, get back into the flow slowly. If you —"

Avery's sharp gasp stopped him. He followed the direction of her gaze to the life-size portrait of Carole mounted on the opposite wall. "What's the matter?"

A hand at her throat, Avery swallowed and said, "Nothing. It's . . . it's just that I don't look much like that anymore." It was disconcerting to look into the eyes of the one person who knew unequivocally that she was an impostor. Those dark, knowing eyes mocked her.

Looking away from them, she smiled up at Tate timorously and ran a hand through her short hair. "I guess I'm not completely used to the changes yet. Would you mind if I took the portrait down?"

"Why would I mind? This is your room. Do whatever the hell you want with it." He headed for the door. "I'll see you at dinner." He soundly closed the door behind him when he left.

His disregard was unarguable. She felt like she'd been dumped in Antarctica and was watching the last plane out disappear over the horizon. He had deposited her where she belonged and considered that the extent of his duty.

This is your room.

The bedroom was museum clean, like it hadn't been occupied for a long time. She guessed it had been three months—since Carole had left it the morning of the plane crash.

She slid open the closet doors. There were enough clothes hanging inside to outfit an army, but every single article was feminine, from the fur coat to the fussiest peignoir. Nothing in the closet belonged to Tate, nor did anything on the bureau or in any of the many drawers.

Avery dejectedly lowered herself to the edge of the wide, king-size bed. *Your room*, he had said. Not *our* room.

Well, she thought dismally, she didn't have to entertain any more qualms about the first time he claimed conjugal rights, did she? That worry could be laid aside. She wouldn't be intimately involved with Tate because he no longer shared that kind of relationship with his wife.

Given his attitude over the last several weeks, it came as no surprise, but it was a vast disappointment. Coupled with her disappointment, however, was shame. It hadn't been her intention to sleep with him under false pretenses; she didn't even know if she wanted that. It would be wrong—very wrong. Yet. . . .

She glared up at the portrait. Carole Rutledge seemed to be smiling down at her with malicious amusement. "You bitch," Avery whispered scathingly. "I'm going to undo whatever you did that caused him to stop loving you. See if I don't."

"You getting enough to eat down there?"

When Avery realized that Nelson was addressing her, she smiled at him down the length of the table. "Plenty, thank you. As good as the food was at the clinic, this tastes delicious."

"You've lost a lot of weight," he observed. "We've got to fatten you up. I don't tolerate puniness in my family."

She laughed and reached for her wine. She didn't like wine, but obviously Carole had. A glass had been poured for her without anyone asking if she wanted it or not. By sipping slowly throughout the meal, she had almost emptied the glass of burgundy that had accompanied the steak dinner.

"Your boobs have practically disappeared." Seated across from Avery, Fancy was balancing her fork between two fingers, insolently wagging it up and down as she made the snide observation.

"Fancy, you'll refrain from making rude remarks, please," Zee admonished.

"I wasn't being rude. Just honest."

"Tact is as admirable a trait as honesty, young lady," her grandfather said sternly from his chair at the head of the table.

"Jeez, I just—"

"And it's unbecoming for any woman to take the Lord's name in vain," he added coldly. "I certainly won't have it from you."

Fancy dropped her fork onto her plate with a loud clatter. "I don't get it. Everybody in this family has been talking about how skinny she is. I'm the only one with enough guts to say something out loud, and I get my head bitten off."

Nelson shot Jack a hard look, which he correctly took as his cue to do something about his daughter's misbehavior. "Fancy, please be nice. This is Carole's homecoming dinner."

Avery read her lips as she mouthed, "Big fuckin' deal." Slouching in her chair, she lapsed into sullen silence and toyed with her remaining food, obviously killing time until she could be excused from the table.

"I think she looks damn good."

"Thank you, Eddy." Avery smiled across the table at him.

He saluted her with his wineglass. "Anybody catch her performance on the steps of the clinic this morning? They aired it on all three local stations during the news."

"Couldn't have asked for better coverage," Nelson remarked. "Pour me some coffee, please, Zee?"

"Of course."

She filled his cup before passing the carafe down the table. Dorothy Rae declined coffee and reached instead for the wine bottle. Her eyes locked with Avery's across the table. Avery's sympathetic smile was met with rank hostility. Dorothy Rae defiantly refilled her wineglass.

She was an attractive woman, though excessive drinking had taken its toll on her appearance. Her face was puffy, particularly around her eyes, which otherwise were a fine, deep blue. She'd made an attempt to groom herself for dinner, but she hadn't quite achieved neatness. Her hair had been haphazardly clamped back with two barrettes, and she would have looked better without any makeup than she did in what had been ineptly and sloppily applied. She didn't enter the conversation unless specifically spoken to. All her interactions were with an inanimate object—the wine bottle.

Avery had readily formed the opinion that Dorothy Rae Rutledge was an extremely unhappy woman. Nothing had changed that first impression. The reason for Dorothy Rae's unhappiness was still unknown, but Avery was certain of one thing, she loved her husband. She responded to Jack defensively, as now, when he tried to discreetly place the wine bottle beyond her reach. She swatted his hand aside, lunged for the neck of the bottle, and topped off the portion already in her glass. In unguarded moments, however, Avery noticed her watching Jack with palpable desperation.

"Did you see those mock-ups of the new posters?" Jack was asking his brother.

Avery was flanked by Tate on one side and Mandy on the other. Though she had been conversant with everybody during the meal, she had been particularly aware of the two of them, but for distinctly different reasons.

After Avery had cut Mandy's meat into bite-size chunks, the child had eaten carefully and silently. Avery's experience with children was limited, but whenever she had observed them, they were talkative, inquisitive, fidgety, and sometimes annoyingly active.

Mandy was abnormally subdued. She didn't complain. She didn't entreat. She didn't do anything except mechanically take small bites of food.

Tate ate efficiently, as though he resented the time it took to dine. Once he had finished, he toyed with his wineglass between sips, giving Avery the impression that he was anxious for the others to finish.

"I looked at them this afternoon," he said in response to Jack's question. "My favorite slogan was the one about the foundation."

" 'Tate Rutledge, a solid new foundation,' " Jack quoted.

"That's the one."

"I submitted it," Jack said.

Tate fired a fake pistol at his brother and winked. "That's probably why I liked it best. You're always good at cutting to the heart of the matter. What do you think, Eddy?"

"Sounds good to me. It goes along with our platform of getting Texas out of its current economic slump and back on its feet. You're something the state can build its future on. At the same time, it subtly suggests that Dekker's foundation is crumbling."

"Dad?"

Nelson was thoughtfully tugging on his lower lip. "I liked the one that said something about fair play for all Texans."

"It was okay," Tate said, "but kinda corny."

"Maybe that's what your campaign needs," he said, frowning.

"It has to be something Tate feels comfortable with, Nelson," Zee said to her husband. She lifted the glass cover off a multilayered coconut cake and began slicing it. The first slice went to Nelson, who was about to dig in before he remembered what the dinner was commemorating.

"Tonight, the first slice belongs to Carole. Welcome home." The plate was passed down to her.

"Thank you."

She didn't like coconut any more than she did wine, but apparently Carole had, so she began eating the dessert while Zee served the men and the men resumed their discussion about campaign strategy.

"So, should we go with that slogan and have them start printing up the posters?"

"Let's hold off making a definite decision for a couple of days, Jack." Tate glanced at his father. Though Nelson was appreciatively demolishing his slice of cake, he was still wearing a frown because his favorite slogan hadn't met with their approval. "I only glanced at them today. That was just my first impression."

"Which is usually the best one," Jack argued.

"Probably. But we've got a day or two to think about it, don't we?"

Jack accepted a plate with a slice of cake on it. Dorothy Rae declined the one passed to her. "We should get those posters into production by the end of the week."

"I'll give you my final decision well before then."

"For God's sake. Would somebody please . . ." Fancy was waving her hand toward Mandy. Getting the cake from plate to mouth had proved to be too much of a challenge for the three-year-old. Crumbs had fallen onto her dress and frosting was smeared across her mouth. She had tried to remedy the problem by wiping it away, but had only succeeded in getting her hands coated with sticky icing. "It's just too disgusting to watch the little spook eat. Can I be excused?"

Without waiting for permission, Fancy scraped her chair back and stood, tossing her napkin into her plate. "I'm going into Kerrville and see if there's a new movie on. Anybody want to go?" She included everybody in the invitation, but her eyes fell on Eddy. He was studiously eating his dessert. "Guess not." Spinning around, she flounced from the room.

Avery was glad to see the little snot go. How dare she speak to a defenseless child so cruelly? Avery scooped Mandy into her lap. "Cake is just too good to eat without dropping a few crumbs, isn't it, darling?" She wrapped a corner of her linen napkin around her index finger, dunked it into her water glass, and went to work on the frosting covering Mandy's face.

"Your girl is getting out of hand, Dorothy Rae," Nelson observed. "That skirt she was wearing was so short, it barely covered her privates."

Dorothy Rae pushed her limp bangs off her forehead. "I try, Nelson. It's Jack who lets her get by with murder."

"That's a goddamn lie," he exclaimed in protest. "I've got her going to work every day, don't I? That's more constructive than anything you've been able to get her to do."

"She should be in school," Nelson declared. "Never should have let her up and quit like that without even finishing the semester. What's going to become of her? What kind of life will she have without an education?" He shook his head with dire premonition. "She'll pay dearly for her bad choices. So will you. You reap what you sow, you know."

Avery agreed with him. Fancy was entirely out of control, and it was no doubt her parents' fault. Still, she didn't think Nelson should discuss their parental shortcomings with everybody else present.

"I don't think anything short of a bath is going to do Mandy any good," she said, grateful for the excuse to leave the table. "Will you please excuse us?"

"Do you need any help?" Zee asked.

"No, thank you." Then, realizing that she was usurping the bedtime ritual from Zee, who must have enjoyed it very much, she added, "Since this is my first night home, I'd like to put her to bed myself. It was a lovely dinner, Zee. Thank you."

"I'll be in to tell Mandy good night later," Tate called after them as Avery carried the child from the dining room.

"Well, I see that nothing's changed."

Dorothy Rae weaved her way across the sitting room and collapsed into one of two chairs parked in front of a large-screen TV set. Jack was occupying the other chair. "Did you hear me?" she asked when several seconds ticked by and he still hadn't said anything.

"I heard you, Dorothy Rae. And if by 'nothing's changed' you mean that you're shit-faced again tonight, then you're right. Nothing's changed."

"What I mean is that you can't keep your eyes off your brother's wife."

Jack was out of his chair like a shot. He slapped his palm against the switch on the TV, shutting up Johnny Carson in midjoke. "You're drunk and disgusting. I'm going to bed." He stamped into the connecting bedroom. Dorothy Rae struggled to get out of her chair and follow him. The hem of her robe trailed behind her.

"Don't try to deny it," she said with a sob. "I was watching you. All through dinner, you were drooling over Carole and her pretty new face."

Jack removed his shirt, balled it up, and flung it into the clothes hamper. He bent over to unlace his shoes. "The only one who drools in this family is you, when you get so drunk you can't control yourself."

Reflexively, she wiped the back of her hand across her mouth. People who had known Dorothy Rae Hancock when she was growing up wouldn't believe what she had become in middle age. She'd been the belle of Lampasas High School; her rein had lasted all four years.

Her daddy had been a prominent attorney in town. She, his only child, was the apple of his eye. The way he doted on her had made her the envy of everybody who knew her. He'd taken her to Dallas twice a year to shop at Neiman-Marcus for her seasonal wardrobes. He'd given her a brand new Corvette convertible on her sixteenth birthday.

Her mother had had a fit and said it was too much car for a young girl to be driving, but Hancock had poured his wife another stiff drink and told her that if he'd wanted her worthless opinion about anything, he would have asked for it.

After graduating from high school, Dorothy Rae had gone off in a blaze of glory to enter the University of Texas in Austin. She met Jack Rutledge during her junior year, fell madly in love, and became determined to have him for her very own. She'd never been denied anything in her life, and she didn't intend to start with missing out on the only man she would every truly love.

Jack, struggling through his second year in law school, was in love with Dorothy Rae, too, but he couldn't even think about marriage until after he finished school. His daddy expected him not only to graduate, but to rank high in his class. His daddy also expected him to be chivalrous where women were concerned.

So when Jack finally succumbed to temptation and re-lieved Dorothy Rae Hancock of her virginity, he was in a quandary as to which had priority—chivalry toward the lady or responsibility toward parental expectations. Dorothy Rae spurred him into making a decision when she weepily told him that she was late getting her period.

Panicked, Jack figured that an untimely marriage was better than an untimely baby and prayed that Nelson would figure it that way, too. He and Dorothy Rae drove to Oklahoma over the weekend, wed in secret, and broke the glad tidings to their parents after the fact.

Nelson and Zee were disappointed, but after getting Jack's guarantee that he had no intention of dropping out of law school, they welcomed Dorothy Rae into the family.

The Hancocks of Lampasas didn't take the news quite so well. Her elopement nearly killed Dorothy Rae's daddy. In fact, he dropped dead of a heart attack one month after the nuptials. Dorothy Rae's unstable mother was committed to an alcohol abuse hospital. On the day of her release several weeks later, she was deemed dried out and cured. Three days later, she ran her car into a bridge abutment while driving drunk. She died on impact.

Francine Angela wasn't born until eighteen months after Dorothy Rae's marriage to Jack. It was either the longest pregnancy in history or she had tricked him into marriage.

He had never accused her of either, but, as though in self-imposed penance, she had had two miscarriages in quick succession when Fancy was still a baby.

The last miscarriage had proved to be life-threatening, so the doctor had tied her tubes to prevent future pregnancies. To blunt the physical, mental, and emotional pain this caused her, Dorothy Rae began treating herself to a cocktail every afternoon. And when that didn't work, she treated herself to two.

"How can you look yourself in the mirror," she demanded of her husband now, "knowing that you love your brother's wife?"

"I don't love her."

"No, you don't, do you?" Leaning close, she poisoned the air between them with the intoxicating fumes of her breath. "You hate her because she treats you like dirt. She wipes her feet on you. You can't even see that all these changes in her are just—"

"What changes?" Instead of hanging his pants on the hanger in his hand, he dropped them into a chair. "She explained about using her left hand, you know."

Having won his attention, Dorothy Rae pulled herself up straight and assumed the air of superiority that only drunks can assume. "Other changes," she said loftily. "Haven't you noticed them?"

"Maybe. Like what?"

"Like the attention she's showering on Mandy and the way she's sucking up to Tate."

"She's been through a lot. She's mellowed."

"Ha!" she crowed indelicately. "Her? Mellowed? God above, you're blind where she's concerned." Her blue eyes tried to focus on his face. "Since that plane crash, she's like a different person, and you know it. But it's all for show," she stated knowingly.

"Why should she bother?"

"Because she wants something." She swayed toward him and tapped his chest for emphasis. "Probably, she's playing the good little senator's wife so she'll get to move to Washington with Tate. What'll you do then, Jack? Huh? What'll you do with your sinful lust then?"

"Maybe I'll start drinking and keep you company."

She raised a shaky hand and pointed her finger at him. "Don't get off the subject. You want Carole. I know you do," she finished with another sob.

Jack, once more bored with her inebriated rambling, finished hanging up his clothes, then methodically went around the room, switching off lamps and turning down the bed. "Come to bed, Dorothy Rae," he said wearily.

She caught his arm. "You never loved me."

"That's not true."

"You think I tricked you into marrying me."

"I never said that."

"I thought I was pregnant. I did!"

"I know you did."

"Because you didn't love me, you thought it was okay to go after other women." Her eyes narrowed on him accusingly.

"I know there have been others. You've cheated on me so many times, it's no wonder I drink."

Tears were streaming down her face. Ineffectually, she slapped his bare shoulder. "I drink because my husband doesn't love me. Never did. And now he's in love with his brother's wife."

Jack crawled into bed, turned onto his side, and pulled the covers up over himself. His nonchalance enraged her. On her knees, she walked to the center of the bed and began pounding on his back with her fists. "Tell me the truth. Tell me how much you love her. Tell me how much you despise me."

Her anger and strength were rapidly exhausted, as he had known they would be. She collapsed beside him, losing consciousness instantly. Jack rolled to his side and adjusted the covers over her. Then, heaving an unhappy sigh, he lay back down and tried to sleep.

SIXTEEN

"I thought she would be in bed by now."

Tate spoke from the doorway of Mandy's bathroom. Avery was kneeling beside the tub, where Mandy was worming her fingers through a mound of bubbles.

"She probably should be, but we went a little overboard with the bubble bath."

"So I see."

Tate came in and sat down on the lid of the commode. Mandy smiled up at him.

"Do your trick for Daddy," Avery told her.

Obediently, the child cupped a handful of suds and blew on them hard, sending clumps of white foam flying in all directions. Several landed on Tate's knee. He made a big deal of it. "Whoa, there, Mandy, girl! You're taking the bath, not me."

She giggled and scooped up another handful. This time a dollop of suds landed on Avery's nose. To Mandy's delight, she sneezed. "I'd better put a stop to this before it gets out of hand." She bent over the tub, slid her hands into Mandy's armpits, and lifted her out.

"Here, give her to me." Tate was waiting to wrap up his daughter in a towel.

"Careful. Slippery when wet."

Mandy, bundled in soft pink terry cloth, was carried into her adjoining bedroom and set down beside her bed. Her chubby little feet sank into the thick rug. Its luxuriant nap swallowed all ten toes. Tate sat down on the edge of her bed and began drying her with experienced hands.

"Nightie?" he asked, looking up at Avery expectantly.

"Oh, yes. Coming right up." There was a tall, six-drawer chest and a wide, three-drawer bureau. Where would the nighties be kept? She moved toward the bureau and opened the top drawer. Socks and panties.

"Carole? Second drawer."

Avery responded with aplomb. "She'll need underwear, too, won't she?" He unwound the towel from around Mandy and helped her step into her underwear, then pulled the nightgown over her head while Avery turned down her bed. He lifted Mandy into it.

Avery brought a hairbrush from the bureau, sat down beside Tate on the edge of the bed, and began brushing Mandy's hair. "You smell so clean," she whispered, bending down to kiss her rosy cheek once she'd finished with her hair. "Want some powder on?"

"Like yours?" Mandy asked.

"Hmm, like mine." Avery went back to the bureau for the small music box of dusting powder she'd spotted there earlier. Returning to the bed, she opened the lid. A Tchaikovsky tune began to play. She dipped the plush puff into the powder, then applied it to Mandy's chest, tummy, and arms. Mandy tilted her head back. Avery stroked her exposed throat with the powder puff. Giggling, Mandy hunched her shoulders and dug her fists into her lap.

"That tickles, Mommy."

The form of address startled Avery and brought tears to her eyes. She pulled the child into a tight hug. It was a moment before she could speak. "Now you really smell good, doesn't she, Daddy?"

"She sure does. 'Night, Mandy." He kissed her, eased her back onto the pillows, and tucked the summer-weight covers around her.

"Good night." Avery leaned down to softly peck her cheek, but Mandy flung her arms around Avery's neck and gave her mouth a smacking, moist kiss. She then turned onto her side, pulled a well-loved Pooh Bear against her, and closed her eyes.

Somewhat dazed by Mandy's spontaneous show of affection, Avery replaced the music box, turned out the light, and preceded Tate through the doorway and down the hall toward her own room.

"For our first day—"

She got no further before he grabbed her upper arm and shoved her inside her bedroom and against the nearest wall. Keeping one hand firmly around her biceps, he closed the door so they wouldn't be overheard and flattened his other palm against the wall near her head.

"What's the matter with you?" she demanded.

"Shut up and listen to me." He moved in closer, his face taut with anger. "I don't know what game you're playing with me. What's more, I don't give a shit. But if you start messing with Mandy, I'll kick you out so fast your head will spin, understand?"

"No. I don't understand."

"The hell you don't," he snarled. "This sweetness and light act is a bunch of crap."

"*Act?*"

"I'm an adult."

"You're a bully. Let go of my arm."

"I recognize your act for what it is. But Mandy is a child. To her it's real, and she'll respond to it." He inclined his body even closer. "Then, when you go back to being your old self, you'll leave her irreparably damaged."

"I—"

"I can't let that happen to her. I won't."

"You give me very little credit, Tate."

"I give you none."

She sucked in a quick, harsh breath.

He looked her over rudely. "Okay, so this morning you dazzled the press on my behalf. Thank you. You took my hand during the press conference. Sweet. We're wearing matching wedding bands. How romantic," he sneered.

"You've even got members of my family, who should know better, speculating that you had some kind of conversion experience in the hospital—found Jesus or something."

He lowered his head to within inches of hers. "I know you too well, Carole. I know that you are at your sweetest and kindest just before you go in for the kill." Increasing the pressure on her arm, he added, "I know that for a fact, remember?"

Distressed, Avery said fervently, "I have changed. I am different."

"Like hell. You've just changed tactics, that's all. But I don't care how well you play the part of the perfect candidate's wife, you're out. What I told you before the crash still stands. After the election, no matter the outcome, you're gone, baby."

His threat of dispossession didn't frighten her. Avery Daniels had been dispossessed of everything already—even her identity. What stunned Avery was that Tate Rutledge, on whose integrity she would have staked her life, was a phony after all.

"You would manipulate the public that way?" she hissed. "You'd go through this campaign with me playing your devoted wife, standing at your side, waving and smiling and delivering silly speeches that are composed for me, only as a means of getting more votes?" Her voice had risen a full octave. "Because a happily married candidate has a better chance of winning than one caught up in a divorce procedure. Isn't that right?"

His eyes turned as hard as flint. "Good try, Carole. Shift the blame to me if it makes you feel better about your own manipulations. You know damn good and well why I didn't kick you out a long time ago. I want this election for myself and for the following I've cultivated. I won't let those voters down. I can't do anything that might prevent me from winning, even if it means pretending to live in wedded bliss with you.''

Once again he subjected her to a contemptuous once-over. ''Your surgery made the packaging look fresher, but you're still rotten on the inside.''

Avery was having a difficult time keeping the aspersions he was casting on Carole separate from herself. She took each insult to heart, as though it were aimed at her and not his late wife. She wanted to defend herself against his criticism, to fight back with a woman's weapons. Because, while his fierce temperament was intimidating, it was also arousing.

His anger only intensified his sexiness. It emanated from him as potently as the scent of his after-shave. His mouth looked hard and cruel. It became Avery's goal to soften it.

She raised her head, defying his resentful glare. ''Are you sure I'm the same?''

''Damn sure.''

Sliding her arms over his shoulders, she clasped her hands behind his neck. ''Are you sure, Tate?'' Coming up on tiptoes, she brushed her parted lips across his. ''Absolutely sure?''

''Don't do this. It only makes you more of a whore.''

''I'm not!''

The insult smarted. In a way, she was prostituting herself with another woman's husband for the sake of a story. But that wasn't motivating her as much as a growing sexual need more powerful than any she had ever experienced. With or without her story, she had a genuine desire to give Tate the tenderness and love that had been missing from his marriage to Carole.

''I'm not the woman I was before. I swear to you I'm not.''

She tilted her head to one side and aligned her lips with his. Her hands cupped the back of his head, her fingers curling through his hair and drawing him down. If he really wanted to, he could resist, Avery assured herself.

But he allowed his head to be drawn closer to hers.

Encouraged, she daintily used the moist tip of her tongue to probe at his lips. His muscles tensed, but it was a sign of weakness, not endurance.

"Tate?" She gently nipped his lower lip with her teeth. "Christ."

The hand bracing him against the wall fell away. Avery was propelled backward when she absorbed the weight of his body, becoming sandwiched between him and the wall. One arm curled hard and tight around her waist. His other hand captured her jaw, almost crushing it between his strong fingers. It held her head in place while he kissed her ravenously. He sealed her open mouth to his with gentle suction, then burrowed his tongue into the silky wet cavity.

Leaving her gasping for breath, he angled his head the opposite way and tormented her with quick, deft flicks of his tongue across her lips and barely inside them. Her hands moved to his cheeks. She laid her palms against them and ran her fingertips across his cheekbones as she gave herself totally to his kiss.

He fumbled with her clothing, thrusting his hand beneath her skirt, into her underpants, and filling it with soft woman flesh. She moaned pleasurably when he tilted her middle up against his swollen pelvis and ground it against her cleft.

Avery felt fluid and feverish. Her sex was wet and warm. Her breasts ached. The nipples tingled.

Then she was abruptly deserted.

She blinked her eyes into focus. Her head landed hard against the wall behind her. She flattened her hands against it to keep herself from sliding to the floor.

"I'll grant you that it's a polished act," he said woodenly. His cheeks were flushed and his eyes were dilated. His breathing was rapid and shallow. "You're not as blatant as you used to be, but classier. Different, but just as sexy. Maybe even sexier."

She looked down at the distended fly of his jeans, a look that made words superfluous.

"Okay, I'm hard," he admitted with an angry growl. "But I'll die of it before I'll sleep with you again."

He walked out. He didn't slam the door behind him, but left it standing open, more of an insult than if he had stormed out. Heartsick and wounded, Avery was left alone in Carole's room, with Carole's chintz, Carole's mess.

Everyone in the family had noticed the puzzling inconsistencies in Carole's personality, but her odd behavior was keeping one person in particular awake at night. After hours of prowling the grounds surrounding the house, looking for answers in the darkness, the insomniac posed a question to the moon.

What is the bitch up to?

No radical changes in her could be pinpointed. The differences in her face were subtle, the result of the reconstructive surgery. Shorter hair made her look different, but that was inconsequential. She had lost a few pounds, making her appear slimmer than before, but it was certainly no drastic weight loss. Physically, she was virtually the same as before the crash. It was the nonphysical changes that were noticeable and so damned baffling.

What is the bitch up to?

Judging by her behavior since the crash, one would think her brush with death had given her a conscience. But that couldn't be. She didn't know the meaning of the word. Although for all the goodwill she was dispensing, that's apparently what she wanted everybody to believe.

Could Carole Rutledge have had a change of heart? Could she be seeking her husband's approval? Could she ever be a loving, attentive mother?

Don't make me laugh.

She was stupid to switch tactics now. She'd been doing fine at what she'd been hired to do: destroy Tate Rutledge's soul, so that by the time that bullet exploded in his head, it would almost be a blessing to him.

Carole Navarro had been perfect for the job. Oh, she'd had to be scrubbed down, tidied up, dressed correctly, and taught not to spike her speech with four-letter words. But by the time the overhaul had been completed, she had been a stunning package of wit, intellect, sophistication, and sexiness that Tate hadn't been able to resist.

He hadn't known that her wit had been cleansed of all ribaldry, that her intellect was only refined street smarts, her

sophistication acquired, and her sexiness tempered with
false morality. Just as planned, he'd fallen for the package,
because it had promised everything he had been looking for
in a wife.

Carole had perpetuated the myth until after Mandy was
born—that had also been according to plan. It had been a
relief for her to put phase two into action and start having
affairs. The shackles of respectability had been chafing her
for a long time. Her patience had worn thin. Once let loose,
she performed beautifully.

God, it had been marvelous fun to witness Tate in his
misery!

Except for that indiscreet visit in the hospital ICU, there'd
been no mention made of their secret alliance since she was
introduced to Tate four years ago. Neither by word or deed
had they given away the pact they had made when she had
been recruited for the job.

But since the crash, she'd been even more evasive than
usual. She bore watching—closely. She was doing some
strange and unusual things, even for Carole. The whole
family was noticing the unfamiliar personality traits.

Maybe she was acting strange for the hell of it. That
would be like her. She enjoyed being perverse for perversi-
ty's sake alone. That wasn't serious, but it rankled that she
had seized the initiative to change the game plan without
prior consultation.

Perhaps she hadn't had an opportunity to consult yet.
Perhaps she knew something about Tate that no one else was
privy to and which needed to be acted upon immediately.

Or perhaps the bitch—and this was the most likely
possibility—had decided that being a senator's wife was
worth more to her than the payoff she was due to receive the
day Tate was laid in a casket. After all, her metamorphosis
had coincided with the primary election.

Whatever her motive, this new behavior pattern was as
annoying as hell. She'd better watch herself, or she'd be cut
out. At this point, it could all go down with or without her
participation. Didn't the stupid bitch realize that?

Or had she finally realized that a second bullet was
destined for her?

SEVENTEEN

"Mrs. Rutledge, what a surprise."

The secretary stood up to greet Avery as she entered the anteroom of the law office Tate shared with his brother. To learn where it was, she had had to look up the address in the telephone directory.

"Hello. How are you?" She didn't address the secretary by name. The nameplate on the desk read "Mary Crawford," but she was taking no chances.

"I'm fine, but you look fabulous."

"Thank you."

"Tate told me that you were prettier than ever, but seeing is believing."

Tate had told her that? They hadn't engaged in a private conversation since the night he had kissed her. She found it hard to believe that he'd said something flattering about her to his secretary.

"Is he in?" He was. His car was parked out front.

"He's with a client."

"I didn't think he was handling any cases."

"He's not." Mary Crawford smoothed her skirt beneath her hips and sat back down. "He's with Barney Bridges. You know what a character he is. Anyway, he pledged a hefty donation to Tate's campaign, so when he hand delivered it, Tate made time to see him."

"Well, I've come all this way. Will they be long? Shall I wait?"

"Please do. Have a seat." The secretary indicated the grouping of waiting room sofas and chairs upholstered in burgundy and navy striped corduroy. "Would you like some coffee?"

"No thanks. Nothing."

She often passed up coffee now, preferring none at all to the liberally sweetened brew Carole had drunk. Sitting down in one of the armchairs, she picked up a current issue of *Field and Stream* and began idly thumbing through it. Mary resumed typing, as she'd been doing before Avery had come in.

This impetuous visit to Tate's law office was chancy, but it was a desperation measure she felt she had to take or go mad. What had Carole Rutledge done all day?

Avery had been living in the ranch house for over two weeks, and she had yet to discover a single constructive activity that Tate's wife had been involved in.

It had taken Avery several days to locate everything in her bedroom and the other rooms of the house to which she had access. She was constantly looking over her shoulder, not wanting to alert anyone to what she was doing. Eventually, she felt comfortable with the house's layout and where everyday items were stored.

Gradually, she began to learn her way around outside, as well. She took Mandy with her on these missions so they would appear to be nothing more than innocent strolls.

Carole had driven an American sports car. To Avery's consternation, it had a standard transmission. She wasn't too adept at driving standard transmissions. The first few times she took the car out, she nearly gave herself whiplash and stripped all the gears.

But once she felt adequate, she invented errands that would get her out of the house. Carole's way of life was dreadfully boring. Her routine lacked diversion and spontaneity. The ennui was making Avery Daniels crazy.

The day she had discovered an engagement calendar in a nightstand drawer, she had clutched it to her chest like a miner would a gold nugget. But a scan of its pages revealed very little except the days that Carole had had her hair and nails done.

Avery never called for an appointment. It would be a luxury to spend several hours a week being pampered in a

salon—something Avery Daniels had never had time for—
but she couldn't risk letting Carole's hairdresser touch her
hair or a manicurist her nails. They might detect giveaways
that others couldn't.

The engagement book had shed no light on what Carole did
to fill her days. Obviously, she wasn't a member of any clubs.
She had few or no friends because no one called. That came
both as a surprise and a relief to Avery, who had been afraid
that a covey of confidantes would descend, expecting to pick
up where they had left off before Carole's accident.

Apparently, no such close friends existed. The flowers
and cards she had received during her convalescence must
have come from friends of the family.

Carole had held no job, had no hobbies. Avery reasoned
that she should be thankful for that. What if Carole had
been an expert sculptress, artist, harpist, or calligrapher? It
had been difficult enough teaching herself in private to write
and eat with her right hand.

She was expected to do no chores, not even make her
own bed. Mona took care of the house and did all the
cooking. A yard man came twice a week to tend to the
plants in the courtyard. A retired cowboy, too old to herd
cattle or to rodeo, managed the stable of horses. No one
encouraged her to resume an activity or interest that had
been suspended as a result of her injuries.

Carole Rutledge had been a lazy idler. Avery Daniels was
not.

The door to Tate's private office opened. He emerged in
the company of a barrel-chested, middle-aged man. They
were laughing together.

Avery's heart accelerated at the sight of Tate, who was
wearing a genuinely warm smile. His eyes were crinkled at
the corners with the sense of humor he never shared with
her. Eddy constantly nagged him to trade in his jeans,
boots, and casual shirts for a coat and tie. He refused unless
he was making a scheduled public appearance.

"Who am I trying to impress?" he had asked his perturbed
campaign manager during a discussion relating to his wardrobe.

"Several million voters," Eddy had replied.

"If I can't impress them by what I'm standing for, they

sure as hell aren't going to be impressed by what I'm standing in.''

Nelson had drolly remarked, ''Unless it's bullshit.''

Everybody had laughed and that had been the end of the discussion.

Avery was glad Tate dressed as he did. He looked sensational. His head was bent at the listening angle that she had come to recognize and find endearing. One lock of hair dipped low over his forehead. His mouth was split in a wide grin, showing off strong, white teeth.

He hadn't seen her yet. At unguarded moments like this, she reveled in looking at him before contempt for his wife turned his beautiful smile into something ugly.

''Now, this is a treat!''

The booming bass voice snapped Avery out of her love-struck daze. Tate's visitor came swiftly toward her on short, stocky legs that were reminiscent of Irish. She was scooped up into a smothering bear hug and her back was hammered upon with exuberant affection. ''Gawddamn, you look better than you ever have, and I didn't think that was possible.''

''Hello, Mr. Bridges.''

'' 'Mr. Bridges?' Shee-ut. Where'd that come from? I told Mama when we saw you on the TV that you're prettier now than you were before. She thought so, too.''

''I'm glad I have your approval.''

He wagged two stubby fingers, holding a cigar, near the tip of her nose. ''Now you listen to ol' Barney, darlin','' those polls don't meant a gawddamn thing, you hear? Not a gawddamn thing. I told Mama just the other day that those polls ain't worth shee-ut. You think I'd put my money on the boy here,'' he said, walloping Tate between the shoulder blades, ''if I didn't think he was gonna put the screws to that gawddamn Dekker on election day? Huh?''

''No sir, not you, Barney,'' she replied, laughing.

''You're gawddamn right I wouldn't.'' Cramming the cigar into the corner of his mouth, he reached for her and gave her another rib-crunching hug. ''I'd purely love to take y'all to lunch, but I got a deacons' meetin' at the church.''

''Don't let us keep you,'' Tate said, trying to keep a straight face. ''Thank you again for the contribution.''

Barney waved away the thanks. "Mama's mailin' hers in today."

Tate swallowed with difficulty. "I . . . I thought the check was from both of you."

"Hell no, boy. That was only my half. Gotta go. The church is a long way from here, and Mama gets pissed if I drive the Vette over seventy in town, so I promised not to. Too many gawddamn crazies on the road. Y'all take care, you hear?"

He lumbered out. After the door had closed behind him, the secretary looked up at Tate and wheezed, "Did he say half?"

"That's what he said." Tate shook his head in disbelief. "Apparently he really believes that the polls aren't worth shee-ut."

Mary laughed. So did Avery. But Tate's smile had disappeared by the time he had ushered her into his office and closed the door. "What are you doing here? Need some money?"

When he addressed her in that curt, dismissive tone of voice, which he reserved for the times when they were alone, each word was like a shard of glass being gouged into her vitals. It made her ache. It also made her mad as hell.

"No, I don't need any money," she said tightly as she sat down in the chair opposite his desk. "As you suggested, I went to the bank and signed a new card. I explained about the change in my handwriting," she said, flexing her right hand. "So I can write a check against the account whenever I get low on cash."

"So, why are you here?"

"I need something else."

"What's that?"

"Something to do."

Her unexpected statement served its purpose. It won her his undivided attention. Skeptically holding her stare, he leaned back in his chair and raised his boots to the corner of his desk. "Something to do?"

"That's right."

He laced his fingers together across his belt buckle. "I'm listening."

"I'm bored, Tate." Her frustration boiled over. Restlessly, she left the chair. "I'm stuck out there on the ranch all day with nothing productive to do. I'm sick of being idle. My mind's turning to mush. I'm actually beginning to discuss the soap operas with Mona."

As she aimlessly roamed his office, she made note of several things—primarily that there were framed photographs of Mandy everywhere, but none of Carole.

Framed diplomas and photographs were attractively arranged on the wall behind the credenza. Looking for clues into his past, she paused in front of an eight-by-ten blowup of a snapshot taken in Vietnam.

Tate and Eddy were standing in front of a jet bomber, their arms draped across each other's shoulders in a pose of camaraderie. One's grin was as cocky as the other's. Avery had inadvertently learned that they'd been college roommates until Tate had postponed his education to enlist in the air force. Until now, she hadn't realized that Eddy had accompanied him to war.

"Since when have you been concerned with your mind?" he asked her, bringing her around.

"I need activity."

"Join an aerobics class."

"I did—the same day the doctor examined my tibia and gave me the go-ahead. But the class only lasts one hour three times a week."

"Join another one."

"Tate!"

"What? What the hell is all this about?"

"I'm trying to tell you. You're stubbornly refusing to listen."

He glanced at the closed door, mindful of the secretary seated just beyond it. Lowering his voice, he said, "You enjoy riding, but you haven't saddled up once since you got home."

No, she hadn't. Avery enjoyed riding, too, but she didn't know how good an equestrian Carole had been and hadn't wanted to tip her hand by being either too adept or too inexperienced.

"I've lost interest," she said lamely.

"I thought you would," he said sardonically, "just as soon as you cut the price tags off all that expensive gear."

Avery had seen the riding clothes in Carole's closet and wondered if she had ever actually worn the jodhpurs and short, tailored jacket. "I'll go back to it eventually." Giving herself time to collect her thoughts, she gazed at a picture of Nelson with Lyndon B. Johnson while he was still a congressman. Impressive.

There were several photos of Nelson in uniform, providing her a chronicle of his military career. One picture in particular caught her eye because it was reminiscent of the snapshot of Tate and Eddy.

In the photo, Nelson's arm was draped companionably around another Air Force cadet—a young man as strikingly handsome and cavalier as young Nelson. Looming in the background, like a behemoth, was a monstrous bomber plane. Typed neatly across the bottom of the photograph was "Majors Nelson Rutledge and Bryan Tate, South Korea, 1951."

Bryan Tate. A relative of Nelson's? A friend? Presumably, because Nelson had named his son after him.

Avery turned again to face him, trying not to show more interest in the photograph than it should warrant for someone already familiar with it. "Put me to work at campaign headquarters."

"No."

"Why? Fancy's working there."

"Which is reason enough to keep you out. There might be bloodshed."

"I'll ignore her."

He shook his head. "We've got a slew of new volunteers. They're stepping over each other. Eddy's inventing work to accommodate all of them."

"I've got to get involved in something, Tate."

"Why, for God's sake?"

Because Avery Daniels performed best under pressure, she was accustomed to moving at a hectic pace, and couldn't tolerate inactivity. The sedentary life Carole Rutledge had lived was driving her insane.

She could neither protect him from assassination or do a story on the attempt if he continued to keep her at a safe distance. Her future, as well as his, hinged on her becoming as actively involved in his campaign as all the suspects.

"I feel like I should be helping you in some way."

He barked a short laugh. "Who do you think you're kidding?"

"I'm your wife!"

"Only for the time being!"

His sharp put-down silenced her. Tate, seeing her wounded expression, swore beneath his breath. "Okay, if you want to do something for me, continue being a decent mother to Mandy. She's opening up a little, I think."

"She's opening up a lot. And I intend for her to improve further every day."

She braced her hands on his desk and leaned over it, as she had when she had appealed to Irish for permission to pursue a story that met with his disapproval. "Even Mandy and her problems don't consume enough time. I can't be with her constantly. She goes to nursery school three mornings a week."

"You agreed with the psychologist that she should."

"I still do. Interaction with other children is extremely beneficial to her. She needs to develop social skills. But while she's at school, I wander through the house, killing time until it's time to pick her up. Every afternoon she takes a long nap." She leaned farther forward. "Please, Tate. I'm withering on the vine."

He held her stare for a long moment. Eventually, his eyes ventured down into the gaping vee of her silk shirt, but he quickly raised them and looked annoyed with himself for even that merest slip of his control.

He cleared his throat and asked crossly, "Okay, what do you suggest?"

Her tension eased somewhat. At least he was open to discussing it. She straightened up. "Let me work at headquarters."

"Nix."

"Then let me accompany you on that campaign trip next week."

"No," he said with taut finality.

"Please."

"I said no." Angrily he swung his feet to the floor, stood up, and rounded the desk.

"Why not?"

"Because you're not a trouper, Carole, and I won't put up with the disharmony you create."

"Like what?"

"Like what?" he demanded, incredulous that her memory didn't serve her. "When you went before, you complained about the rooms, the banquet food, everything. You ran consistently late when you knew how tightly Eddy wanted to keep to schedule. You made wisecracks to the press, which you considered cute and everybody else thought were tasteless and unbecoming. And that was only a three-day trip to test the waters before I had made my final decision to run."

"It won't be like that this time."

"I won't have any time to entertain you. When I'm not making a speech, I'll be writing one. Hours into the trip, you'd be whining that I was ignoring you and that you had nothing to do."

"I'll find things to do. I can make coffee, order sandwiches, sharpen pencils, take calls, return calls, run errands."

"Menial labor. We've got gofers and hangers-on who do all that."

"I can do *something*." She had been following closely on his heels as he moved around the office. When he stopped abruptly, she collided with him from behind.

He turned. "The novelty would wear off after the first day, and you'd be tired of it, complaining, wanting to come home."

"No, I won't."

"Why do you want to become involved all of a sudden?"

"Because," she said with rising ire, "you're running for a Senate seat, and it's my responsibility as your wife to help you win."

"Bullshit!"

There were three sharp raps on the door. Seconds later it was opened to admit Eddy and Jack. "Excuse us," the former said, "but we heard all the shouting when we came in and thought you might need us to referee."

"What's going on?" Jack closed the door behind them. "What are you doing here?"

"I came to see my husband," Avery retorted. "If that's all right with you, Jack." She pushed her bangs off her forehead, a belligerent gesture that dared him to make something of it.

"Calm down, for crissake. I was just asking." Jack sat down on the short sofa against the wall.

Eddy shoved his hands into his pants pockets and stared at the Oriental rug between his gleaming shoes. Tate returned to his desk and sat down. Avery was too keyed up to sit, so she crossed to the credenza and backed against it, supporting herself on her hips.

"Carole wants to go on the campaign trip with us next week," Tate said.

Jack said, "Jesus, not again."

Avery cried, "Well, why not?"

Eddy said, "Let's discuss it."

Tate took them in turn. "You don't like the idea, Jack?"

Jack glared at her, then shrugged and swore beneath his breath. "She's your wife."

Tate's attention moved to Avery. "You already know my objections."

"Some of them are justified," she said in a conciliatory tone, admiring him for not criticizing his wife in front of other men. "I'll do better this time, now that I know what to expect and what is expected of me."

"Eddy?"

Eddy's contemplation of the rug ended when Tate spoke his name. He raised his head. "There's no doubt that a handsome couple is an easier package to sell than a handsome man alone."

"Why?"

"Image, mainly. A couple represents all the things America stands for—hearth and home, the American dream. Marriage signifies that once you get to Washington you aren't going to squander taxpayers' money on bimbo secretaries who can't type.''

"At least in theory," Jack said with a guffaw.

Eddy smiled crookedly and conceded, "At least in theory. Women voters will respect you for being a faithful husband and conscientious father. Men will like that you aren't either gay or on the make.

"For all our modern sophistication, voters might feel uneasy about voting a suspected homosexual into office. A good-looking candidate is inherently resented by male voters. Having a wife by your side makes you one of the guys."

"In other words, misery loves company," Avery said snidely.

Eddy gave a helpless lift of his shoulders and apologetically replied, "I didn't make up the rules, Carole."

She divided her disgusted look among the three of them. "So, what's the verdict?"

"I have a suggestion."

"You have the floor, Eddy." As before, Tate's feet were resting on the corner of his desk, and he was reclining in the tall leather chair. Avery was tempted to sweep his boots off the desk just to unbalance his posture and his insouciance.

Eddy said, "On Carole's behalf, I declined her invitation to attend that dinner coming up this Friday night."

"The southern governors' thing in Austin?"

"Right. I excused her from going by saying that for all the progress she's made, she wasn't quite up to a black tie evening."

He turned toward her. "I could call them back and accept. It's a bipartisan group, so there'll be no active campaigning, just a chance to glad-hand, see, and be seen. We'll see how that evening goes and make a decision about the trip based on that."

"An audition, in other words," Avery said.

"If that's how you want to see it," Eddy returned calmly. He looked toward Jack and Tate. "She did a pretty good job at that press conference when she left the hospital."

Eddy's opinion mattered a great deal to Tate, but final decisions were always left to him. He glanced at his older brother, who had remained irascibly silent. "What do you think, Jack?"

"I guess it'd be okay," he said, glancing at her resentfully. "I know Mom and Dad would rather the two of you present a unified front."

"Thank you both for your advice."

They took the subtle hint. Jack left the office without saying another word. Eddy nodded an unspoken good-bye to Avery and closed the door behind himself.

Tate held her stare for several moments. "All right," he said grudgingly. "You've won a chance to convince me that you'd be more of an asset than a liability when we begin campaigning in earnest."

"You won't be disappointed, Tate. I promise."

He frowned doubtfully. "Friday night. We'll leave the house at seven sharp. Be ready."

EIGHTEEN

"I'll get it."

The front doorbell had rung twice. Avery was the first to reach it. She grabbed the knob and pulled it open. Van Lovejoy stood between the pots of geraniums.

Avery froze. Her expectant, welcoming smile turned to stone, her knees to water. Her stomach tightened.

Van reacted with similar disquiet. His slumped posture was instantly corrected. A cigarette fell from between his fingers. He blinked numerous times.

Avery, hoping that his pupils had been dilated by marijuana and not shock, mustered as much composure as she could. "Hello."

"Hi, uh . . ." He closed his eyes for a moment and shook his head of stringy hair. "Uh, Mrs. Rutledge?"

"Yes?"

He covered his heart with a bony hand. "Jesus, for a minute there, you looked just like—"

"Come in, please." She didn't want to hear him speak her name. She had barely curbed her impulse to joyously cry out his. It had been nearly impossible to keep from hugging him fiercely and telling him that she was onto the hottest story of her career.

From the beginning, however, she had been in this alone. Telling Van would place him in danger, too. As comforting as it would be to have an ally, she couldn't afford the luxury. Besides, she didn't want to risk blowing the opportunity by confiding in him. Van wasn't all that trustworthy.

She stepped aside and he joined her in the entry. It would have been natural for him to gaze around at the unfamiliar and impressive surroundings, but instead, he stared into her face. Avery pitied him his confusion. "You are . . . ?"

"Oh, sorry." He rubbed his palms self-consciously on the seat of his jeans, then extended his right hand. She shook it quickly. "Van Lovejoy."

"I'm Carole Rutledge."

"I know. I was there the day you left the clinic. I work for KTEX."

"I see."

Even though he was making an attempt at normal conversation, his eyes hadn't left her. It was agony to be this close to a friend and not be able to behave normally. She had a million and one questions to ask him, but settled for the one that Carole would logically ask next.

"If you're here representing the television station, shouldn't you have cleared it first with Mr. Paschal, my husband's campaign manager?"

"He knows I'm coming. The production company sent me over."

"Production company?"

"I'm shooting a TV commercial here next Wednesday. I came today to scout my locations. Didn't anybody tell you I was coming?"

"I—"

"Carole?"

Nelson moved into the hallway, subjecting Van to a glare of stern disapproval. Nelson was always military neat. He never had a wrinkle in his clothing or a single gray hair out of place.

Van was the antithesis. His dingy T-shirt had come from a Cajun restaurant that specialized in oysters on the half shell. The lewdly suggestive slogan on the shirt read, "Shuck me, suck me, eat me raw." His jeans had gone beyond being fashionably ragged to downright threadbare. There were no laces in his scuffed jogging shoes. Avery doubted he owned a pair of socks because he always went without.

He looked unhealthy and underfed to the point of emaciation. Sharp shoulder blades poked against the T-shirt. If he had stood up straight, each rib would have been delineated. As it was, his back bowed over a concave torso.

Avery knew that those nicotine-stained hands with the chipped and dirty fingernails were gifted in handling a video camera. His vacuous eyes were capable of incredible artistic insight. All Nelson could see, however, was an eternal hippie, a wasted life. Van's talent was as well disguised as her real identity.

"Nelson, this is Mr. Lovejoy. Mr. Lovejoy, Colonel Rutledge." Nelson seemed reluctant to shake hands with Van and made short business of it. "He's here to look over the house in preparation for the television commercial they're taping next week."

"You work for MB Productions?" Nelson asked stiffly.

"I freelance for them sometimes. When they want the best."

"Hmm. They said somebody would be out today." Apparently, Van wasn't what Nelson had expected. "I'll show you around. What do you want to see—indoors or out?"

"Both. Any place that Rutledge, his wife, and his kid might spend an average day. Folksy is what they said they wanted. Sentimental crap."

"You can see all of the house you want, but you'll have no access to my family, Mr. Lovejoy. My wife would be affronted by the crude wording on your shirt."

"She's not wearing it, so why the fuck should she care?"

Nelson's blue eyes turned arctic. He was accustomed to being treated with more deference by anyone he considered of inferior rank. Avery wouldn't have been surprised if Nelson had grabbed him by the seat of his pants and the scruff of his neck and thrown him out. If Van's business hadn't dealt directly with Tate's campaign, he probably would have.

As it was, he said, "Carole, I apologize for what you just heard. You'll excuse us?"

Van turned back to her. "See you around, Mrs. Rutledge. Sorry I stared, but you look so much like—"

"I'm used to people staring at my face now," she interrupted quickly. "Everyone's naturally curious about it."

Nelson impatiently inclined his head. "This way, Lovejoy."

Van gave one last puzzled shake of his head before ambling off down the hallway behind Nelson. Avery retreated to her room, leaning against the door after she had closed it behind her. She breathed deeply and blinked back tears of nervousness and remorse.

She had wanted to grab Van's skinny arm and, after a jubilant reunion, pump him for information. How was Irish? Was he still grieving over her death? Was he taking care of himself? What had become of the new weatherman? Had he been canned or had he left of his own volition? Had the pregnant secretary delivered a boy or a girl? What was the latest gossip from the sales department? Was the general manager still cheating on his wife with the socialite?

She realized, however, that Van might not be as glad to see her as she was to see him. Oh, he'd be thrilled that she was alive, but once he'd recovered from the shock, she could almost hear him saying, "Just what the fuck do you think you're doing?"

Frequently, she had been asking herself that same question. She wanted the story, yes, but her motivation wasn't entirely self-fulfilling.

Saving Tate's life had been her ultimate reason for taking the place of his late wife. But was that still operative? Where was the threat that was supposed to exist?

Since coming home, she had been a curious observer.

There was some discord between Jack and Dorothy Rae. Fancy could provoke a saint. Nelson was autocratic. Zee was aloof. Eddy was competent to a fault. But none had exhibited anything but adoration and love toward Tate. She wanted to rout out a potential killer, and get the story that would win back the respect and credibility that had been so stupidly sacrificed to poor judgment. Seeing Van had served as a reminder of that.

He'd brought with him the realization that she wasn't concentrating as much on the incredible story as she was on the people living it. That wasn't surprising. Detachment had always been the most difficult aspect of her career. It was the only essential element of journalism that had escaped her.

She had inherited journalistic interest and skill from her father. But his ability to discount the human factor hadn't been part of his legacy. She tried to develop objectivity but so far she had failed. She feared that she wasn't going to learn it by becoming involved with the Rutledges.

But she could not leave now. The biggest flaw in her carefully laid plan was that she hadn't left herself an escape route. Short of ripping the whole thing wide open, she had no choice but to stay and take things as they came—even surprise visits from old friends.

Friday arrived. Avery whiled away the long hours of the afternoon by playing with Mandy in her room after she woke up from her nap. Seated at a small table, they made clay dinosaurs until Mandy got hungry and was turned over to Mona.

At five o'clock Avery bathed. While she applied her evening makeup, she nibbled from a snack plate that Mona had brought her.

She styled her hair with mousse. It was still short and chic, but not as severe as it had been. The top had grown out long enough for her to creatively style it. She accented the smart, sexy, final results with a lavish pair of diamond earrings.

By quarter of seven, fifteen minutes ahead of schedule,

she was ready. She was in her bathroom, dabbing fragrance behind her ears, when Tate suddenly strode in.

His unheralded and unprecedented appearance stunned her. He slept on the convertible sofa in the study/parlor next to her room. There was a connecting door between them, but it was always kept shut and locked from his side.

The study was decorated in subdued, masculine tones resembling a gentleman's club. It had a small adjoining bathroom. The sink was no bigger than a dentist's basin, the shower barely large enough to accommodate an adult. Yet Tate preferred those cramped facilities to sharing his wife's spacious bedroom and bathroom, which had two large dressing areas connected by a wall of mirrors, a marble Roman tub with a skylight overhead, and yards of plush carpeting.

Avery's first sinking thought when he barged in was that he had changed his mind and had come to tell her that she couldn't go with him. He didn't appear angry, however, only harassed. He was brought up short when he spied her image in the mirror.

Gratified to know that her efforts had paid off, Avery turned to face him and held her arms out to her sides. "Like it?"

"The dress? The dress is great."

"Our Frost Brothers bill will reflect just how great."

She knew it was a terrific dress. Black illusion, irregularly sprinkled with sequins, covered her chest, shoulders, upper back, and arms, down to the wrists. From the first suggestion of cleavage, the knee-length sheath was lined with black silk. The dress was further enhanced by bands of black iridescent sequins at her neck and around her wrists.

It was a sexy dress, but in a respectable way, reminiscent of Audrey Hepburn. She hadn't splurged on it for selfish reasons. She hadn't wanted to wear anything belonging to Carole tonight. She had wanted to be new for Tate, different, unlike Carole had ever been.

Besides, all Carole's formal dresses had been low-cut and flamboyant, not to Avery's liking. She had needed something seasonably lightweight, but with long sleeves. She was very conscientious about revealing too much skin, which might give her false identity away. This dress had offered it all.

"Money well spent," Tate muttered reluctantly.

"Did you want something in particular? Or did you come to see if I was running late?"

"I'm the one who's late, I'm afraid. I can't find my studs. Have you seen them?"

It hadn't escaped her notice that he was only partially dressed. There was a speck of fresh blood on his chin, attesting to a quick, close shave. He was still barefoot, his hair was still damp and uncombed after a haphazard towel drying, and his starched, pleated shirt was unbuttoned. The long shirttail hung over his dark tuxedo trousers.

The sight of his hairy, bare chest made her mouth water. His belly was as tight and flat as a drum. Since he hadn't yet fastened the fly to his trousers, she had an unrestricted view all the way down, past his navel, to the white elastic waistband of his briefs.

Reflexively, she moistened her lips. Her heart was beating so hard she could actually feel the fabric of her dress moving against her skin. "Studs?" she asked faintly.

"I thought I might have left them in here."

"Feel free to look." She gestured toward the dressing area, where she had discovered a cache of masculine toiletries and grooming utensils during one of her explorations.

He rifled through two drawers before finding the black jewelry box with the flip-top lid. A set of onyx studs and a pair of matching cuff links were inside. "Do you need help?"

"No."

"Yes." She moved to block his exit from the room.

"I can do it."

"And wrinkle your shirt while wrestling with them. Let me." Waving away his protests and his hands, she inserted the first stud. Her knuckles brushed against the dense hair on his chest. It was soft, damp. She wanted to bury her face in it.

"What's all that?" She glanced up at him, then followed his indicating chin. "Oh. Mandy's artwork." There were several scribbled pictures attached to her mirror with strips of Scotch tape. "Didn't she give you some?"

"Sure. I just didn't expect yours to be so prominently displayed. You used to say you couldn't stand the clutter. Finished?" He bent his head down to check her slow progress. They almost bumped heads.

"One more. Stand still. Is that your stomach growling? Help yourself to a snack."

He paused for a moment, then reached toward the snack plate for an apple slice and a chunk of cheese. His teeth crunched into the apple. The sound of his munching was wildly erotic.

"Cuff links?"

He passed them to her and extended his left arm. She speared the cuff link through the holes, then flipped it open so it would hold. She patted it into place. "Next?" He gave her his right arm. After it was done, she declined to put distance between them. Instead, she angled her head back and looked up at him from close range.

"What about your bow tie?"

He swallowed the food. "In my room."

"Can you handle it?"

"I'll manage. Thanks."

"Any time."

Then, when he could leave, he didn't. He stayed for several moments longer, staring down at her, with the lingering mist of her long bath and the smell of her perfume swirling around them.

Finally, he stepped back and moved toward the door. "I'll be out in five minutes."

Tate felt like he had just made a narrow escape when he reentered the room he slept in. His shower must have been too hot. Why else couldn't he cool down? He blamed his clumsiness on necessary haste and the important evening facing him.

He bungled tying his tie several times before getting it right; he couldn't find matching socks; it took him ten minutes to finish dressing. However, when his wife emerged from her bedroom after his soft tap on her door, she didn't remark on the delay.

Together they went into the living room, where Zee was reading Mandy a story. Nelson was watching his favorite TV detective chase down the bad guys and bring them to justice.

He glanced up when they walked in and gave a long wolf whistle. "You two look like the bride and groom on the wedding cake."

"Thanks, Dad," Tate answered for both of them.

"She hardly looks like a bride in that black dress, Nelson."

Tate was sure his mother hadn't meant for her comment to be insulting, but that's how it sounded. It was followed by an awkward pause that was finally broken when Zee added, "But you do look very nice, Carole."

"Thank you," she replied in a subdued voice.

From the day they were introduced, Zee had been reserved in her relationship with Carole. She would have preferred that their love affair had died before it had come to marriage, though she would never have said so.

She had warmed up to Carole while she was carrying Mandy, but that maternal affection soon cooled. For months prior to the plane crash, Zee had been more openly critical than before. Tate knew why, of course. Neither of his parents was stupid or blind, and they had always disparaged anything that hurt Jack or him.

Tonight, however, he had hoped that everything would go smoothly. It already promised to be a strained evening. While his mother's thoughtless comment hadn't ruined it entirely, it certainly hadn't helped relieve any tension.

Mandy revived the festive mood somewhat when she slid from her grandmother's lap and shyly approached them. He knelt down. "Come give me a big hug." Mandy placed her arms around him and buried her face in his neck.

To his surprise, Carole crouched down beside them. "I'll come kiss you when we get home. Okay?"

Mandy raised her head and nodded solemnly. "Okay, Mommy."

"Be a good girl for Grandma and Grandpa."

Mandy nodded again, then removed her arms from Tate's neck and hugged Carole. "Bye-bye."

"Bye-bye. Give me good night sugars."

"Do I have to go to bed now?"

"No, but I want my sugars ahead of time."

Mandy kissed Carole's mouth noisily, then scampered back to her grandmother. Ordinarily, Carole complained when Mandy ruined her makeup or mussed her clothing. All she did now was lightly dab at her lips with a Kleenex.

He couldn't figure it, except that she was playing the good-mother role to the hilt. God only knew what her motive was. This newfound affection for Mandy was probably phony as hell. No doubt she had picked up pointers from talk shows and magazine articles during her convalescence.

He placed his hand beneath her elbow and guided her toward the front door. "It might be late before we're back."

"Drive carefully," Zee called after them.

Nelson left his detective with gun drawn and followed them to the door. "If this was a beauty contest and ballots were handed out tonight, y'all would win. Can't tell you how proud and pleased I am to see the two of you stepping out with each other all dressed up."

Was his father suggesting that whatever had come between them should be forgiven and forgotten? Tate appreciated his concern; he just didn't think he could oblige him. Forgive? He'd always found that hard to do. Forget? It just wasn't in his nature.

But as he seated Carole in the silver leather interior of his car, he wished he could. If he could erase all the anger, pain, and contempt, and start over with this woman tonight, would he want to?

Tate had always been as scrupulously honest with himself as he was with everyone. Looking and behaving as Carole did tonight, yes, he told himself, he would want to make a new start.

Plainly, he wanted her. He liked her when she was like this, soft-spoken and even-tempered and sexy. He didn't expect her to be a doormat. She had too much vivacity and intelligence to be a silent, submissive partner. He didn't want her to be. He liked sparks—of anger, of humor. Without them, a relationship was as bland as unseasoned food.

She smiled at him as he slid behind the wheel. "Nelson's right. You look very nice tonight, Tate."

"Thanks." And just because he was weary of being scornful all the time, he added, "So do you."

She dazzled him with a smile. In the old days, he would have said, "Screw being late, I'm going to make love to my wife," and taken her right there in the car.

A fantasy of doing that flashed into his mind: nuzzling her flushed breasts; sinking into her deep, wet heat; hearing her gasps of pleasure when she came.

He groaned, quickly covering it with a cough.

He missed the spontaneity, the fun of having hot sex with someone he loved.

To conceal the fierce light in his eyes, which she would instantly recognize as arousal, he slid on his sunglasses, even though the sun had already set.

Driving away from the house, he admitted that he missed what they had had, but he didn't miss *her*. Because while the sex had been hot and good and frequent, there had been little real intimacy. That cerebral exchange and spiritual bonding had been lacking in their marriage from the very beginning, though he hadn't put a name to the missing component until much later.

He couldn't miss what he'd never had, but he still yearned for it. Winning the Senate seat was going to be sweet. It would mark the beginning of what he hoped would be a lifetime career in public service. But the victory would be tainted by his marital unhappiness.

It would be much sweeter, and his political future would look much brighter, if he could share it with a loving, supportive wife.

He might just as well wish for the moon, he thought. Even if Carole had that kind of love to give, which she didn't, he wouldn't take it. She had destroyed any possibility of that long ago.

The physical attraction was still there, inexplicably stronger than ever, but the emotional attachments were dead. And he'd be damned if he would accept one while being cheated of the other.

He figured the resolution just hadn't reached his cock yet.

He glanced at Carole from out of the corner of his eye. She looked fantastic. His mother had called it correctly. She had too much poise and sophistication and sexiness for a bride.

She looked like a well-loved, well-sated wife—very unlike Carole.

NINETEEN

Eddy Paschal stepped out of his shower. He quickly patted the towel over his arms and chest and down both legs. Flinging it over his shoulder, he caught the other end and rubbed it back and forth across his back as he moved from bathroom to bedroom. As soon as he cleared the door, he drew up short. "What the—"

"Hi, there. Didn't know you were into dirty pictures."

Fancy was stretched diagonally across his bed. She was propped up on one elbow, thumbing through the *Penthouse* she had found lying on his nightstand. After a dispassionate glance at one particularly provocative pose, she looked up at him and smiled slyly. "You naughty boy, you."

"What the hell are you doing in here?" He hastily secured the towel around his middle.

Fancy stretched with feline laziness. "I was sunbathing out by the pool and came in here to get cool."

Eddy lived in an apartment over the ranch's garage. Shortly after he was hired to be Tate's campaign manager, he had asked if he could rent the efficiency. The Rutledges had vehemently protested.

Zee had been the most vocal. "Servant's quarters? I wouldn't hear of it."

Tate had added his own protests, stating that if Eddy was going to live at the ranch, he would live in the house with the family.

Eddy had explained that he needed the convenience of living close to them while maintaining his privacy. The garage apartment satisfied both requirements. They had relented and he had moved in.

His privacy had now been invaded. "Why cool off in here?" he asked querulously. "Is the air conditioner in the house on the blink?"

"Don't be tacky." Fancy tossed the magazine aside and came to a sitting position. "Aren't you glad to see me?"

"There's certainly plenty to see," he muttered, ruffling his wet hair. It was fine, straight, and pale. "I've seen Band-Aids bigger than that bikini. Does Nelson approve of you running around like that?" Abundant flesh was overflowing the skimpy swimsuit.

"Grandpa doesn't approve of anything erogenous," she snorted. "I swear I don't know how my daddy and Uncle Tate ever got conceived. I bet Grandpa sings 'The Battle Hymn of the Republic' while he's balling Grandma. Or maybe 'Off We Go, into the Wild, Blue Yonder.' " She drew a thoughtful expression. "I just can't imagine her coming, can you?"

"You're hopeless, Fancy." In spite of himself, he chuckled at the images she had conjured. Then he propped his hands on his hips and looked at her reprovingly. "Will you please scram so I can dress? I told Tate I'd meet him and Carole at the Waller Creek, and I'm already running late."

"Can I go with you?"

"No."

"Why?" she wheedled.

"No more tickets."

"You could manage it." He shook his head no. "Why not? I could get ready in a jiff."

"It'll be a stuffy, grown-up affair, Fancy. You'd be bored stiff."

"You'd be stiff if I went along. But I guarantee you wouldn't be bored." She gave him a licentious wink.

"Are you going to leave, or what?"

"What, I think," she replied flippantly. She unclasped her bikini bra and let it fall. Leaning back, she propped herself up on her elbows. "How do you like my. . . tan?"

Her breasts were full and soft, rising from a band of baby pinkness between her suntanned chest and stomach. The areolas were oversized, and her nipples were rosy and raised.

Tilting his face ceilingward, Eddy pinched his eyes shut. "Why are you doing this now? Come on, get up. Put your top back on and get the hell out of here."

He moved toward the bed and extended his hand down to assist her up. Fancy took his hand, but she didn't use it as leverage. Instead, she carried it to her breast and pressed his palm against the distended center. Her eyes were alight with mischief and arousal. As she slowly rotated his palm over her nipple, she used her other hand to pull away his towel and affected a gasp of surprised pleasure.

"Hmm, Eddy, you have a beautiful cock."

She gazed at it avidly as she inched to the edge of the bed. Her fingers encircled his penis, then she squeezed it through her fist, elongating and stretching it. "So big. Who are you saving it for? That ugly redhead down at headquarters? Or my Aunt Carole?"

She flung her head back and looked up the length of his torso. The cold glint in his eyes alarmed her for an instant before she decided that she liked him best when he was being a bastard. He posed more of a challenge that way.

"I can and will do more for you than either of them." Having made that breathy pledge, she bent her head over him to prove it.

At the first deft, damp stroke of her tongue, Eddy's knees buckled. In seconds, Fancy was on her back in the middle of his bed and he was lying above her, his tongue inside her mouth, spearing toward the back of her throat.

"Oh, God. Oh, Jesus. Yes. Yes," Fancy panted when his hands roughly caressed her.

He threw her arms behind her head and attacked her

breasts with his mouth, sucking ardently, biting hungrily, licking furiously while the girl writhed beneath him. She became so lost in his rowdy foreplay that it took several seconds for her to realize that he was no longer doing it.

She opened her eyes. Once again he was standing at the foot of the bed, smiling with amusement.

"Wha—"

Only when she tried to sit up did she discover that her arms were tied above her head. She swung them forward. Her bikini bra was wrapped around her wrists, the ends knotted.

"You son of a bitch," she yelled. "Untie my fuckin' hands."

Calmly, Eddy went to the bureau and took a pair of briefs from the top drawer. As he pulled them on, he made a tsking sound. "Such language."

"Untie me, you bastard."

"I'm sure that a resourceful young *lady*," he stressed with one eyebrow skeptically raised, "will think of a way to free herself."

He took his rented tuxedo out of the plastic bag and began dressing. For as long as that took, Fancy lambasted him with every epithet her fertile mind and unlimited vocabulary could produce.

"Save it," Eddy said tersely when the crude tirade had ceased to be amusing. "I just want to know one thing."

"Screw you."

"What did you mean by that remark about Carole and me?"

"What do you think?"

He reached the bed in three strides, grabbed a handful of Fancy's hair, and wound it around his fist until it pulled against her scalp. "I don't know what to think. That's why I'm asking."

He frightened her. She lost some of her defiance. "You're getting it from somewhere. Why not from Aunt Carole?"

"First and foremost, because she doesn't appeal to me."

"That's bullshit."

"Why bullshit?"

"Because you watch her like a hawk, especially since she came home."

Eddy continued to stare at her coldly. "She's my best friend's wife. They've had their problems. I'm concerned how their marriage might effect the outcome of the campaign."

"Some marriage," Fancy scoffed. "He can't stand her because she's screwed around on him. My true blue Uncle Tate won't put up with that kind of crap from his wife. He's only staying married to her until the election is over."

Then Fancy smiled. She was almost purring. "But, you know what? If you do want in Carole's pants, I think you're out of luck. I think they're patching things up. I think she's giving to him—if he wants it—what she was giving to you before the airplane crash."

Gradually, his hand relaxed and he released her hair. "That's quite a theory, Fancy." His voice was cool and calm. He moved to the dresser, stuffed a handkerchief into his pants pocket, and slid on his wristwatch. "It just happens to be wrong. There never has been or will be anything between Carole and me."

"I might ask her and see what she says."

"If I were you," he said softly, addressing her over his shoulder, "I'd keep my jealous speculations to myself."

Without the benefit of her hands to assist her, Fancy wiggled off the bed and came to her feet. "This is getting old, Eddy. Untie my hands."

He angled his head to one side, as though giving her demand careful consideration. "No, I don't believe so. I think I'd rather put some distance between us before you get loose."

"I can't leave here until I get my hands free."

"That's right."

She padded after him to the door. "Please, Eddy," she wailed. Tears formed in her large blue eyes. "You're being cruel. This isn't a game to me. I know you think I'm a slut for throwing myself at you, but I felt like I had to make the first move or you never would. I love you. Please love me back. Please."

He laid his hand in the curve of her waist and squeezed it

gently. "I'm sure you can find some other guy who'll appreciate me warming you up for him."

Her cheeks bloomed scarlet. "You son of a bitch." The wheedling humility vanished. Her low voice now vibrated with rage. "You're goddamn right I'll find a man. I'll fuck his brains out. I'll suck him dry. I'll—"

"Have a good evening, Fancy." Unceremoniously, he pushed her out of his way and jogged down the exterior stairs to his parked car.

Fancy put her foot to the door and slammed it hard behind him.

As Avery came out of the ladies' room, she didn't even notice the man at the pay telephone. She was anxious to get back to the party. The banquet had been interminable, the after-dinner speaker ponderous.

However, once they were free to mingle, Tate had been the center of attention. It seemed that everyone in the room wanted to meet him and shake his hand, whether they shared a party affiliation or not. Even political rivals were friendly. None was hostile—certainly not enough to want him dead.

He was respected even if his ideas weren't unanimously popular. It was a heady feeling just to be standing next to him as his wife. Each time he made an introduction, he did so with a certain degree of pride that thrilled her. She hadn't made any social blunders. She had covertly taken her cues from him when someone Carole would have known approached. Everything was going splendidly.

Tate had touched her arm briefly as she excused herself to go to the powder room, as though he dreaded even that brief a separation.

Now, as she passed the bank of telephones, a hand shot out and manacled her wrist. She emitted a cry of astonishment and spun around to confront the man who had accosted her. He was wearing a tuxedo, signifying that he belonged to the crowd in the banquet hall.

"How's it going, baby?" he drawled.

"Let go of me." Taking him for someone who'd had too

much to drink, she made a painful attempt to wrench her arm free.

"Not so fast, Mrs. Rutledge." He slurred the name insultingly. "I want to get a close-up look at the new face I've heard so much about." He pulled her closer. "Except for your hair, you look the same. But tell me what I really want to know. Are you still as hot?"

"Let me go, I said."

"What's the matter? Afraid your husband is going to catch you? He won't. He's too busy campaigning."

"I'll scream bloody murder if you don't release my arm this instant."

He laughed. "Are you pissed because I didn't come see you in the hospital? Now, would it have been seemly for one of your lovers to elbow your husband away from your bedside?"

She glared at him with cold fury. "Things have changed."

"Oh, yeah?" He put his face close to hers. "Doesn't your pussy itch like it used to?"

Incensed and afraid, she renewed her struggle to release her arm, which only seemed to incite him. He bent her arm up behind her and hauled her against the front of his body. His breath was humid and boozy against her face. She tried to turn her head away, but he trapped her jaw with his free hand.

"What's with you, Carole? Do you think you're high and mighty now that Tate's actually in the race? What a joke! Rory Dekker's gonna kick his ass, you know." He closed his fingers, hurting her jaw. She whimpered with pain and outrage.

"Now that you think he might make it to Washington, you're really sucking up to him, aren't you? Tonight you looked straight through me. Just who the hell do you think you are, bitch, to ignore me like that?"

He ground a hard kiss upon her lips, smearing her fresh lipstick and making her sick by poking his tongue between her lips. She doubled up her fists and pushed with all her might against his shoulders. She tried to drive a knee into his crotch, but her slim skirt prevented that. He was strong;

she couldn't budge him. He consumed all her air. She felt herself weakening, growing faint.

Dimly at first, and then louder, she heard approaching voices. So did he. He shoved her away and gave her a smirking smile. "You'd do well to remember who your friends are," he sneered. He rounded the corner seconds ahead of two women who were on their way to the powder room.

Their conversation died when they saw Avery. She quickly turned her back and fumbled with the telephone receiver as though she were about to place a call. They went past and entered the ladies' room. As soon as the door swished closed behind them, she collapsed against the shelf beneath the public phone.

She broke a nail in her haste to undo the clasp on Carole's beaded evening bag in search of a Kleenex. Finding one, she wiped her mouth, rubbing it hard, ridding it of the smeared lipstick and any taste of the hateful kiss she had endured from Carole's ex-lover. She unwrapped a peppermint and put it in her mouth, then dabbed her tearful eyes with the tissue. During the tussle an earring had come off; she clipped it back on.

The two women came out, speaking in hushed tones as they walked past. Avery murmured needlessly into the receiver, feeling like a fool for enacting such a ridiculous charade.

But then, she had become very good at playing charades, hadn't she? She'd fooled one of Carole's lovers.

When she finally felt composed enough to face the crowd again, she hung up the telephone receiver and turned to go. As she did, a man quickly rounded the corner and ran right into her. Seeing only the front of his tux, she cried out in fear.

"Carole? For God's sake, what's wrong?"

"Tate!"

Avery slumped against him, tightly wrapping her arms around his waist. Resting her cheek on his lapel, she closed her eyes to block out the vision of the other man.

Hesitantly, Tate placed his arms around her. His hands stirred the silk against her body as he stroked her back.

''What's the matter? What happened? A lady drew me aside and said you looked upset. Are you sick?''

He had immediately deserted the limelight and rushed to her assistance, even though she was an unfaithful wife. Whatever scruples she had had against sleeping with another woman's husband vanished in that single moment. Carole hadn't deserved him.

''Oh, Tate, I'm sorry.'' She lifted her face to his. ''So sorry.''

''For what?'' He took her firmly by the shoulders and shook her lightly. ''Will you tell me what the hell is going on?''

Because she couldn't tell him the truth, she foundered for a logical explanation. When she arrived at one, she realized that it wasn't entirely untrue. ''I guess I'm not ready to be surrounded by so many people. The crowd was overwhelming me. I felt smothered.''

''You seemed to be doing fine.''

''I was. I was enjoying it. But all of a sudden everybody seemed to close in. It was like being wrapped up in those bandages again. I couldn't breathe, couldn't—''

''Okay. I get the picture. You should have said something. Come on.'' He took her by the arm.

She dug her heels in. ''We don't have to leave.''

''The party's breaking up anyway. We'll beat everybody to the valet parking.''

''You're sure?'' She wanted to leave. To return to the banquet hall and possibly confront that gloating face again would be untenable. However, this was her audition. She didn't want to blow it and be left at the ranch when he went campaigning.

''I'm sure. Let's go.''

They didn't say much on the way home. Avery tucked her feet beneath her hips and turned in the seat to face him. She wanted to touch him, to comfort and be comforted, but she satisfied herself with simply facing him.

Everyone was in bed when they arrived home. Silently they went together to Mandy's room, and, as they had promised, kissed her good night. She mumbled sleepily in response but didn't wake up.

As they moved down the hallway toward their respective bedrooms, Tate said offhandedly, "We'll be attending several formal functions. You probably should take that dress on the trip."

Avery spun around to face him. "You mean you want me to go?"

He looked at a spot beyond her head. "Everybody thinks it would be a good idea."

Unwilling to let him off that lightly, she gave his lapel a tug. His eyes connected with hers. "I'm only interested in what you think, Tate."

He deliberated for several tense moments before giving her his answer. "Yeah, I think it's a good idea. Eddy'll give you an itinerary in a day or two so you'll know what else to pack. Good night."

Bitterly disappointed in his lukewarm enthusiasm, Avery watched him walk down the hall and enter his room. Dejectedly, she went into hers alone and prepared for bed. She examined her dress, looking for damage done by Carole's ex-lover, whoever he'd been, but thankfully found none.

She was exhausted by the time she turned off the lamps, but when an hour went by and she still hadn't fallen asleep, she got out of bed and left her room.

Fancy decided to enter through the kitchen in case her grandfather had set up an ambush in the living room. She unlocked the door, disengaged the alarm system, and quietly reset it.

"Who's that? Fancy?"

Fancy nearly jumped out of her skin. "Jesus Christ, Aunt Carole! You scared the living shit out of me!" She reached for the light switch.

"Oh, my God." Avery sprang from her chair at the kitchen table and turned Fancy's face up toward the light. "What happened to you?" She grimaced as she examined the girl's swollen eye and bleeding lip.

"Maybe you can lend me your plastic surgeon," Fancy quipped before she discovered that it hurt to smile. Touching the bleeding cut with the tip of her tongue, she disengaged herself from her aunt. "I'll be all right." She moved to the refrigerator, took out a carton of milk, and poured herself a glass.

"Shouldn't you see a doctor? Do you want me to drive you to the emergency room?"

"Hell, no. And would you please keep your voice down? I don't want Grandma and Grandpa to see this. I'd never hear the end of it."

"What happened?"

"Well, it was like this." She scraped the cream filling out of an Oreo with her lower front teeth. "I went to this shit-kicker's dance hall. The place was swinging. Friday night, you know—payday. Everybody was in a party mood. There was this one guy with a really cute ass." She ate the two disks of chocolate cookie and dug into the ceramic jar for another.

"He took me to a motel. We drank some beer and smoked some grass. He got a little too sublime, I guess, because when we got down to business, he couldn't get it up. Naturally, he took it out on me." As she summed up the tale, she dusted her hands of cookie crumbs and reached for the glass of milk.

"He hit you?"

Fancy gaped at her, then gave a semblance of a laugh. "'He hit you?'" she mimicked. "What the hell do you think? Of course he hit me."

"You could have been seriously hurt, Fancy."

"I can't believe this," she said, rolling her eyes ceilingward in disbelief. "You always enjoyed hearing about my romantic interludes, said they gave you a vicarious thrill, whatever the hell that means."

"I'd hardly classify getting hit in the face romantic. Did he tie you up, too?"

Fancy followed her aunt's gaze down to the red circles around each of her wrists. "Yeah," she answered bitterly, "the bastard tied my hands together." Carole didn't have to know that the "bastard" she referred to wasn't the drunken, impotent cowboy.

"You're crazy to go to a motel room with a stranger like that, Fancy."

"I'm crazy? You're the one stuffing ice cubes in a Baggie."

"For your eye."

Fancy slapped away the makeshift ice pack. "Don't do me any favors, okay?"

"Your eye is turning black and blue. It's about to swell shut. Do you want your parents to see it like that and have to tell them the story you just told me?"

Irritably, Fancy snatched up the ice pack and held it against her eye. She knew her aunt was right.

"Do you want some peroxide for your lip? An aspirin? Something for the pain?"

"I had enough beer and grass to dull the pain."

Fancy was confused. Why was Carole being so nice to her? Since coming home from that luxury palace of a clinic, she had been freaking weird. She didn't yell at the kid anymore. She looked for things to do instead of sitting on her ass all day. She actually seemed to like Uncle Tate again.

Fancy had always considered Carole stupid for playing Russian roulette with her marriage. Uncle Tate was good-looking. All the girls she knew drooled over him. If her instincts in this field were any good, and she believed them to be excellent, he'd be terrific in bed.

She wished she had somebody who loved her as much as Uncle Tate had loved Carole when they had first gotten married. He'd treated her like a queen. She had been a fool to throw that away. Maybe she had reached that conclusion herself and was trying to win him back.

Fat chance, Fancy thought derisively. Once you crossed Uncle Tate, you were on his shit list for life.

"What are you doing up so late," she asked, "sitting all by yourself in the dark?"

"I couldn't sleep. I thought cocoa might help." There was a half-empty cup of chocolate on the table.

"Cocoa? That's a hoot."

"A proper insomnia remedy for a senator's wife," she replied with a wistful smile.

Fancy, never one to beat around the bush, asked, "You're mending your ways, aren't you?"

"What do you mean?"

"You know damn well what I mean. You're changing your image in the hopes that Uncle Tate will get elected and keep you on when he goes to Washington." She assumed a confidential, just-between-us-girls pose. "Tell me, did you give up humping all your boyfriends, or just Eddy?"

Her aunt's head snapped up. Her face went pale. She pulled her lower lip between her teeth and wheezed, "What did you say?"

"Don't play innocent. I suspected it all along," Fancy said breezily. "I confronted Eddy with it."

"And what did he say?"

"Nothing. Didn't deny it. Didn't admit it. He responded as a gentleman should." Snorting rudely, she headed for the door that led to the other rooms of the house. "Don't worry. There's enough shit flying around here already. I'm not going to tell Uncle Tate. Unless . . ."

She spun around, her attitude combative. "Unless you pick up your affair with Eddy again. It's me he's gonna be screwing from now on, not you. G'night."

Feeling smug and satisfied for having made herself so unequivocally understood, Fancy sashayed from the kitchen. One look in the mirror over her bedroom dresser confirmed that her face was a mess.

It didn't occur to Fancy until days later that Carole was the only one in the family who had even noticed that she was sporting a black eye and a busted lip, and that she hadn't ratted on her.

TWENTY

Van Lovejoy's apartment was *House Beautiful*'s worst nightmare. He slept on a narrow mattress supported by concrete building blocks. Other pieces of furniture were just as ramshackle, salvaged from flea markets and junk stores.

There was a sad, dusty piñata, a sacrilegious effigy of Elvis Presley, dangling from the light fixture. It was a souvenir he'd brought back from a visit to Nuevo Laredo. The goodies inside—several kilos of marijuana—were but a memory. Except for the piñata, the apartment was unadorned.

The otherwise empty rooms were filled with videotapes. That and the equipment he used to duplicate, edit, and play back his tapes were the only things of any value in the apartment, and their worth was inestimable. Van was better equipped than many small video production companies.

Video catalogs were stacked everywhere. He subscribed to all of them and scoured them monthly in search of a video he didn't already have or hadn't seen. Nearly all his income went to keeping his library stocked and updated.

His collection of movies rivaled any video rental store. He studied directing and cinematographic techniques. His taste was eclectic, ranging from Orson Welles to Frank Capra, Sam Peckinpah to Steven Spielberg. Whether filmed in black and white or Technicolor, camera moves fascinated him.

Besides the movies, his collection included serials and documentaries, along with every inch of tape he had shot himself in the span of his career. It was known throughout the state that if stock footage of an event was needed and it couldn't be found elsewhere, Van Lovejoy of KTEX in San Antonio would have it.

He spent all his free time watching tapes. Tonight, his fascination was centered on the raw footage he had shot at the Rocking R Ranch a few days earlier. He'd delivered the tapes to MB Productions, but not before making copies of them for himself. He never knew when something he'd shot years earlier might prove useful or valuable, so he kept copies of everything.

In post-production, MBP would write scripts, edit, record voice-overs, mix music, and end up with slick, fully produced commercials of varying lengths. Van's camera work would look sterilized and staged by the time the commercials went out over the air. He didn't care. He'd been paid. What interested him were the candid shots.

Tate Rutledge was charismatic on or off camera. Handsome and affluent, he was a walking success story—the kind of man Van usually despised on principle. But if Van had been a voter, the guy would get his vote just because he seemed to shoot straight from the hip. He didn't bullshit, even when what he was saying wasn't particularly what people wanted to hear. He might lose the election, but it wouldn't be because he lacked integrity.

He kept thinking that there was something wrong with the kid. She was cute enough, although, in Van's opinion, one kid looked like another. He usually wasn't called upon to videotape children, but when he was, his experience had been that they had to be threatened or cajoled into settling down, behaving, and cooperating, especially when shooting retakes or reverse questions.

That hadn't been the case with the Rutledge kid. She was quiet and didn't do anything ornery. She didn't do anything, period, unless she was told to, and then she moved like a little wind-up doll. The one who got the most response out of her was Carole Rutledge.

It was she who really held Van enthralled.

Time and again he had played the tapes—those he'd shot of her at the ranch, and those he'd shot on the day she left the clinic. The lady knew what to do in front of a camera.

He'd had to direct Rutledge and the kid, but not her. She was a natural, always turning toward the light, knowing instinctively where to look. She seemed to know what he was about to do before he did it. Her face begged for close-ups. Her body language wasn't stilted or robotized, like most amateurs.

She was a pro.

Her resemblance to another pro he had known and worked with was damned spooky.

For hours he had sat in front of his console, replaying the tapes and studying Carole Rutledge. When she did make an awkward move, he believed it was deliberate, as if she realized just how good she was and wanted to cover it up.

He ejected one tape and inserted another, one he had shot

so it could be played back in slow motion. He was familiar with the scene. It showed the threesome walking through a pasture of verdant grass, Rutledge carrying his daughter, his wife at his side. Van had planned his shot so that the sun was sinking behind the nearest hill, casting them in silhouette. It was a great effect, he thought now as he watched it for the umpteenth time.

And then he saw it! Mrs. Rutledge turned her head and smiled up at her husband. She touched his arm. His smile turned stiff. He moved his arm—slightly, but enough to shrug off her wifely caress. If the tape hadn't been in slow motion, Van might not have even noticed the candidate's subtle rejection of his wife's touch.

He didn't doubt when the post-production was done, the shot would be edited out. The Rutledges would come out looking like Ozzie and Harriet. But there was something wrong with the marriage, just like there was something wrong with the kid. Something stunk in Camelot.

Van was a cynic by nature. It came as no surprise to him that the marriage was shaky. He figured they all were, and he didn't give a flying fig.

Yet the woman still fascinated him. He could swear that she had recognized him the other day before he had introduced himself. He was constantly aware of expressions and reactions, and he couldn't have mistaken that momentary widening of her eyes or the quick rush of her breath. Even though the features weren't identical, and the hairstyle was wrong, the resemblance between Carole Rutledge and Avery Daniels was uncanny. Carole's moves were right on target and the subconscious mannerisms eerily reminiscent.

He let the tape play out. Closing his eyes, Van pinched the bridge of his nose between two of his fingers until it hurt, as if wanting to force the notion out of his head, because what he was thinking was just too weird—''Twilight Zone'' time. But the idea was fucking with his mind something fierce and he couldn't get rid of it, crazy as it was.

Several days ago he'd walked into Irish's office. Dropping into one of the armchairs, he'd asked, ''Get a chance to watch that tape I gave you?''

Irish, as usual, was doing six different things at once. He ran his hand over his burred gray hair. "Tape? Oh, the one of Rutledge? Who've we got on that human bone pile they found in Comal County?" he had shouted through his office door to a passing reporter.

"What'd you think about it?" Van asked, once Irish's attention swung back to him.

Irish had taken up smoking again since Avery wasn't there to hound him about it. He seemed to want to make up for lost time. He lit a new cigarette from the smoldering butt of another and spoke through the plume of unfiltered smoke. "About what?"

"The tape," Van said testily.

"Why? You moonlighting as a pollster?"

"Jesus," Van had muttered and made to rise. Irish cantankerously signaled him to sit back down. "What'd you want me to look at? Specifically, I mean."

"The broad."

Irish coughed. "You got the hots for her?"

Van remembered being annoyed that Irish hadn't noticed the similarities between Carole Rutledge and Avery Daniels. That should have been an indication of just how ridiculous his thinking was, because nobody knew Avery better than Irish. He had known her for two decades before Van had ever laid eyes on her. Mulishly, however, Irish's flippancy compelled him to prove himself right.

"I think she looks a lot like Avery."

Irish had been pouring himself a cup of viscous coffee from the hot plate on his littered credenza. He gave Van a sharp glance. "So, what else is new? Somebody remarked on that as soon as Rutledge got into politics and we started seeing him and his wife in the news."

"Guess I wasn't around that day."

"Or you were too stoned to remember."

"Could be."

Irish returned to his desk and sat down heavily. He worked harder than ever, putting in unnecessarily long hours. Everybody in the newsroom talked about it. Work was a panacea for his bereavement. A Catholic, he wouldn't commit suicide outright, but he would eventually kill himself through too much work, too much booze, too much smoking, too much stress—all the things about which Avery had affectionately berated him.

"You ever figure out who sent you her jewelry?" Van asked. Irish had confided that bizarre incident to him, and he had thought it strange at the time, but had forgotten about it until he had stood eyeball to eyeball with Carole Rutledge.

Irish thoughtfully shook his head. "No."

"Ever try?"

"I made a few calls."

Obviously, he didn't want to talk about it. Van was persistent. "And?"

"I got some asshole on the phone who didn't want to be bothered. He said that following the crash, things were so chaotic just about anything was possible."

Like mixing up bodies? Van wondered.

He wanted to ask that question, but didn't. Irish was coping as best he could with Avery's death, and he still wasn't doing very well. He didn't need to hear Van's harebrained hypothesis. Besides, even it it were possible, it made no sense. If Avery were alive, she'd be living her life, not somebody else's.

So he hadn't broached the possibility with Irish. His imagination had run amok, that's all. He'd compiled a bunch of creepy coincidences and shaped them into an outlandish, illogical theory.

Irish would probably have said that his brains were fried from doing too much dope, which was probably the truth. He was nothing but a bum—a washout. A reprobate. What the fuck did he know?

But he loaded another of the Rutledge tapes into the VCR anyway.

The first scream woke her. The second registered. The third prompted her to throw off the covers and scramble out of bed.

Avery grabbed a robe, flung open the door to her bedroom, and charged down the hall toward Mandy's room.

Within seconds of leaving her bed, she was bending over the child's. Mandy was thrashing her limbs and screaming.

"Mandy, darling, wake up." Avery dodged a flailing fist. "Mandy?"

Tate materialized on the other side of the bed. He dropped to his knees on the rug and tried to restrain his daughter. Once he had captured her small hands, her body bucked and twisted while her head thrashed on the pillow and her heels pummeled the mattress. She continued to scream.

Avery placed her hands on Mandy's cheeks and pressed hard. "Mandy, wake up. Wake up, darling. Tate, what should we do?"

"Keep trying to wake her up."

"Is she having another nightmare?" Zee asked as she and Nelson rushed in. Zee moved behind Tate. Nelson stood at the foot of his granddaughter's bed.

"We could hear her screams all the way in our wing," he said. "Poor little thing."

Avery slapped Mandy's cheeks lightly. "It's Mommy. Mommy and Daddy are here. You're safe, darling. You're safe."

Eventually, the screams subsided. As soon as she opened her eyes, she launched herself into Avery's waiting arms. Avery gathered her close and cupped the back of her head, pressing the tear-drenched face into her neck. Mandy's shoulders shook; her whole body heaved with sobs.

"My God, I had no idea it was this bad."

"She had them nearly every night while you were still in the hospital," Tate told her. "Then they started tapering off. She hasn't had one for several weeks. I was hoping that once you got home they would stop altogether." His face was drawn with concern.

"Is there anything you want us to do?"

Tate glanced at Nelson. "No. I think she'll calm down now and go back to sleep, Dad, but thanks."

"You two need to put a stop to this. Immediately." He took Zee's arm and propelled her toward the door. She seemed reluctant to leave and looked at Avery anxiously.

"She'll be all right," Avery said, rubbing Mandy's back. She was still hiccuping sobs, but the worst was over.

"Sometimes they come back," Zee said uneasily.

"I'll stay with her for the rest of the night." When she and Tate were left alone with the child, Avery said, "Why didn't you tell me her nightmares were this severe?"

He sat down in the rocking chair near the bed. "You had your own problems to deal with. The dreams stopped happening with such regularity, just like the psychologist predicted they would. I thought she was getting over them."

"I still should have known."

Avery continued to hold Mandy tight against her, rocking back and forth and murmuring reassurances. She wouldn't let go until Mandy indicated that she was ready. Eventually, she raised her head.

"Better now?" Tate asked her. Mandy nodded.

"I'm sorry you had such a bad dream," Avery whispered, wiping Mandy's damp cheeks with the pads of her thumbs. "Do you want to tell Mommy about it?"

"It's going to get me," she stammered on choppy little breaths.

"What is, darling?"

"The fire."

Avery shuddered with her own terrifying recollections. They seized her sometimes unexpectedly and it often took several minutes to recover from them. As an adult, she found it hard to deal with her memories of the crash. What must it be like for a child?

"I got you out of the fire, remember?" Avery asked softly. "It's not there anymore. But it's still scary to think about, isn't it?" Mandy nodded.

Avery had once done a news story with a renowned child psychologist. During the interview she recalled him saying that denying the authenticity of a child's fears was the worst thing a parent could do. Fears had to be acknowledged before they could be dealt with and, hopefully, overcome.

"Maybe a cool, damp cloth would feel good on her face," Avery suggested to Tate. He left the rocker, and returned shortly with a washcloth. "Thank you."

He sat down beside her as she bathed Mandy's face. In a move that endeared him to Avery, he picked up the Pooh

Bear and pressed it into Mandy's arms. She clutched it to her chest.

"Ready to lie back down?" Avery asked her gently.

"No." Apprehensively, her eyes darted around the room.

"Mommy's not going to leave you. I'll lie down with you."

She eased Mandy back, then lay down beside her, facing her as their heads shared the pillow. Tate pulled the covers over both of them, then bridged their pillow with his arms and leaned down to kiss Mandy.

He was wearing nothing but a pair of briefs. His body looked exceptionally strong and beautiful in the soft glow of the night-light. As he started to stand up, his eyes locked with Avery's. Acting on impulse, she laid her hand on his furry chest and raised her head to lightly kiss his lips. "Good night, Tate."

He straightened up slowly. As he did, her hand slid down his chest; over the hard, curved muscles; across the nipple; through the dense, crisp hair; to the smoother plane of his belly; until her fingertips brushed against the elastic waistband of his briefs before falling away.

"I'll be right back," he mumbled.

He was gone only a few minutes, but by the time he returned, Mandy was sleeping peacefully. He had pulled on a lightweight robe, but had left it unbelted. As he lowered himself into the rocking chair, he noticed that Avery's eyes were still open. "That bed's not meant for two. Are you comfortable?"

"I'm fine."

"I don't think Mandy would know if you got up now and went to your own room."

"I would know. And I told her I'd stay with her the rest of the night." She stroked Mandy's flushed cheek with the back of her finger. "What are we going to do, Tate?"

Resting his elbows on his knees, he sat forward and dug his thumbs into his eye sockets. A tousled lock of hair fell over his forehead. With stubble surrounding it, the vertical cleft at the edge of his chin seemed more pronounced. He sighed, expanding his bare chest beneath the open robe. "I don't know."

"Do you think the psychologist is doing her any good?" He raised his head. "Don't you?"

"I shouldn't second-guess the choice you and your parents made while I was indisposed."

She knew she shouldn't get involved at all. This was a personal problem and Avery Daniels had no right to poke her nose into it. But she couldn't just stand by and let a child's emotional stability deteriorate.

"If you have an opinion, be my guest and say so," Tate urged. "This is our child we're talking about. I'm not going to get petty about who had the best idea."

"I know of a doctor in Houston," she began. One of his eyebrows arched inquisitively. "He . . . I saw him on a talk show once and was very impressed with what he had to say and how he conducted himself. He wasn't pompous. He was very straightforward and practical. Since the current doctor isn't making much progress, maybe we should take Mandy to see him."

"We haven't got anything to lose. Make an appointment."

"I'll call tomorrow." Her head sank deeper into the pillow, but she kept her eyes on him. He sat back in the rocking chair and rested his head against the stuffed pink cushion. "You don't have to sit there all night, Tate," she said softly.

Their eyes met and held. "Yes, I do."

She fell asleep watching him watch her.

TWENTY-ONE

Avery woke up first. It was very early, and the room was dim, although the night-light still burned. She smiled wistfully when she realized that Mandy's small hand was resting on her cheek. Her muscles were cramped from lying so long in one position; otherwise, she probably would have gone back to sleep. Needing to stretch, she eased Mandy's hand off her face and laid it on the pillow. Taking agonizing care not to awaken the child, she got up.

Tate was asleep in the rocker. His head was lying at such an angle to one side that it was almost resting on his shoulder. It looked like a very uncomfortable position, but his abdomen was rising and falling rhythmically, and she could hear his even breathing in the quiet room.

His robe lay parted, revealing his torso and thighs. His right leg was bent at the knee; the left was stretched out in front of him. His calves and feet were well-shaped. His hands were heavily veined and sprinkled with hair. One was dangling from the arm of the chair, the other lay against his stomach.

Sleep had erased the furrow of concern from between his brows. His lashes formed sooty crescents against his cheeks. Relaxed, his mouth looked sensual, capable of giving a woman enormous pleasure. Avery imagined that he would make love intently, passionately, and well, just as he did everything. Emotion brimmed inside Avery's chest until it ached. She wanted badly to cry.

She loved him.

As much as she wanted to make recompense for her professional failures, she realized now that she had also assumed the role of his wife because she had fallen in love with him before she could even speak his name. She had loved him when she had had to look at him through a veil of bandages and rely only on the sound of his voice to inspire her to fight for her life.

She was playing his wife because she wanted to *be* his wife. She wanted to protect him. She wanted to heal the hurts inflicted on him by a selfish, spiteful woman. She wanted to sleep with him.

If he claimed his conjugal rights, she would gladly oblige him. That would be her greatest lie yet — one he wouldn't be able to forgive when her true identity was revealed. He would despise her more than he had Carole because he would think she had tricked him. He would never believe her love was genuine. But it was.

He stirred. When he brought his head upright, he winced. His eyelids fluttered, came open with a start, then focused on her. She was standing within touching distance.

"What time is it?" he asked with sleepy huskiness.

"I don't know. Early. Does your neck hurt?" She ran her hand through his tousled hair, then curved her hand around his neck.

"A little."

She squeezed the cords of his neck, working the kinks out.

"Hmm."

After a moment, he yanked his robe together, folding one side over the other. He drew in his extended leg and sat up straighter. She wondered if her tender massage had given him an early morning erection he didn't want her to see.

"Mandy's still asleep," he commented rhetorically.

"Want some breakfast?"

"Coffee's fine."

"I'll make breakfast."

Dawn was just breaking. Mona wasn't even up yet and the kitchen was dark. Tate began spooning coffee into the disposable paper filter of a coffeemaker. Avery went to the refrigerator.

"Don't bother," he said.

"Aren't you hungry?"

"I can wait for Mona to get up."

"I'd like to cook you something."

Turning his back, he said nonchalantly, "All right. A couple of eggs, I guess."

She was familiar enough with the kitchen by now to assemble the makings for breakfast. Everything went fine until she started whisking eggs in a bowl.

"What are you doing?"

"Making scrambled eggs. F . . . for me," she bluffed when he gave her a puzzled look. She had no idea how he liked his eggs. "Here. You finish this and let me get the toast started."

She busied herself with buttering the slices of toast as they popped from the toaster while covertly watching him fry two eggs for himself. He slid them onto a plate and brought it to the table, along with her serving of scrambled eggs.

"We haven't had breakfast together in a long time." She bit into a slice of toast, scooped a bite of egg into her mouth, and reached for her glass of orange juice before she realized that she was the only one eating. Tate was sitting across from her with his chin propped in his hands, elbows on the table.

"We've never eaten breakfast together, Carole. You hate breakfast."

It was difficult for her to swallow. Her hand clenched the glass of juice. "They made me eat breakfast while I was in the hospital. You know, after I got the dental implants and could eat solid food. I had to gain my weight back."

His gaze hadn't wavered. He wasn't buying it.

"I . . . I got used to eating it and now I miss it when I don't." Defensively, she added, "Why are you making such a big deal of it?"

Tate picked up his fork and began to eat. His movements were too controlled to be automatic. He was angry. "Save yourself the trouble."

She was afraid he meant the trouble of lying to him. "What trouble?"

"Cooking my breakfast is just another of your machinations to worm your way back into my good graces."

Her appetite deserted her. The smell of the food now made her nauseated. "Machinations?"

Apparently he, too, had lost his appetite. He shoved his plate away. "Breakfast. Domesticity. Those displays of affection like touching my hair, rubbing my neck."

"You seemed to enjoy them."

"They don't mean a goddamn thing."

"They do!"

"The hell they do!" He sat back, glowering at her, his jaw working with pent-up rage. "The touches and sweet good-night kisses I can stomach if I have to. If you want to pretend that we're a loving, affectionate couple, go ahead. Make a fool of yourself. Just don't expect me to return the phony affection. Even the Senate seat wouldn't be enough inducement to get me into bed with you again, so that should tell you just how much I despise you." He paused for breath. "But the thing that really galls me is your sudden concern for Mandy. You put on quite a show for her last night."

"It wasn't a show."

He ignored her denial. "You'd damn sure better plan to follow through with the maternal act until she's completely cured. She couldn't take another setback."

"You sanctimonious . . ." Avery was getting angry in her own right. "I'm as interested in Mandy's recovery as you are."

"Yeah. Sure."

"You don't believe me?"

"No."

"That's not fair."

"You're a fine one to talk about fair."

"I'm worried to death about Mandy."

"Why?"

"*Why?*" she cried. "Because she's our child."

"So was the one you aborted! That didn't stop you from killing it!"

The words knifed through her. She actually laid an arm across her middle and bent forward as though her vital organs had been impaled. She held her breath for several seconds while she stared at him speechlessly.

As though loath to look at her, he got up and turned his back. At the counter he refilled his coffee cup. "I would have found out eventually, of course." His voice sounded as cold as ice. When he turned back around to confront her, his eyes looked just as piercingly cold.

"But to be informed by a stranger that my wife was no longer pregnant . . ." Seething, he glanced away. Again, it was as though he couldn't bear looking at her. "Can you imagine how I felt, Carole? Jesus! There you were, close to death, and I wanted to kill you myself." He swung his head back around and, as his eyes bore into hers, he clenched his free hand into a fist.

Out of her cottony memory, Avery conjured up voices. Tate's: *The child . . . effects on the fetus?*

And someone else's: *Child? Your wife wasn't pregnant.*

The fractured conversation had meant nothing. Its significance had escaped her. It had blended into the myriad confusing conversations she had overheard before she had fully regained consciousness. She had forgotten it until now.

"Didn't you think I'd notice that you failed to produce a baby? You were so eager to flaunt it in my face that you were pregnant, why didn't you let me know about your abortion, too?"

Avery shook her head miserably. She had no words to say to him. No excuses. No explanations. But now she knew why Tate hated Carole so.

"When did you do it? It must have been just a few days before your scheduled trip to Dallas. Didn't want to be hampered by a baby, did you? It would have cramped your style."

He bore down on her and loudly slapped the surface of the table. "Answer me, damn you. Say something. It's about time we talked about this, don't you think?"

Avery stammered, "I . . . I didn't think it would matter so much." His expression turned so ferocious, she thought he might actually strike her. Rushing to her own defense, she lashed out, "I know your policy on abortion, Mr. Rutledge. How many times have I heard you preach that it's a woman's right to choose? Does that pertain to every woman in the state of Texas except your wife?"

"Yes, dammit!"

"How hypocritical."

He grabbed her arm and hauled her to her feet. "The principle that applies to the public at large doesn't necessarily carry over into my personal life. *This* abortion wasn't an *issue*. It was my baby."

His eyes narrowed to slits. "Or was it? Was that another lie to keep me from throwing you out, along with the other trash?"

She tried to imagine how Carole might have responded. "It takes two to make a baby, Tate."

As she had hoped, she had struck a chord. He released her arm immediately and backed away from her. "I sorely regret that night. I made that clear as soon as it happened. I'd sworn never to touch your whoring body again.

"But you've always known which buttons to push, Carole. For days you'd been curling up against me like a cat in heat, mewing your apologies and promises to be a loving wife. If I hadn't had too much to drink that night, I would have recognized it for the trap it was."

He gave her a scornful once-over. "Is that what you're doing now, laying another trap? Is that why you've been the model wife since you got out of the hospital?

"Tell me," he said, propping his hands on his hips, "did you slip up that night and get pregnant by accident? Or was getting pregnant and having an abortion part of your plan to torment me? Is that what you're trying to do again—make me want you? Prove that you can get me into your bed again, even if it means sacrificing your own daughter's welfare in order to prove it?"

"No," Avery declared hoarsely. She couldn't endure his hatred, even though it wasn't intended for her.

"You no longer have any power over me, Carole. I don't even hate you anymore. You're not worth the energy it requires to hate you. Take all the lovers you want. See if I give a damn.

"The only way you could possibly hurt me now is through Mandy, and I'll see you in hell first."

That afternoon she went horseback riding. She needed the space and open air in which to think. Feeling silly wearing the formal riding clothes, she asked the stable hand to saddle her a mount.

The mare shied away from her. As the aging cowboy gave her a boost up, he said, "Guess she hasn't forgotten the whipping you gave her last time." The mare was skittish because she didn't recognize her rider's smell, but Avery let the man believe what he wanted.

Carole Rutledge had been a monster—abusive to her husband, her child, everything she had come into contact with, it seemed. The scene over breakfast had left Avery's nerves raw, but at least she knew what she was up against. The extent of Tate's contempt for his wife was understandable now. Carole had planned to abort his child—or one she claimed was his—though whether she had done so before the crash would forever remain a mystery.

Avery pieced together the scenario. Carole had been unfaithful and had made no secret of it. Her faithlessness would be intolerable to Tate, but with his political future at risk, he decided to remain married until after the election.

For an unspecified period of time, he hadn't slept with his wife. He'd even moved out of their bedroom. But Carole had seduced him into making love to her one more time.

Whether the child was Tate's or not, Carole's abortion *was* a political issue, and Avery believed she had planned it that way. It made her ill to think about the negative publicity and grave repercussions if anyone ever found out. The public effect on Tate would be as profound as the personal one.

When Avery returned from her ride, Mandy was assisting Mona with baking cookies. The housekeeper was very good with Mandy, so Avery complimented Mandy's cookies and left her in the older woman's care.

The house was quiet. She had seen Fancy roar off in her Mustang earlier. Jack, Eddy, and Tate were always in the city at this time of day, working at either the campaign headquarters or the law office. Dorothy Rae was secluded in her wing of the house, as usual. Mona had told her that Nelson and Zee had gone into Kerrville for the afternoon. Reaching her room, Avery tossed the riding quirt onto the bed and used the bootjack to remove the tall riding boots. She padded into the bathroom and turned on the taps of the shower.

Not for the first time, an eerie feeling came over her. She sensed that someone had been in the rooms during her absence. Goose bumps broke out over her arms as she examined the top of her dressing table.

She couldn't remember if she had left her hairbrush lying there. Had her bottle of hand lotion been moved? She was certain she hadn't left the lid of the jewelry box opened with a strand of pearls spilling out. She noticed things in the bedroom, too, that had been disturbed while she was out. She did something she hadn't done since moving into Carole's room—she locked the door.

She showered and pulled on a thick robe. Still uneasy and distressed, she decided to lie down for a while before dressing. As her head sank into the pillow, it crackled.

A sheet of paper had been slipped between the pillow and the pillowcase.

Avery studied it with misgivings. The paper had been folded twice, but nothing was written on the outside. She dreaded opening it. What had the intruder expected to find? What had he been searching for?

One thing was certain—the note was no accident. It had been cleverly and deliberately placed where she, and only she, would find it.

She unfolded it. There was one line typed in the center of the white, unlined sheet:

Whatever you're doing, it's working on him. Keep it up.

"Nelson?"

"Hmm?"

His absent reply drew a frown from Zinnia. She laid her hairbrush aside and swiveled on her dressing table stool. "This is important."

Nelson tipped down the corner of his newspaper. Seeing that she was troubled, he folded the paper and depressed the footrest of his lounge chair, bringing himself to a sitting position. "I'm sorry, darling. What'd you say?"

"Nothing yet."

"Is something wrong?"

They were in their bedroom. The ten o'clock news, which they watched ritualistically, was over. They were preparing for bed.

Zee's dark hair was shining after its recent brushing. The silver streak was accented by the lamplight. Her skin, well tended because of the harsh Texas sun, was smooth. There weren't many worry lines to mar it. There weren't many laugh lines, either.

"Something is going on between Tate and Carole," she said.

"I think they had a tiff today." He left his chair and began removing his clothing. "They were both awfully quiet at supper."

Zee had also noticed the hostility in the air tonight. Where her younger son's moods were concerned, she was particularly sensitive. "Tate wasn't just sullen, he was mad."

"Carole probably did something that didn't sit well with him."

"And when Tate is mad," Zee continued as though he hadn't spoken, "Carole is usually her most ebullient. Whenever he's angry, she antagonizes him further by being frivolous and silly."

Nelson neatly hung his trousers in the closet on the rod where all his other trousers were hung. Messiness was anathema. "She wasn't frivolous tonight. She barely said a word."

Zee gripped the back of her vanity stool. "That's my point, Nelson. She was as edgy and upset as Tate. Their fights never used to be like that."

Dressed only in his boxer shorts now, he neatly folded back the bedspread and climbed into bed. He stacked his hands beneath his head and stared at the ceiling. "I've noticed several things here lately that aren't like Carole at all."

"Thank God," Zee said. "I thought I was losing my mind. I'm relieved to know somebody besides me has noticed." She turned out the lamps and got into bed beside her husband. "She's not as superficial as she used to be, is she?"

"That close call with death sobered her up."

"Maybe."

"You don't think so?"

"If that were all, I might think that was the reason."

"What else?" he asked.

"Mandy, for one. Carole's a different person around her. Have you ever seen Carole as worried about Mandy as she was last night after her nightmare? I remember once when Mandy was running a temperature of a hundred and three. I was frantic and thought she should be taken to the emergency room. Carole was blasé. She said that all kids ran fevers. But last night, Carole was as shaken as Mandy."

Nelson shifted uncomfortably. Zee knew why. Deductive

reasoning annoyed him. Issues were either black or white. He believed only in absolutes, with the exception of God, which, to him, was an absolute as sure as heaven and hell. Other than that, he didn't believe in anything intangible. He was skeptical of psychoanalysis and psychiatry. In his opinion, anyone worth his salt could solve his own problems without whining for help from someone else.

"Carole's growing up, that's all," he said. "The ordeal she was put through matured her. She's looking at things in a whole new light. She finally appreciates what she's got—Tate, Mandy, this family. 'Bout time she got her head on straight."

Zee wished she could believe that. "I only hope it lasts."

Nelson rolled to his side, facing her, and placed his arm in the hollow of her waist. He kissed her hairline where the gray streak started. "What do you hope lasts?"

"Her loving attitude toward Tate and Mandy. On the surface, she seems to care for them."

"That's good, isn't it?"

"If it's sincere. Mandy is so fragile I'm afraid she couldn't handle the rejection if Carole reverted to her short-tempered, impatient self. And Tate." Zee sighed. "I want him to be happy, especially at this turning point in his life, whether he wins the election or not. He deserves to be happy. He deserves to be loved."

"You've always seen to the happiness of your sons, Zee."

"But neither of them has a happy marriage, Nelson," she stated wistfully. "I had hoped they would."

His finger touched her lips, trying to trace a smile that wasn't there. "You haven't changed. You're still so romance-minded."

He drew her delicate body against his and kissed her. His large hands removed her nightgown and possessively caressed her naked flesh. They made love in the dark.

TWENTY-TWO

Avery agonized for days over how to contact Irish.

Once she had reached the soul-searching conclusion that she needed counsel, she was faced with the problem of how to go about informing him that she hadn't died a fiery death in the crash of Flight 398.

No matter how she went about it, it would be cruel. If she simply appeared on his doorstep, he might not survive the shock. He would think a phone call was a prank because her voice no longer sounded the same. So she settled on sending a note to the post office box where she had mailed her jewelry weeks earlier. Surely he had puzzled over receiving that through the mail without any explanation. Wouldn't he already suspect that there had been mysterious circumstances surrounding her death?

She deliberated for hours over how to word such an unprecedented letter. There were no guidelines that she knew of, no etiquette to follow when you informed a loved one who believed you to be dead that you were, in fact, alive. Straightforwardness, she finally decided, was the only way to go about it.

Dear Irish,
    I did not die in the airplane crash. I will explain the bizarre sequence of events next Wednesday evening at your apartment, six o'clock.
    Love, Avery.

She wrote it with her left hand—a luxury these days—so that he would immediately recognize her handwriting, and mailed it without a return address on the envelope.

Tate had barely been civil to her since their argument over breakfast the previous Saturday. She was almost glad. Even though his antipathy wasn't aimed at her, she bore the brunt of it for her alter ego. Distance made it easier to endure.

She dared not think about how he would react when he discovered the truth. His hatred for Carole would pale against what he would feel for Avery Daniels. The best she could hope for was an opportunity to explain herself. Until then, she could only demonstrate how unselfish her motives were. Early Monday morning, she made an appointment with Dr. Gerald Webster, the famed Houston child psychologist. His calendar was full, but she didn't take no for an answer. She used Tate's current celebrity in order to secure an hour of the doctor's coveted time. For Mandy's sake, she pulled rank with a clear conscience.

When she informed Tate of the appointment, he nodded brusquely. "I'll make a note of it on my calendar." She had made the appointment to coincide with one of the days their campaign would have them in Houston anyway.

Beyond that brief exchange, they'd had little to say to each other. That gave her more time to rehearse what she was going to say when she stood face-to-face with Irish.

However, by Wednesday evening, when she pulled her car to a stop in front of his modest house, she still had no idea what to say to him or even how to begin.

Her heart was in her throat as she went up the walk, especially when she saw movement behind the window blinds. Before she reached the front porch, the door was hauled open. Irish, looking ready to tear her limb from limb with his bare hands, strode out and demanded, "Who the fuck are you and what the fuck is your game?"

Avery didn't let his ferocity intimidate her. She continued moving forward until she reached him. He was only a shade taller than she. Since she wore high heels, they met eye to eye.

"It's me, Irish." She smiled gently. "Let's go inside."

At the touch of her hand on his arm, his militancy evaporated. The furious Irishman wilted like the most fragile of flower petals. It was a pathetic sight to see. In a matter of seconds he was transformed from a belligerent pugilist into a confused old man. The icy disclaimer in his blue eyes was suddenly clouded by tears of doubt, dismay, joy.

"Avery? Is it . . .? How . . .? Avery?"

"I'll tell you everything inside."

She took his arm and turned him around because it seemed he had forgotten how to use his feet and legs. A gentle nudge pushed him over the threshold. She closed the door behind them.

The house, she noted sadly, looked as much a wreck as Irish, whose appearance had shocked her. He'd gained weight around his middle, yet his face was gaunt. His cheeks and chin were loose and flabby. There was a telltale tracery of red capillaries in his nose and across his cheekbones. He'd been drinking heavily.

He had never been a fashion plate, dressing with only decency in mind, but now he looked downright seedy. His dishevelment had gone beyond an endearing personality trait. It was evidence of character degeneration. The last time she'd seen him, his hair had been salt-and-pepper. Now it was almost solid white.

She had done this to him.

"Oh, Irish, Irish, forgive me." With a sob, she collapsed against him, wrapping her arms around his solid bulk and holding on tight.

"Your face is different."

"Yes."

"And your voice is hoarse."

"I know."

"I recognized you through your eyes."

"I'm glad. I didn't change on the inside."

"You look good. How are you?" He set her away from him and awkwardly rubbed her arms with his large, rough hands.

"I'm fine. Mended."

"Where have you been? By the Blessed Virgin, I can't believe this."

"Neither can I. God, I'm so glad to see you."

Clinging to each other again, they wept. At least a thousand times in her life, she had run to Irish for comfort. In her father's absence, Irish had kissed scraped elbows, repaired broken toys, reviewed report cards, attended dance recitals, chastised, congratulated, commiserated.

This time, Avery felt like the elder. Their roles had been reversed. He was the one who clung tightly and needed nurturing.

Somehow, they stumbled their way to his sofa, though neither remembered later how they got there. When the crying binge subsided, he wiped his wet face with his hands, briskly and impatiently. He was embarrassed now.

"I thought you might be angry," she said after indelicately blowing her nose into a Kleenex.

"I am—damn angry. If I weren't so glad to see you, I'd paddle your butt."

"You only paddled me once—that time I called my mother an ugly name. Afterward, you cried harder and longer than I did." She touched his cheek. "You're a softy, Irish McCabe."

He looked chagrined and irascible. "What happened? Have you had amnesia?"

"No."

"Then, what?" he asked, studying her face. "I'm not used to you looking like that. You look like—"

"Carole Rutledge."

"That's right. Tate Rutledge's wife—late wife." A light bulb went on behind his eyes. "She was on that flight, too."

"Did you identify my body, Irish?"

"Yes. By your locket."

Avery shook her head. "It was her body you identified. She had my locket."

Tears formed in his eyes again. "You were burned, but it was your hair, your—"

"We looked enough alike to be mistaken for sisters just minutes before the attempted takeoff."

"How—"

"Listen and I'll tell you." Avery folded her hands around his, a silent request that he stop interrupting. "When I regained consciousness in the hospital, several days after the crash, I was bandaged from head to foot. I couldn't move. I could barely see out of one eye. I couldn't speak.

"Everyone was calling me Mrs. Rutledge. At first I

thought maybe I did have amnesia because I couldn't remember being Mrs. Rutledge or Mrs. Anybody. I was confused, in pain, disoriented. Then, when I remembered who I was, I realized what had happened. We'd switched seats, you see.''

She talked him through the agonizing hours she had spent trying to convey to everyone else what only she knew. ''The Rutledges retained Dr. Sawyer to redo my face—Carole's face—using photographs of her. There was no way I could alert them that they were making a mistake.''

He pulled his hands from beneath hers and dragged them down his loose jowls. ''I need a drink. Want one?''

He returned to the couch moments later with a tumbler three-quarters full of straight whiskey. Avery said nothing, though she eyed the glass meaningfully. Defiantly, he took a hefty draught.

''Okay, I follow you so far. A gross error was made while you were unable to communicate. Once you *were* able to communicate, why didn't you? In other words, why are you still playing Carole Rutledge?''

Avery stood up and began roaming the untidy room, making ineffectual attempts to straighten it while she arranged her thoughts. Convincing Irish that her charade was viable and justified was going to be tricky. His contention had always been that reporters reported the news, they did not make it. Their role was to observe, not participate. That point had been a continual argument between him and Cliff Daniels.

''Somebody plans to kill Tate Rutledge before he becomes a senator.''

Irish hadn't expected anything like that. His hand was arrested midway between the coffee table and his mouth as he was raising the glass of whiskey. The liquor sloshed over the rim of the tumbler onto his hand. Absently, he wiped it dry on his trousers leg.

''What?''

''Somebody plans—''

''Who?''

''I don't know.''

''Why?''

''I don't know.''

"How?"

"I don't know, Irish," she said, raising her voice defensively. "And I don't know where or when, either, so save your breath and don't ask. Just hear me out."

He shook his finger at her. "I may give you that spanking yet for sassing me. Don't test my patience. You've already put me through hell. Pure hell."

"It hasn't exactly been a picnic for me, either," she snapped.

"Which is the only reason I've restrained myself this long," he shouted. "But stop bullshitting me."

"I'm not!"

"Then, what's this crap about somebody wanting to kill Rutledge? How the bloody hell do you know?"

His mounting temper was reassuring. This Irish she could deal with much more easily than the woebegone shell he'd been minutes earlier. She'd had years of practice sparring with him. "Somebody told me he was going to kill Tate before he took office."

"Who?"

"I don't know."

"Shit," he cursed viciously. "Don't start that again."

"If you'll give me a chance, I'll explain."

He took another drink, ground his fist into his other palm, and finally relaxed against the back of the sofa, relaying that he was ready to sit still and listen.

"Believing me to be Carole, somebody came to me while I was still in the ICU. I don't know who it was. I couldn't scc because my eye was bandaged and he was standing beyond my shoulder." She recounted the incident, repeating the threat verbatim.

"I was terrified. Once I was able to communicate who I really was, I was afraid to. I couldn't tip my hand without placing my life, and Tate's, in jeopardy."

Irish was silent until she had finished. She returned to the sofa and sat down beside him. When he did speak, his voice was skeptical.

"What you're telling me, then, is that you took Mrs. Rutledge's place so you could prevent Tate Rutledge from being assassinated."

"Right."

"But you don't know who plans to kill him."

"Not yet, but Carole did. She was part of it, although I don't know her relationship with this other person."

"Hmm." Irish tugged thoughtfully on the flaccid skin beneath his chin. "This visitor you had—"

"Has to be a member of the family. No one else would have been admitted into the ICU."

"Someone could have sneaked in."

"Possibly, but I don't think so. If Carole had hired an assassin, he would simply have vanished when she became incapacitated. He wouldn't have come to warn her to keep quiet. Would he?"

"He's your assassin. You tell me."

She shot to her feet again. "You don't believe me?"

"I believe you believe it."

"But you think it was my imagination."

"You were drugged and disoriented, Avery," he said reasonably. "You said so yourself. You were half blind in one eye and—forgive the bad joke couldn't see out of the other. You think the person was a man, but it *could* have been a woman. You think it was a member of the Rutledge family, but it *could* have been somebody else."

"What are you getting at, Irish?"

"You probably had a nightmare."

"I was beginning to think so myself until several days ago." She took the sheet of paper she'd found in her pillowcase from her purse and handed it to him. He read the typed message.

When his troubled eyes connected with hers, she said, "I found that in my pillowcase. He's real, all right. He still thinks I'm Carole, his coconspirator. And he still intends to do what they originally planned."

The note had drastically altered Irish's opinion. He cleared his throat uncomfortably. "This is the first contact he's had with you since that night in the hospital?"

"Yes."

He reread the message, then remarked, "It doesn't say he's going to kill Tate Rutledge."

Avery gave him a retiring look. "This has been a well-thought-out assassination attempt. The plans were long-range. He'd hardly risk spelling it out. Naturally, he made the note obscure, just in case it was intercepted. The seemingly innocent words would mean something entirely different to Carole.''

''Who has access to a typewriter?''

''Everybody. There's one at a desk in the family den. That was the one used. I checked.''

''What does he—or she—mean by 'whatever you're doing'?''

Avery looked away guiltily. ''I'm not sure.''

''Avery?''

Her head snapped around. She had never been able to fudge the truth with Irish. He saw through it every time. ''I've been trying to get along better with Tate than his wife did.''

''Any particular reason why?''

''It was obvious to me from the beginning that there was trouble between them.''

''How'd you figure that?''

''By the way he treats her. Me. He's polite, but that's all.''

''Hmm. Do you know why?''

''Carole either had, or was planning to have, an abortion. I only found out about that last week. I'd already discovered that she was a selfish, self-centered woman. She cheated on Tate and was a disaster of a parent to her daughter. Without raising too much suspicion, I've been trying to bridge the gap that had come between him and his wife.''

Again Irish asked, ''Why?''

''So I'd know more about what is going on. I had to get to the source of their problem before I could begin to find a motive for a killer. Obviously, my attempts to improve their marriage have been noticed. The killer figures that it's Carole's new tactic to put Tate off guard.''

She chafed her arms as though suddenly chilled. ''He's real, Irish. I know it. There's the proof,'' she said, nodding down at the note.

Not yet committing himself one way or the other, Irish tossed the sheet of paper down on the coffee table. ''Let's assume there is a killer. Who's gonna ice him?''

"I have no idea," she replied with a defeated sigh. "They're one big, happy family."

"According to you, somebody out there at the Rocking R ain't so happy."

She provided him with a verbal run-down of names and each person's relationship to Tate. "Each has his ax to grind, but none of those axes has anything to do with Tate. Both his parents dote on him. Nelson's the undisputed head of the family. He rules, being stern and affectionate by turns.

"Zee isn't so easy to pigeonhole. She's a good wife and loving mother. She remains aloof from me. I think she resents Carole for not making Tate happier."

"What about the others?"

"Carole might have had an affair with Eddy."

"Eddy Paschal, Rutledge's campaign manager?"

"And best friend since college. I don't know for sure. I'm only going by Fancy's word on that."

"What a cliché. How does this Paschal character treat you?"

"He's civil, nothing more. Of course, I haven't put out the signals Carole did. If they were having an affair, maybe he just assumes it ended with the accident. In any event, he's dedicated to Tate winning the election."

"The girl?"

Avery shook her head. "Fancy is a spoiled brat with no more morals than an alley cat in heat. But she's too flighty to be a killer. Not that she's above it; she just wouldn't expend the energy."

"The brother? Jack, is it?"

"He's extremely unhappy with his marriage," she mused, frowning thoughtfully, "but Tate doesn't figure into that. Although . . ."

"Although?"

"Jack's rather pathetic, actually. You think of him as being competent, good-looking, charming, until you see him next to his younger brother. Tate's the sun. Jack is the moon. He reflects Tate's light but has none of his own. He works as hard as Eddy on the campaign, but if anything goes wrong, he usually gets blamed for it. I feel sorry for him.''

''Does he feel sorry for himself? Enough to commit fratricide?''

''I'm not sure. He keeps his distance. I've caught him watching me and sense a smoldering hostility there. On the surface, however, he seems indifferent.''

''What about his wife?''

''Dorothy Rae might be jealous enough to kill, but she would go after Carole before she would Tate.''

''What makes you say that?''

''I was browsing through family photo albums, trying to glean information. Dorothy came into the living room to get a bottle from the liquor cabinet. She was already drunk. I rarely see her, except at dinner, and then she hardly says anything. That's why I was so surprised when, out of the blue, she began accusing me of trying to steal Jack. She said I wanted to pick up with him where I'd left off before the crash.''

''Carole was sleeping with her brother-in-law, too?'' Irish asked incredulously.

''It seems that way. At least she was trying to.'' The notion had distressed Avery very much. She had hoped it was only an alcohol-inspired delusion that Dorothy Rae had drummed up while sequestered in her room with her bottles of vodka. ''It's preposterous,'' she said, thinking aloud. ''Carole had Tate. What could she possibly have wanted with Jack?''

''There's no accounting for taste.''

''I guess you're right.'' Avery was so lost in her own musings, she missed his wry inflection. ''Anyway, I denied having any designs on Dorothy Rae's husband. She called me a bitch, a whore, a home wrecker—things like that.''

Irish ran a hand over his burred head. ''Carole must have really been something.''

''We don't know for certain that she wanted either Jack or Eddy.''

''But she must have put out some mighty strong signals if that many people picked up on them.''

''Poor Tate.''

"What does 'poor Tate' think of his *wife*?"

Avery lapsed into deep introspection. "He thinks she aborted his baby. He knows she had other lovers. He knows she was a negligent parent and put emotional scars on his daughter. Hopefully, that can be reversed."

"You've taken on that responsibility, too, haven't you?"

His critical tone of voice brought her head erect. "What do you mean?"

Leaving her to stew for a moment, Irish disappeared into the kitchen and returned with a fresh drink. Feet spread and firmly planted, he stood before her. "Are you leveling with me about that midnight caller you had in the hospital?"

"How can you even doubt it?"

"I'll tell you how I can doubt it. You came to me, what was it, almost two years ago, with your tail tucked between your legs, needing a job—any job. You'd just been fired from the network for committing one of the worst faux pas in journalism history."

"I didn't come here tonight to be reminded of that."

"Well, maybe you should be reminded! Because I think that's what's behind this whole damned scheme of yours. You plunged in that time over your head, too. Before you got your facts straight, you reported that a a junior congressman from Virginia had killed his wife before blowing his own brains out."

She pressed her fists against her temples as that horrible sequence of events unfolded like a scroll in her memory.

"First reporter on the scene, Avery Daniels," Irish announced with a flourish, showing her no mercy. "Always hot on the trail of a good story. You smelled fresh blood."

"That's right, I did! Literally." She crossed her arms over her middle. "I saw the bodies, heard those children screaming in terror over what they had discovered when they had come home from school. I saw them weeping over what their father had done."

"Had *allegedly* done, dammit. You never learn, Avery. He *allegedly* killed his wife before blasting his own brains onto the wallpaper." Irish took a quick drink of whiskey. "But you went live with a report, omitting that technical little legal word, leaving your network vulnerable to a slander suit.

"You lost it on camera, Avery. Objectivity took a flying leap. Tears streamed down your face and then—*then*—as if all that wasn't enough, you asked your audience at large how any man, but especially an elected public official, could do such a beastly thing."

She raised her head and faced him defiantly. "I know what I did, Irish. I don't need you to remind me of my mistake. I've tried to live it down for two years. I was wrong, but I learned from it."

"Bullshit," he thundered. "You're doing the same damn thing all over again. You're diving in where you have no authority to go. You're making news, not reporting it. Isn't this the big break you've been waiting for? Isn't this the story that's going to put you back on top?"

"All right, yes!" she flung up at him. "That was part of the reason I went into it."

"That's been your reason for doing everything you've ever done."

"What are you saying?"

"You're still trying to get your daddy's attention. You're trying to fill his shoes, live up to his name, which you feel like you've failed to do." He moved toward her. "Let me tell you something—something you don't want to hear." He shook his head and said each word distinctly. "He's not worth it."

"Stop there, Irish."

"He was your father, Avery, but he was my best friend. I knew him longer and a whole lot better than you did. I loved him, but I viewed him with far more objectivity than you or your mother ever could."

He braced one hand on the arm of the sofa and leaned over her. "Cliff Daniels was a brilliant photographer. In my book, he was the best. I'm not denying his talent with a camera. But he didn't have a talent for making the people who loved him happy."

"I was happy. Whenever he was home—"

"Which was a fraction of your childhood—a small fraction. And you were disconsolate every time he waved good-bye. I watched Rosemary endure his long absences. Even when he was home she was miserable, because she knew it would be for only a short time. She spent that time dreading his departure.

"Cliff thrived on the danger. It was his elixir, his life force. To your mother, it was a disease that ate away her youth and vitality. It took his life quickly, mercifully. Her death was agonizing and slow. It took years. Long before the afternoon she swallowed that bottle of pills, she had begun dying.

"So, why does he deserve your blind adoration and dogged determination to live up to his name, Avery? The most valuable prize he ever won wasn't the fucking Pulitzer. It was your mother, only he was too stupid to realize that."

"You're just jealous of him."

Steadily, Irish held her gaze. "I was jealous of the way Rosemary loved him, yes."

The starch went out of her then. She groped for his hand, pressed it to her cheek. Tears trickled over the back of it. "I don't want us to fight, Irish."

"I'm sorry then, because you've got a fight on your hands. I can't let you continue this."

"I've got to. I'm committed."

"Until when?"

"Until I know who threatened to kill Tate and can expose him."

"And then what?"

"I don't know," she groaned miserably.

"And what if this would-be assassin never goes through with it? Suppose he's blowing smoke? Will you stay Mrs. Rutledge indefinitely? Or will you simply approach Rutledge one day and say, 'Oh, by the way'?"

Admitting to him what she had admitted to herself only a few days earlier, she said, "I haven't figured that out yet. I didn't leave myself a graceful escape hatch."

"Rutledge has got to know, Avery."

"No!" She surged to her feet. "Not yet. I can't give him up yet. You've got to swear you won't tell him."

Irish fell back a step, dumbfounded by her violent reaction. "Jesus," he whispered as the truth dawned on him.

"So that's what this is really about. You want another woman's husband. Is that why you want to remain Mrs. Rutledge—because Tate Rutledge is good in bed?"

TWENTY-THREE

Avery turned her back to keep from slapping him. "That was ugly, Irish."

She moved to the window and was alarmed to notice that it had already grown dark. At the ranch, they'd be finished with dinner. She had told them she was going to shop through the dinner hour. Still, she needed to leave soon.

"It was ugly, yes," Irish conceded. "It was meant to be. Every time I feel like going soft on you, I think about the countless nights following the crash when I drank myself into a stupor. You know, I even considered cashing it all in."

Avery came around slowly, her face no longer taut with anger. "Please don't tell me that."

"I figured, fuck this life. I'll take my chances in the next one. I had lost Cliff and Rosemary. I had lost you. I asked God, 'Hey, who needs this abuse?' If I hadn't feared for my immortal soul, such as it is . . .'' He smiled ruefully.

She placed her arms around him and rested her cheek on his shoulder. "I love you. I suffered for you, too, believe it or not. I knew how my death would affect you."

He gathered her into a hug, not for the first time wishing she was truly his daughter. "I love you, too. That's why I can't let you go on with this, Avery."

She leaned away from him. "I have no choice now."

"If there is somebody who wants Rutledge dead—"

"There is."

"Then you're in danger, too."

"I know. I want to be a different Carole for Tate and Mandy, but if I'm too different, her coconspirator will figure she's betrayed him. Or," she added soberly, "that Carole isn't really Carole. I live in fear of giving myself away."

"You might have failed already and don't know it."

She shivered. "I realize that, too."

"Van noticed."

She reacted with a start, then expelled her breath slowly. "I wondered. I nearly had a heart attack when I opened the door to him."

Irish related his conversation with Van. "I was busy and didn't pay much attention to him at the time. I thought he was just being his usual, obnoxious self. Now, I think he was trying to tell me something. What should I say if he brings it up again?"

"Nothing. The fewer who know, the better—for their sakes, as well as mine. Van knew Avery Daniels. The Rutledges didn't. They don't have anyone to compare the new Carole to. They're attributing the changes in her to the crash and its traumatic aftermath."

"It's still shallow," he said worriedly. "If there is no assassination plot—and I pray to heaven that there isn't—the best you can hope to get out of this is a broken heart."

"If I gave it up now and managed to come out alive, I would have done it for nothing. I haven't got the whole story yet. And what if Tate *were* assassinated, Irish? What if I could have prevented it and didn't? Do you think I could live with that the rest of my life?"

He lightly scrubbed her jaw with his knuckles. "You love him, don't you?"

Closing her eyes, she nodded.

"He hated his wife. Therefore, he hates you."

"Right again," she said with a mirthless laugh.

"What's it like between you?"

"I haven't slept with him."

"I didn't ask."

"But that's what you wanted to know."

"Would you?"

"Yes," she replied without equivocation. "From the time I regained consciousness until the day I left the clinic, he was wonderful—absolutely wonderful. The way he treats Carole in public is above reproach.''

"What about how he treats her in private?"

"Chilly, like a betrayed husband. I'm working on that.''

"What will happen then? If he gives in and makes love to you, don't you think he'll know the difference?''

"Will he?" She tilted her head to one side and tried to smile. "Don't men say that all cats are gray in the dark?''

He gave her a reproving glare. "Okay, let's say he doesn't notice. How will you feel about him making love to you while thinking you're somebody else?''

That hadn't occurred to her. Thinking about it now caused her to frown. "I'll want him to know it's me. I know it's wrong to trick him, but . . ."

Her voice trailed off as she wrestled with the question she hadn't yet found an answer for. Leaving it unresolved again, she said, "And then there's Mandy. I love her, too, Irish. She desperately needs a caring mother.''

"I agree. What will happen to her when your job is done and you desert her?''

"I won't just desert—"

"And how do you think Rutledge is going to feel when you do an exposé on his family?''

"It won't be an exposé.''

"I'd hate to be around when you try and explain that to him. He'll think you've used him." He paused for emphasis. "He'll be right, Avery.''

"Not if I saved his life in the process. Don't you think he could find it within himself to forgive me?''

He swore beneath his breath. "You missed your calling. You should have been a lawyer. You'd argue with the devil himself.''

"I can't let my career end in disgrace, Irish. I've got to make restitution for the mistake I made in Washington and earn back my credibility as a journalist. Maybe I am only trying to be daddy's little girl, but I've got to do it.'' Her eyes appealed to him for understanding. "I didn't pursue this golden opportunity. It was forced on me. I've got to make the best of it.''

"You're going about it the wrong way," he said gently,

tilting her chin up with his index finger. "You're too emotionally involved, Avery. You've got too much heart to remain detached. By your own admission, you care for these people. You love them."

"All the more reason for me to stay. Someone wants to kill Tate and make Mandy an orphan. If it's within my power, I've got to prevent that from happening."

His silence was as good as waving a white flag of surrender. She consulted his wall clock. "I must go. But first, do you have something belonging to me?"

In under a minute she was slipping the gold chain of her locket over her head. Monetarily it wasn't worth much, but it was her most valued possession.

Her father had brought it back to her from Egypt in 1967, when he had been hired by *Newsweek* to document the conflict between that country and Israel.

Avery depressed the spring and the two disks parted. She gazed at the photographs inside. One was of her father. In the photograph, he was dressed in battle fatigues, a 35-mm camera draped around his neck. It was the last picture taken of him. He had been killed a few weeks later. The other picture was of her mother. Rosemary, lovely and dainty, was smiling into the camera, but sadly.

Hot, salty tears filled Avery's eyes. She closed the locket and squeezed it in her palm. Not everything had been taken away from her. She still had this, and she still had Irish.

"I hoped you had it," she told him gruffly.

"It was in the dead woman's hands."

Avery nodded, finding it difficult to speak. "Mandy had noticed it around my neck. I had given it to her to look at. Just as we were about to take off, Carole became annoyed because Mandy was twirling the chain. She took it away from her. That's the last thing I remember before the crash."

He showed her Carole's jewelry. "Shook my gizzard when I opened that envelope you sent. You *did* send it, didn't you?"

She told him how that had come about. "I didn't know what else to do with it."

"Why didn't you just throw it away?"

"I guess I secretly wanted to make contact with you."

"You want her jewelry?"

She shook her head no, glancing down at the plain gold band on her left ring finger. "Its sudden reappearance would require an explanation. I have to keep things as simple as possible."

He cursed with impatience and apprehension. "Avery, call it off—now. Tonight."

"I can't."

"Hell and damnation," he swore. "You've got your father's ambition and your mother's compassion. It's a dangerous combination—lethal under these circumstances. Unfortunately, you inherited a stubborn will from both of them."

Avery knew he had capitulated completely when he asked regretfully, "What do you want me to do?"

Tate was standing in the hallway when she returned. Avery thought he'd probably been waiting and watching for her, but he tried to pass it off as a coincidence.

"Why are you so late?" he asked, barely looking in her direction.

"Didn't Zee give you my message? I told her I had some last-minute things to get for the trip."

"I thought you'd be back sooner than this."

"I had a lot of shopping to do." She was loaded down with shopping bags—purchases she had made before her meeting with Irish. "Could you help me get this stuff to the bedroom, please?"

He relieved her of some of the bags and followed her down the hall. "Where's Mandy?" she asked.

"She's already asleep."

"Oh, I was hoping I'd get back in time to read a bedtime story to her."

"Then you should have come home sooner."

"Did she get a story?"

"Mom read her one. I tucked her in and stayed until she'd gone to sleep."

"I'll check on her in a while." She noticed as she passed the hall windows that Nelson, Jack, and Eddy were conversing over one of the patio tables in the courtyard. Zee was reclined in a lounger reading a magazine. Fancy was cavorting in the pool. "You're missing the conference."

"Eddy's going over the itinerary again. I've already heard it a thousand times."

"Just set those bags on the bed." She slid off her linen jacket, tossed it down beside the shopping bags, and stepped out of her pumps. Tate hovered close, looking ready to pounce.

"Where did you go shopping?"

"The usual places."

He had asked a dumb question, since the glossy sacks had familiar logos on them. For one horrifying moment, she wondered if he had followed her to Irish's house. He couldn't have. She had taken a circuitous route, constantly checking her rearview mirror to make sure she wasn't being followed.

Safety measures like that, which would have seemed absurdly melodramatic months ago, had become second nature. She didn't like living dishonestly, being constantly on guard. Tonight, especially, after the emotionally draining visit with Irish, her nerves were shot. Tate had picked the wrong night to interrogate her and put her on the defensive.

"Why are you giving me the third degree about going shopping?"

"I'm not."

"The hell you're not. You're sniffing like a bloodhound." She came a step closer to him. "What did you expect to smell on me? Tobacco smoke? Liquor? Semen? Something that would confirm your nasty suspicions that I spent the afternoon with a lover?"

"It's happened," he said tightly.

"Not anymore!"

"What kind of sap do you take me for? Do you expect me to believe that an operation on your face has turned you into a faithful wife?"

"Believe what you bloody well want to," she shouted back. "Just leave me alone while you're believing it."

She moved to her closet and almost derailed the sliding door as she angrily shoved it open. Her hands were trembling so badly that her fingers couldn't manage the buttons on the back of her blouse. She softly cursed her unsuccessful efforts to unbutton them.

"Let me."

Tate spoke from close behind her, an underlying apology in his tone. He tipped her head forward, leaving her neck exposed. His hands captured hers and lowered them to her sides, then unbuttoned the blouse.

"It would have been a familiar scene," he remarked as he undid the last button.

The blouse slid off her shoulders and down her arms. She caught it against her chest and turned to face him. "I don't respond well to inquisitions, Tate."

"No better than I respond to adultery."

She bowed her head slightly. "I deserve that, I suppose." For a moment, she stared at his throat and the strong pulse beating there. Then she lifted her eyes to his again. "But since the airplane crash, have I given you any reason to doubt my devotion to you?"

The corner of his lips jerked with a tiny spasm. "No."

"But you still don't trust me."

"Trust is earned."

"Haven't I earned yours back yet?"

He didn't answer. Instead, he raised his hand and, with his index finger, traced the gold chain around her neck. "What's this?"

His touch almost melted her. Taking a real chance by revealing more skin than she ever had, she let the blouse slip from her hands to the floor. Her locket lay nestled in the cleft between her breasts, enhanced by the engineering of her sheer bra. She heard the sharp breath he took.

"I found it in a secondhand jewelry store," she lied. "Pretty, isn't it?" Tate was staring at the delicate gold piece with the hunger of a starved man for the last morsel of food on earth. "Open it."

After a moment's hesitation, he scooped the locket into his palm and depressed the clasp. The two tiny frames were empty. She'd removed the photographs of her mother and father and left them in Irish's safekeeping.

"I want to put pictures of you and Mandy in it."

He searched her eyes. Then he looked long at her mouth while rubbing the locket between his thumb and finger. When he snapped it closed, the sound seemed inordinately loud.

He laid the golden disk back into place against her breasts. His hand lingered. His fingertips skimmed the soft curves, barely maintaining contact with her skin, but where they touched, she burned.

Still touching her, Tate turned his head away. He was fighting a war within himself, attested to by the flexing of his jaw, the turbulent indecision in his eyes, his shallow breathing.

"Tate." Her plaintive inflection brought his gaze back to meet hers. On a whisper, she said, "Tate, I never had an abortion." She raised her fingertips to his lips before they could form an argument. "I never had an abortion because there never was a baby."

The irony of it was that it was the unvarnished truth, but she would have to confess to a lie in order for him to believe it.

This germ of an idea had been cultivating in her mind for days. She had no idea if Carole had conceived and aborted a baby or not. But Tate would never know, either. A lie would be easier for him to forgive than an abortion, and since that seemed to be the thickest barrier to their reconciliation, she wanted to tear it down. Why should she pay the penalty for Carole's sins?

Once committed to it, the rest of the lie came easily. "I only told you I was pregnant for the very reason you cited the other morning. I wanted to flaunt it. I wanted to provoke you." She laid her hands against his cheeks. "But I can't let you go on believing that I destroyed your child. I can see that it hurts you too much."

After a long, deep, probing stare, he broke contact and stepped back. "The flight to Houston leaves at seven o'clock on Tuesday. Will you be able to handle that?"

She had hoped her news would release a tide of forgiveness and suppressed love. Trying not to let her disappointment show, she asked, "Which? The early hour or the flight itself?"

"Both."

"I'll be all right."

"I hope so," he said, moving toward the door. "Eddy wants everything to go like clockwork."

On Monday evening, Irish summoned KTEX's political reporter into his office. "You all set for this week?"

"Yeah. Rutledge's people sent over a schedule today. If we cover all this, you'll have to give Dekker equal time."

"Let me worry about that. Your job is to document what's going on in Rutledge's campaign. I want daily reports. By the way, I'm sending Lovejoy with you instead of the photographer originally assigned."

"Jesus, Irish," the reporter whined. "What have I done to deserve him, huh? He's a pain in the ass. He's unreliable. Half the time he smells bad."

He continued with a litany of objections. He preferred to be paired with just about anybody over Van Lovejoy. Irish listened silently. At the conclusion of the reporter's petition, he repeated, "I'm sending Lovejoy with you." The reporter slunk out. Once Irish said something twice, there was no use arguing.

Irish had arrived at that decision several days earlier. Before he had even begun, the reporter hadn't had a chance in hell of changing Irish's mind.

Avery might not think she was in any imminent danger, but she was impetuous and headstrong and often made snap judgments for which she later paid dearly. He couldn't believe the mess she'd made for herself now. God almighty, he thought, she had become another woman! It was too late for him to talk her out of assuming Carole Rutledge's identity, but he was going to do all he could to see that she didn't pay for this impersonation with her life.

They had agreed to contact each other through his post office box if telephoning proved risky. He had given her his extra key to the box. Fat lot of good that would do her if she needed immediate help. That safety net was no more substantial than a spiderweb, but she had refused his offer to loan her a handgun.

The whole cloak-and-dagger routine made him nervous as

hell. Just thinking about it made him reach for his bottle of antacid. These days he was drinking as much of that stuff as he was whiskey. He was too old for this, but he couldn't just stand by, do nothing, and let Avery get herself killed.

Since he couldn't be her guardian angel, he would do the next best thing—he'd send Van along. Having Van around would no doubt make her nervous, but if she got into trouble while on the campaign trail, she'd have somebody to run to. Van Lovejoy wasn't much, but for the time being, he was the best Irish could do.

TWENTY-FOUR

The first glitch in Eddy's carefully orchestrated campaign trip occurred on the third day. They were in Houston. Early that morning Tate had made an impassioned breakfast speech to a rowdy audience of longshoremen. He was well received.

Upon their return to the downtown hotel, Eddy went to his room to answer telephone calls that had come in during their absence. Everyone else gathered in Tate's suite. Jack buried himself in the morning newspapers, scouring them for stories relating to Tate, his opponent, or the election in general. Avery sat on the floor with Mandy, who was scribbling in a Mickey Mouse coloring book.

Tate stretched out on the bed, propping the pillows behind his head. He turned on the television set to watch a game show. The questions were asinine, the contestants frenzied, the host obnoxious, but often something that inane relaxed his mind and opened up new avenues of thought. The best ideas came to him when he wasn't concentrating.

Nelson and Zee were working a crossword puzzle together. Eddy interrupted the restful scene. He barged into the room, as excited as Tate had ever seen him. "Switch that thing off and listen."

Tate used the remote control to silence the TV set. "Well," he said with an expectant laugh, "you've got everybody's attention, Mr. Paschal."

"One of the largest Rotary Clubs in the state is meeting at noon today. It's their most important meeting of the year. New officers are being sworn in, and wives are invited. Their scheduled speaker called in sick this morning. They want you."

Tate sat up and swung his long legs over the side of the bed. "How many people?"

"Two-fifty, three hundred." Eddy was riffling through the papers in his briefcase. "These are top businessmen and professionals—pillars of the community. Oldest Rotary Club in Houston. Its members have lots of money, even in these depressed times. Here," he said, thrusting several sheets of paper at Tate, "this was a hell of a speech you gave in Amarillo last month. Glance over it. And for God's sake, get out of that chambray and denim and put on a conservative suit."

"This crowd sounds more like Dekker people."

"They are. That's why it's important that you go. Dekker's made you out to be a kid with his head in the clouds, at best, or a wacko liberal, at worst. Show them you've got both feet on the ground and that you don't have horns and a pointed tail." He glanced over his shoulder. "You're invited, too, Carole. Look your charming best. The women—"

"I can't be there."

Everyone's attention abruptly shifted from Eddy to her, where she still sat on the floor with Mandy, holding a selection of crayons in her hand and a picture of Donald Duck in her lap. "Mandy's appointment with Dr. Webster is at one o'clock today."

"Crap." Tate plowed his hand through his hair. "That's right. I'd forgotten."

Eddy divided his disbelieving gaze between them. "You can't even consider throwing away this opportunity. We're up one point in the polls this week, Tate, but we're still trailing by a dismal margin. This speech could mean a lot of campaign dollars—dollars we need to buy TV commercial time.''

Jack tossed his folded newspaper aside. "Make another appointment with this doctor."

"What about it, Carole?" Tate asked.

"You know how hard this one was to come by. I probably wouldn't be able to get another one for weeks. Even if I could, I don't believe it would be in Mandy's best interest to postpone."

Tate watched his brother, father, and campaign manager exchange telling glances. They wanted him to make a speech to this influential crowd of Rotarians, and they were right. These conservatives, staunch Dekker supporters, needed to be convinced that he was a viable candidate and not a hotheaded upstart. When he looked down at his wife, however, he could feel the strength behind her calm gaze. He would be damned either way he went. "Christ."

"I could go to the psychologist's office with Carole," Zee offered. "Tate, you make your speech. We can fill you in later on what the doctor has to say about Mandy."

"I appreciate the offer, Mom, but she's my daughter."

"And this could mean the election," Eddy argued, raising his voice.

Jack stood and hiked up the waistband of his pants, as though he was about to engage in a fistfight. "I agree with Eddy one hundred percent."

"One speech isn't going to cost the election. Dad?"

"I think your mother had the most workable solution. You know I don't put much stock in shrinks, so I wouldn't mind a bit going to hear what this one has to say about my granddaughter."

"Carole?"

She had let the dispute revolve around her without contributing anything to it, which was uncharacteristic. As long as Tate had known her, she had never failed to express her opinion.

"They're both terribly important, Tate," she said. "It has to be your decision."

Eddy swore beneath his breath and shot her a glance of supreme annoyance. He would rather her rant and rave and fight to get her way. Tate felt the same. It had been much easier to say no to Carole when she was being obstreperous and inflexible. Lately, she used her dark, eloquent eyes to express herself more than she used a strident voice.

Whatever his choice, it would be met with disapproval. The deciding factor was Mandy herself. He looked down into her solemn little face. Even though she couldn't have understood what the controversy was about, she seemed to be apologizing to him for causing such a fuss.

"Call them back, Eddy, and graciously decline." Carole's posture relaxed, as though she'd been holding herself in breathless anticipation of his answer. "Tell them Mrs. Rutledge and I have a previous engagement."

"But—"

Tate held up his hand to ward off a barrage of protests. He gave his friend a hard, decisive stare. "My first obligation is to my family. I was guaranteed your understanding, remember?"

Eddy gave him a hard, exasperated stare, then stormed out. Tate couldn't blame him for being pissed. He didn't have a child. He was responsible to no one but himself. How could he possibly understand divided loyalties?

"I hope you know what you're doing, Tate." Nelson stood and reached for Zee's hand. "Let's go try to calm down our frustrated campaign manager." They left together.

Jack was just as agitated as Eddy. He glared at Carole. "Satisfied?"

"Enough, Jack," Tate said testily.

His brother aimed an accusing finger at her. "She's manipulating you with this good-mother routine."

"What goes on between Carole and me is none of your damned business."

"Ordinarily, no. But since you're running for public office, your private life is everybody's business. Whatever affects the campaign is my business. I've devoted years to getting you elected."

"And I appreciate everything you've done. But today I'm taking an hour off for my daughter's sake. I don't think that's asking too much, and even if it is, don't give me an argument about it."

After casting another hostile glance at Carole, Jack left the suite, slamming the door behind him.

She came to her feet. "Is that what you think, Tate? That this is just a good-mother routine?"

The hell of it was that he didn't know what to think. Since his first sexual conquest at age fifteen, Tate had exercised control over all his relationships with women. Women liked him. He liked them in return. He also respected them. Unlike most men to whom romantic encounters came easily, his friends among the female sex numbered as many as his lovers, although many in the first category secretly lamented that they'd never joined the ranks of the second.

His most serious involvement had been with a San Antonio divorcée. She sold commercial real estate, very successfully. Tate had lauded her success, but didn't love her enough to compete with it for her time and attention. She had also made it clear from the beginning that she didn't want children. After a two-year courtship, they had parted as friends.

Jack did most of the hiring and firing at their law firm, but when Carole Navarro had applied, he had solicited Tate's opinion. No living man could look at Carole impassively. Her large, dark eyes captivated his attention, her figure his imagination, her smile his heart. He had given her his stamp of approval and Jack had put her on the payroll as a legal assistant.

Soon, Tate had violated his own business ethics and invited her out to dinner to celebrate a case the jury had found in favor of their client. She had been charming and flirtatious, but the evening had ended at the door of her apartment with a friendly good-night handshake.

For weeks, she had kept their dates friendly. One night, when Tate had withstood the buddy system as long as he could, he had taken her in his arms and kissed her. She had returned his kiss with gratifying passion. They made a natural progression to bed, and the sex had been deeply satisfying for both.

Within three months the law firm had lost an employee, but Tate had gained a wife.

Her pregnancy came as a shock. He had quickly and

agreeably adapted to the idea of having a child sooner than they had planned; Carole had not. She complained of feeling shackled by an unwelcome responsibility. Her engaging smile and infectious laughter became memories.

Her sexual performance had turned so obligatory that Tate didn't miss it when it was suspended altogether. They had had blistering arguments. Nothing he did pleased or interested her. Eventually, he gave up trying to and devoted his time and energy to the election, which was still years away.

As soon as Mandy was born, Carole dedicated herself to getting her figure back. She exercised with fiendish diligence. He wondered why. Then the reason behind the zeal became apparent. He knew almost to the day when she took her first lover. She made no secret of it, nor of any of the infidelities that followed. His defense was indifference, which, by that time, was genuine. In retrospect, he wished he had gone ahead and divorced her then. A clean break might have been better for everybody.

For months they occupied the same house, but lived separate lives. Then, one night, she had visited him in his room, looking her sexiest. He never knew what had prompted her to come to him that night—probably boredom, maybe spite, maybe the challenge of seducing him. Whatever her reason, sexual abstinence and imprudent drinking with his brother during a poker game had caused him to take advantage of her offer.

During the blackest hours of their estrangement, he had considered resuming his affair with the realtor or cultivating another relationship just for the physical release it would afford him. Ultimately, he had denied that luxury to himself. A sexual dalliance was a pitfall to any married man. To a political candidate, it was an inescapable abyss. Falling into it and getting caught was career suicide.

Whether he got caught or not, vows meant something to him, though they obviously didn't mean anything to his wife. Like a dolt, he had remained faithful to Carole and to the words he had recited to her during their wedding ceremony.

Weeks after that night, she had belligerently announced that she was pregnant again. Although Tate had seriously doubted that the child was his, he had had no choice but to take her word for it.

"I didn't want to be stuck with another kid," she had yelled.

That's when he knew he didn't love her anymore, hadn't for a long time, and never could again. He had reached that momentous conclusion one week to the day before she boarded Flight 398 to Dallas.

Now he shook his head to bring himself out of his unpleasant reverie. He was going to ignore her question about the good-mother routine, just as he had ignored her claim that there had never been a child. He was afraid of the old bait-and-switch con. He wasn't going to commit himself one way or the other until he knew that Carole's recent transformations were permanent.

"Why don't you order up lunch so we won't have to go out before our meeting with Dr. Webster," he suggested, changing the subject.

She seemed just as willing to let the matter drop. "What would you like?"

"Anything. A cold roast beef sandwich would be fine."

As she sat down on the bed to use the phone on the nightstand, she mechanically crossed her legs. Tate's stomach muscles clenched at the sound of her stockings scratching together.

If he still distrusted her, why did he want to have sex with her so badly?

She deserved an A for effort. He would grant her that. Since coming home, and even before, she had done her best to reconcile with him. She rarely lost her temper anymore. She made a concerted effort to get along with his family, and had taken an unprecedented and inordinate amount of interest in their comings and goings, their habits, their activities. She was the antithesis of the impatient, ill-tempered parent she'd been before.

"That's right, a peanut butter sandwich," she was saying into the receiver. "With grape jelly. I know it's not on the room service menu, but that's what she likes to eat for lunch." Mandy's unwavering love affair with peanut butter and jelly sandwiches was a joke between them. Over her shoulder, Carole flashed him a smile.

God, he wanted to taste that smile.

Recently, he had. Her mouth hadn't tasted of deceit and lies and unfaithfulness. The kisses she returned were sweet and delicious and . . . different. Analyzing them—and he had done that a lot lately—he realized that kissing her had been like kissing a woman for the first time.

What should have been familiar had been unique. Their few kisses had jolted him and left indelible impressions. He had exercised monastic self-discipline to stop with a few, when what he had wanted to do was explore her mouth at leisure until he found an explanation for this phenomenon.

Or maybe it wasn't so phenomenal. She looked different with her hair short. Maybe the plastic surgery had altered her face just enough to make her seem like an entirely different woman.

It was a good argument, but he wasn't convinced.

"They'll be right up," she told him. "Mandy, pick up the crayons and put them back in the box, please. It's time for lunch."

She stooped to help her. As she bent over, the narrow skirt of her suit was pulled tight across her derriere. Desire ripped through him. Blood rushed to his loins. That was understandable, he reasoned quickly. He hadn't been with a woman in so damn long.

But he didn't really believe that, either.

He didn't want just any woman. If that were the case, he could solve his problem with a single phone call.

No, he wanted this woman, this Carole, this wife he was only now becoming acquainted with. Sometimes, when he gazed into her eyes, it was as though he'd never known her before and the antagonism between them had happened to someone else. Impossible as it was to believe, he liked this Carole. Even more impossible to believe, he had fallen a little in love with her.

But he would deny it with his dying breath.

* * *

"I'm glad you came with us," Avery said, giving Tate a tentative smile. A receptionist had seated them in Dr. Webster's office to await their private consultation.

"It was the only decision I could make."

The psychologist had been with Mandy for almost an hour. Waiting for his prognosis was taking its toll on them. The idle conversation was an attempt to relieve their nervous tension.

"Will Eddy stay mad at me for the rest of the trip?"

"I spoke with him before we left the hotel. He wished us luck with Mandy. I guess Mom and Dad calmed him down. Anyway, he never really gets mad."

"That's odd, isn't it?"

Tate consulted his wristwatch. "How long does his session with her last, for crissake?" He looked at the door behind him as though willing it to open. "What did you say?"

"About Eddy never getting mad."

"Oh, right." He shrugged. "It's just his temperament. He rarely loses control."

"Iceman," she murmured.

"Hmm?"

"Nothing."

She fiddled with the strap of her handbag, weighing the advisability of pursuing the subject. Irish had advised her to learn as much as she could about these people. Her career had been built on her ability to pose pertinent questions, but to phrase them subtly. She had been adroit at squeezing information out of people who were sometimes reluctant to impart their secrets. She decided to test her talent and see if it was still intact.

"What about women?"

Tate tossed aside the magazine he had just picked up. "What women?"

"Eddy's women."

"I don't know. He doesn't discuss them with me."

"He doesn't discuss his sex life with his best friend? I thought all men swapped success stories."

"Boys might. Men don't need to. I'm not a voyeur and Eddy's not an exhibitionist."

"Is he heterosexual?"

Tate hit her with an icy blast of his eyes. "Why? Did he turn you down?"

"Damn you!"

The door swung open. The two of them guiltily sprang apart. The receptionist said, "The doctor is finishing up with Mandy. He'll be in shortly."

"Thank you."

After she withdrew, Avery leaned forward from her chair again. "I'm only asking about Eddy because your niece is throwing herself at him, and I'm afraid she'll get hurt."

"My niece? Fancy?" He laughed with incredulity. "She's after Eddy?"

"She told me so the other night, when she came home with a battered face." His smile disappeared. "That's right, Tate. She picked up a cowboy in a bar. They got high. When he couldn't maintain an erection, he blamed it on Fancy and beat her up."

He expelled a long breath. "Jesus."

"Didn't you notice her black eye and swollen lip?" He shook his head. "Well, don't feel too badly. Neither did her own parents," she said bitterly. "Fancy's like a piece of furniture. She's there, but no one really sees her... unless she's behaving outrageously. Anyway, she has her sights fixed on Eddy now. How do you think he'll reciprocate?"

"Fancy's just a kid."

Avery gave him an arch look. "You might be her uncle, but you're not blind."

He rolled his shoulders uncomfortably. "Eddy had his share of coeds while we were at UT. He visited the whorehouses in Nam. I know he's straight."

"Is he currently seeing anyone?"

"He goes out with some of the women who work at headquarters, but it's usually a platonic, group thing. I haven't heard any scuttlebutt that he's sleeping with one of them. Several would probably be willing if he asked.

"But Fancy?" Tate shook his head doubtfully. "I don't think Eddy would touch her. He wouldn't get involved with a woman almost twenty years his junior, particularly Fancy. He's too bright."

"I hope you're right, Tate." After a thoughtful pause, she

glanced up at him and added, "And not because I'm interested in him myself."

He didn't have time to comment before the doctor opened the door and entered the office.

TWENTY-FIVE

"Don't feel too bad, Mrs. Rutledge. Your guilt over past mistakes won't help Mandy now."

"How am I supposed to feel, Dr. Webster? You've all but said that I'm responsible for Mandy's retarded social development."

"You made some mistakes. All parents do. But you and Mr. Rutledge have already taken the first step toward reversing that trend. You're spending more time with Mandy, which is excellent. You're praising even her smallest achievements and minimizing her failures. She needs that kind of positive reinforcement from you."

Tate was frowning. "That doesn't sound like much."

"On the contrary, it's a lot. You'd be amazed how important parental approval is to a child."

"What else should we do?"

"Ask for her opinion often. 'Mandy, do you want vanilla or chocolate?' Force her to make choices and then commend her decisions. She should be made to vocalize her thoughts. My impression is that up till now she's been discouraged to."

He regarded them from beneath rust-colored eyebrows that would have better befitted a cattle rustler with a six-shooter strapped to his hip than a child psychologist with a benign demeanor.

"Your little girl has a very low opinion of herself." Avery pressed her fist to her lips and rolled them inward. "Some children manifest low self-esteem with bad behavior, drawing attention to themselves in that way. Mandy has retreated into herself. She considers herself transparent—of little or no significance.''

Tate's head dropped between his shoulders. Bleakly, he glanced at Avery. Tears were rolling down her cheeks. ''I'm sorry,'' she whispered. She was apologizing for Carole, who didn't deserve his forgiveness.

''It's not all your fault. I was there, too. I let lots of things slide when I should have intervened.''

''Unfortunately,'' Dr. Webster said, directing their attention back to him, ''the airplane crash only heightened Mandy's anxiety. How did she behave on the flight here the other day?''

''She raised quite a ruckus when we tried to buckle her into her seat,'' Tate said.

''I was having a difficult time buckling my own seat belt,'' Avery confessed honestly. ''If Tate hadn't talked me through it, I doubt I could have stood the takeoff.''

''I understand, Mrs. Rutledge,'' he said sympathetically. ''How was Mandy once you took off?''

They glanced at each other, then Avery answered. ''Come to think of it, she was fine.''

''That's what I figured. See, she remembers you fastening her into her seat, Mrs. Rutledge, but doesn't remember anything beyond the crash. She doesn't remember you rescuing her.''

Avery laid a hand against her chest. ''You're saying she blames me for putting her through the crash?''

''To an extent, I'm afraid so.''

Shuddering, she covered her mouth with her hand. ''My God.''

''It will be a real breakthrough when she allows her mind to live through that explosion again. Then she'll remember you rescuing her.''

''That would be hell for her.''

''But necessary for a complete cure, Mr. Rutledge. She's fighting her memory of it. My guess is that her recurring nightmares lead her right up to the moment of impact.''

''She said the fire was eating her,'' Avery said softly,

remembering Mandy's last nightmare. "Is there anything we can do to prod her memory?"

"Hypnosis is a possibility," the doctor said. "What I'd rather do, however, is let her memory evolve naturally. Next time she has one of these nightmares, don't wake her up."

"Christ."

"I know that sounds cruel, Mr. Rutledge, but she's got to experience the crash again to get to the other side of it, to reach safety in the arms of her mother. The terror must be exorcised. She won't overcome her subconscious fear and dread of your wife until then."

"I understand," Tate said, "but it's going to be tough."

"I know." Dr. Webster stood, signaling that their time was up. "I don't envy you having to stand by and let her relive that horrifying experience. I'd like to see her back in two months, if that's convenient."

"We'll make it convenient."

"And before that, if you think it's necessary. Feel free to call anytime."

Tate shook hands with Dr. Webster, then assisted Avery from her chair. She wasn't the mother Mandy had the subconscious fear and dread of, but she might just as well be. Everyone would lay Carole's blame on her. Even with the support of Tate's hand beneath her elbow, she could barely find the wherewithal to stand.

"Good luck with your campaign," the psychologist told Tate.

"Thank you."

The doctor clasped Avery's hands, sandwiching them between his. "Don't make yourself ill with guilt and remorse. I'm convinced that you love your daughter very much."

"I do. Did she tell you that she hated me?"

The question was routine. He heard it a dozen times a day, particularly from mothers harboring guilt. In this instance, he could provide a positive answer. He smiled a good ole boy's smile. "She speaks very highly of her mommy and only gets apprehensive when referring to events that took place before the crash, which ought to tell you something."

"What?"

"That you've already improved as a parent." He patted her shoulder. "With your continued tender loving care, Mandy will get through this and go on to be an exceptionally bright, well-adjusted child."

"I hope so, Dr. Webster," she said fervently. "Thank you."

He escorted them to the door and pulled it open. "You know, Mrs. Rutledge, you gave me quite a start when I first met you. A young woman did a television interview with me about a year ago. She bears a remarkable resemblance to you. In fact, she's from your area. By any chance, do you know her? Her name is Avery Daniels."

Avery Daniels, Avery Daniels, Avery Daniels.

The crowd was chanting her real name as she and Tate made their way through the crowd toward the dais.

Avery Daniels, Avery Daniels, Avery Daniels.

There were people everywhere. She stumbled and became separated from Tate. He was swallowed by the crowd. "Tate!" she screamed. He couldn't hear her over the demonic recitation of her name.

Avery, Avery, Avery.

What was that? A shot! Tate was covered with blood. Tate turned to her and, as he fell, he sneered, 'Avery Daniels, Avery Daniels, Avery Daniels."

"Carole?"

Avery Daniels.

"Carole? Wake up."

Avery sat bolt upright. Her mouth was gaping open and dry. She was wheezing. "Tate?" She fell against his bare chest and threw her arms around him. "Oh God, it was awful."

"Were you having a bad dream?"

She nodded, burrowing her face in the fuzzy warmth of his chest. "Hold me. Please. Just for a minute."

He was sitting on the edge of her bed. At her request, he inched closer and placed his arms around her. Avery snuggled closer still and clung to him. Her heart was racing, thudding against his chest. She couldn't eradicate the image of a blood-drenched Tate turning to her with contempt and accusation burning in his eyes.

"What brought this on?"

"I don't know," she lied.

"I think I do. You haven't been yourself since Dr. Webster mentioned Avery Danicls." She whimpered. Tate threaded his fingers up through her hair and closed them around her scalp. "I can't believe he didn't know she died in that crash. He was so embarrassed by mentioning it, I felt sorry for him. He had no way of knowing how much the comparison would upset you."

Or why, she thought. "Did I behave like a fool?" All she remembered after the doctor had spoken her name was the clamorous ringing in her ears and the wave of dizziness that had knocked her against Tate.

"Not like a fool, but you almost fainted."

"I don't even remember leaving his office."

He set her away from him. Her hands slid onto his biceps. "It was a bizarre coincidence that you were on the same airplane with the Daniels woman. Strangers often mistook you for her, remember? It's surprising that no one has mentioned her to you before now."

So he had known who Avery Daniels was. That made her feel better somehow. She wondered if he had liked watching her on TV. "I'm sorry I caused a scene. I just get . . ." She wished he was still holding her. It was easier to talk when she didn't have to look him in the eye.

"What?"

She laid her head on his shoulder. "I get tired of people staring at my face all the time. It's an object of curiosity. I feel like the bearded lady in a sideshow."

"Human nature. No one means to be cruel."

"I know, but it makes me extremely self-conscious. Sometimes I feel like I'm still wrapped in bandages. I'm on the inside looking out, but no one can see past my face into me." A tear trickled from the corner of her eye and splashed onto his shoulder.

"You're still upset over the dream," he said, easing her up again. "Would you like something to drink? There's some Bailey's in the bar."

"That sounds wonderful."

He divided the small bottle of Irish cream between two drinking glasses and returned to the bed with them. If he was self-conscious about having only his underwear on, he gave no outward sign of it.

It pleased her that he sat back down on her bed, not the one he had been sleeping in before her nightmare woke him up. Only a narrow space separated the beds, but it might just as well have been the Gulf of Mexico. It had taken an emergency to get him to cross it.

"To your victory, Tate." She clinked her glass with his. The liquor slid easily down her throat and spread warmly through her belly. "Hmm. This was a good idea. Thanks."

She welcomed this quiet interlude. They shared all the problems inherent to any married couple, but none of the intimacy. Because of the campaign, they were always in the public eye and under constant scrutiny. That put an additional strain on an already difficult relationship. They shared no counterbalancing pleasure in each other.

They were married, yet they weren't. They occupied the same space, but existed in separate spheres. Until tonight, Mandy had served as a buffer between them in the confines of the hotel room. She'd slept with Avery.

But tonight Mandy wasn't here. They were alone. It was the middle of the night. They were sipping Irish cream together and discussing their personal problems. For any other couple, the scene would result in lovemaking.

"I miss Mandy already," she remarked as she traced the rim of her glass with her fingertip. "I'm not sure we did the right thing by letting her go home with Zee and Nelson."

"That's what we had planned all along—that they'd take her home after her appointment with Webster."

"After talking to him, I feel like I should be with her constantly."

"He said a few days of separation wouldn't hurt, and Mom knows what to do."

"How did it happen?" Avery mused aloud. "How did she become so introverted, so emotionally bruised?" She asked the questions rhetorically, without expecting a response. Tate, however, took them literally and provided her with answers.

"You heard what he said. He told you how it happened. You didn't spend enough time with her. What time you did spend with her was more destructive than not."

Her temper surged to the surface. In this instance, Carole was getting a bum deal, and Avery felt compelled to take up for her. "And where were you all that time? If I was doing such a rotten job of mothering, why didn't you step in? Mandy has two parents, you know."

"I realize that. I admitted it today. But every time I made the slightest suggestion, you got defensive. Seeing us fight sure as hell wasn't doing Mandy any good. So I couldn't step in, as you put it, without making a bad situation even worse."

"Maybe your approach was wrong." Giving Carole the benefit of the doubt, she played devil's advocate.

"Maybe. But I've never known you to take criticism well."

"And you do?"

He set his glass on the nightstand and reached for the lamp switch. Avery's hand shot out and grabbed his. "I'm sorry. Don't . . . don't go back to bed yet. It's been a long, tiring day for many reasons. We're both feeling the pressure. I didn't mean to lash out at you."

"You probably should have gone home with Mom and Dad, too."

"No," she said quickly, "my place is with you."

"Today was just a sample of what it's going to be like between now and November, Carole. It's only going to get tougher."

"I can handle it." Smiling, she impulsively reached up and ran her finger across the cleft in his chin. "I wish I had a nickel for every time today you said, 'Hi, I'm Tate Rutledge, running for U.S. senator.' Wonder how many hands you shook?"

"This many." He held up his right hand. It was bent into a cramped claw.

She laughed softly. "I believe we bore up very well

during that visit to the Galleria, considering we'd just ended our visit with Dr. Webster and told Mandy good-bye.''

As soon as they had returned to the hotel from the psychologist's office, they had given Mandy over to her grandparents. Zee went beyond being a white-knuckle flier. She refused to fly altogether, so they had come to Houston by car. They had wanted to start the drive home so they would arrive before dark.

No sooner had she and Tate waved them off than Eddy hustled them into a car and sped toward the sprawling, multilayered shopping mall.

Volunteers, under Eddy's supervision, had heralded their arrival. Tate made a short speech from a raised platform, introduced his wife to the crowd that had gathered, then moved among them, shaking hands and soliciting votes.

It had gone so well that Eddy was mollified after having to decline the Rotary Club's invitation. Even that had turned out well. The civic club had extended Tate an invitation to speak at one of their meetings later in the month.

"Eddy went nuts over all the television coverage you got today," Avery said, reflecting on it.

"They gave us twenty seconds during the six o'clock broadcast. Doesn't sound like much, but I'm told that's good."

"It is. So I'm told," she hastily added.

She'd been stunned to see Van Lovejoy and a political reporter from KTEX at the longshoremen's breakfast. All day, they'd stayed hot on Tate's trail. "Why did they come all the way from San Antonio?" she had asked Eddy.

"Don't knock the free publicity. Smile into the camera every chance you get."

Instead, she tried to avoid Van's camera. But he seemed bent on getting her image on tape. The cat-and-mouse game she played with him all day, coupled with the shock Dr. Webster had dealt her, had chafed her nerves raw. She had been so nervous that, later, when she couldn't find a pair of earrings, she had overreacted.

"I know they were in here the day before I left," she cried to Tate.

"Look again."

She did better than that. She upended the satin pouch and raked through the contents. "They're not here."

"What do they look like?"

They were due to leave for a fund-raising barbecue dinner being hosted by a wealthy rancher outside the city. Tate had been dressed and waiting for half an hour. She was running late.

"Big silver loops." Tate gave the room a cursory once-over. "You won't find them lying on the surface," she had told him with exasperation. "I haven't worn them yet. I brought them specifically for this outfit."

"Can't you substitute something else?"

"I guess I'll have to." She made a selection from the pile of jewelry she'd spilled onto the dresser. By then she was so flustered, she had had difficulty fitting the post into the back. Three attempts proved to be misses. "Shit!"

"Carole, for heaven's sake, calm down," Tate said, raising his voice. Up till then he'd been infuriatingly calm. "You forgot a pair of earrings. It's not the end of the world."

"I didn't forget them." Drawing a deep breath, she faced him. "This isn't the first time something has mysteriously disappeared."

"You should have told me. I'll call hotel security right away."

She caught his arm before he could reach for the telephone. "Not just here. At home, too. Somebody's been sneaking into my room and going through my things."

His reaction was what she had expected. "That's ridiculous. Are you crazy?"

"No. And I'm not imagining it, either. I'm missing several things—small, insignificant things. Like this pair of earrings that I know damn good and well I packed. I checked and double-checked my accessories before I put them in the suitcases."

Sensitive to any criticism of his family, he folded his arms across his chest. "Who are you accusing of stealing?"

"I don't mind the missing objects so much as the violation of my privacy."

Just then a knock had sounded on their door—the perfect

culmination for a frazzling day. "Case in point," she had said irritably. "Why can't we ever finish a private conversation before we're interrupted?"

"Keep your voice down. Eddy'll hear you."

"To hell with Eddy," she had said, meaning it.

Tate pulled the door open and Eddy came striding in. "Ready, guys?"

By way of explanation for their being late, Tate said, "Carole lost her earrings."

She shot him a look that clearly stated she had not lost them.

"Well, wear some others or go without, but we've got to get downstairs." Eddy held the door open. "Jack's waiting with the car. It's an hour's drive."

They rushed for the elevator. Thankfully, another hotel guest saw them coming and politely held it for them. Jack was pacing the length of the limo parked in the porte cochere.

For the duration of the drive they discussed polls and campaign strategy. She could have been invisible, for all the attention she was given. Once, when she offered an unsolicited opinion, it was met with three impassive stares, then summarily ignored.

Surprisingly, the party had been fun. No press was allowed. Since she didn't have to concentrate on dodging Van's camera, she relaxed and enjoyed herself. There was a plethora of good Texana food, friendly people who likened Tate to a young John Kennedy, and live music. She even got to dance with Tate. Eddy had pressured him into it.

"Come on. It'll look good to the crowd."

For the time Tate held her in his arms and twirled her around the dance floor, she pretended it had been his idea. Heads thrown back, they had smiled at each other as their feet kept time to the lively tune. She believed he was actually enjoying himself. As the music reached a crescendo, he lifted her against him and whirled her around to the exuberant applause of everyone watching. Then he had bent down and kissed her cheek.

When he pulled back, there was an odd expression on his face. He appeared surprised by his own spontaneity.

On the return trip into the city, however, she sat in the corner of the limousine's backseat, staring through the dark patch of tinted window while he, Jack, and Eddy analyzed how well the day had gone and assessed what effect it might have on the outcome of the election.

She had gone to bed feeling exhausted and glum. She'd had difficulty falling asleep. The nightmare—and she could count on one hand the others she had had in her lifetime—was the product of a physically and emotionally taxing day.

She treasured this uninterrupted moment with Tate. They were continually surrounded by other people. Even in their own suite, they were rarely alone.

"I think the Bailey's is going to do the trick." She handed him her empty glass and lay back against the pillows.

"Feeling sleepy?"

"Hmm." She flung her arms up so that her hands were lying on either side of her head, palms up, fingers curled inward, a position both provocative and defenseless. Tate's eyes turned dark as they moved from her face down the front of her body.

"Thank you for dancing with me," she said drowsily. "I enjoyed you holding me."

"You used to say I had no rhythm."

"I was wrong."

He continued to watch her for a moment, then switched out the lamp. He was about to leave her bed when she laid a restraining hand on his bare thigh. "Tate?"

He froze. His motionless silhouette was limned by the bluish light leaking through the drapes from the parking lot. Invitingly, she repeated his name on a breath of a whisper.

Slowly, he lowered himself to the mattress again and leaned over her. With a soft exclamation, she bicycled her legs to kick off the covers so there would be nothing between them.

"Tate, I—"

"Don't," he commanded gruffly. "Don't say anything to change my mind." His head moved so close that she felt his breath against her lips. "I want you, so don't say a word."

Fiercely possessive, his lips rubbed hers apart. His tongue

probed and explored, dipping into her mouth on deep and daring forays. Avery clutched handfuls of his hair and pressed her mouth up into his kiss.

He relaxed his arms, which had been stiffly bridging her head. Gradually, his body stretched out along hers. His hard thigh crowded her hip; she turner her lower body into it. He nudged her moist cleft with his knee.

"Is it me you're wet for?"

Avery gasped, unspeakably aroused by his boldness. "You told me not to say anything."

"Who are you wet for?"

She ran her hand down his thigh, placed it beneath his hip, and invitingly drew him closer.

Groaning in need, he ended the kiss with several rough glances of his lips across hers. He kissed his way down her throat and chest and nuzzled her breasts as he filled his hands with them. His open mouth sought the raised center of one and tugged on it through the fabric of her gown. It beaded against his flicking tongue.

Reflexively, her body bowed off the bed. His hands slid between the pillow and her head, his palms cradling it, his thumbs meeting beneath her chin. He tilted her face up and fastened his mouth to hers again, giving her a scorching, searching kiss as he moved to lie between her spreading thighs.

Avery's body quickened to the splendor of feeling the full extension of his sex stroking the dell of her femininity. There was even a certain sexiness to the friction of his cotton briefs sliding against her silk underpants.

Heat shimmied through her and was conveyed to him through her skin. His kiss delved deeper, and the rocking motions of his body grew more desperate. Too impatient to be leisurely and inquisitive, her hands clutched his sleek, supple back. She fitted his calf muscles into the arches of her feet and receptively angled her hips up.

Hostile, hard, and hot, Tate slid his hand into the damp silk prohibiting his entrance.

The telephone rang.

He withdrew his hand, but she still lay trapped beneath

him. While they lay breathing heavily against each other, the phone continued to ring.

Eventually, Tate rolled to the edge of the bed and jerked the receiver to his ear. "Hello?" After a brief pause, he cursed. "Yeah, Jack," he growled. "I'm awake. What is it?"

Avery emitted a small, anguished cry and moved to the far side of the bed, putting her back to him.

TWENTY-SIX

"I'm coming."

Eddy left his comfortable hotel room chair and rounded the matching hassock. Stacked on top if it were computer readouts, newspaper clippings, demographic charts. Thinking the knock signaled the arrival of his room service order, he pulled the door open without first checking the peephole.

Fancy stood on the threshold. "I'd pay to see that."

Not bothering to conceal his annoyance, he barred her entrance by placing his forearm on the doorjamb. "See what?"

"You coming."

"Cute."

"Thanks," she replied cheekily. Then her blue eyes darkened. "Who were you expecting?"

"None of your business. What are you doing so far away from home, little girl?"

The bell on the elevator down the hall chimed, and the room service waiter emerged, carrying a tray on his shoulder. He approached them on soundless footsteps. "Mr. Paschal?"

"Here." When Eddy stepped aside to let him in, Fancy slipped inside, too. She went into the bathroom and locked the door. Eddy scrawled his signature on the bottom of the tab and showed the waiter to the door.

"Have a good night." The youth gave him an elbow-in-the-ribs grin and a sly wink.

Eddy closed the door a little too suddenly and a little too loudly to be polite. "Fancy?" He rapped on the bathroom door.

"I'll be out in a sec."

He heard the commode flush. She opened the door while still tugging the tight, short skirt of her tube dress over her hips. The dress was made of stretchy, clingy stuff that conformed to her body like a second skin. It had a wide cuff across the top that could be worn off the shoulders. She was wearing it way off.

The dress was red. So was her lipstick, her high-heeled pumps, and the dozens of plastic bangle bracelets encircling her arms. With her mane of blond hair even more unruly than usual, she looked like a whore.

"What did you order? I'm starved."

"You're not invited." Eddy intercepted her on her way toward the room service tray the waiter had left on the table near the easy chair. He gripped her upper arm. "What are you doing here?"

"Well, first I was peeing. Now I'm going to scope out what you've got to eat."

His fingers pinched tighter and he strained her name through his teeth. "What are you doing in Houston?"

"It got boring at home," she said, wresting her arm free, "with nobody but Mona and Mother around. Mother's in a stupor half the time. The other half she's crying over Daddy not loving her anymore. Frankly, I doubt he ever did. You know he thought she was knocked up with me when they got married." She lifted the silver metal lid off one of the plates and picked up a cherry tomato—a garnish for his club sandwich.

"What's . . . hmm, a chocolate sundae," she cooed with pleasure as she investigated beneath another lid. "How do you eat like this late at night and keep your belly so nice and flat?"

Her practiced eyes moved down his smooth, muscled

torso, seen through his unbuttoned shirt. Suggestively, Fancy licked her lips.

"Anyway, Mother believes Daddy has the hots for Aunt Carole, which I think is downright scandalous, don't you?" She shivered—not from repugnance, but with delight. "It's so, so Old Testament for a man to covet his brother's wife."

"The sin of the week, by Fancy Rutledge."

She giggled. "Mother's positively morose and Mona looks at me with the same regard she would have for a cockroach in her sugar canister. Grandma, Grandpa, and the little spook were due back, which would only make things worse, so I decided to split and come here, where all the action is."

Wryly, he said, "As you can see, there's not much going on tonight."

Undaunted, she curled up in the easy chair he'd been occupying and popped the tomato into her mouth. It was the same vibrant color as her lips. Her teeth sank into it. The juice squirted inside her mouth.

"The truth of the matter is, Eddy darlin', I ran out of cash. The automatic teller said it couldn't give me any money 'cause my account's overdrawn. So," she said, raising her arms over her head and stretching languorously, "I came to my best friend for a little loan."

"How little?"

"A hundred bucks?"

"I'll give you twenty just to get rid of you." He withdrew a bill from his pants pocket and tossed it into her lap.

"Twenty!"

"That'll buy you enough gas to get home."

"With nothing left over."

"If you want more, you could get it from your old man. He's in room twelve-fifteen."

"Do you think he'd be pleased to see me? Especially if I told him I'd just come from your room?"

Not deigning to answer, Eddy consulted his watch. "If I were you, I'd start home before it gets any later. Be careful driving back." He headed for the door to let her out.

"I'm hungry. Since you've been so stingy with your loan, I won't be able to afford supper. I believe that entitles me to some of this sandwich." She took a wedge of the triple-decker sandwich from the plate and bit into it.

"Help yourself." He pulled a straight chair from beneath the table, sat down, and began eating a wedge of the sandwich. He perused one of the computer readouts while he chewed.

Fancy slapped at it, knocking it out of his hand. "Don't you dare ignore me, you bastard."

The glint in his eyes looked dangerous. "I didn't invite you here, you little whore. I don't want you here. If you don't like it here, you're welcome to leave any time—the sooner the better—and good riddance."

"Oh, Eddy, don't talk like that."

Her knees landed on the carpet as she scooted out of the chair. Suddenly contrite, she walked forward on them until she reached him. She stretched her arms up and slipped her hands inside his shirt, laying them on his bare chest. "Don't be mean to me. I love you."

"Cut it out, Fancy."

His request went unheeded. She wedged herself between his knees and kissed his stomach. "I love you so much." Her mouth and tongue moved avidly over his sleek, hairless belly. "I know you love me, too."

He grunted with involuntary pleasure as her long nails lightly scratched his nipples. She unbuckled his belt and unfastened his trousers.

"Jesus," he moaned when she lifted his hard flesh out of his underwear. His fingers dove into her wealth of blond hair. He roughly twisted bunches of it around his knuckles. From above, he watched her red, red lips slide down over his stiff organ. Her mouth was avaricious, without temperance, modesty, or conscience—an amoral mouth that had never been denied or disciplined.

He gasped her name twice. She raised her head and appealed to him, "Love me, Eddy, please."

He struggled to his feet, drawing her up with him, against him. Their mouths met in a carnal kiss. While her hands worked frantically to get his shirt off, he reached beneath the tube for her panties. Flimsy things, they came apart in his hands.

She cried out with surprise and pain when he crammed two fingers up inside her, but she rode them with crude pleasure. She had already shoved his trousers and underwear past his knees. He pushed them to his ankles and walked out of them as he lifted her to straddle his lap.

Together they fell onto the bed. He shoved up her dress and buried his face in the delta of her body while she wormed her way out of the stretchy tube. Before she had even gotten the dress over her head completely, he began squeezing her breasts, sucking and biting and twisting her nipples.

Fancy writhed beneath him, exulting in his rowdy foreplay. She raked her nails down his back and dug them into his buttocks hard enough to draw blood. He cursed her, called her ugly gutter names. When she drew back her knees, the stiletto heel of her shoe cut a jagged, six-inch gash into the bedspread, but neither noticed or would have cared.

Eddy splayed her thighs wide and thrust into her with enough impetus to drive her into the headboard. His body was already slick with sweat when she wrapped her limbs around him and matched his frenzied bucking. Their bodies slammed together, again and again.

Eddy's face contorted with a grimace of ecstasy. Arching his back, he put all his strength behind his final lunge. Fancy climaxed simultaneously.

"God, that was great!" she sighed as they rolled apart moments later.

She recovered first, sat up, and frowned at the sticky moisture on her inner thighs. She left the bed in search of the small purse she had brought in with her. She took from it a package of condoms and tossed it at him. "Use one of these next time."

"Who says there'll be a next time?"

Fancy, who was unabashedly admiring her naked body in the dresser mirror, gave his reflection an arch smile. "I'm gonna be black and blue tomorrow." She proudly touched the teeth marks on her breasts like they were small trophies. "I can already feel the bruises."

"Don't let on like you're bothered by it. You get off on being punished."

"I didn't hear you complaining, Mr. Paschal."

Still in her heels and bracelets, she strutted to the table and inspected the remnants of the tray. There was nothing left of the sundae except a puddle of white foam muddied by chocolate syrup, with a cherry floating on top.

"Oh, piss," she muttered, "the ice cream's melted."

From the bed, Eddy began to laugh.

Avery woke up before Tate. The room was deeply shadowed. It was still very early, but she knew she wouldn't go back to sleep. She tiptoed into the bathroom and showered. He was still asleep when she came out.

She took the ice bucket and the room key with her and slipped out the door in her robe. Tate enjoyed jogging every morning, even when he was out of town. When he returned, he consumed quarts of ice water. It wasn't always easy to come by in a hotel. She had started having it waiting there for him when he returned from his jog, hot and dehydrated.

She filled the bucket from the ice machine down the hall and was on her way back to their room when another door opened. Fancy stepped out and quietly closed the door behind her. She turned toward the elevators, but drew up short when she saw Avery.

Avery was shocked by the girl's appearance. Her hair was hopelessly tangled. What was left of her makeup was smudged and streaked. Her lips were bruised and swollen. There were scratches on her neck and across her chest, none of which she had made an attempt to hide. In fact, after recovering from her initial shock of seeing Avery, she defiantly tossed back her hair and threw out her chest to better display her wounds. "Good morning, Aunt Carole." Her sweet smile was in vile contrast to her debauched appearance.

Avery flattened herself against the corridor wall, at a loss for words. Fancy swept past her. She smelled unwashed and used. Avery shuddered with disgust.

The elevator arrived almost immediately after Fancy

summoned it. Before stepping into it, she shot Avery a gloating smile over her bare, bruised shoulder.

For several seconds Avery stared at the elevator's closed doors, then looked toward the room Fancy had come out of, although she already knew who it belonged to.

Tate was wrong about his best friend. Eddy wasn't as scrupulous as Tate believed. Nor was he as bright.

TWENTY-SEVEN

From Houston the campaign went to Waco, and from Waco to El Paso, where Tate was the undisputed champion of the Hispanic voters. The Rutledges were received like visiting royalty. At the airport, Avery was handed a huge bouquet of fresh flowers. "*Señora Rutledge, como está?*" one of their greeters asked.

"*Muy bien, gracias. Y usted? Como se llama?*"

Her smile over the cordial welcome faltered when the man turned away and she happened to lock gazes with Tate.

"When did you learn to speak Spanish?"

For several heartbeats, Avery couldn't think of a credible lie in any language. She had minored in Spanish in college and was still comfortable with it. Tate spoke it fluently. It had never occurred to her to wonder if Carole had spoken it or not.

"I . . . I wanted to surprise you."

"I'm surprised."

"The Hispanic vote is so important," she continued, limping through her explanation. "I thought it would help if I could at least swap pleasantries, so I've been studying it on the sly."

For once, Avery was glad they were surrounded by people. Otherwise, Tate might have pressed her for details on where and when she had acquired her knowledge of Spanish. Thankfully, no one else had overheard their conversation. Tate was the only one she could trust completely.

Being with Jack, Eddy, and a few of the campaign volunteers as they traveled from city to city had provided her with no more clues as to who Carole's coconspirator was.

Carefully placed questions had revealed little. Innocently, she had asked Jack how he had managed to get into the ICU the night she regained consciousness. He had looked at her blankly. "What the hell are you talking about?"

"Never mind. Sometimes the sequence of events still confuses me."

He was either innocent or an adroit liar.

She had tried the same ploy with Eddy. He had answered by saying, "I'm not family. What would I be doing in the ICU?"

Making threats on Tate's life, she had wanted to say.

She couldn't say that, so she had mumbled something about her confusion and let it go at that, turning up nothing in the way of opportunity for either of them.

She hadn't been luckier in discerning a motive. Even when Tate disagreed with his confidants and advisers, as he often did, they all seemed devoted to him and his success at the polls.

In lieu of a campaign contribution, a private businessman had loaned the entourage his private jet. As they flew from El Paso to Odessa, where Tate was scheduled to speak to independent oil men, the key personnel aired some of their differences.

"At least talk to them, Tate." Eddy was being his most persuasive. "It won't hurt to listen to their ideas."

"I won't like them."

The argument over whether or not to hire professional campaign strategists was becoming a frequent one. Weeks earlier, Eddy had suggested retaining a public relations firm that specialized in getting candidates elected to public office. Tate had been vehemently opposed to the idea and remained so.

"How do you know you won't like their ideas until you've heard what they are?" Jack asked.

"If the voters can't elect me for what I am—"

"The voters, the voters," Eddy repeated scoffingly. "The voters don't know shit from Shinola. What's more, they don't want to. They're lazy and apathetic. They want somebody to tell them who to vote for. They want it drummed into their feeble little minds so they won't have to make a decision on their own."

"Great confidence you're showing in the American public, Eddy."

"I'm not the idealist, Tate. You are."

"Thank God I am. Rather that than a cynic. I believe that people do care," he shouted. "They do listen to the issues. They respond to straight talk. I want to get the issues across to the voters without having to filter the language and phraseology through some bullshitting P.R. jargon."

"Okay, okay." Eddy patted the air between them. "Since that subject is a sore spot, let's table it for now and talk about the Hispanics."

"What about them?"

"Next time you're addressing an audience of them, don't lean so hard on their integrating into our society."

"*Our* society?"

"I'm thinking like an Anglo voter now."

"It's important that they integrate into American society," Tate argued, not for the first time. "That's the only way we can keep society from being distinguished as yours, ours, or theirs. Haven't you been listening to my speeches?"

"Stress that they maintain their own customs."

"I did. I said that. Didn't I say that?" he asked everyone within hearing distance.

"He said that." It was Avery who spoke up. Eddy ignored her.

"I just think it's important that you don't broadcast the message that they should give up their culture in favor of Anglo America's."

"If they live here, Eddy—if they become citizens of this country—they've got to assume some of the customs, primarily the English language."

Eddy was undeterred. "See, the Anglos don't like hearing that their society is going to be invaded by the Hispanics, any better than the Hispanics like having Anglo customs crammed down their throat, including a new language. Get elected first and then make a point of that integration bit, okay? And try to avoid addressing the drug trafficking problem that exists between Texas and Mexico."

"I agree," Jack said. "When you're a senator you can do something about it. Why wave the drug problem like a red flag now? It gives everybody room to criticize that you're either too harsh or too soft."

Tate laughed with disbelief and spread his hands wide. "I'm running for the U.S. Senate, and I'm not supposed to have an opinion on how to handle the illegal flow of drugs into my own state?"

"Of course you're supposed to have an opinion," Jack said, as though he were humoring a child.

"Just don't bring up your plans to remedy the problem unless specifically asked to. Now, as for this Odessa crowd," Eddy said, consulting his notes.

Eddy was never without notes. Watching him organize them, Avery studied his hands. Had those hands inflicted the scratches and bruises on Fancy, or had she come to him for refuge after another cowboy had worked her over?

"For God's sake, try to be on time to every engagement."

"I explained why we were late to that breakfast speech this morning. Carole had been trying to reach Mom and Dad, and finally caught them at home. They wanted to know everything that was going on, then we each had to talk to Mandy."

Eddy and Jack looked at her. As always, she felt their unspoken criticism, although she had done her best not to cause them any inconvenience on the trip. Out of spite, she said to Jack, "Dorothy Rae and Fancy sent you their love."

"Oh, well, thanks."

She slid a glance at Eddy when she mentioned Fancy's name. His eyes focused on her sharply, but he returned his attention to Tate. "Before we land, get rid of that tie."

"What's the matter with it?"

"It looks like shit, that's what's the matter with it."

For once, Avery sided with Eddy. Tate's necktie wasn't the most attractive one she'd ever seen, but she resented Eddy being so tactless about pointing it out.

"Here, switch with me," Jack suggested, tugging at the knot of his tie.

"No, yours is worse," Eddy said with characteristic candor. "Switch with me."

"Fuck you both and fuck the tie," Tate said. He flopped back in the airplane's plush seat. "Leave me alone." Resting his head on the cushion, he closed his eyes, effectively shutting out everybody.

Avery applauded him for telling them off, even though he had shut her out, too. Since the night in Houston when they had come so close to making love, Tate had taken even greater strides to keep his distance from her. That wasn't always easy because they had to share a bathroom, if not a bed. They went to ridiculous pains to avoid being seen unclothed. They never touched. When they spoke, they usually snapped at each other like two animals who had been sharing the same cage for too long.

Tate's even breathing could soon be heard over the drone of the airplane's engines. He could fall asleep almost instantly, sleep for several minutes, and wake up refreshed—a skill he had developed while in Vietnam, he had told her. She liked watching him sleep and often did so during the night when she found her mind too troubled to give over to unconsciousness.

"Do something."

Eddy had leaned across the narrow aisle of the airplane and roused her from her woolgathering. He and Jack were glaring at her like interrogators. "About what?"

"About Tate."

"What do you want me to do? Start picking out his neckties?"

"Convince him to let me retain that P.R. firm."

"Don't you feel that you're doing an adequate job, Eddy?" she asked coolly.

Belligerently, he thrust his face close to hers. "You think I'm ruthless? Those guys wouldn't take any of your crap."

"What crap?" she shot back.

"Like your screening Tate's calls."

"If you're referring to last night, he was already asleep when you phoned. He needed the rest. He was exhausted."

"When I want to talk to him, I want to talk to him right then," he said, jabbing the space between them. "Got that, Carole? Now, about these professionals—"

"He doesn't want them. He thinks they build a phony, plastic image and so do I."

"Nobody asked you," Jack said.

"When I have an opinion about my husband's campaign, I'll bloody well express it, and you can go to the devil if you don't like it!"

"Do you want to be a senator's wife or not?"

A silent moment elapsed while they collectively cooled their tempers. Eddy went on in a conciliatory tone, "Do whatever it takes to get Tate out of this rotten, short-tempered mood, Carole. It's self-destructive."

"The crowds don't know he's in a foul mood."

"But the volunteers do."

"Jack's right," Eddy said. "Several have noticed and commented on it. It's demoralizing. They want their hero on top of the world and radiating a lust for life, not moping around. Get him right with the world, Carole." Having concluded his pep talk, Eddy resumed his seat and went back to scanning his notes.

Jack frowned at her. "You're the one who's put him in this blue funk. You're the only one who can get him out. Don't play like you don't know how, because we all know better."

The heated exchange left Avery feeling frustrated and unable to do anything about a bad situation they clearly blamed on her.

It was a relief to land and leave the compact jet. She plastered on a smile for the crowd that had gathered to meet them. Her smile dissipated, however, when she spotted Van Lovejoy among the press photographers. He turned up everywhere Tate Rutledge went these days. His presence never failed to unnerve Avery.

As soon as it was feasible, she stepped into the back-ground, where it would be harder for the lens of a camera to find her. From that vantage point, she looked out over the crowd, constantly on the alert for anyone looking suspicious. This crowd was largely comprised of media, Rutledge supporters, and curious onlookers.

A tall man standing at the back of the crowd arrested her attention, only because he looked familiar. He was dressed in a tailored western suit and cowboy hat, and she first took him for one of the oil men Tate was there to address.

She couldn't pinpoint where or when she had seen him before, but she didn't think he'd been dressed as he was now. She would have remembered the cowboy hat. But she had seen him recently, she was sure of that. The barbecue in Houston, perhaps? Before she could cite the time and place, he faded into the throng and was lost from sight.

Avery was hustled toward the waiting limousine. At her side, the mayor's wife was gushing like a fountain. She tried to pay attention to what the other woman was saying, but her mind had been diverted by the gray-haired man who had so adroitly disappeared an instant after they'd made eye contact.

As soon as the immediate area was cleared of the senatorial candidate, his entourage, and the media jackals, the well-dressed cowboy emerged from the telephone cubicle. Tate Rutledge was an easy target to follow through the airport. They were both tall, but while Tate wanted to be seen, the cowboy prided himself on his ability to merge into a crowd and remain virtually invisible.

For such a large man, he moved with grace and ease. His carriage alone commanded respect from anyone who happened to fall into his path. At the car rental office, the clerk was exceptionally polite. His bearing seemed to demand good service. He laid down a credit card. It had a false name on it, but it cleared the electronic check system it was run through.

He thanked the clerk as she dropped the tagged key into his hand. "Do you need a map of the area, sir?"

"No, thank you. I know where I'm going."

He carried his clothes in one bag, packed efficiently and

economically. The contents were untraceable and disposable; so was the rented sedan, if that became necessary.

The airport was located midway between Midland and Odessa. He headed toward the westernmost city, following the limousine carrying Rutledge at a safe, discreet distance.

He mustn't get too close. He was almost certain Carole Rutledge had picked him out of the crowd while her husband was shaking hands with his local supporters. It was unlikely that she had recognized him from that distance, but in his business, nothing could be taken for granted.

TWENTY-EIGHT

A king-size bed.

"I don't envy the women of Texas. Like the women of every state in this nation, they're faced with serious problems— problems that require immediate solutions. Daily solutions. Problems such as quality child care."

Even as Tate waxed eloquent at a luncheon meeting of professional women, his mind was on that one large bed in the room at the Adolphus Hotel.

After landing at Love Field, they had rushed to check in, freshen up, and make the luncheon on time. The hectic schedule hadn't dimmed his one prevalent thought: tonight he would be sharing a bed with Carole.

"Some corporations, many of which I'm pleased to say are located here in Dallas, have started day-care programs for their employees. But these companies with vision and innovative ideas are still in the minority. I want to see something done about that."

Over the applause, Tate was hearing in his mind the accommodating bellman ask, "Will there be anything else, Mr. Rutledge?"

That's when he should have said, "Yes. I'd prefer a room with separate beds."

The applause died down. Tate covered his extended pause by taking a sip of water. From the corner of his eye, he could see Carole looking up at him curiously from her place at the head table. She looked more tempting than the rich dessert he had declined following lunch. He would decline her, too.

"Equal pay for equal work is a tired subject," he said into the microphone. "The American public is weary of hearing about it. But I'm going to keep harping on it until those who are opposed to it are worn down. Obliterated. Banished."

The applause was thunderous. Tate smiled disarmingly and tried to avoid looking up the skirt of the woman in the front row who was offering him a spectacular view.

While they had scrambled to get ready in the limited time allowed, he'd caught an accidental glimpse of his wife through a crack in the partially opened bathroom door.

She was wearing a pastel brassiere. Pastel hosiery. Pastel garter belt. She had a saucy ass. Soft thighs.

She had leaned into the mirror and dusted her nose with a powder puff. He'd gotten stiff and had stayed that way through the wilted salad, mystery meat, and cold green beans.

Clearing his throat now, he said, "The crimes against women are of major concern to me. The number of rapes is increasing each year, but the number of offenders who are prosecuted and brought to trial is lamentably low.

"Domestic violence has been around as long as there have been families. Thankfully, this outrage has finally come to the conscience of our society. That's good. But is enough being done to reverse this rising trend?

"Mr. Dekker suggests that counseling is the answer. Toward reaching a final solution, yes, I agree. But I submit that police action is a necessary first step. Legal separation from the source and guaranteed safety for the victims—most frequently women and children—is mandatory. Then and only then should counseling and reconciliation be addressed."

When the applause subsided, he moved into the final

fervent paragraphs of his speech. As soon as this meeting concluded, they were scheduled to go to a General Motors assembly plant in neighboring Arlington, to mingle with the workers as they changed shifts.

After that they would return to the hotel, watch the evening news, peruse the newspapers, and dress for the formal dinner being held in his honor at Southfork. And late tonight, they would return to the king–size bed.

"I'll be expecting your support in November. Thank you very much."

He received an enthusiastic standing ovation. He signaled for Carole to join him at the podium. She took her place beside him. He slid his arm around her waist, as expected. What wasn't expected was the thrill he got from having her that close, feeling small and feminine against his side. She tilted her head back and smiled up at him with what appeared to be admiration and love.

She could put on a hell of an act.

It was almost half an hour later before Eddy was able to separate them from the adoring crowd that was reluctant to let them go. The September heat struck them like a blast furnace as they exited the meeting hall.

"Jack is holding a call for me back there," Eddy explained as he herded them toward a car parked at the curb. "Some glitch about tonight. Nothing serious. We'll follow you out to the assembly plant. If you don't leave right now you won't make it in time. Know where it is?"

"Off I-30, right?" Tate shrugged off his suit jacket and tossed it into the backseat of the rented car.

"Right." Eddy detailed the directions. "You can't miss it. It'll be on your right." He glanced at Carole. "I'll call you a cab back to the hotel."

"I'm going with Tate." She slid beneath his arm into the passenger seat.

"I think—"

"It's okay, Eddy," Tate said. "She can come with me."

"She'll stick out like a sore thumb. That's no ladies' club out there."

"Tate wants me there and I want to go," she argued.

"All right," he conceded, but Tate could tell he was none

too pleased. "We'll catch up with you shortly." He closed
Carole's passenger door and they sped off.

"He never passes up an opportunity to make me feel like
a useless appendage, does he?" she said. "I'm surprised he
approved of you marrying me."

"He didn't have a chance. We couldn't track him down,
remember?"

"Of course I remember," she said crossly. "I only
meant . . . oh, never mind. I don't want to talk about Eddy."

"I know he's not one of your favorite people. Sometimes
his nagging can be a real pain in the ass. But his instincts
are rarely wrong."

"I trust his instincts," she said. "I'm not so sure I trust
him."

"What's he ever done to make you mistrust him?"

She averted her head and gazed out the windshield.
"Nothing, I guess. Lord, it's hot."

Leaning as far forward as the seat belt would allow, she
pulled off her suit jacket. Beneath it was a matching silk
blouse. Beneath that, her breasts filled up the lacy yellow
brassiere he'd seen while peeping through the bathroom
door.

"You were brilliant, Tate," she remarked. "Not conde-
scending or patronizing. They wouldn't have condoned that.
As it was, they were eating out of your hand." She glanced
at him sideways. "Especially the one in the bright blue
dress on the front row. What color were her panties?"

"She wasn't wearing any."

The blunt retort knocked the props out from under her.
She hadn't been expecting it. Her teasing smile evaporated.
Again, she turned her head forward and stared through the
windshield.

He could tell she was wounded. Well, that was fair,
wasn't it? He'd been nursing this ache in his groin for days.
Why should he be the only one to suffer? An imp was sitting
on his shoulder goading him to make her as miserable as he
was.

"I avoided the abortion issue. Did you notice?"

"No."

"I didn't know what to say. Maybe I should have called

you to the lectern. You could have given us a firsthand account of what it's like.''

When she faced him, there were tears in her eyes. "I told you I'd never had an abortion.''

"But I'll never know for certain which time you were lying, will I?''

"Why are you being this way, Tate?''

Because there is a *king-size bed* in our room, he thought. Before I share it with you, I've got to remind myself of all the reasons I despise you.

He didn't say that, of course.

He took the cloverleaf at the highway interchange at an indiscriminate speed. Once again on a straightaway, he speeded up even more. If it hadn't been for some quick thinking and daredevil driving, he would have overshot the exit.

There was a delegation waiting for them at the gate to the automotive plant. Tate parked a distance away so he'd have time to collect himself before having to be civil. He felt like a brawl. He wanted to slug it out. He didn't feel like smiling and promising to solve labor's problems when he couldn't even solve his own marital dilemma. He didn't want any part of his wife except *that* part, and he wanted it with every masculine fiber of his body.

"Put your jacket back on," he ordered her, even though he was removing his tie and rolling up his shirtsleeves.

"I intend to," she replied coolly.

"Good. Your nipples are poking against your blouse. Or is that what you had in mind?''

"Go to hell," she said sweetly as she shoved open her car door.

He had to give her credit. She recovered admirably from his stinging insults and conversed intelligently with the union bosses who were there to greet them. Eddy and Jack arrived about the time the shift changed and the doors of the plant began to disgorge workers. Those coming to work converged on them from the parking lot. Tate shook hands with everyone he could reach.

Each time he glanced at Carole, she was campaigning just as diligently as he. She listened intently to whomever was speaking with her. As Eddy had said, dressed in her yellow silk, she did stick out in this crowd. Her dark hair reflected the sunlight like a mirror. Her flawless face didn't distance people, but attracted women workers as well as men.

Tate looked for something to criticize, but could find nothing. She reached for dirty hands and gave them a friendly shake. Her smile was unflagging, even though the crowd was rambunctious and the heat unbearable.

And she was the first one to reach his side when something struck him and he went down.

TWENTY-NINE

Avery happened to be watching Tate when his head suddenly snapped backward. Reflexively, he raised his hand to his forehead, reeled, then fell.

"No!"

There were only a few yards separating them, but the crowd was dense. It seemed to take forever for her to push her way through the people. She ruined her stockings and skinned her knees when she landed on the hot pavement beside Tate.

"Tate! Tate!" Blood was oozing from a wound on the side of his head. "Get a doctor, somebody. Eddy! Jack! Somebody do something. He's hurt!"

"I'm all right." He struggled to sit up. Swaying dizzily, he groped for support, found Avery's arm, and held on tight.

Since Tate could speak and make an effort to sit up, she was sure that the bullet had only grazed him and not penetrated his skull. She cushioned his head on her breasts. His blood ran warm and wet down the front of her clothing, but she didn't even notice.

"Jesus, what happened?" Eddy finally managed to elbow his way through the crowd to them. "Tate?"

"I'm okay," he mumbled. Gradually, Avery released her hold on his head. "Give me a handkerchief."

"They're calling an ambulance."

"No need to. Something hit me." He glanced around him, searching through a forest of feet and legs. "That," he said, pointing to the broken beer bottle lying nearby on the pavement.

"Who the hell threw it?"

"Did you see him?" Avery was prepared to do battle with the attacker.

"No, I didn't see anything. Give me a handkerchief," he repeated. Eddy took one from his pocket. Avery snatched it from him and pressed it to the bleeding gash near Tate's hairline. "Thanks. Now help me up."

"I'm not sure you should try and stand," she cautioned.

"I'm okay." He smiled unsteadily. "Just help me get up off my ass, okay?"

"I could throttle you for joking at a time like this."

"Sorry. Somebody beat you to it."

As she and Eddy helped him to his feet, Jack ran up, huffing for breath. "A couple of the workers don't like your politics. The police have arrested them."

There was a commotion at the far corner of the parking lot. Anti-Rutledge picket signs bobbed up and down like pogo sticks. "Rutledge is a pinko fag," read one. "Vote for a bleeding liberal? You're bleeding crazy!" read another. And "Rutledge is a rutting commie."

"Let's go," Eddy ordered.

"No." Tate's lips were stiff and white from a combination of anger and pain. "I came here to shake hands and ask for votes, and that's what I'm going to do. A couple of bottle throwers aren't going to stop me."

"Tate, Eddy's right." Avery clutched his arm tightly. "This is a police matter now."

She had died a thousand deaths on her headlong rush to reach him. She had thought, "This is it. This is what I wanted to prevent, and I have failed to." The incident brought home to her just how vulnerable he was. What kind of protection could she offer him? If someone wanted to kill him badly enough, he could. There wouldn't be a damn thing she or anyone else could do to prevent it.

"Hello, I'm Tate Rutledge, running for the U.S. Senate." Stubbornly, Tate turned to the man standing nearest him. The UAW member looked down at Tate's extended hand, then glanced around uncertainly at his co-workers. Finally, he shook Tate's hand. "I would appreciate your vote in November," he told the man before moving to the next. "Hi, I'm Tate Rutledge."

Despite his advisers, Tate moved through the crowd, shaking hands with his right hand, holding the blood-stained handkerchief to his temple with the left. Avery had never loved him so much.

Nor had she ever been more afraid for him.

"How do I look?"

Tate asked for her opinion only after dubiously consulting his reflection in the mirror. He'd remained on the parking lot of the assembly plant until those going off duty had left for home and those reporting to work had gone inside.

Only then had he allowed Eddy and her to push him into the backseat of the car and rush him to the nearest emergency room. Jack, who followed in the second car, joined them there, where a resident physician took three stitches and covered them with a small, square white bandage.

Avery had placed a call to Nelson and Zee from the emergency room, knowing that if they heard about the incident on the news they would be worried. They insisted on speaking with Tate. He joked about the injury, although Avery saw him gratefully accept the painkiller the nurse gave him.

A horde of reporters was waiting for them in the lobby of the Adolphus when they returned. They surged forward en masse. "Be sure they get pictures of the blood on your dress," Eddy had told her out the side of his mouth.

For that insensitive remark, she could easily have scratched his eyes out. "You bastard."

"I'm just doing my job, Carole," he said blandly. "Making the most of every situation—even the bad ones."

She had been too incensed to offer a comeback. Besides, they were battling their way through microphones and cameras toward the elevators. At the door to their room, she confronted Jack and Eddy, who were about to follow them inside.

"Tate is going to lie down and let that pain pill take effect," she told them, barring any arguments to the contrary. "I'm going to tell the switchboard not to put any calls through."

"He's got to make some kind of statement."

"You write it," she said to Jack. "You would rewrite whatever he said anyway. Just remember what he told us on the drive back. He doesn't intend to press charges against the man who threw the bottle, although he abhors violence and considers it a base form of self-expression. Nor does he blame the UAW as a group for the actions of a few members. I'm sure you can elaborate on that."

"I'll pick you up here at seven-thirty," Eddy said as he turned to go. Over his shoulder, he added peremptorily, "Sharp."

Tate had dozed for a while, then watched the news before getting up to shower and dress. Now he turned away from the bureau mirror and faced her, lifting his hands away from his sides. "Well?

Tilting her head, she gave him a thoughtful appraisal. "Very rakish." His hair dipped attractively over the wound. "The bandage adds a cavalier dash to your very proper tuxedo."

"Well, that's good," he muttered, tentatively touching the bandage, "because it hurts like bloody hell."

Avery moved nearer and gazed up at him with concern. "We don't have to go."

"Eddy would shit a brick."

"Let him. Everyone else would understand. If Michael Jackson can cancel a concert because of a stomach virus, disappointing thousands of adoring fans, you can cancel a dinner and disappoint a couple hundred."

"But have Michael Jackson's fans paid two hundred dollars a plate?" he quipped. "He can afford to cancel. I can't."

"At least take another pill."

He shook his head. "If I go, I've got to be in full command of my faculties."

"Lord, you're stubborn. Just like you were about staying there this afternoon."

"It made great video on the evening news."

She frowned at him. "You sound like Eddy now. You're running for public office, not best target of the year for every kook with a grudge against the system. You shouldn't place your life in jeopardy just because it makes for good film at six and ten."

"Listen, it's only because I'm running for public office that I didn't go after that son of a bitch who threw the bottle and beat the crap out of him myself."

"Ah, that's what I like. A candidate who really speaks his mind."

They laughed together, but after a moment their laughter died. Tate's warm gaze held hers. "That's still my favorite dress. You look terrific."

"Thank you." She was wearing the black cocktail dress he had admired before.

"I, uh, behaved like a jerk this afternoon."

"You said some hurtful things."

"I know," he admitted, blowing out a gust of air. "I meant to. Partially because—"

A knock sounded. "Seven-thirty," Eddy called through the door.

Tate looked annoyed. Avery, at the height of frustration, yanked up her evening bag and marched toward the door. Her senses were sizzling. Her nerves were shot. She felt like screaming.

She almost did when one of the first people she spotted among the crowd at Southfork was the man she'd noticed once before, at the Midland/Odessa Airport.

The ranch house made famous by the television series "Dallas" was ablaze with lights. Since this was a special night, the house was open and partygoers were allowed to walk through it. The actual dinner was being held in the adjacent barnlike building that was frequently leased for large parties.

The turnout was better than expected. As soon as they arrived they were informed that it was a capacity crowd. Many had offered to pay more than two hundred dollars for the opportunity to attend and hear Tate speak.

"No doubt as a result of that fantastic news story today," Eddy said. "All the networks and local channels led with it on their six o'clock telecasts." He flashed Avery a complacent smile.

She slid her arm through the crook of Tate's elbow, an indication that he was more important to her than any news story, or even the election itself. Eddy's grin merely widened.

Avery was liking him less every day. His inappropriate dalliance with Fancy was reason enough for her to distrust his Boy Scout cleanliness.

Tate, however, trusted him implicitly. That's why she hadn't mentioned seeing Fancy coming out of Eddy's room, even when Tate had provided her an opportunity to. She could sense a softening in Tate's attitude toward her and didn't want it jeopardized by bad-mouthing his trusted best friend.

She tried to put aside Eddy's remark and all other worries as she walked into the cavernous building with Tate. He would need her to bolster him tonight. The injury was probably causing him more discomfort than he let on. An enthusiastic local supporter approached them. He bussed Avery on the cheek and pumped Tate's hand. It was as she tossed back her head to laugh at a comment he made that she caught sight of the tall, gray-haired man on the fringes of the crowd.

She did a double take, but almost instantly lost sight of him. Surely she was mistaken. The man at the airport had been wearing a western suit and Stetson. This man was dressed in formal clothing. They were probably just coincidental look-alikes.

While trying to appear attentive to the people approaching them to be introduced, she continued to scan the crowd, but didn't catch sight of the man again before dinner. From the head table it was difficult to see into the darkest corners of the enormous hall. Even though it was a formal dinner, people were milling about. Frequently, she had television lights blindingly trained on her.

"Not hungry?" Tate leaned toward her and nodded down at her virtually untouched plate.

"Too much excitement."

Actually, she was sick with worry and considered warning Tate of the danger he was in. She regarded the bandage on his forehead as an obscenity. Next time it might not be an empty beer bottle. It might be a bullet. And it might be deadly.

"Tate," she asked hesitantly, "have you seen a tall, gray-haired man?"

He laughed shortly. "About fifty of them."

"One in particular. I thought he looked familiar."

"Maybe he belongs in one of those memory pockets that hasn't opened up for you yet."

"Yes, maybe."

"Say, are you all right?"

Forcing a smile, she raised her lips to his ear and whispered, "The candidate's wife has to go to the ladies' room. Would that be kosher?"

"More kosher than the consequences if she doesn't."

He stood to assist her out of her chair. She excused herself. At the end of the dais, a waiter took her hand and helped her down the shaky portable steps. As unobtrusively as possible, she searched the crowd for the man with gray hair while making her way toward an exit.

As she cleared the doorway, she felt both frustrated and relieved. She was almost positive he had been the same man she'd spotted in West Texas. On the other hand, there were tens of thousands of tall Texans with gray hair. Feeling a little foolish over her paranoia, she smiled to herself ruefully.

Her smile congealed when someone moved in close behind her and whispered menacingly, "Hello, Avery."

THIRTY

At midnight, the McDonald's restaurant at the corner of Commerce and Griffin in downtown Dallas looked like a goldfish bowl. It was brightly lit. Through the plate glass windows, everyone inside was as clearly visible as actors standing on center stage.

The cashier was taking an order from a somber loner. A wino was sleeping it off in one of the booths. Two giddy teenage couples were squirting catsup on each other.

Breathless from having walked three blocks from the hotel, Avery approached the restaurant cautiously. Her formal attire distinguished her from everyone else who was out and about. It was foolhardy for a woman to be walking the downtown streets alone at this hour anyway.

From across the street, she peered into the capsulized brilliance of the dining room. She saw him, sitting alone in a booth. Fortunately, the booth was adjacent to the windows. As soon as the traffic light changed, she hurried across the broad avenue, her high heels clacking on the pavement.

"Mmm-mmm, mama, lookin' good!" A black youth licentiously wagged his tongue at her. With punches and guffaws, his two chums congratulated him. On the corner, two women, one with orange hair, the other with burgundy, competed for the attentions of a man in tight leather pants. He was leaning against the traffic light post, looking bored, until Avery walked by. He gave her a carnivorous once-over. The orange-haired woman spun around, propped her hands on her hips, and shouted at Avery, "Hey, bitch, keep your ass outta his face or I'll kill you."

Avery ignored them all as she walked past, moving along

the sidewalk toward the booth. When she drew even with it, she knocked on the window. Van Lovejoy looked up from his chocolate milk shake, spotted her, and grinned. He indicated the other bench of the booth. Avery angrily and vehemently shook her head no and sternly pointed down at the grimy sidewalk beneath her black satin shoes.

He took his sweet time. She impatiently followed his unhurried progress through the restaurant, out the door, and around the corner, so that by the time he reached her, she was simmering with rage.

"What the hell are you up to, Van?" she demanded.

Feigning innocence, he curled both lanky hands in toward his chest. "*Moi*?"

"Did we have to meet here? At this time of night?"

"Would you rather I had come to your room—the room you're sharing with another woman's husband?" In the ensuing silence, he casually lit a joint. After two tokes, he offered it to Avery. She slapped his hand aside.

"You can't imagine the danger you placed me in by speaking to me tonight."

He leaned against the plate glass window. "I'm all ears."

"Van." Miserably, she caught her head with her hand and massaged her temples. "It's too difficult to explain—especially here." The women at the corner were loudly swapping obscenities while the man in leather cleaned his fingernails with a pocketknife. "I slipped out of the hotel. If Tate discovers that I'm gone—"

"Does he know you're not his wife?"

"No! And he mustn't."

"How come?"

"It'll take a while to explain."

"I'm under no deadline."

"But I am," she cried, clutching his skinny arm. "Van, you can't tell anybody. Lives would be put in danger."

"Yeah, Rutledge just might be pissed off enough to kill you."

"I'm talking about Tate's life. This isn't a game, trust me. There's a lot at stake. You'll agree when I've had a chance to explain. But I can't now. I've got to get back."

"This is quite a gig, Avery. When did you decide to do it?"

"In the hospital. I was mistaken for Carole Rutledge. They had done the reconstructive operation on my face before I could tell them otherwise."

"When you could, why didn't you?"

Frantically, she groped for an expeditious way to tell him. "Ask Irish," she blurted out.

"Irish!" he croaked, choking on marijuana smoke. "That cagy son of a bitch. He knows?"

"Not until recently. I had to tell somebody."

"So that's why he sent me on this trip. I wondered why we were covering Rutledge like he was fuckin' royalty or something. It was you Irish wanted me to keep an eye on."

"I guess. I didn't know he was going to assign you this detail. I was stunned when I saw you in Houston. It was bad enough when I answered the door that day at the ranch and you were standing on the porch. Is that when you first recognized me?"

"The day you left the clinic, I noticed how Mrs. Rutledge's mannerisms in front of a camera were similar to yours. It was spooky the way she wet her lips and made that movement with her head just like you used to. After that day of taping at the ranch, I was almost convinced. Tonight I was so sure of it, I decided to let you know that I was in on your little secret."

"Oh, Lord."

"What?"

Over Van's shoulder Avery had spotted a patrolman approaching them on foot.

"Okay, what is it?" Tate asked his brother irritably.

Jack closed the door to his hotel room and shrugged out of his formal jacket. "Drink?"

"No thanks. What's up?"

The moment they entered the lobby of the Adolphus, Jack had cupped Tate's elbow and whispered that he needed to see him alone.

"What, now?"

"Now."

Tate didn't feel like holding a closed-door session with his brother tonight. The only one he wanted to speak with privately was his wife, who had been behaving strangely since their arrival at Southfork. Before that, she had been fine.

Over dinner, she had mentioned a gray-haired man— obviously someone from her past who had inconveniently showed up at the banquet. Whoever he was, he must have confronted her when she had gone to the ladies' room, because she had returned to the head table looking pale and shaken.

She'd been as jumpy as a cat for the remainder of the evening. Several times he had caught her nervously gnawing on her lower lip. When she did smile, it was phony as hell. He hadn't had an opportunity to get to the bottom of it. He wanted to now—right now.

But for the sake of harmony within the camp, he decided to humor Jack first. While they were waiting for an elevator, he had turned to her and said, "Jack wants to see me for five minutes." He shot his brother a meaningful glance that said, "No more than five minutes."

"Oh, now?" she had asked. "In that case, I'm going back to the concierge and ask for some brochures and, uh, hotel stationery to take to Mandy. I won't be long. I'll see you in the room."

The elevator had arrived. She'd dashed off. He'd gone up with Jack and Eddy. Eddy had said good night and gone to his own room, leaving the two brothers alone.

Tate waited expectantly as Jack withdrew a white envelope from the breast pocket of his tux and passed it to him. It had his name handwritten on it. He slid his index finger beneath the flap and ripped it open. After reading the message twice, he looked up at his brother from beneath his brows.

"Who gave you this?"

Jack was pouring himself a nightcap from a bottle of brandy. "Remember the lady—woman—in blue at the luncheon this afternoon? Front row."

Tate hitched his chin toward the liquor bottle. "I changed my mind." Jack handed him a drink. Tate held the note at arm's length and reread it as he polished off the brandy in one long swallow.

"Why'd she ask you to deliver it?" he asked his brother.

"I guess she didn't think it would be proper for her to deliver it herself."

"Proper?" Tate scoffed, glancing again at the brazen wording of the note.

Not even attempting to conceal his amusement, Jack asked, "May I hazard a guess what it's about?"

"Bingo."

"May I offer a suggestion?"

"No."

"It wouldn't hurt to accept her invitation. In fact, it might help."

"Has it escaped your attention that I'm married?"

"No. It also hasn't escaped my attention that your marriage isn't worth shit right now, but you wouldn't welcome my comments about either your wife or your marriage."

"That's right. I wouldn't."

"Don't get defensive, Tate. I've got your interests at heart. You know that. Take advantage of this invitation. I don't know what's going on between Carole and you." He lowered one eyelid shrewdly. "But I know what *isn't*. You're not sleeping together and haven't since long before the crash. There's not a man alive, not even you, who can function at his optimum best if his dick's unhappy."

"Speaking from experience?"

Jack lowered his head and concentrated on the swirling contents of his glass. Tate raked his fingers through his hair, wincing when it pulled against the sutured gash on his temple. "Sorry. That was uncalled for. Forgive me, Jack. It's just that I resent everybody meddling in my business."

"Comes with the territory, little brother."

"But I'm sick of it."

"It's only started. It won't end when you get into office."

Tate propped his hips against the dresser. "No, I guess not." Silently, he studied the nap of the carpet. After a moment, a small laugh started in his chest and gradually worked its way out.

"What?" Jack failed to see the humor in their conversation.

"Not too long ago, Eddy offered to find me a woman to work my frustrations out on. Where were the two of you when I was young and single and could have used a couple of good pimps?"

Jack smiled wryly. "I guess I deserve that. It's just that

you've been so uptight lately, I thought a harmless roll in the hay with a lusty, willing broad would do you good.''

''It probably would, but no thanks.'' Tate moved toward the door. ''Thanks for the drink, too.'' With his hand on the doorknob, he asked as an afterthought, ''Talked with your family recently?''

''Speaking of 'drink,' hey?''

''It just came out that way,'' Tate replied, looking chagrined.

''Don't worry about it. Yes, I talked to Dorothy Rae today. She said everything was fine. She can tell that Fancy's up to mischief, but doesn't yet know what it is.''

''God only knows.''

''Maybe God knows. Sure as hell nobody else does.''

''Good night, Jack.''

''Uh, Tate?'' He turned back. ''Since you're not interested . . .'' Tate followed his brother's gaze down to the note he still held in his hand. Jack shrugged. ''She might be willing to settle for second best.''

Tate balled up the paper and tossed it to his brother, who caught it with one hand. ''Good luck.''

Tate had already removed his jacket, tie, and cummerbund by the time he opened the door to his room. ''Carole? I know that took longer than five minutes, but . . . Carole?''

She wasn't there.

When she saw the policeman, Avery averted her head. The sequin trim on her dress seemed to glitter as brilliantly as the golden arches outside the restaurant. ''For heaven's sake, put out that cigarette,'' she said to Van. ''He'll think . . .''

''Forget it,'' her friend interrupted, smiling crookedly. ''If you were a whore, I couldn't afford you.'' He pinched out the burning tip of the joint and dropped it back into his shirt pocket.

While the policeman was busy breaking up the shouting match at the corner, Avery indicated with her head that they should slip around the corner and head back toward the Adolphus. With his slouching gait, Van fell into step beside her.

''Van, I need your promise that you won't reveal my

identity to anyone. One night next week, when we're back home, I'll arrange a meeting between Irish, you, and me. He'll want to hear about my trip anyway. I'll fill in the blanks then.''

''What do you think Dekker would pay for this information?''

Avery came to an abrupt halt. She roughly grabbed Van's arm. ''You can't! Van, please. My God, you can't.''

''Until you make me a better offer, I might.'' He threw off her hand and turned away, calling back, ''See ya, Avery.''

They were even with the hotel now, but across the street. She trotted after him and caught his arm again, swinging him around. ''You don't know how high the stakes are, Van. I'm begging you, as my friend.''

''I don't have any friends.''

''Please don't do anything until I've had a chance to explain the circumstances.''

He pulled his arm free again. ''I'll think about it. But your explanation better be damn good, or I'm cashing in.''

She watched his sauntering retreat down the sidewalk. He seemed not to have a care in the world. Her world, by contrast, had caved in. Van was holding all the aces and he knew it.

Feeling like she'd just been bludgeoned, she crossed the street toward the hotel. Just before she reached the opposite curb, she raised her head.

Tate was standing in the porte cochere, glaring at her.

THIRTY-ONE

His expression was murderous. After a few faltering steps, Avery moved toward him with the undaunted carriage of a criminal who knows the jig is up but is still unwilling to confess.

"There she is, Mr. Rutledge," the doorman said cheerfully. "I told you she would probably be back any second."

For the doorman's benefit, Tate kept his voice light. "I was getting worried, Carole." His fingers wrapped around her upper arm with the strength of a python.

He "escorted" her through the lobby. In the elevator, they faced forward, saying nothing, while anger arced between them. He unlocked the door to their room and let her precede him inside.

The security lock had a final, metallic sound when he flipped it forward. Neither reached for a light. Neither thought to. For illumination, they relied solely on the weak night-light burning in the bathroom behind a *faux* nautilus shell.

"Where the hell did you go?" Tate demanded without preamble.

"To the McDonald's on the corner. Remember, I didn't eat much dinner at the banquet. I was hungry. As long as you were with Jack, I thought—"

"Who was the guy?"

She started to play dumb, but thought better of it. He had obviously seen her with Van, but hadn't recognized him. While she was deliberating on whether to shoot straight or lie, he advanced on her. "Was he a dealer?"

Her jaw went slack with astonishment. "A drug dealer?"

"I know that on occasion you and Fancy have smoked pot. I hope to God that's all you've done, but a senatorial candidate's wife doesn't buy grass off the street from an unknown pusher, Carole. For God's sake, he could have been an undercover—"

"That was Van Lovejoy!" she shouted angrily. Obviously the name didn't ring any bells. He gave her a blank stare. "The cameraman from KTEX. He shot the video for your TV commercial. Remember?"

She knocked him aside and swept past him, moved to the dresser and began removing her jewelry, dropping the pieces onto the surface with little regard for their value or delicacy.

"What were you doing with him?"

"Walking," she said flippantly, addressing his reflection behind her own in the mirror. In the dim light he appeared dark and intimidating. She refused to be cowed. "I ran into him at McDonald's. He and the station's reporter are staying at the Holiday Inn, I believe he said." Lying was becoming easier. She was getting lots of practice. "Anyway, he chided me for walking alone and insisted on seeing me back to the hotel."

"Smart fellow. A hell of a lot smarter than you. What the hell were you thinking of to go out alone at this time of night?"

"I was hungry," she said, raising her voice.

"Ever think of room service?"

"I needed air."

"So open a window."

"What does it matter to you if I went out? You were with Jack. Jack and Eddy. Laurel and Hardy. Tweedledee and Tweedledum." She wagged her head from side to side in time to her words. "If it's not one who has something urgent to discuss with you, it's the other. One of them is always knocking on your door."

"Don't get off the subject. We're talking about you, not Jack or Eddy."

"What about me?"

"What made you so nervous tonight?"

"I wasn't nervous."

She tried to sidestep him again, but he wouldn't have it. He blocked her path and caught her by the shoulders. "Something's wrong. I know there is. What have you done this time? You'd better tell me before I find out from somebody else."

"What makes you think I've done something?"

"Because you won't look me in the eye."

"I'm avoiding you, yes. But only because I'm mad, not because I've committed what you would consider a transgression."

"That's been your routine in the past, Carole."

"Don't call me—" Avery caught herself just in time.

"Don't call you what?"

"Nothing." She hated having him address her as Carole.

"Don't call me a liar," she amended. Defiantly, she flung her head back. "And just so you'll know from me before you hear it from somebody else, Van Lovejoy was smoking a joint. He even offered it to me. I refused. Now, do I pass muster, Mr. Senator?"

Tate was furiously rocking back and forth on the balls of his feet. "Don't wander off by yourself like that again."

"Don't put me on a short leash."

"I don't care what you do, dammit," he growled, gripping her shoulders harder. "It's just not safe for you to be alone."

"Alone?" she repeated in a harsh, mirthless tone. "Alone? We're never alone."

"We're alone right now."

It occurred to them simultaneously that they were standing chest to chest. One was breathing with as much agitation as the other. Their blood was running hot and their tempers were high. Avery felt her nerves sizzle like fallen hot wires that snaked across a rain-slick street.

His arms went around her, met at the center of her back, and jerked her against him. Avery went limp with desire. Then, moving as one, their mouths came together in a ravenous kiss. She folded her arms around his neck and provocatively arched her body into his. His hands slid over her derriere and roughly drew her up high and hard against the front of his body.

Their breathing was loud. So was the rustle of their evening clothes. Their mouths twisted against each other; their tongues were too greedy to exercise finesse.

Tate walked her backward into the wall, which then served the original purpose of his hands by keeping her middle cemented to him. His fingers curved tightly around her head and held it in place while he gave her a hungry kiss.

The kiss was carnal. It had a dark soul. It touched off elemental sparks that were as exciting to Avery as the first tongues of flame were to primal man. It conveyed that much heat, that much promise.

She attacked the studs on his pleated shirt. One by one they landed soundlessly in the carpeting. She peeled the shirt wide and bared his chest. Her open mouth found the very center of it. He swore with pleasure and reached behind her for the fastenings on her dress.

They eluded his fumbling fingers. Fabric was ripped. Beads scattered. Sequins rained down. Neither was mindful of the damage. He worked the dress down her shoulders and planted a fervent kiss on the upper curve of her breast, then reached for the clasp of her strapless brassiere.

Avery panicked when it fell open. *He would know!* But his eyes were closed. His lips were his sensors, not his eyes. He kissed her breasts, stroking the tips with his tongue, drawing them into his mouth.

He needed her. She wanted him to need her. She couldn't give enough.

She tugged his cuffs over his hands without even unhooking his cuff links. He flapped his arms until he was entirely free of his shirt, then slipped his hands beneath the hem of her dress. They smoothed up her thighs, caught the elastic of her underwear, and worked it down. Then his palm was on her, his fingers inside her, and she was gasping hoarse, whimpering, wanting sounds.

"You're my wife," he said thickly. "You deserve a little better than to be banged against the wall."

He released her and stepped away. In seconds he was out of his shoes and socks, leaving his trousers in a heap on the carpet.

Avery shimmied out of her dress, kicked off her shoes, and quickly moved to the bed. The housekeeper had already turned it down. She brushed the chocolate mints off the pillow and slid between the sheets. The lacy black garter belt came off with a snap. Her stockings had barely cleared her toes when Tate reached for her.

She went willingly as he pulled her against his warm, hairy nakedness. Their mouths met for another deep, wet kiss. His sex was hard and smooth. It probed the softness of her belly, nestled in the vee of dark curls.

He cupped her breast, lifted it, ran this thumb lightly back and forth over her nipple, and applied his tongue to it. With no resistance from her, he separated her thighs. The cleft between them was soft and sensitive and creamy. She gasped several short, choppy breaths as his fingers played over her.

Then he rolled her to her back and guided his rigid erection into the moist, oval opening. Her body received him coyly because he was very large and hard and she was very small and soft. Man and woman. As it should be. His power was reduced to weakness; her vulnerability was made strong.

She marveled at the absoluteness of his possession. It was invasive but sweet, unencumbered yet yearning. Her back and throat arched in total surrender. He went farther, touched deeper, reached higher than she believed possible.

Above her, he was straining to withhold his climax, to sustain the pleasure, but that was asking too much of his body, which had been imprisoned by self-imposed abstinence for so long.

He sank into her only a few times before he climaxed.

The room was so silent she could hear the ticking of his wristwatch where his hand lay beside her head on the pillow. She didn't dare look at him. Touching him wasn't even a remote possibility. She lay there and listened as his breathing returned to normal. Except for the rising and falling of his chest, he lay motionless.

It was over.

Eventually she rolled to her side, facing away from him. She tucked the pillow beneath her cheek and drew her knees against her chest. She was hurting, but she couldn't specify how or where or why.

Several minutes elapsed. When she first felt the stroking movement of his hand on her waist, she thought it was because she had wished it so badly that her imagination had made her feel it.

His hand settled in the curve of her waist and applied enough pressure to bring her over to her back again. She gazed up into his face, her eyes large and inquisitive and brimming with misgiving.

"I've always been fair," he whispered.

He drew his knuckles across her cheek, then over her lips. They'd been scraped by his beard stubble. At his tender touch, Avery swallowed emotionally. Her lips parted, but she couldn't speak aloud what she felt in her heart.

Tate lowered his head and kissed her softly. He paused, then kissed her again with the same delicacy. His cheeks were very hot against hers. Acting on instinct and overwhelming need, she reached up and touched the bandage at his hairline. Affectionately, her fingers sifted through his tousled hair. She traced the cleft in his chin with her fingernail.

God, she loved this man.

His lips settled against hers with purpose. His tongue slipped between her lips. Gently, erotically, he worked it in and out, making love to her mouth. She made a small, wanton sound. He responded by drawing her closer to him, close enough for his softened penis to nestle in the humid warmth between her thighs.

He kept kissing her mouth, her neck, her shoulders, while he fondled her breasts. His stroking fingers made the nipples stiff for his mouth. Hotly, wetly, he sucked them with tempered greed, until she was moving beneath him restlessly. He kissed her stomach, her undulating abdomen, the sensitive space between her pelvic bones.

Avery, lost to the touch of his mouth on her skin, threaded her fingers through his hair and held on tight.

Between her thighs, she was absurdly slippery, but his fingers dipped into her without intimidation. He discovered that tiny, distended nubbin of flesh between the pouting lips. He pressed it, feathered it, gently rolled it between his fingers.

She spoke his name on a serrated sigh. Her body quickened. Small shudders began to ripple through her. Reflexively she drew her knees up.

"I'm hard again."

His voice was tinged with wonder. Unintentionally he had spoken aloud the realization that had him mystified. He hadn't expected to need her again so soon, nor to ever need her as violently as he did now.

His entrance was surer than before, yet he took more When he was fully buried inside her, he turned his her neck and gently pulled her skin between his teeth. Avery's body responded instantly. Her inner muscles flexed, tightly squeezing him. With a low sound, he mindlessly began rocking his hips forward and backward.

She clung to him. Each rhythmic stroke propelled her closer to the light glimmering at the end of a dark tunnel. Her eyelids fluttered. She raced, harder and faster.

The light exploded around her brilliantly and she was consumed.

Tate released a long, low moan. His whole body tensed. He came and came and came, scalding and fierce, until he was completely empty.

He said nothing when he disengaged his body from hers. He turned away, giving her his back and drawing the sheet over his sweat-beaded shoulders.

Avery faced the opposite wall, trying to keep her crying silent. Physically it had been the finest sex imaginable, far surpassing anything she had ever experienced from the few lovers she'd had. There had been pitifully few. Relationships required time, and she'd sacrificed most of hers to the pursuit of her career. The obvious difference with this time was the love she had for her partner.

But for Tate it had started and ended as a biological release. Anger had been his turn-on, not love or even affection. He'd given her a climax, but that had been an obligation considerately fulfilled and nothing more.

The foreplay had been technically excellent but impersonal. They hadn't luxuriated in their repletion, though she'd longed to explore his naked body, familiarize her eyes and hands and mouth with every nuance of it. No endearments had been whispered. No vows of love had been pledged. He hadn't once spoken her name.

He didn't even know it.

THIRTY-TWO

"Tate, I need a minute of your time."

Avery barreled through the previously closed door, interrupting the conference being held in the large den at the ranch house.

Jack, who had been speaking when she made her peremptory entrance, was left standing in the midst of them with his hand frozen in a gesture and his mouth hanging open.

"What is it?" Tate asked, looking particularly ill-tempered.

Eddy was frowning with annoyance; Jack was cursing beneath his breath. Nelson's displeasure was just as clear, but he made an attempt at civility. "Is it an emergency? Mandy?"

"No, Nelson. Mandy's at nursery school."

"Is it something Zee can help you with?"

"I'm afraid not. I need to speak privately to Tate."

"We're in the middle of something here, Carole," he said testily. "Is it important?"

"If it weren't important, I wouldn't have interrupted you."

"I'd rather you wait until we get finished or handle the crisis yourself."

She felt her cheeks grow warm with indignation. Since their return home several days earlier, he had gone out of his way to avoid her. It had come as a vast disappointment but only a mild surprise that he hadn't moved back into the yellow bedroom she occupied. Instead, he'd resumed sleeping alone in the adjoining study.

Their lovemaking hadn't drawn them closer. Rather, it had widened the gap between them. The morning following it, they'd barely made eye contact. Words had been few.

The mood had been subdued, as though something nefarious had transpired and neither party involved wanted to own up to it. She had taken her cue from Tate and pretended that nothing had happened in that wide bed, but the effort to remain impassive had made her cantankerous.

He had acknowledged it only once, as they waited for the bellman to come for their luggage. "We didn't use anything last night," he had said in a low, strained voice as he gazed out over the Dallas skyline.

"I don't have AIDS," she had snapped waspishly, wanting to prick his seemingly impenetrable aloofness. She succeeded.

He came around quickly. "I know. They would have discovered it while you were in the hospital."

"Is that why you felt it was okay to touch me? Because I was disease-free?"

"What I want to know," he ground out, "is if you could get pregnant."

Glumly, she shook her head. "Wrong time of the month. You're safe on all accounts."

That had been the extent of the conversation about their lovemaking, although that term elevated the act into something it hadn't actually been, at least for Tate. She felt like a one-night stand—an unpaid prostitute. Any warm, female body would have suited him. For the time being, he was sated. He wouldn't need her for a while.

She resented being so disposable. Used once—well, twice, actually—then thrown away. Perhaps Carole's unfaithfulness had been justified. Avery was beginning to wonder if Tate got off just as easily on the heady thought of becoming a senator as he did on sex. He certainly spent more time in pursuit of that than he did cultivating a loving relationship with his wife, she thought peevishly.

"All right," she said now, "I'll handle it."

She pulled the den door closed with a hard slam. Less than a minute later she was slamming another door in the house—this one to Fancy's bedroom. The girl was sitting on her bed, painting her toenails fire-engine red. A cigarette was burning in the nightstand ashtray. Condensation was collecting on the cold drink can beside the ashtray. Stereo headphones were bridging her head. Her jaws were working a piece of Juicy Fruit to the rhythm of the music.

She couldn't possibly have heard the slamming door over the acid rock being blasted into her ears, but she must have felt the vibration of the impact because she glanced up and saw Avery glaring down at her, holding a gum wrapper in her hand.

Fancy replaced the brush in the bottle of nail polish and draped the headphones around her neck. "What the hell are you doing in my room?"

"I came to retrieve my belongings."

Giving Fancy no more warning than that, Avery marched to the closet and slid open a louvered panel.

"Just a freaking minute!" Fancy exclaimed. She tossed the headphones down onto the bed and came charging off it.

"This is mine," Avery said, yanking a blouse off a hanger. "And this skirt. And this." She removed a belt from a hook. Finding nothing more in the closet, she crossed to Fancy's dressing table, which was littered with candy wrappers, chewing gum foil, perfume bottles, and enough cosmetics to stock a drugstore.

Avery raised the lid of a lacquered jewelry box and began riffling through earrings, bracelets, necklaces, and rings. She found the silver earrings she had reported missing in Houston, a bracelet, and the watch.

It was an inexpensive wristwatch—costume jewelry, really— but Tate had bought it for her. It hadn't been a bona fide gift. They had been browsing through a department store during a break in the campaign trip. She had seen the watch, remarked on its attractive green alligator band, and Tate had passed the star struck salesgirl his credit card.

Avery treasured it because he had bought it for *her*, not for Carole. She had noticed its disappearance from her jewelry box that morning. That had prompted her to storm the meeting in search of Tate. Since he had declined to advise her on how to deal with Fancy's kleptomania, she had taken matters into her own hands.

"You're a lousy thief, Fancy."

"I don't know how your stuff got into my room," she said loftily.

"You're an even lousier liar."

"Mona probably—"

"*Fancy!*" Avery shouted. "You've been sneaking into my room and taking things for weeks. I know it. Don't insult my intelligence by denying it. You leave unmistakable clues behind."

Fancy looked down at the incriminating gum wrapper now lying on the bed. "Are you going to tattle to Uncle Tate?"

"Is that what you want me to do?"

"Hell, no." She flopped back down on the bed and began vigorously shaking the bottle of nail polish. "Do whatever the hell you want to. Just do it someplace else besides my room."

Avery was on her way out when she reconsidered. Turning back, she approached the bed and sat down. Taking the silver earrings, she pressed them into Fancy's hand and folded her fingers around them.

"Why don't you keep these? I would have loaned them to you if you had just asked."

Fancy flung the earrings as far as she could throw them. "I don't want your goddamn charity." Her beautiful blue eyes turned ugly with dislike. "Who the hell are you to offer me your sorry leftovers? I don't want the earrings or anything else you've got."

Avery withstood the verbal attack. "I believe you. It's not the earrings or any of this stuff that you wanted," she said, nodding down at the possessions she had gathered. "What you wanted was to get caught."

Fancy scoffed. "You've been out in the sun too long, Aunt Carole. Don't you know the sun's bad for your plastic face? It might cause it to melt."

"You can't insult me," Avery returned blandly. "You don't have the power. Because I'm on to you."

Fancy regarded her sulkily. "What do you mean?"

"You wanted my attention. You got it by stealing. Just like you get your parents' attention by doing things you know they'll disapprove of."

"Like fucking Eddy?"

"Like fucking Eddy."

Fancy was taken aback by Avery's calm echo of her cheeky question. She quickly recovered, however. "I'll bet you nearly shit when you saw me coming out of his hotel room. Didn't know I was anywhere near Houston, did you?"

"He's too old for you, Fancy."

"We don't think so."

"Did he invite you to join him in Houston?"

"Maybe, maybe not." She sprayed fixative on her scarlet toenails, then waggled them as she admired her handiwork. Hopping off the bed, she moved to a drawer and took out a bikini. She peeled her nightgown over her head. Her body was marred by bruises and scratches. Her shapely buttocks were striped with them. Avery glanced away, a sick feeling rising in her stomach.

"I've never had a lover like Eddy before," Fancy said dreamily as she stepped into the bikini trunks.

"Oh? What kind of lover is he?"

"Don't you know?" Avery said nothing. She didn't know if Carole had slept with her husband's best friend or not. "He's the best." Fancy hooked the bikini bra, then leaned into the mirror, selected a lipstick off the dressing table, and spread it across her mouth. "Jealous?"

"No."

They made eye contact in the mirror. Fancy looked skeptical. "Uncle Tate's still sleeping in that other room."

"That's none of your business."

"Doesn't matter to me," she said with a malicious grin, "as long as you don't try and take up the slack with Eddy."

"You sound very proprietary."

"He's not sleeping with anybody else." She bent at the waist and, flipping her hair forward, began pulling a brush through the thick, dark-blond strands.

"Are you sure of that?"

"I'm sure. I don't leave him the energy to screw around on me."

"Tell me about him."

Fancy swept her hair to one side and slyly looked up at Avery from her upside down position. "I get it. Not jealous, just curious."

"Maybe. What do you and Eddy find to talk about?"

"Do you chat with the guys you're balling?" She laughed

out loud. "Say, you wouldn't happen to have any grass, would you?"

"No."

"Guess not," she said, sighing with disgust as she came erect and threw her hair back. "Uncle Tate went berserk when he caught us smoking that time. Wonder what he would have thought if he'd caught us sharing that cowboy?"

Avery blanched and looked away. "I . . . don't do things like that anymore, Fancy."

"No shit? For real?" She seemed genuinely curious.

"For real."

"You know, when you first came home from the hospital, I thought you were faking it. You were Miss Goody Two Shoes all of a sudden. But now, I believe you really changed after that airplane crash. What happened? Are you afraid you're gonna die and go to hell, or what?"

Avery changed the subject. "Surely Eddy's told you something about himself. Where did he grow up? What about his family?"

Fancy propped her hands on her hips and regarded Avery strangely. "You know where he grew up, same as I do. Some podunk town in the Panhandle. He didn't have any family, remember? Except for a grandma who died while he and Uncle Tate were still at UT."

"What did he do before he came to work for Tate?"

Fancy had already grown impatient with the questions. "Look, we screw, okay? We don't talk. I mean, he's a real private person."

"For instance?"

"He doesn't like me going through his stuff. One night I was searching in his drawers for a shirt to put on and he got really pissed, said for me not to meddle in his stuff again, so I don't. I don't pry, period. We all need our privacy, you know."

"He's never mentioned what he did between Vietnam and when he came back to Texas?"

"All I've ever asked was if he'd been married. He told me he hadn't. He said he'd spent a lot of time finding himself. I said, 'Were you lost?' I meant it like a joke, but Eddy got this funny look on his face and said something like, 'Yeah, for a while there, I was.' "

"What do you think he meant by that?"

"Oh, I suspect he freaked after the war," Fancy said with breezy unconcern.

"Why?"

"Probably because of Uncle Tate saving his life after their plane crashed. I guess Eddy relives bailing out, being wounded, and having Uncle Tate carry him around in the jungle until a chopper could pick them up. If you've ever seen him naked, you must've noticed the scar on his back. Pretty gruesome, huh?

"He must've been scared shitless they were gonna get captured by the Cong. Eddy begged Uncle Tate to leave him to die, you know, but Uncle Tate wouldn't."

"Surely he didn't think Tate would," Avery exclaimed.

"Well, you know the fighter pilots' motto—'Better dead than look bad.' Eddy must've taken it to heart more than most. Uncle Tate was the hero. Eddy was just another casualty. That must still play on his mind."

"How do you know all this, Fancy?"

"Are you kidding? Haven't you heard Grandpa tell it often enough?"

"Oh, sure, of course. You just seem to know so many of the fine details."

"No more than you. Look, I'm going out to the pool. Do you mind?"

Inhospitably, she walked to the door and pulled it open. Avery joined her there. "Fancy, the next time you want to use something of mine, just ask." She rolled her eyes, but Avery ignored her insolence. Touching the girl's shoulder briefly, she added, "And be careful."

"Of what?"

"Of Eddy."

"She said for me to be careful of you."

The motel room was cheap, dusty, and dank. But as Fancy bit into a fried chicken drumstick, she didn't seem to notice or mind. She'd become accustomed to the shabby surroundings in the last several weeks.

She would rather have had her trysts with Eddy in a more elegant hotel, but the Sidewinder Inn was located on the interstate between campaign headquarters and the ranch, so it was a convenient place for them to meet before going home. The motel catered to illicit lovers. Rooms were rented by the hour. The staff was discreet—out of indifference, not empathy.

Because they had worked through the dinner hour this evening, Fancy and Eddy were sharing their time together with a bucket of Colonel Sanders's best. Naked, they were sitting amid the rumpled sheets, eating fried chicken and discussing Carole Rutledge.

"Careful of me?" Eddy asked. "Why?"

"She said I shouldn't be getting involved with a man so much older," Fancy said, tearing off a bite of meat. "But I don't think that's the real reason."

Eddy broke apart a chicken wing. "What's the real reason?"

"The real reason is because she's eaten up with jealousy. See, she wants to play the good wife for Uncle Tate, just in case he wins and goes to Washington. But in case he doesn't, she wants to have someone waiting in the wings. Even though she pretends not to, I know Aunt Carole craves your body." Playfully, she tapped his chest with the drumstick.

Eddy didn't respond. He was staring absently into space, frowning. "I still wish she didn't know about you and me."

"Let's not have another fight about that, okay? I couldn't help it. I walked out of your room and there she was, clutching that stupid ice bucket to her chest and looking like she'd just swallowed her tongue."

"Has she told Tate?"

"I doubt it." A piece of golden-brown crust fell onto her bare belly. She moistened her fingertip, picked up the crumb, then licked it off. "I'll tell you something else," she said in a mysterious whisper, "I don't think she's quite right in the head yet."

"What do you mean?"

"She asks the dumbest questions."

"Like what?"

"Yesterday I mentioned something she should have a vivid memory of, even if she did suffer a concussion."

"What?"

"Well," Fancy drawled, dragging the nearly clean drum-

stick across her lips, "another ranch was buying some
horses from Grandpa. When the cowboy came to look at
them, nobody was around. I took him into the stable
myself. He was real cute."

"I get the picture," Eddy said drolly. "What does Carole
have to do with it?"

"She discovered us screwing like rabbits in one of the
stalls. I thought I was sunk, see, because this was a couple
of years ago and I was barely seventeen. But Carole and the
cowboy connected immediately. You know, snap, crackle,
pop. The next thing I know, she's as naked as we are and
rolling around in the hay with us."

She fanned her face theatrically. "God, it was fantastic!
What an afternoon. But yesterday, when I mentioned it, she
looked ready to puke or something. You want some more
chicken?"

"No thanks." Fancy tossed her cleaned bone into the box
and took out the last chicken leg. Eddy encircled her ankle
with his hard fingers. "You didn't give away any of my
secrets, did you?"

She laughed and nudged him in the butt with her bare
foot. "I don't know any of your secrets."

"So what did you and Carole talk about regarding me?"

"I just told her you were the best I'd ever had." She
leaned forward and gave him a greasy kiss on the lips. "You
are, you know. You've got a cock of solid iron. And there's
something about you that's so exciting—dangerous, almost."

He was amused. "Finish your chicken. It's time you
headed home."

Disobediently, Fancy looped her arms around his neck
and kissed him languorously. She left her lips in place as
she whispered, "I've never done it doggie fashion before."

"I know."

She drew her head back sharply. "Didn't I do it good?"

"You did it fine. But I could tell you were surprised at
first."

"I love surprises."

Eddy cupped the back of her head and gave her a searing
kiss. Together they fell back onto the sour-smelling pillows.
"The next time your Aunt Carole starts asking questions

about me," he panted as he pulled on a rubber, "tell her to mind her own frigging business." He plowed into her.

"Yes, Eddy, yes," she chanted, beating on his back with the drumstick she still had clutched in one hand.

THIRTY-THREE

"What the hell," Van Lovejoy said resignedly. He took a final drag on a cigarette he had smoked down to his stained fingertips. "I wouldn't be any better at blackmailing than I am at anything else. I would have fucked up."

"You threatened her with blackmail?" Irish stared at the video photographer with contempt. "You failed to mention that when you told me about your meeting with Avery."

"It's all right, Irish." Avery laid a calming hand on the older man's arm. With a trace of a grin, she added, "Van was miffed at us for not including him in our secret."

"Don't joke about it. This secret is giving me chronic indigestion." Irish left his sofa in pursuit of another shot of whiskey, which he poured into his glass from a bottle on the kitchen table.

"Bring me one of those," Van called to him. Then to Avery, he said, "Irish is right. You're up shit creek and you don't even know it."

"I know it."

"Got any paddles?"

She shook her head. "No."

"Jesus, Avery, are you nuts? Why'd you do such a damn fool thing?"

"Do you want to tell him, or should I?" she asked Irish as he resumed his seat next to her on the couch.

"This is your party."

While Irish and Van sipped their whiskey, Avery related

her incredible tale again. Van listened intently, disbelievingly, glancing frequently at Irish, who verified everything she said with a somber nod of his grizzled head.

"Rutledge has no idea?" Van asked when she had brought him up to date.

"None. At least as far as I can tell."

"Who's the traitor in the camp?"

"I don't know yet."

"Have you heard from him anymore?"

"Yes. Yesterday. I received another typed communiqué."

"What'd it say?"

"Virtually the same as before," she answered evasively, unable to connect with Irish's shrewd blue eyes.

The succinct note, found in her lingerie drawer, had read, *You've slept with him. Good work. He's disarmed.*

It had made her queasy to think of that unknown someone crowing over what had happened at the Adolphus. Had Tate discussed their lovemaking with his traitorous confidant? Or was he so close to Tate that he had sensed his mood swing and made a lucky guess into the reason for it? She supposed she should be glad that he thought it was a ploy and hadn't figured it for an act of love.

"Whoever he is," she told her friends now, "he still means to do it." Her arms broke out in chill bumps. "But I don't think he's going to do the actual killing." The word was almost impossible for her to speak aloud. "I think someone's been hired to do it. Did you bring the tapes I asked for?"

Van nodded toward an end table where he had stacked several videotapes when he arrived, just a few minutes ahead of Avery. "Irish passed along the note you sent me through his post office box."

"Thanks, Van." Leaving her place on the sofa, she retrieved the tapes, then went to Irish's TV set and VCR and turned them on. She inserted one of the videos and returned to the sofa with a remote control transmitter. "This is everything you shot during our trip?"

"Yep. From your arrival at Houston to your return home. If we're going to watch unedited home movies, I've got to have another drink."

"Next time, bring your own bottle," Irish muttered as Van sauntered into the kitchen.

"Screw you, McCabe."

Taking no offense, Irish leaned forward and propped his elbows on his knees. On the television screen Tate was seen emerging from a jetway. Avery and Mandy were at his side. The rest of the entourage was in the background.

"You've got the kid, but where are his parents?" Van asked, returning with a fresh drink.

"They drove down. Zee refuses to fly."

"Funny for an air force wife, isn't it?"

"Not so much. Nelson flew bombing missions in Korea while she was left at home with baby Jack. Then he did some test piloting. I'm sure she was afraid of being widowed. And Nelson's buddy—Tate's named after him—was lost at sea when his plane crashed."

"How'd you learn all that?"

"I went to Tate's office when I knew he wouldn't be there, with the excuse of wanting to have all the pictures reframed. I manipulated his secretary into conversation about the people in—Wait! Stop!"

Realizing that she was controlling the TV with the transmitter, she stopped the tape, backed it up, and replayed it. Very quietly, fearfully, she said, "He was at the airport when we arrived in Houston, too."

"Who?" Irish and Van asked in unison.

Again Avery rewound the tape. "This is still Hobby Airport, right, Van?"

"Right."

"There! See the tall man with gray hair?"

"Yellow polo shirt?"

"Yes."

"Where? I don't see him," Irish grumbled.

"What about him?" Van asked.

Avery rewound the tape. "Does this thing have a stop action?"

"Hell, yes." Irish snatched the transmitter from her hands. "Say when. I haven't seen a goddamn thing to—"

"When!"

He depressed the button, freezing the action on the

screen. Avery knelt in front of the TV set and pointed the
man out to Irish. He was standing in the background, at the
periphery of the crowd.

"He was in our hotel," she declared as the realization
struck her. "We were rushing off to a rally and he held an
elevator for us."

That's why she had noticed him in Midland. She had just
seen him in Houston, although it hadn't registered at the
time that the sweaty man who'd come from a workout in the
hotel gym was the same as the man in the western suit.

"So?"

"So he was in Midland, too. He was at the airport when
we landed. And I saw him later, in Dallas, at the fund-
raising dinner at Southfork."

Van and Irish exchanged worried glances. "Coincidence?"

"Do you really think so?" Avery demanded angrily.

"All right, an avid Rutledge supporter."

"I had just about convinced myself of that," she said,
"but I've been dropping by campaign headquarters nearly
ever day since we got back, and I haven't seen him among
the volunteers. Besides, he never approached us while we
were away. He was always at the edge of the crowd."

"You're jumping to conclusions, Avery."

"Don't." It was probably the harshest tone of voice she'd
ever used with Irish. It startled them both, but she modified
it only slightly when she added, "I know what you're
thinking and you're wrong."

"What am I thinking?"

"That I'm plunging in, jumping to conclusions before
I've lined up all the facts, reacting emotionally instead of
pragmatically."

"You said it." Van sat back on his curved spine and
propped his tumbler of whiskey on his concave abdomen.
"You're good at that."

Avery drew herself up. "Let's look at all the tapes and
see just how wrong I am."

When the final tape went to snow on the screen, a
sustained silence followed, ameliorated only by the whistling sound made by the video recorder as it rewound the
tape.

Avery came to her feet and turned to face them. She didn't waste time by rubbing it in how right she'd been. The tapes spoke for themselves. The man had shown up in nearly every one.

"Does he look familiar to either of you?"

Van said, "No."

"He was in every single city we were," Avery mused out loud. "Always lurking in the background."

"Not 'lurking.' Standing," Irish corrected.

"Standing and staring intently at Tate."

"So were you, most of the time," Van quipped. "You're not going to ice him."

She shot him a baleful look. "Don't you think it's a little odd that a man would follow a senatorial candidate around the state if he weren't actually part of the election committee?"

They glanced at each other and shrugged warily. "It's odd," Irish conceded, "but we don't have any pictures of him with his finger on a trigger."

"Did you see him at the GM plant?" Van wanted to know.

"No."

"That was one of the largest, most hostile crowds Tate addressed," Irish said. "Wouldn't that have been a likely spot for the guy to make his move?"

"Maybe the bottle thrower beat him to it."

"But you said you didn't see Gray Hair there," Van pointed out.

Avery gnawed her lip in consternation. That eventful day was a blur in her memory, punctuated by vivid recollections, like Tate sitting in the emergency room, his shirt stained with his blood. The wound had healed in a matter of days; the small scar was faint and hidden by his hair. She shuddered to think how much worse it could have been if Gray Hair—

"Wait! I just remembered," she exclaimed. "I read that day's agenda before we left the hotel," she recalled excitedly. "The trip to the GM plant wasn't printed on the schedule because it was squeezed in later. Nobody except Eddy, Jack, and the union bosses at the plant knew we were going to be there. So even if Gray Hair had intercepted a schedule, he couldn't have known that Tate was going to be in Arlington.''

"You two sound like you're talking about a goddamn Indian," Irish said cantankerously. "Look, Avery, this thing is getting too dangerous. Tell Rutledge who you are, what you suspect, and get the hell out."

"I can't." She drew in a catchy breath and repeated with soft emphasis, "I can't."

They argued with her for another half hour, but got nowhere. She enumerated the reasons why she couldn't give up now and rebuked their arguments that she was just doing it for the notoriety it would bring her when it was over.

"Don't you understand? Tate needs me. So does Mandy. I'm not deserting them until I know they're safe, and that's final."

As she prepared to leave, rushing because time had gotten away from her, she hugged them both. "It'll be a comfort to know you're around," she told Van. Irish had assured her that he would assign Van to the Rutledge campaign permanently until after the election. "Be the eyes in the back of my head. Scan the crowds. Let me know immediately if you see Gray Hair."

"Not with the Indian names again," Irish groaned. He pulled her into a bear hug. "You've given me the worst bellyache of my life," he said gruffly. "But I still don't want to lose you again."

She hugged him back and kissed his cheek. "You won't."

Van said, "Cover your ass, Avery."

"I will, I promise."

She left quickly and sped home. But she wasn't speedy enough.

THIRTY-FOUR

"This is becoming an all-too-familiar scene." Tate angrily confronted Avery the moment she cleared Mandy's bedroom door. "I'm pacing the floor, not knowing where the hell you are."

Breathless, she rushed across the room and gingerly lowered herself to the edge of the bed. Mandy was sleeping, but there were tear tracks on her cheeks. "I'm sorry. Zee told me she had another nightmare." Tate's mother had been waiting for her in the hall when she came in.

Tate appeared even more agitated than Zee had been. His face was drawn and haggard, his hair uncombed. "It happened about an hour ago, shortly after she'd fallen asleep."

"Did she remember anything?" she asked, looking up at him hopefully.

"No," he replied in a clipped voice. "Her own screams woke her up."

Avery smoothed back Mandy's hair and murmured, "I should have been here."

"You damn sure should have. She cried for you. Where were you?"

"I had errands to run." His imperative tone of voice grated on her, but she was presently more interested in the child than in arguing with Tate. "I'll stay with her now."

"You can't. The men from Wakely and Foster are here."

"Who?"

"The consultants we hired to oversee the campaign. Our meeting was interrupted by Mandy's nightmare, and their time is expensive. We've kept them waiting long enough."

He propelled her from Mandy's bedroom and toward one

of the doors that opened onto the central courtyard. Avery dug in her heels. "What are you most upset over, Tate—your daughter's nightmare, or keeping the bigwigs waiting?"

"Don't test my temper now, Carole," he said, straining the words through clenched teeth. "I was here to comfort her, not you."

She conceded him the argument by guiltily glancing away. "I thought you were against using professional consultants for your campaign."

"I changed my mind."

"Eddy and Jack changed it for you."

"They had their input, but I made the final decision. Anyway, they're here, waiting to talk strategy with us."

"Tate, wait a minute," she said, laying a restraining hand on his chest when he made to move past her. "If you don't feel right about this, just say no to them. Up till now, your campaign has been based on *you*—who you are and what you stand for. What if these so-called experts try to change you? Won't you feel diluted? Homogenized? Even the best advisers can be wrong. Please don't be pressured into doing something you don't want to do."

He removed her hand from the front of his shirt. "If I could be pressured into doing something, Carole, I would have divorced you a long time ago. That's what I was advised to do."

The following morning she stepped out of her tub and loosely wrapped a bath sheet around herself. As she stood in front of the mirror, towel-drying her hair, she thought she saw movement in the bedroom through the partially opened door. Her first thought was that it might be Fancy. She flung open the door, but rapidly recoiled.

"Jack!"

"I'm sorry, Carole. I thought you heard my knock."

He was standing well beyond the door to her room. If he had knocked, she certainly wouldn't have given him permission to come in. He was lying. He hadn't knocked. More angry than embarrassed, she drew the bath sheet tighter around her.

"What do you want, Jack?"

"Uh, the guys left this for you."

Without taking his eyes off her, he tossed a plastic binder on her bed. His intense gaze made her very uncomfortable. It was prurient, but it was also incisive. The bath sheet left her legs and shoulders bare. Could he detect the difference in her body from Carole's? Did he know what Carole's body had looked like?

"What guys?" she asked, trying not to let her discomfort show.

"From Wakely and Foster. They didn't have a chance to give it to you last night before you stormed out of the meeting."

"I didn't storm out of the meeting. I came inside to check on Mandy."

"And stayed until after they'd left." She offered no apology or denial. "You didn't like them, did you?"

"Since you asked, no. I'm surprised you do."

"Why?"

"Because they're usurping your position."

"They work for us, not the other way around."

"That's not what it sounded like to me," she said. "They were autocratic and mandatory. I don't respond to that kind of high-handedness, and I'll be amazed if Tate tolerates it for any significant length of time."

Jack laughed. "Feeling as you do about them and their high-handed advice, you're going to have a tough time stomaching this." He gestured down at the folder.

Curious, Avery approached the bed and picked up the folder. She opened it and scanned the first several sheets of paper. "A list of dos and don'ts for the candidate's wife."

"That's right, Mrs. Rutledge."

She slapped shut the folder's cover and dropped it back onto the bed.

Again Jack laughed. "I'm glad I'm just the errand boy. Eddy's going to be pissed if you don't read and digest everything in there."

"Eddy can go to hell. And so can you. And so can anybody who wants to make Tate a baby-kissing, hand-shaking, plastic automaton who can turn a glib phrase but says absolutely nothing worth listening to."

"You've become quite a crusader for him, haven't you? All of a sudden you're his staunchest ally."

"Damn right."

"Who the hell do you think you're kidding, Carole?"

"I'm his wife. And the next time you want to see me, Jack, knock louder."

He took a belligerent step toward her, his face congested with anger. "Playact all you want in front of everybody else, but when we're alone—"

"Mommy, I drew you a picture." Mandy came bounding in, waving a sheet of construction paper.

Jack glowered at Avery, then wheeled around and strode from the room. She congratulated herself on holding up remarkably well, but now her weak knees buckled and she sank onto the edge of the bed, gathering Mandy against her and holding on tight. She pressed her lips against the top of the child's head. It would be difficult to tell who was drawing comfort from whom.

"Mommy?"

"What did you draw? Let me see." Avery released her and studied the colorful slashes Mandy had made across the page. "It's wonderful!" she exclaimed, smiling tremulously.

In the weeks since her visit with Dr. Webster, Mandy had made tremendous progress. She was gradually emerging from the shell she had sequestered herself in. Her mind was fertile. Her sturdy little body seemed imbued with energy. Though her self-confidence was still fragile, it didn't seem quite so breakable as before.

"It's Daddy. And here's Shep," she chirped, pointing to a dark blue blob on the paper.

"I see."

"Can I have some chewing gum? Mona said to ask you."

"One piece. Don't swallow it. Bring it to me when you don't want it anymore."

Mandy kissed her moistly. "I love you, Mommy."

"I love you, too." Avery gave her another tight hug, sustaining it until Mandy squirmed free and rushed off in quest of her chewing gum.

Avery followed her to the door and closed it. She considered turning the lock. There were those in the house whom she wanted to shut out.

But there were those she had to leave her door open for, just in case. Mandy, for one. And Tate.

Van opened a can of tuna and carried it with him back to his video console. His stomach had finally communicated to his brain that one had to have sustenance to stay alive. Otherwise, he would have been so engrossed in what he was doing, he would never have remembered to eat. He conveyed chunks of the oily fish from can to mouth via a reasonably clean spoon.

Clamping the bowl of the spoon in his mouth, he used both hands at once to eject one tape from one machine and insert a new tape into another. In this capacity, he functioned like a well-coordinated octopus.

He replaced the first tape in its labeled box and turned his attention to the one now playing. The color bars appeared on the screen, then the countdown.

Van swallowed the food he'd been holding in his mouth, took a puff of his smoldering cigarette, a gulp of whiskey, then scooped up another bite of tuna as he leaned back in his desk chair and propped his feet on the edge of the console.

He was watching a documentary he had shot several years earlier for a station in Des Moines. The subject was kiddie porn. This wasn't the watered-down, edited version that had gone out over the air. This was his personal copy—the one containing all the footage he'd shot over a twelve-week period while following around a features producer, a reporter, a grip, and a sound man. It was only one tape of the hundreds in his extensive personal library.

So far, none that he'd watched had justified the niggling notion that he'd seen someone in Rutledge's entourage before, and it wasn't the gray-haired man that had Avery so concerned. Van wasn't even certain what he was looking for, but he had to start somewhere. He wouldn't stop until he found it—whatever "it" was. Until he went back on the campaign trail with Rutledge, he didn't have anything better to do except get wasted.

He could always do that later.

                        *   *   *

"Where's Eddy?" Nelson asked from his place at the head of the dining table.

"He had to stay late," Tate replied. "He said not to wait dinner on him."

"It seems that we're never all together at dinner anymore," Nelson remarked with a frown. "Dorothy Rae, where's Fancy?"

"She's . . . she's . . ." Dorothy Rae was at a loss as to the whereabouts of her daughter.

"She was still at headquarters when I left," Tate said, coming to his sister-in-law's rescue.

Jack smiled at his parents. "She's been putting in a lot of long hours there, right, Mom?"

Zee gave him a tepid smile. "She's been more dedicated than I expected."

"The work's been good for her."

"It's a start," Nelson grumbled.

Avery, sitting across from Jack, held her peace. She doubted Fancy was working during all the hours she spent at campaign headquarters. She seemed the only one to attach any significance to Fancy and Eddy often coming in late together.

Mandy asked for help buttering her roll. When Avery finished and raised her head, she caught Jack watching her. He smiled, as though they shared a naughty secret. Avery quickly looked away and concentrated on her plate while the conversation eddied around her.

Fancy arrived several minutes later and flopped into her chair, her disposition as sour as her expression.

"Haven't you got a civil word for anybody, young lady?" Nelson asked sternly.

"Jesus, cauliflower," she mumbled, shoving the serving bowl to the other side of the table.

"I will not abide that kind of language," Nelson thundered.

"I forgot," she shouted with asperity.

His face turned an angry red. "Nor will I put up with any of your sass." He shot meaningful glances at Jack, who ducked his head, and Dorothy Rae, who reached for her wineglass. "Show some manners. Sit up properly and eat your dinner."

"There's never anything decent to eat around here," Fancy complained.

"You should be ashamed of yourself, Francine."

"I know, I know, Grandpa. All those starving kids in Africa. Save the sermon, okay? I'm going to my room."

"You'll stay where you are," he barked. "You're part of the family, and in this family, everyone has dinner together."

"There's no need to shout, Nelson," Zee said, touching his sleeve.

Fancy's face swelled up. She glared at her grandfather mutinously, at her parents contemptuously, but she remained seated.

As though nothing had happened, Nelson picked up the conversation where it had left off when she had come in. "The Wakely and Foster team is setting up another trip for Tate." He imparted this piece of information for the benefit of the women, who hadn't heard it firsthand.

Avery looked at Tate. "I just found out this afternoon," he said defensively, "and didn't have time to tell you before dinner. You'll get a schedule."

"Where are we going?"

"Just about every corner of the state."

Zee blotted her mouth. "How long will you be away?"

"A little over a week."

"Don't worry about Mandy, Carole," Nelson said. "Grandpa'll take care of her. Won't he, Mandy?"

She grinned at him and bobbed her head up and down. The child never minded being left with them. Ordinarily, Avery would have had no qualms about leaving her. However, Mandy had had another nightmare the night before—the second that week. If she were on the brink of a breakthrough, Avery hated to be away from her. Perhaps Mandy could go with them. It was something she needed to discuss with Tate before final plans were made.

Eddy suddenly appeared in the arched opening of the dining room. Mona, who was clearing away the main course dishes, told him she had kept his dinner warm. "I'll bring it right out."

"Never mind." His eyes darted around the table, lighting briefly on everyone seated. "I'll have to eat later."

Fancy's mood brightened considerably. A light came on behind her sullen eyes. Her sulky pout lifted into a smile. She sat up straight in her chair and looked at him with admiration and lust.

"I hate to ruin everyone's dinner," he began.

Nelson waved his hand dismissively. "You seem upset."

That was a gross understatement, Avery thought. Eddy was bristling with rage.

"What's the matter? Did we slip in the polls?"

"Is something wrong?"

"I'm afraid so," Eddy said, choosing Zee's question to respond to. "Ralph and Dirk are with me, but I told them to wait in the living room until I'd had a chance to speak with the family privately."

Ralph and Dirk were the two men from Wakely and Foster who were assigned to Tate's campaign. Their names frequently cropped up in conversation. Avery always dreaded hearing them referred to, because she usually had a negative reaction to whatever was subsequently said.

"Well?" Nelson prompted impatiently. "Best to get bad news over with."

"It concerns Carole." Every eye in the room moved to where she sat between Tate and Mandy. "Her abortionist is about to tell all."

THIRTY-FIVE

A quality necessary to bomber pilots is the ability not to crack under pressure. Nelson didn't. Avery reflected on his aplomb later when she reviewed those heart-stopping moments following Eddy's appalling announcement.

His lack of response was remarkable to her, because she had felt like she might very well shatter. She'd been rendered speechless, motionless, unable to think. Her brain shut down operation. It seemed the planet had been yanked from beneath her, and she floated without the security of gravity in an airless, black void.

Nelson, with admirable resilience, scooted back his dining chair and stood up. "I believe we should move this discussion to the living room."

Eddy nodded his head once, glanced at Tate with a mix of pity and exasperation, then left the room.

Zee, drastically pale but almost as composed as her husband, stood also. "Mona, we'll skip dessert tonight. Please entertain Mandy. We might be occupied for some time."

Dorothy Rae reached for her wineglass. Jack took it away from her and returned it to the table. He caught her beneath the arm, lifted her from her chair, and pushed her toward the hall. Fancy went after them. She was fairly bubbling now.

When they reached the archway, Jack said to his daughter, "You stay out of this."

"No way. This is the most exciting thing that's ever happened," she said with a giggle.

"It's none of your concern, Fancy."

"I'm part of this family, too. Grandpa just said so. Besides that, I'm a campaign worker. I have every right to sit in on the discussion. Even more right than her," she said, gesturing toward her mother.

Jack dug a fifty-dollar bill out of his pants pocket and pressed it into Fancy's hand. "Find something else to do."

"Son of a bitch," she mouthed before stamping off.

Tate's face was white with wrath. His movements were carefully controlled as he folded his napkin and laid it next to his plate. "Carole?"

Avery's head snapped up. Denials were poised and ready to be spoken, but the sheer fury burning in his eyes silenced them. Under his firmly guiding hand, she left the dining room and walked across the hall toward the large living room.

It was still twilight. The living room afforded a spectacular view of the western sky, streaked with the vivid shades of sunset. The vista was breathtaking, one Avery often sat and enjoyed. This evening, however, the endless horizon made her feel exposed and alone.

There wasn't a single friendly face to greet her when she entered the room. The men representing the public relations firm were particularly hostile.

Dirk was tall, thin, saturnine, and had a perpetual, blue-black five o'clock shadow. He looked the stereotype of a hit man from a gangster movie. It appeared that his face would crack if he even tried to smile.

Ralph was Dirk's antithesis. He was round, stout, and jolly. He was always cracking jokes, more to everyone's annoyance than amusement. When nervous, he jangled change. The coins in his pocket were getting a workout now. They rang as noisily as sleigh bells.

Neither of these men, to her knowledge, had ever professed to having a last name. She sensed that omission was to promote a friendly working relationship between them and their clients. As far as she was concerned, the gimmick didn't work.

Nelson took charge. "Eddy, please clarify what you just told us in the dining room."

Eddy went straight to the heart of the matter and turned to Avery. "Did you have an abortion?"

Her lips parted, but she couldn't utter a sound. Tate answered for her. "Yes, she did."

Zee jumped as if her slender body had just been struck with an arrow. Nelson's brows pulled together into a steep frown. Jack and Dorothy Rae only stared at Avery in stunned disbelief.

"You knew about it?" Eddy demanded of Tate.

"Yes."

"And you didn't tell anybody?"

"It wasn't anybody's business, was it?" Tate snapped furiously.

"When did this happen?" Nelson wanted to know. "Recently?"

"No, before the plane crash. Just before."

"Great," Eddy muttered. "This is just fuckin' great."

"Mind your language in front of my wife, Mr. Paschal!" Nelson roared.

"I'm sorry, Nelson," the younger man shouted back,

"but do you have any idea what this will do to the Rutledge campaign if it gets out?"

"Of course I do. But we have to guard against responding in a knee-jerk fashion. What good will flying tempers do us now?" After tempers had cooled, Nelson asked, "How did you find out about this . . . this abomination?"

"The doctor's nurse called headquarters this afternoon and asked to speak to Tate," Eddy told them. "He had already left, so I took the call. She said Carole had come to them six weeks pregnant and asked for a D and C to terminate pregnancy."

Avery sank down onto the padded arm of the sofa and folded her arms across her middle. "Do we have to talk about this with them in here?" She nodded toward the public relations duo.

"Beat it." Tate nodded them toward the door.

"Wait a minute," Eddy objected. "They have to know everything that's going on."

"Not about our personal lives."

"Everything, Tate," Dirk said. "Right down to the deodorant you use. No surprises, remember? Especially not unpleasant ones. We told you that from the beginning."

Tate looked ready to explode. "What did this nurse threaten to do?"

"Tell the media."

"Or?"

"Or we could pay her to keep quiet."

"Blackmail," Ralph said, playing a tune with the change in his pocket. "Not very original."

"But effective," Eddy said curtly. "She got my attention, all right. You might have ruined everything, you know," he shot at Avery.

Trapped in her own lie, Avery had no choice now but to bear their scorn. She didn't care what any of the others thought of her, but she wanted to die when she thought of how betrayed Tate must feel.

Eddy strode to the liquor cabinet and poured himself a straight scotch. "I'm open to suggestions."

"What about the doctor?" Dirk asked him.

"The nurse doesn't work for him anymore."

"Oh?" Ralph stopped jingling coins. "How come?"

"I don't know."

"Find out."

Avery, who had given the sharp command, came to her feet. She saw only one way to redeem herself in Tate's eyes and that was to help get him out of this mess. "Find out why she no longer works for the doctor, Eddy. Maybe he fired her for incompetency."

"He? It's a woman doctor. Jesus, don't you even remember?"

"Do you want my help with this or not?" she fired back, bluffing her way through a dreadful error. "If the nurse has been fired, she wouldn't be a very believable extortionist, would she?"

"Carole's got something there," Ralph said, glancing around the circle of grave faces.

"You got us into this jam," Eddy said, advancing on Avery. "What do you plan to do, brazen it out?"

"Yes," she said defiantly.

She could almost hear the wheels of rumination turning throughout the room. They were giving it serious consideration.

Zee broke the silence. "What if she has your medical records?"

"Records can be falsified, especially copied ones. It would still be my word against hers."

"We can't lie about it," Tate said.

"Why the hell not?" Dirk demanded.

Ralph laughed. "Lying's part of it, Tate. If you want to win, you've got to lie more convincingly than Rory Dekker, that's all."

"If I become a senator, I've still got to look myself in the mirror every morning," Tate said, scowling.

"I won't have to lie. Neither will you. No one will ever know about the abortion." Avery stepped in front of Tate and laid her hands on his arms. "If we call her bluff, she'll back down. I can almost guarantee that no local television station would listen to her, especially if she has been dismissed from the doctor's staff."

If the nurse took her story to Irish McCabe—and KTEX

would probably be her first choice, because it had the highest ratings—he would nip the story in the bud. If she took it someplace else . . .

Avery suddenly turned to Eddy and asked, "Did she say she had someone to corroborate her story?"

"No."

"Then no credible journalist would break it."

"How the hell would you know?" Jack asked from across the room.

"I saw *All the President's Men*."

"The tabloids would print it without corroboration."

"They might," she said, "but they have no credibility whatsoever. If we nobly ignored a scandalous story like that, readers would consider it a sordid lie."

"What if it got leaked to Dekker's staff? He'd blast it from Texarkana to Brownsville."

"What if he did?" Avery asked. "It's an ugly story. Who would believe I'd do such a thing?"

"Why did you?"

Avery turned to Zee, who had asked the simple question. She looked stricken, suffering for her son's sake. Avery wished she could provide her with a satisfactory answer to her question, but she couldn't.

"I'm sorry, Zee, but that's between Tate and me," she said finally. "At the time, it seemed like the thing to do."

Zee shuddered with repugnance.

Eddy didn't care about the sentimental aspects of their dilemma. He was pacing the rug. "God, Dekker would love to have this plum. He's got the zealous pro-lifers in his back pocket already. They're fanatics. I hazard to think what he could do with this. He'd paint Carole as a murderess."

"It would look like he was slinging mud," Avery said, "unless he can prove it beyond a shadow of a doubt, which he can't. Voter sympathy would swing our way."

Dirk and Ralph looked at each other and shrugged in unison. Dirk said, "She's brought up some valid points, Eddy. When you hear from the nurse again, call her bluff. She's probably grasping at straws and will scare easily."

Eddy gnawed his inner cheek. "I don't know. It's chancy."

"But it's the best we can do." Nelson got up from his

seat and extended a hand down to Zee. "Y'all sort out the
rest of this ugliness. I never want to hear it mentioned
again." Neither he or Zee deigned to look at Avery as they
went out.

Dorothy Rae headed for the liquor cabinet. Jack was
glaring so malevolently at his brother's wife that he didn't
notice or try to stop her.

Apparently, no one in the family had known about Carole's
pregnancy and abortion until tonight. This development had
come as a shock to everyone, even to Avery, who hadn't
known for certain herself and had lost by gambling on no
one ever finding out.

"You got any more skeletons rattling around in your
closet?"

Tate spun around and confronted his brother with more
anger than Avery had ever seen him exhibit for anyone in
his family. His hands were balled into fists at his sides.
"Shut up, Jack."

"Don't tell him to shut up," Dorothy Rae cried, slamming the vodka decanter back onto the cabinet. "It's not his
fault your wife's a slut."

"Dorothy Rae!"

"Well, isn't she, Jack? She got rid of a baby on purpose,
while mine . . . mine . . ." Tears welled up in her eyes. She
turned her back to the room.

Jack blew out his breath, lowered his head, and mumbled, "Sorry, Tate."

He went to his weeping wife, placed his arm around her
waist, and led her from the room. For all the aversion she
felt toward Jack, Avery was touched by this kind gesture.
So was Dorothy Rae. She gazed up at him with gratitude
and love.

Dirk and Ralph, impervious to the family drama, had
been talking between themselves. "You'll sit this trip out,"
Dirk told Avery peremptorily.

"I second that," Eddy said.

"That's up to Tate," she said.

His face was cold and impassive. "You stay."

Tears were imminent, and she'd be damned before she

cried in front of Dirk, his sidekick, and the indomitable iceman, Eddy Paschal. "Excuse me."

Proudly, but quickly, she walked out. Tate followed her from the room. He caught up with her in the hallway and brought her around to face him. "There's just no limit to your deceit, is there, Carole?"

"I know it looks bad, Tate, but—"

"*Bad*?" Bitter and incredulous, he shook his head. "If you'd already done it, why didn't you just own up to it? Why tell me there'd never been a child?"

"Because I could see how much it was hurting you."

"Bullshit. You saw how much it was hurting you!"

"No," she said miserably.

"Call her bluff. No corroborating witness. Falsified records," he said, quoting her previous suggestions. "If you got caught, you had your escape route all thought out, didn't you? How many other tricks have you got up your sleeve?"

"I made those suggestions so you'd be protected. You, Tate."

"Sure you did." His lips curled with cynicism. "If you'd wanted to do something for me you wouldn't have had an abortion. Better yet, you wouldn't have gotten pregnant in the first place. Or did you think a baby would be your ticket to Washington?"

He released her suddenly, flinging off his hands as though he couldn't bear to touch her. "Stay out of my way. I can't stand the sight of you."

He returned to the living room, where his advisers were waiting for him. Avery slumped against the wall and covered her mouth with her hands to hold back the sobs.

In another attempt to atone for Carole's sins, she had only driven Tate farther away.

The following morning, Avery woke up feeling groggy. Her head was muzzy, and her eyes were swollen and stinging from crying herself to sleep. Pulling on a light robe, she stumbled toward the bathroom.

As soon as she cleared the door, she flattened herself against the wall and, with horror, read the message that had been written on the mirror with her own lipstick.

Stupid slut. You almost ruined everything.

Fear held her paralyzed for several moments, then galva-
nized her. She ran to the closet and dressed hastily. Pausing
only long enough to wipe the message off the mirror, she
fled the room as through chased by demons.

It took only a few minutes in the stable for her to saddle a
horse. She streaked across the open pasture at a full gallop,
putting distance between her and the lovely house that
harbored such treachery. Even though the sun's first rays
warmed her skin, goose bumps broke out on Avery's arms
when she thought of someone sneaking into her bedroom
while she slept.

Perhaps Irish and Van were right. She was certifiably
insane to continue with this charade. She might pay with her
life for another woman's manipulations. Was any story
worth that? It was foolish not to leave before she was
discovered.

She could disappear, go someplace else, assume a new
identity. She was smart and resourceful. She was interested
in many things. Journalism wasn't the only worthwhile field
of endeavor.

But those were options generated by panic and fear.
Avery knew she would never act upon them. She couldn't
withstand another professional failure, especially one of this
magnitude. And what if Tate's life were lost as a conse-
quence? He and Mandy were now worth more to her than
any acclaim. She must stay. With the election only several
weeks away, the end was in sight.

As attested to by the message on her mirror, Carole's
recent unpredictability had made Tate's enemy angry and
nervous. Nervous people made mistakes. She would have to
be watchful for giveaways, and at the same time guard
against giving herself away.

The stable was still deserted when she returned her mount
to his stall. She unsaddled him, gave him a bucket of feed,
and rubbed him down.

"I've been looking for you."

Alarmed, she dropped the currycomb and spun around.
"Tate!" She splayed a hand across her thudding heart. "I
didn't hear you come in. You startled me."

He was standing at the opening of the stall. Shep sat obediently at his feet, tongue lolling.

"Mandy's demanding your French toast for breakfast. I told her I'd come find you."

"I went riding," she said, stating the obvious.

"What happened to the fancy britches?"

"Pardon?"

"Those . . ." He gestured along the outside of his thighs.

"Jodhpurs?" Her jeans and boots weren't fancy, by any means. The shirttail of her simple cotton shirt was hanging loosely over her hips. "I feel silly in them now."

"Oh." He turned to go.

"Tate?" When he came back around, she nervously moistened her lips. "I know everyone is furious with me, but your opinion is the only one that matters. Do you hate me?"

Shep lay down on the cool cement floor of the stable and propped his head on his front paws, looking up at her with woeful eyes.

"I'd better get back to Mandy," Tate said. "Coming?"

"Yes, I'll be right there."

Yet neither made a move to leave the stable. They just stood there, staring at each other. Except for the occasional stamping of a shod hoof against the floor or the snuffling of a horse, the stable was silent. Dust motes danced in the stripes of sunlight coming through the windows. The air was still and thick with the pleasing smells of hay and horseflesh and leather. And lust.

Avery's clothes suddenly seemed constricting. Her hair felt too heavy for her head, her skin too small to contain her teeming body. She ached to go to Tate and place her arms around his waist. She wanted to rest her cheek on his chest and feel the beating of his heart as it had pulsed when he was inside her. She wanted him to reach for her with need and passion again, even if short-term gratification was all he wanted from her.

The desire swirling within her was coupled with despair. The combination was unbearable. She looked away from him and idly reached out to stroke the gelding's velvet muzzle. He turned away from his oats to affectionately bump her shoulder.

"I don't get it."

Her eyes swung back to Tate. "What?"

"He used to breathe fire if you came anywhere near him. You wanted us to sell him to the glue factory. Now you nuzzle each other. What happened?"

She met Tate's gray eyes directly and said softly, "He learned to trust me."

He got the message. There was no mistaking that. He held her stare for a long time, then nudged the large dog with the toe of his boot. "Come on, Shep." Over his retreating shoulder he reminded her, "Mandy's waiting."

THIRTY-SIX

"Be a sweet girl for Daddy." Tate knelt in front of his daughter and gave her a tight hug. "I'll be back before you know it and bring you a present."

Ordinarily, Mandy's grin would have caused Avery to smile, but she found that impossible to do this morning, the day of Tate's departure. He stood up. "Call me if she has any breakthroughs."

"Of course."

"Or any regressions."

"Yes."

"The entire staff's been put on notice that if a call comes in concerning Mandy, I'm to be summoned immediately, no matter what."

"If anything happens, I promise to call right away."

Jack tooted the car horn. He was waiting impatiently behind the steering wheel. Eddy was already sitting in the passenger seat, speaking into the cellular phone that had recently been installed.

"About that other," Tate said, keeping his tone confidential. "Eddy did as you suggested and asked the nurse for irrefutable proof that you'd had an abortion. He grilled her good, gave her a taste of what she would be up against if she went to the press or to Dekker's people with her story.

"He also did some investigating. As you guessed, she was fired from her job and wanted to embarrass the doctor even more than us. Eddy used that as leverage, too, and threatened all kinds of litigation. For the time being, she's cowed."

"Oh, I'm so glad, Tate. I would have hated to have that darken your campaign."

He gave a short laugh. "It couldn't look much darker than it already does."

"Don't get discouraged," she said, laying her hand on his sleeve. "The polls aren't gospel. Besides, they can be reversed at any time."

"They'd better be damn quick about it," he said grimly. "November's going to be here before we know it."

Between now and then, his life was in danger and she couldn't even warn him of it. During this trip she wouldn't be there watching for a tall, gray-haired man. Maybe she should mention that—just give him that much head start against his enemies.

"Tate—" she began. Jack honked the horn again.

"Got to go." He bent from the waist and kissed Mandy's cheek again. "Good-bye, Carole." She didn't get a kiss, or a hug, or even a backward glance before he got into the car and was driven away.

"Mommy? Mommy?"

Mandy must have addressed her several times. By the time Avery stopped staring at the curve in the road where the car had disappeared from view and looked down at her, her little face was perplexed.

"I'm sorry. What is it, darling?"

"How come you're crying?"

Avery brushed the tears off her cheeks and forced a wide smile. "I'm just sad because Daddy's leaving. But I've got you to keep me company. Will you do that while he's gone?''

Mandy nodded vigorously. Together they went inside. If Tate was temporarily beyond her help, she could at least do the best she could for his daughter.

The days crawled by. She spent most of her time with Mandy, but even the activities she invented for them weren't enough to absorb the endless hours. She hadn't been exaggerating when she had told Tate all those weeks earlier that she needed something constructive to do. She wasn't accustomed to inactivity. On the other hand, she seemed to lack the energy to motivate herself into doing anything more than staring into space and worrying about him.

She watched the evening news every night, anxiously looking for the gray-haired man in the crowd shots. Irish would wonder why she hadn't accompanied Tate on this trip, so she had called him from a public phone booth in Kerrville and explained about the abortion crisis.

"His advisers, starting with Eddy, recommended that I stay behind. I'm a pariah now."

"Even to Rutledge?"

"To an extent, yes. He's as polite as ever, but there's a definite chill there."

"I've heard of political experts like Wakely and Foster. They give a command and Rutledge barks, is that it?"

"They give a command, Tate snarls at them, then barks."

"Hmm, well, I'll notify Van and tell him to keep his eye out for that guy you seem to think is significant."

"I *know* he's significant. Tell Van to call me the instant he spots him."

"If he does."

Apparently he hadn't, because Van hadn't called. But all the news stories broadcast by KTEX featured at least one crowd shot. Van was sending her a message. Gray Hair wasn't in the crowds surging around Tate.

That did little to relieve Avery's anxiety, however. She wanted to be beside Tate to see for herself that he was in no imminent danger. At night she experienced graphic visions of him dying a bloody death. During the day, when she wasn't involved with Mandy, she wandered restlessly through the rooms of the house.

"Still in the dumps?"

Avery raised her head. Nelson had come into the living room without her hearing him. "Does it show?" she asked with a wan smile.

"Plain as day." He lowered himself into one of the easy chairs.

"Admittedly, I haven't been very good company lately."

"Missing Tate?"

The family's subtle snubbing had made the time pass even more slowly. It had been a little over a week since Tate had left. It seemed eons.

"Yes, Nelson, I miss him terribly. I suppose you find that hard to believe. Zee does. She'll barely look at me."

He stared straight into her eyes, hard enough and incisively enough to make her squirm. He said, "That abortion business was hideous."

"I had no intention of anyone ever finding out."

"Except Tate."

"Well, he had to know, didn't he?"

"Did he? Was the baby his?"

She hesitated for only a second. "Yes."

"And you wonder why we aren't feeling too kindly toward you?" he asked. "You destroyed our grandbaby. I find that impossible to forgive, Carole. You know how Zee feels about Tate. Did you expect her to embrace you for what you did?"

"No."

"Being the kind of mother she's been to the boys, she can't imagine doing what you did. Frankly, neither can I."

Avery glanced down at the photo album that was spread open over her lap. The pictures she had been looking at when he had come in were from early years. Zee was very young and very beautiful. Nelson looked dashing and handsome in his air force blues. Jack and Tate were pictured as youngsters in various stages. They typified the all-American family.

"It couldn't have been easy for Zee when you went to Korea."

"No, it wasn't," he said, settling more comfortably into his chair. "I had to leave her alone with Jack, who was just a baby."

"Tate was born after the war, right?"

"Just after."

"He was still a baby when you moved to New Mexico," she said, consulting the album again, hoping he would elaborate on the few bare facts she knew through painstaking investigation.

"That's where the Air Force sent me, so that's where I went," Nelson said. "Desolate place. Zee hated the desert and the dust. She also hated the work I was doing. In those days, test pilots were disposable commodities."

"Like your friend Bryan Tate."

His features softened, as though he was mentally reliving good times. Then, sadly, he shook his head. "It was like losing one of the family. I gave up test piloting after that. My heart just wasn't in it anymore, and if your heart's not in it, you can get killed quicker. Maybe that's what happened with Bryan. Anyway, I didn't want to die. There was still too much I wanted to do.

"The air force sent me to Lackland. This was home, anyway. Good place to raise the boys. My daddy was getting old. I retired from the air force after he died and took over the ranching business."

"But you miss the flying, don't you?"

"Yeah—hell, yeah," he said with a self-deprecating laugh. "Old as I am, I still remember what it was like up there. No feeling in the world to rival it. Nothing like swapping beers and stories with the other fliers, either. A woman can't understand what it's like to have buddies like that."

"Like Bryan?"

He nodded. "He was a good pilot. The best." His smile faded. "But he got careless and paid the price with his life." His vision cleared as he focused on Avery again. "Everybody pays for his mistakes, Carole. You might get away with them for a while, but not forever. Eventually, they'll catch up with you."

She looked away uncomfortably. "Is that what you think is happening with me and the abortion?"

"Don't you?"

"I suppose so."

He leaned forward and propped his forearms on his thighs. "You've already had to pay by bearing the shame of it. I'm just hoping that Tate doesn't have to pay for your mistake by losing this election."

"So do I."

He studied her for a moment. "You know, Carole, I've jumped to your defense many times since you became part of this family. I've given you the benefit of the doubt on more occasions than one."

"Your point?"

"Everyone's noticed the changes in you since you came back after your accident."

Avery's heartbeat quickened. Had they been discussing these changes among themselves? "I have changed. For the better, I think."

"I agree, but Zee doesn't think the changes are real. She believes you're putting on an act—that your interest in Mandy is phony and your sudden regard for Tate is merely a tactic to stay in his good graces so he'll take you with him to Washington."

"Not a very flattering commendation from a mother-in-law," she mused aloud. "What do you think?"

"I think you're a beautiful, smart young woman—too smart to lock horns with me." He pointed a blunt finger at her. "You better be everything you've pretended to be." For several moments, his expression remained foreboding. Then he broke into a wide grin. "But if you're sincerely trying to make up for past mistakes, I commend you for it. To get elected, Tate needs his family, especially his wife, behind him one hundred percent."

"I am behind his getting elected one hundred percent."

"That's no more than should be expected." He rose from his chair. At the door he turned back. "Behave like a senator's wife and you'll get no trouble from me."

Apparently he spoke to Zee, because at dinner that evening, Avery noticed a slight thawing in Zee's attitude toward her. Her interest seemed genuine when she asked, "Did you enjoy your ride this afternoon, Carole?"

"Very much. Now that it's cooler, I can stay out longer."

"And you're riding Ghostly. That's odd, isn't it? You've always despised that animal, and vice versa."

"I think I was afraid of him before. We've learned to trust each other."

Mona stepped into the dining room at that moment to call Nelson to the phone. "Who is it?"

"It's Tate, Colonel Rutledge."

Avery squelched a pang of regret that Tate hadn't asked to speak to her, but just knowing that he was on the telephone in the next room made her insides flutter. Nelson was gone for several minutes. When he returned, he looked extremely pleased.

"Ladies," he said, addressing not only his wife and Avery, but Dorothy Rae, Fancy, and Mandy, too. "Get your bags packed tonight. We're leaving for Fort Worth tomorrow."

Their reactions were varied.

Zee said, "All of us?"

Dorothy Rae said, "Not me. Me?"

Fancy leaped from her chair, giving a wild whoop of irrepressible joy. "God, it's about time something good and fun happened around here."

Mandy looked at Avery for a clarification of why everybody had suddenly become so excited.

Avery asked, "Tomorrow? Why?"

Nelson addressed her question first. "The polls. Tate's slipping, losing ground every day."

"That's not much cause to celebrate," Zee said.

"Tate's advisers think the family should be more visible," Nelson explained, "so he doesn't look like such a maverick. I, for one, am glad we're all going to be together again."

"They've changed their minds about me staying in the background?" Avery asked.

"Obviously."

"I'll pack for Mandy and me." All negative thoughts were dispelled by the knowledge that she would soon be with Tate. "What time are we leaving?"

"Soon as everybody's ready." Nelson glanced down at Dorothy Rae, who was obviously panic-stricken. Her face was the color of cold oatmeal and she was wringing her hands. "Mona, please help Dorothy Rae get her things together."

"Do I have to go?" she asked in a quavering voice.

"That's what I was told." Nelson divided a stern stare between her and Fancy, who, unlike her mother, was ebullient. "I don't think I need to remind anyone to be on her best behavior. We're moving into the final days of the campaign. All the Rutledges are going to be under public scrutiny, constantly living under a magnifying glass. Conduct yourselves accordingly."

THIRTY-SEVEN

It was raining in Fort Worth when they arrived.

Nelson drove straight to the downtown hotel, but because the trip from the hill country had taken longer than expected due to the inclement weather and frequent stops, Jack, Eddy, and Tate had already left for the political rally being held that evening.

The travel-weary group checked into their rooms as quickly as possible. Mandy was tired and cranky. She threw a temper tantrum and nothing pacified her—not even the room service meal that was promptly delivered.

"Mandy, eat your dinner," Zee said.

"No," she said petulantly, poking out her lower lip. "You said I could see Daddy. I want to see Daddy."

"He'll be here later," Avery explained for the umpteenth time.

"Come on now, this is your favorite," Zee said cajolingly. "Pizza."

"I don't like it."

Nelson impatiently glanced at his military wristwatch.

"It's almost seven. We've got to leave now or get there late."

"I'll stay with her," Dorothy Rae volunteered, her expression hopeful.

"Big help you'd be," Fancy said scornfully. "I say let the little wretch starve."

"Fancy, please," Zee remonstrated. "One difficult child at a time is enough." She pleaded fatigue herself and offered to skip the rally and stay with Mandy.

"Thank you, Zee," Avery said. "That would be a help. I don't think she's fit to meet the public tonight. Nelson, you take Dorothy Rae and Fancy now. I'll come along later."

Nelson began to protest. "Dirk and Ralph said to—"

"I don't care what they said," Avery said, butting in. "Tate wouldn't want me to leave Mandy with Zee while she's behaving this badly. Once she's in bed, I'll take a cab. Tell them I'll get there as soon as I can."

The three of them filed out of Mandy's bedroom, part of a three-room suite assigned to Tate's family. "Now, Mandy," Avery said reasonably, "eat your supper so I can brag to Daddy how good you've been."

"I want my surprise."

"Eat your dinner, dear," Zee pleaded.

"No!"

"Then would you like a nice, warm bath?"

"No! I want my surprise. Daddy said I'd get a surprise."

"Mandy, stop this," Avery said sternly, "and eat your dinner."

Mandy gave the room service tray a push. It went crashing to the floor. Avery shot to her feet. "That settles it." She yanked Mandy out of her chair, spun her around and swatted her bottom hard several times. "I won't put up with that from you, young lady."

At first Mandy was too stunned to react. She looked up at Avery with wide, round eyes. Then her lower lip began to quiver. Enormous tears rolled down her cheeks. She opened her mouth and let out a wail that would awake the dead.

Zee reached for her, but Avery edged her aside and gathered Mandy against her. The child's arms wrapped around her neck. She burrowed her wet face into Avery's shoulder.

Avery rubbed her back soothingly. "Aren't you ashamed of yourself for having to get a spanking? Daddy thinks you're a good girl."

"I *am* a good girl."

"Not tonight. You're being very naughty and you know it."

The crying jag lasted for several minutes. When it finally abated, Mandy raised her blotchy face. "Can I have my ice cream now?"

"No, you can't." Avery pushed back strands of Mandy's hair that tears had plastered to her cheeks. "I don't believe you deserve a treat, do you?" Her lower lip continued to tremble, but she shook her head no. "If you behave now, when Daddy gets here tonight, I'll let him wake you up to give you your surprise. Okay?"

"I want some ice cream."

"I'm sorry," Avery said shaking her head no. "Bad behavior doesn't get rewarded. Understand Mommy?"

Mandy nodded regretfully. Avery eased her off her lap. "Now, let's go take a bath and put your pajamas on so you and Grandma can go to bed. The faster you go to sleep, the sooner Daddy will get here."

Twenty minutes later, Avery tucked her in. Mandy was so tired, she was almost asleep by the time her head hit the pillow. Avery was also exhausted. The incident had sapped her stamina. She was in no frame of mind to quarrel with Zee, whose compact body was quaking with disapproval.

"Tate will hear about the spanking," she said.

"Good. I believe he should."

She was on her way into the connecting room when the telephone rang. It was Tate. "Are you coming, or what?" he demanded without preamble.

"Yes, I'm coming. I had a problem with Mandy, but she's in bed now. I'll get a cab and be there—"

"I'm downstairs in the lobby. Be quick."

She did the best she could in five minutes' time, which was all she dared allow herself. The results weren't spectacular, but good enough to make Tate do a double take as she stepped off the elevator.

The two-piece suit was smart and sassy. The sapphire blue silk enhanced her own vibrant coloring. The curl in her hair had been sacrificed to the humidity, so she'd opted for a sophisticated, dramatic effect and capped it off with a pair of bold, gold earrings.

"What the hell's going on?" Tate asked as he ushered her toward the revolving door. "Dad said Mandy was upset."

"Upset, my foot. Mandy was being an absolute terror."

"Why?"

"She's three years old, that's why. She'd been cooped up in a car all day. I understood why she was behaving the way she was, but understanding only stretches so far. I hate to spoil Zee's surprise, but I spanked her."

They had reached the car parked beneath the porte cochere. He paused with his hand on the passenger door handle. "What happened?"

"It got her attention. It also worked."

He studied her resolute expression for a moment, then bobbed his head and brusquely ordered, "Get in."

He quickly tipped the doorman who'd been keeping an eye on the car, got behind the wheel, and drove cautiously out into the street. The windshield wipers clacked vigorously, but fought a losing battle against the heavy rainfall.

Tate headed north on Main Street, rounded the distinctive Tarrant County Courthouse, then drove across the Trinity River Bridge toward north Fort Worth, where cowboys and cutthroats had made history in its celebrated stockyards.

"Why did you come to get me?" she asked as the car streaked through the stormy night. "I could have taken a cab."

"I wasn't doing anything except hanging around backstage anyway. I thought the time would be better spent doing taxi duty."

"What did Dirk and Ralph say about you leaving?"

"Nothing. They didn't know."

"What!"

"By the time they figure out I'm not there, it'll be too

late for them to do anything about it. Anyway, I was goddamn tired of them editing my speech.''

He was driving imprudently fast, but she didn't call that to his attention. He seemed in no mood to listen to criticism. His disposition seemed black all around. ''Why were we summoned to join you?'' she asked, hoping to find the root of his querulousness.

''Have you been following the polls?''

''Yes.''

''Then you know that a change of strategy is called for. According to my advisers, desperation measures must be taken. We embarked on this trip to pump up enthusiasm, gain support. Instead, I've lost three points since we started.''

''Nelson said something about your maverick image.''

He swore beneath his breath. ''That's how they think I'm coming across.''

''They?''

''Who else? Dirk and Ralph. They thought the bulwark of a family standing behind me would convince voters that I'm not a hothead. A family man projects a more stable image. Shit, I don't know. They go on and on till I don't even hear them anymore.''

He wheeled into the parking lot of Billy Bob's Texas. Touted as the world's largest honky-tonk, complete with an indoor rodeo arena, it had been leased by Tate's election committee for the night. Several country and western performers had donated their time and talent to the fund-raising rally.

Tate nosed the car up to the front door. A cowboy wearing a yellow slicker and dripping felt Stetson stepped from the alcove and approached the car. Tate lowered the foggy window.

''Can't park here, mister.''

''I'm—''

''You gotta move your car. You're in a fire lane.''

''But I'm—''

''There's a parking lot across the street, but because of the crowd, it might already be full.'' He shifted his wad of tobacco from one jaw to the other. ''Anyhow, you can't leave it here.''

"I'm Tate Rutledge."

"Buck Burdine. Pleased to meet ya. But you still can't park here."

Buck obviously had no interest in politics. Tate glanced at Avery. Diplomatically, she was studying her hands where they lay folded in her lap and biting her lip to keep from laughing.

Tate tried again. "I'm running for senator."

"Look, mister, are you gonna move your car, or am I gonna have to kick ass?"

"I guess I'm gonna move my car."

A few minutes later, he parked in an alley several blocks away, between a boot repair shop and a tortilla factory. As soon as he cut the engine, he looked across the interior of the car at Avery. She glanced at him sideways. Simultaneously, they burst out laughing. It lasted for several minutes.

"Aw, Jesus," he said, squeezing the bridge of his nose, "I'm tired. It feels good to laugh. Guess I have Buck Burdine to thank."

Rain was coming down in torrents and sheeting against the windows of the car. The streets were virtually deserted on this rainy weeknight. The businesses that sandwiched them were closed, but their neon signs projected wavering stripes of pink and blue into the car.

"Has it been horrible, Tate?"

"Yeah. Horrible." Mindlessly, he traced the stitching around the padded leather steering wheel. "I'm losing ground every day, not gaining it. My campaign's on the wane here in the final weeks, when it should be picking up momentum by the hour. It looks like Dekker is going to pull it off again." He thumped the steering wheel with his fist.

Avery shut out everything except him. She gave him her undivided attention, knowing that he needed a sounding board that didn't talk back. He hadn't had to tell her that he was tired. Lines of weariness and worry were etched at the sides of his mouth and around his eyes.

"I've never once doubted that it was my destiny to serve this state in the U.S. Senate." He turned his head and looked at her. She nodded in agreement but said nothing, uncertain how she should respond. He wouldn't tolerate banalities and platitudes:

"I even skipped running for state representative and went after what I ultimately wanted. But now, I'm beginning to wonder if I've been listening to people who only told me what I wanted to hear. Have I got delusions of grandeur?"

"Undoubtedly." She smiled when he registered surprise over her candor. "But name one politician who doesn't. It takes someone with enormous self-confidence to assume the responsibility for thousands of people's lives, Tate."

"We're all egomaniacs, then?"

"You have a healthy self-esteem. That's nothing to be ashamed of or apologize for. The ability to lead is a gift, like being musically inclined or having a genius for numbers."

"But no one accuses a mathematical wizard of exploitation."

"Your integrity wouldn't allow you to exploit anyone, Tate. The ideals you espouse aren't just campaign slogans. You believe in them. You're not another Rory Dekker. He's all wind. He's got no substance. In time, the voters are going to realize that."

"You still think I'm going to win?"

"Absolutely."

"Yeah?"

"Yeah."

It became very close and still within the car while the rain continued to beat against the roof and lash at the windows. He reached across the car and laid his hand flat on her chest, his thumb and little finger stretching from collarbone to collarbone.

Avery's eyes closed. She made a slight swaying motion toward him as though being tugged by an invisible string. When she opened her eyes again, he was much nearer. He had moved to the center of the bench seat and his eyes were busily scanning her face.

His hand slid up her throat and curled around the back of her neck. When his lips touched hers, spontaneous combustion consumed them. They kissed madly while their hands battled to gain ground. His smoothed down her chest, over the tailored suit jacket, then up again to knead her breasts through the quality cloth.

Avery caressed his hair, his cheeks, the back of his neck, and his shoulders, then drew him against her as she fell back into the corner of the seat.

He unbuttoned the two buttons on her left shoulder and wrestled with the row of hooks running down that side of her torso. When he shoved open the jacket, the gold locket now containing his and Mandy's pictures slipped into the valley between her breasts. The neon lights made a night-time rainbow of her skin. Streams of rainwater cast fluid shadows across her breasts which were swelling out of her bra.

He bent his head and kissed the full curve, then the dark center. Through the lace, his tongue flicked roughly, hungrily, lustfully.

"Tate," she moaned, as sensations swirled from her breast throughout the rest of her body. "Tate, I want you."

Clumsily, he freed himself from his trousers and carried her hand down. Her fingers encircled the rigid length of his penis. As she caressed its velvety tip with the ball of her thumb, he buried his face between her breasts and gasped snatches of erotic phrases and promises.

His hands slipped beneath her narrow skirt. She helped him get her underpants off. Their lips met in a frantic, passion-driven kiss while they sought a workable position within the impossible confines of the front seat.

"Damn!" he cursed, his voice sounding dry and raw.

Suddenly he sat up and pulled her over his lap. Holding her bottom between his hands beneath her skirt, he positioned her above his erection. She impaled herself. They gave glad cries which, within seconds, diminished to pleasurable groans.

Their lips sought and found each other while their tongues were rampant and quick. He squeezed the taut flesh of her derriere and stroked her thighs above her hosiery and between the lacy suspenders of her garter belt. She used her knees for elevation that teasingly threatened to release his cock before sinking down onto it until it was fully imbedded again. She rode him, milked him.

"Damn, you can fuck."

Having rasped that, he nuzzled his head against her breast until he had worked it free of her brassiere cup. He laved the raised nipple with his tongue, then took it into his mouth. He slid one of his hands between her damp thighs and entwined his fingers in the soft hair, then slipped them into the cleft and stroked the small protuberance.

Avery's breathing became choppy and loud. She bent her head over his shoulder. Tensing around the hardness within her and grinding against the magic stroking finger without, she had a very long, very wet climax that coincided with Tate's.

They didn't move for a full five minutes. Each was too weak. Finally, Avery eased herself off his lap and retrieved her underpants from the floorboard. Wordlessly, Tate passed her a handkerchief.

Self-consciously, she accepted it and said, "Thank you."

"Are you okay? Did I hurt you?"

"No, why?"

"You . . . you feel so small."

Her eyes were the first to fall away after a long, telling stare.

Once she had tidied herself and straightened her helplessly wrinkled clothing, she flipped down the sun visor and looked with dismay at her reflection in the vanity mirror.

Her hairdo had been ravaged. Clumps of moussed hair surrounded her head like a spiked halo. An earring was missing. Carefully outlined lipstick had been smeared over the entire lower third of her face. "I'm a wreck."

Tate made his body as straight as the accommodations would allow and tucked in his shirttail. His necktie was askew and his coat was hanging off one shoulder. He fumbled with his pants zipper and cursed it twice before closing it successfully.

"Do the best you can," he said, passing her the earring he'd just sat down on.

"I'll try." With the cosmetics in her purse, she repaired the damages to her makeup and did what she could with her coiffure. "I guess we can blame my hair on the weather."

"What'll we blame the whisker burns on?" Tate touched the corner of her mouth. "Do they sting?"

She gave a small, unrepentant shrug and smiled shyly. He smiled back, then got out and came around for her.

By the time they reached the backstage area where Eddy was pacing and Ralph was jingling change in both pockets, they truly did look the worse for wear—windblown and rain-spattered, but inordinately happy.

"Where the hell have you been?" Eddy was almost too livid to form the words.

Tate answered with admirable composure. "I went to pick up Carole."

"That's what Zee told us when we called the hotel," Ralph said. He was no longer rattling change. "What possessed you to pull such a damn fool stunt? She said you'd left half an hour ago. What took so long?"

"No place to park," Tate said tersely, disliking this cross-examination. "Where are Jack and the others?"

"Our front trying to keep the hounds at bay. Hear that?" Eddy pointed toward the auditorium, where the crowd could be heard stamping in beat to a patriotic march and chanting, "We want Tate! We want Tate!"

"They'll be all the more glad to see me," Tate said calmly.

"Here's your speech." Eddy tried to thrust several sheets of paper at him, but he refused to take them.

He tapped the side of his head instead and said, "Here's my speech."

"Don't pull that disappearing act again," Ralph warned him bossily. "It's stupid not to let at least one of us know where you are at all times."

Dirk hadn't said a word. His dark face was even darker with fury. It wasn't aimed at Tate, but at Avery. He hadn't taken his beady eyes off her since their breathless arrival. She had withstood his baleful glare with aplomb. When he finally spoke, his voice vibrated with rage. "From now on, Mrs. Rutledge, when you want to be screwed, do it on your time, not ours."

Tate, making a savage, snarling sound, launched himself against the other man. He would have knocked him off his feet if he hadn't flattened him against the nearest wall. His forearm formed a bar as hard as steel against Dirk's throat and his knee plowed high into his crotch. Dirk grunted with surprise and pain.

"Tate, have you gone completely crazy?" Eddy shouted.

He tried to remove Tate's arm from Dirk's throat, but it wouldn't be budged. Tate's nose wasn't even an inch from Dirk's. His face was smooth and blank with the single-mindedness of a man bent on murder. Dirk's face, by contrast, was growing progressively bluer.

"Tate, please," Avery said desperately, laying a hand on his shoulder. "Never mind him. What he says doesn't matter to me."

"For God's sake, Tate." Frantically, Eddy tried to wedge himself between the two men. "Let him go. Now's not the time. Jesus, think!"

"If you ever," Tate said in a slow, throbbing voice, "*ever* insult my wife like that again, you'll die choking on it. You got that, you son of a bitch?" He dug into Dirk's testicles with his knee. The man, whose small eyes were bugging with fear, bobbed his head as much as Tate's arm beneath his chin would permit.

Gradually, Tate's arm relaxed. Dirk bent from the waist, clutching his balls, coughing and sputtering. Ralph rushed to assist his cohort. Tate smoothed back his hair, turned to Eddy, and said coolly, "Let's go." He reached for Avery.

She took his extended hand and followed him on stage.

THIRTY-EIGHT

Mandy insisted on substituting her nightgown for the T-shirt Tate gave her, even though it was long after midnight and closer to breakfast than bedtime.

"Now you're an honorary Dallas Cowboys cheerleader," he said as he slipped it over her head.

She admired the gaudy silver lettering on the front of her new shirt, then smiled up at him beguilingly. "Thank you,

Daddy.'' Yawning hugely, she retrieved Pooh Bear and
dropped back onto her pillow.

"She's learning to be a woman, all right."

"Exactly what does that comment imply?" Avery asked
him as they went into their bedroom on the other side of the
parlor.

"She took the goods, but didn't come across with a hug
or a kiss."

Avery propped her hands on her hips. "Should I warn the
female voters that behind your public feminist stand on
issues, you're nothing but a rotten chauvinist at heart?"

"Please don't. I need all the votes I can get."

"I thought it went very well tonight."

"Once I got there, you mean."

"And before, too." Her confidential inflection brought his
head up. "Thank you for defending my honor, Tate."

"You don't have to thank me for that."

They exchanged a long gaze before Avery turned away
and began removing her clothes. She slipped into the bathroom, took a quick shower, put on a negligee, then relinquished
the bathroom to Tate.

Lying in bed, Avery listened to the water running as he
brushed his teeth. From sharing other hotel suites, she knew
that he never replaced the towel on the bar, but always left it
wadded in a damp heap beside the sink.

When he emerged from the bathroom, she turned her
head, intending to tease him about that bad habit. The
words were never voiced.

He was naked. His hand was on the light switch, but he
was looking at her. She rose to a sitting position, an unspoken
question in her eyes.

"In the past," he said in a hoarse whisper, "I could
block you out of my mind. I can't anymore. I don't know
why. I don't know what you're doing now that you didn't do
before, or what you're not doing that you once did, but I'm
unable to ignore you and pretend that you don't exist. I'll
never forgive you for that abortion, or for lying to me about
it, but things like what happened tonight in the car make it
easier to forget.

"Ever since that night in Dallas, I'm like an addict who's

discovered a new drug. I want you a lot, and I want you constantly. Fighting it is making me crazy and nearly impossible to live with. The last few weeks haven't been fun for me or for anybody around me.

"So, as long as you're my wife, I'm going to exercise my conjugal rights." He paused momentarily. "Is there anything you have to say about that?"

"Yes."

"Well?"

"Turn out the light."

The tension ebbed from his splendid body. A grin tugged at one corner of his lips. He switched out the light, then slid into bed and pulled her into his arms.

Her nightgown seemed to vaporize beneath his caressing hands. Before Avery had time to prepare herself for it, she was lying naked beneath him, and he was stroking her skin with his fingertips. Occasionally his lips left hers to sample a taste of throat, breast, shoulder, belly.

Desire rivered through her, a constant ebbing and flowing of sensation until even her extremities were pulsing. Her body was sensitized to each nuance of his—from the strands of hair that fell over his brow and dusted her skin each time he dipped his head for a kiss, to the power in his lean thighs that entwined with hers before gradually separating them.

When he levered himself above her, poised for entrance, she prolonged the anticipation by bracketing his rib cage between her hands and rubbing her face in his chest hair. Her lips brushed kisses across his nipples. The sound of Tate's hoarse moan was her reward.

Hungrily, their mouths found each other again. His kisses were hot and sweet and deep . . . and that's what he said of her body when he claimed it.

Mandy, riding on Tate's shoulders, squealed as he dipped and staggered as though he were about to fall with her. She gripped double handfuls of his hair, which made him yelp.

"Shh, you two!" Avery admonished. "You'll get us kicked out of this hotel."

They were making their way down the long corridor from the elevator to their suite after having eaten breakfast in the

restaurant downstairs. They'd left Nelson and Zee drinking
coffee, but Mandy had been getting restless. The formal
dining room was no place for an energetic child.

Tate passed Avery the key to their suite. They went
inside. The parlor was full of busy people. "What the hell's
going on in here?" Tate asked as he swung Mandy down.

Eddy glanced up from his perusal of the morning paper
and removed the Danish pastry that he'd been holding
between his teeth. "We needed to meet and you have the
only room with a parlor."

"Make yourselves at home," Tate said sarcastically.

They already had. Trays of juice, coffee, and Danish had
been sent up. Fancy was polishing off a bagel as she sat
crossed-legged on the bed, flipping through a fashion magazine. Dorothy Rae was sipping what looked like a Bloody
Mary and staring vacantly out the window. Jack was on the
phone, a finger plugging one ear. Ralph was watching the
"Today Show." Dirk was riffling through Tate's closet with
the appraising eye of a career shopper at a clearance
sale.

"You got a good review last night," Eddy commented
around the sweet roll.

"Good."

"I'll take Mandy into the other room." Avery placed her
hands on the child's shoulders and steered her toward the
connecting door.

"No, you stay," Dirk said, turning away from the closet.
"No hard feelings about last night, okay? We've all been
under a lot of pressure. Now the air's been cleared."

The man was insufferable. Avery wanted to slap the
phony, ingratiating smile off his dour face. She looked at
Tate. Ignoring the campaign expert, he told her, "I guess
you'd better stick around."

Jack hung up the phone. "All set. Tate's got a live
interview on channel five at five o'clock. We need to have
him there no later than four-thirty."

"Great," Ralph said, rubbing his hands together. "Any
word from the Dallas stations?"

"I've got calls in."

Someone knocked on the door. It was Nelson and Zee. A

man, a stranger to Avery, was with them. Fancy bounded off the bed and embraced her grandparents in turn. Since her arrival in Fort Worth, her mood had been effervescent.

"Good morning, Fancy." Zee cast a disapproving glance at Fancy's denim miniskirt and red cowboy boots, but said nothing.

"Who's he?" Tate asked, nodding at the man lingering on the threshold.

"The barber we sent for." Dirk stepped forward and pulled the dazed man into the room. "Sit down, Tate, and let him get started. He can clip while we talk. Something conservative," he told the barber, who whisked a blue-and-white-striped drape around Tate's neck and took a comb to his hair.

"Here," Ralph said, shoving a sheaf of papers beneath Tate's nose. "Glance over these."

"What are they?"

"Your speeches for today."

"I've already written my speeches." No one listened to or acknowledged him.

The phone rang. Jack answered. "Channel four," he excitedly informed them, covering the mouthpiece.

"Zee, Nelson, find seats, please, and let's get down to business. The morning's getting away." In his element, Dirk took the floor. "As Eddy has said, we had a terrific turnout at Billy Bob's last night and raised a lot of campaign dollars. God knows we need them. Once momentum subsides, supporters stop contributing."

"Even though we're currently behind by a substantial margin, we don't want it to look like we're giving up," Ralph said as he bounced the coins in his pocket.

"The people at channel four said they'd be at General Dynamics to get a sound bite of Tate's speech, but that's all they'll promise," Jack reported as he hung up the phone.

Dirk nodded. "Not great, but better than nothing."

"See, Tate," Ralph said, continuing as though the second conversation weren't going on, "even if you lose, you don't want it to look like you gave up."

"I'm not going to lose." He glanced at Avery and winked.

"Well, no, of course not," Ralph stammered, laughing uncomfortably. "I only meant—"

"You're not taking enough off," Dirk sourly told the barber. "I said *conservative*."

Tate batted the barber's fussing hands away. "What's this?" He pointed to a paragraph in one of the speeches that had been written for him. Again he was ignored.

"Hey, listen to this." Eddy read a passage from the newspaper. "Dekker comes right out and calls you a rabble-rouser, Tate."

"I think he's running scared," Nelson said, drawing Dirk's attention to him.

"Nelson, I want you to be a prominent figure on the podium when Tate speaks at General Dynamics this afternoon. Those military contracts keep them in business. Since you're an ex-flier, you'll be a bonus."

"Am I to go? And Mandy?" Zee asked.

"I'll be glad to stay with Mandy," Dorothy Rae offered.

"Everybody goes." Dirk frowned at the empty glass in Dorothy Rae's hand. "And everybody looks his best. Squeaky-clean America. That means you too, missy," he said to Fancy. "No miniskirt."

"Go screw yourself."

"Francine Rutledge!" Nelson thundered. "You'll be sent home promptly if you use that kind of language again."

"Sorry," she mumbled. "But who's this asshole to tell me how to dress?"

Dirk, unfazed, turned to Avery. "You usually do fine as far as wardrobe goes. Don't wear anything too flashy today. These are working people, wage earners. Tate, I picked the gray suit for you today."

"Don't forget to remind him about his shirt," Ralph said.

"Oh, yes, wear a blue shirt, not white. White doesn't photograph as well on TV."

"All my blue shirts are dirty."

"I told you to send them out to be laundered every day."

"Well, I forgot, okay?" Suddenly he swiveled around and snatched the scissors from the barber's hands. "I don't want my hair cut any more. I like it like this."

In a tone of voice he might have used on Mandy, Dirk said, "It's too long, Tate."

He was out of his chair in an instant. "Who says? The voters? Those workers out at GD? Channel five's viewing audience? Or just you?"

Avery wanted to applaud. Unlike everyone else, she hadn't been caught up in the pandemonium going on around her. She'd been watching Tate. The more he read of the papers Ralph had given him to study, the deeper his scowl had become. She had sensed that his temper was about to erupt and she'd been right.

He whipped the drape from around his neck, sending hair clippings flying. He fished into his pocket and came up with a fifty-dollar bill, foisted it on the barber, and walked him to the door. "Thanks a lot." Tate shut the door on him.

When Tate turned back into the room, his expression was as ominous as the low clouds that still scuttled across the sky. "Next time, Dirk, I'll let *you* know when I need a haircut, if I deem it any of your business, which, frankly, I don't. And I would also appreciate it if you'd stay out of my closet and consult me before moving in on my family's private quarters."

"There was no place else to meet," Eddy said.

"The hell there wasn't, Eddy," he shouted, rounding on his friend, who had dared to intervene. "This hotel has several hundred rooms. But since you're already here," he said, picking up the sheets of paper he'd tossed down on the dresser, "I'd like to know what the hell this is supposed to signify?"

Ralph leaned over and read a few lines. "That's your position on the new education bill."

"Like hell it is. This is bullshit. That's what this is." He slapped the sheet of paper with the back of his hand. "Whitewashed, watered down, wishy-washy bullshit."

Zee left her chair. "I'll take Mandy into the other room to watch TV." She led the child away by the hand.

"I have to go potty, Grandma."

"Okay, darling. Fancy, you might want to come with us."

"Hell, no. I wouldn't budge for ten million bucks," she said from her position in the middle of the bed. She opened a fresh stick of Juicy Fruit and added it to the one already in her mouth.

When the door had been closed behind Zee and Mandy, Ralph ventured forth with a conciliatory explanation. "We simply felt, Tate, that your position on some of the campaign issues should be softened."

"Without consulting me?" Tate demanded, bearing down on the much shorter man. "It's *my* position," he said, thumping his chest. "My position."

"You're trailing in the polls," the man pointed out reasonably.

"I was doing that before you were retained to advise me. I've sunk lower since then."

"Because you haven't been taking our advice."

"Uh-uh," Tate said, stubbornly shaking his head. "I think it's because I've been taking too much of it."

Eddy stood up. "What are you implying, Tate?"

"Not a damn thing. I'm outright stating that I don't need anybody to pick out my shirts and suits or hire my barbers. I'm saying that I don't want anybody to put words in my mouth. I'm saying that I don't want anybody softening my position until it's so soft that even I don't recognize it. The people who have pledged their votes to me on the basis of those positions would think I'd gone crazy. Or worse, that I had betrayed them."

"You're blowing this out of proportion."

Tate confronted his brother. "It's not your hair they're trying to cut, Jack," he said heatedly.

"But it might just as well be," he fired back. "I'm in this as much as you are."

"Then you should know how important it is to me that I'm my own man."

"You are," Eddy said.

"The hell I am! What's wrong with the way I dress?" He gestured down to the clothes he'd worn to breakfast. "Do you really think it matters to those workers out at GD what color shirt I have on? Hell, no! They want to know if I'm for a strong defense program or for cutting the defense budget because my Senate vote may determine whether or not they'll have jobs for the next several years."

He paused to draw a breath and plowed his hand through his hair, which, Avery was glad to see, the barber hadn't gotten too much of. "Look, guys, this is me." He held his arms out perpendicular to his body. "This is the ticket. This is how I originally went to the Texas voters. Change me and they won't recognize me."

"We don't want to change you, Tate," Dirk said expansively. "Only make you better."

He clapped Tate on the shoulder. Tate shrugged off his hand. "Gentlemen, I'd like to speak to my family in private, please."

"If there's something to discuss—"

Tate held up his hand to ward off their objections. "Please." They moved toward the door reluctantly. Dirk shot Eddy a telling glance before they went out.

"Carole, would you pour me a cup of that coffee, please?"

"Certainly." As she rose to do so, Tate dropped into an easy chair. She brought the requested cup of coffee and sat down on the upholstered arm of his chair. Tate took the coffee with one hand and casually draped his other over her knee.

Eddy said, "Well, that was quite a speech."

"I tried it your way, Eddy. Against my better judgment, I let you hire them." His gaze was direct and so was his statement. "I don't like them."

"I'll talk to them, tell them to back off a little."

"Wait," Tate said, as Eddy headed for the door. "That's not good enough. They don't listen."

"Okay, I'll tell them that by the end of this tour we want to see drastic improvements in the polls or else."

"Still not good enough."

"Then what do you suggest?"

Tate looked at everyone in the room before saying, "Give them their walking papers."

"Fire them?" Jack exclaimed. "We can't do that."

"Why not? We hired them, didn't we?"

"You just don't shrug off a company like Wakely and Foster. You'll never be able to use them again."

"I don't consider that any great loss."

"You can't do it," Jack said stubbornly.

Eddy pleaded, "Tate, I beg you to think about this carefully."

"I have. I don't like them. I don't like what they're trying to do."

"Which is?" Jack's tone was snide, his stance belligerent.

"Which is to mold me into what they think I should be, not what I am. Okay, maybe I need some grooming. I could use some coaching, some finesse. But I don't like things to be mandated. I sure as hell don't like words put in my mouth when I don't even agree with them."

"You're only being stubborn," Jack said. "Just like when you were a kid. If I told you you couldn't do something, that's exactly what you became damned and determined to do just to show me up."

Tate expelled a long breath. "Jack, I've listened to your advice, and it's always been sound. I don't want to second-guess you on this decision—"

"But that's what you're doing, isn't it?"

"It was my decision, too," Tate said, raising his voice. "Now I'm changing my mind."

"Just like that?" Eddy said, snapping his fingers. "With the election only a few weeks away, you want to switch horses in the middle of the stream?"

"No, dammit, that's what they were trying to do!" He shot out of his chair and pointed toward the door through which the two under discussion had passed.

"They wanted to bend and shape me until I wouldn't be recognizable to the voters who have backed me from the beginning. I'd be selling out. I'd be no better than Dekker. Slicker than owl shit. Two-faced. Double-dealing." He was met with a wall of silent opposition from Eddy and his brother.

He turned to Nelson. "Dad? Help me out here."

"Why ask for my help now? You've already let your temper get the best of you. Don't ever get mad, Tate. Get even."

"How?"

"Win."

"By keeping my mouth shut and taking their advice?"

"Unless you feel that you're being compromised."

"Well, that's exactly where I am. I'd rather lose the election being myself than win and know I've had to compromise on everything I stand for. I'm sorry if none of you agrees."

"I'm on Eddy's side," Fancy said, "if anybody's interested in my opinion."

"Nobody is," Jack said to her.

"Carole?"

She had refrained from entering the verbal melee. Until Tate asked for her opinion, she intended to withhold it. Now that he had, she raised her head and looked up at him with newly formed intimacy and the wordless communication of lovers.

"Whatever you decide is all right with me, Tate. I'm with you all the way."

"Oh, yeah? Since when?" Jack rounded on Tate. "You talk about compromises. Sleeping with her again is the biggest compromise you ever made, little brother."

"That's enough, Jack!" Nelson bellowed.

"Dad, you know as well as I do that—"

"*Enough!* When you can control your own wife, you can start criticizing Tate."

Jack glared at his father, then at his brother, then hunched his shoulders and stormed out. Dorothy Rae rose from her chair unsteadily and followed him.

"I guess you'll walk next," Tate said to Eddy in the tense aftermath of their departure.

Eddy smiled lopsidedly. "You know better than that. Unlike Jack, I don't take these things personally. I think you're wrong, but . . ." He gave an eloquent shrug. "We'll know on election day." He clapped his friend on the back. "Guess I'd better go break the bad news to our *former* consultants." He left; Fancy was hot on his heels.

Zee brought Mandy in. The atmosphere still crackled with animosity. Uneasily, she remarked, "I heard a lot of shouting."

"We got some things sorted out," Nelson said.

"I hope my decision is okay by you, Dad."

"As you said, it was your decision. I hope you're prepared to live with it."

"For my peace of mind, that's the way it had to be."

"Then stop apologizing for something that's already done."

"I told Mandy we would walk down to Sundance Square for a while," Zee said, interrupting the uncomfortable conversation. "I don't think it's going to rain anymore."

"I'll come along," Nelson said, scooping the child into his arms, his good humor seemingly restored. "I could use the exercise. And we won't mind if it does rain, will we, Mandy?"

"Thanks for backing me up," Tate said to Avery when they were finally alone. "You haven't always."

"As Jack rudely reminded me."

"He was upset."

"More than that, Tate. Jack despises me."

He seemed disinclined to address that. Perhaps he knew, as Avery did, that Jack didn't like Carole, but he desired her. Maybe Tate ignored that calamitous fact in the desperate hope that it would go away.

"Why'd you do it?" he asked. "Why'd you take my side? Did you feel like it was your wifely duty?"

"No," she said, taking umbrage. "I sided with you because I believe you're right. I didn't like them or their meddling or their advice any better than you did."

It had occurred to her that the men from Wakely and Foster might somehow be connected to the plot to assassinate Tate. That was another reason she was so glad to see the last of them.

After the recent heated discussion, the suite suddenly seemed very quiet. Paradoxically, without all the other people, the parlor seemed smaller, not larger. Their silent solitude pressed in on them.

Avery clasped her hands at her waist. "Well, I—"

"Good of Mom and Dad to take Mandy for a walk."

"Yes, it was."

"She'll enjoy the outing."

"And it'll give you a chance to study your speeches without interruption."

"Hmm."

"Although I don't think you really need to study them."

"No, I feel comfortable about today's schedule."

"That's good."

He contemplated the toes of his boots for a moment. When he looked up, he asked, "Do you think it'll rain?"

"I, uh . . ." She gave the window a cursory glance. "I don't think so, no. It—"

He reached for her, pulled her against him, kissed her neck.

"Tate?"

"Hmm?" He walked her backward toward the sofa.

"I thought, after last night, you wouldn't want . . ."

"You thought wrong."

THIRTY-NINE

"Boo!"

Fancy sprang out from behind the door as soon as Eddy entered his hotel room. He didn't even flinch. "How'd you get in here?"

"I bribed a maid."

"With what?"

"Uncle Tate's jockstrap."

"You're sick."

"Don't ya love it?"

"What's that?" He pointed to a table in front of the large window. It was draped with a white cloth and had two place settings laid out on it.

"Lunch. Crab salad in cute little avocado halves."

"You should have asked me first, Fancy."

"Aren't you hungry?"

"It wouldn't matter if I were. I've only got a minute."

He sat down on the edge of the bed and picked up the telephone. After consulting the piece of scrap paper in his shirt pocket, he punched out the number. "Mr. George Malone, please."

Fancy stood on her knees behind him and ground her pelvis against his spine. "Mr. Malone? This is Eddy Paschal, with the Rutledge campaign. You called?" Eddy ducked his head when she leaned over his shoulder and bit his earlobe.

"Mr. Rutledge's schedule is tight, I'm afraid. What did you have in mind? How many people? Uh-huh."

She kissed his neck, lightly sucking the skin up against her teeth. He covered the mouthpiece with his hand. "Cut it out, Fancy. I'm busy."

Pouting, she flounced off the bed. Moving to the bureau mirror, she paused to plump her hair. Bending at the waist, she flung the thick mane upside down. When she straightened up, she was encouraged to notice that Eddy had been looking at her ass. Facing him with her feet widely spaced, she gathered up her short skirt, flirtatiously raising it an inch at a time.

"How soon do you have to know?"

As Eddy continued to speak smoothly into the telephone, she ran her splayed hands up the fronts of her thighs. Her thumbs met at the red satin triangle covering her pubis. She stroked it once, twice, then peeled the panties off and dangled them in front of his nose.

"I'll speak with Mr. Rutledge and get back to you as soon as possible. In any event, we appreciate your interest. Thank you for the invitation."

He hung up. To Fancy's dismay he brushed past her and went to the bathroom, where he combed his hair and washed his hands.

"What the hell's wrong with you?" she demanded when she joined him.

"Nothing. I'm in a hurry, that's all."

"You're mad because Uncle Tate had you fire those assholes, aren't you?"

"Not mad. I just disagree, that's all."

"Well, don't take it out on me."

"I'm not." He straightened his tie and checked his cuff links.

"Quite a scene this morning, wasn't it? I've never seen Uncle Tate so hot. He's kinda cute when he's in that mood. I love it when a man is on the verge of losing his temper." She slipped her arms beneath Eddy's, reached around him, and pressed her hands against his fly. "That potential violence is so sexy."

"I haven't got time for you now, Fancy." He removed her hands and stepped back into the bedroom.

She flopped down on the bed and watched as he sorted through the papers in his briefcase. He looked so handsome when his brow was furrowed with concentration.

Inspired, Fancy scooted up the bed until her back was against the headboard. She peeled her white cotton sweater over her head and tossed it on the floor beside her discarded panties. Then, left only in her miniskirt and red cowboy boots, she softly called his name. He turned. Slowly, she dragged her tongue over her lower lip and whispered, "Ever had a cowgirl?"

"As a matter of fact, I have," he said blandly. "Last night. In the ass. Or don't you remember?"

Fancy's widespread knees snapped together like the jaws of a sprung trap. She rolled to the edge of the bed, picked up her sweater, and worked it over her head, furiously thrusting her arms into the sleeves.

When she confronted him, her eyes were shimmering with tears. "That wasn't very nice."

"You seemed to think so last night."

"That's not what I meant," she yelled.

Eddy calmly closed his briefcase and picked up the jacket of his suit. "*Nice* is a strange word coming from you." He headed for the door.

She caught his sleeve as he moved past her. "Why are you being so hateful to me?"

"I'm in a hurry, Fancy."

"Then you're not mad?"

He sidestepped her. "I'm not mad."

"Will I see you later?"

"At the rally this afternoon." He patted his pocket to

make sure he had his room key, then reached for the doorknob.

She flattened herself against the door. "You know what I mean. Will I see you later?" Smiling seductively, she squeezed him through his trousers.

"Yes, I know what you mean." He brushed aside her caressing hand and opened the door, despite her efforts to keep him from it. "In the meantime, try and stay out of trouble."

As the door closed behind him, Fancy swore liberally. She'd planned an intimate little lunch, then a quick, raunchy tumble. Or, depending on his schedule, a long leisurely afternoon of lovemaking.

So much for that, she thought resentfully. Nobody did or said anything anymore unless it related to the election. She was damn sick and tired of hearing about *the election*. She would be so glad when it was over and done with so Eddy could concentrate solely on her.

She propped herself against the headboard again and turned on the TV. A soap opera couple were smooching beneath satin sheets. Angry and jealous, she mashed the button on the remote control to switch channels. Geraldo Rivera was refereeing a shouting match between a funda-mentalist preacher and a cross-dresser. On another station a group of housewives was sniffing open jars of peanut butter. She went back to the soap opera.

She loved Eddy passionately, but admitted that part of his appeal was his remoteness. She'd known guys who screwed their brains out, literally. The building could fall down around them and they wouldn't know it until after they climaxed.

Not Eddy. His physical performance was excellent, but his mind remained detached from his body. Even the most intimate acts never required emotional involvement from him. His participation was almost that of an observer.

That steely control excited her. It was different, intriguing.

But sometimes she wished Eddy would gaze at her with dopey adoration like the hunky male soap star was gazing into the face of the gorgeous ingenue. His eyes spoke volumes of unqualified love while his lips nibbled her fingertips.

Capturing Eddy Paschal's heart would be a real coup. She would delight in knowing that he couldn't take his eyes off her, that they would hungrily follow her as she moved about a room.

She would love for Eddy to be totally absorbed with her like that.

She would love for him to be absorbed with her the way Uncle Tate was with Aunt Carole.

Dorothy Rae launched her attack while they were sitting in the limousine waiting for the men to rejoin them. One second she was staring docilely out the window at the red, white, and blue bunting flapping in the wind, the next she was hissing at Avery like a she-cat.

"You loved it, didn't you?"

Mandy's head was resting in Avery's lap. The child had become tired and restless at the outdoor rally, so she had returned to the car with her before the program was over. Mandy was asleep now. Dorothy Rae, who had accompanied them back to the car, had been so quiet that Avery had almost forgotten she was there.

"I'm sorry, what?" she asked vaguely.

"I said you loved it."

Her meaning escaped Avery completely. She shook her head in confusion. "Loved what?"

"Loved making Jack look like a fool this morning."

Was she drunk? Avery took a closer look at her. On the contrary, she seemed in desperate need of a drink. Her eyes were clear but had the blazing wildness of someone gone mad. She was wringing a damp Kleenex between her hands.

"How did I make Jack look like a fool?" Avery asked.

"By taking Tate's side."

"Tate is my husband."

"And Jack's mine!"

Mandy was roused, but after opening her eyes once, she fell back asleep instantly. Dorothy Rae lowered her voice. "That hasn't stopped you from trying to steal him away from me."

"I haven't tried to steal him."

"Not lately, maybe," she said, taking a swipe at her leaky eyes with the Kleenex, "but before the crash you did."

Avery said nothing.

"The thing that makes it so despicable," Dorothy Rae continued, "is that you really didn't want him. As soon as he became interested, you spurned him. You didn't care that your rejection crushed his ego. You only wanted to get at Tate by flirting with his brother."

Avery couldn't deny the ugly allegations because they were probably true. Carole wouldn't have had any scruples against having an affair with her husband's brother, or, just short of that, making out like she was open to one. Most of her pleasure would be derived from the disharmony and devastation it would cause within the family. Perhaps that was all part of Carole's scheme to destroy Tate.

"I have no designs on Jack, Dorothy Rae."

"Because he's not the one in the limelight." Her hand clenched Avery's arm like a claw. "He never is. Never was. You knew that. Why didn't you just leave him alone? How dare you play with people's lives like that?"

Avery wrenched her arm from the other woman's grip. "Did you fight me for him?"

Dorothy Rae wasn't prepared for a counterattack. She stared at Avery with stupefaction. "Huh?"

"Did you ever fight me for Jack's attention, or did you just drink yourself into a stupor every day and let it happen?"

Dorothy Rae's face began to work convulsively. Her red-rimmed eyes got redder, wetter. "That's not a very kind thing to say."

"People have been kind to you for too long. Everybody in the family turns a blind eye to your disease."

"I don't have a—"

"You've got a disease, Dorothy Rae. Alcoholism is a disease."

"I'm not an alcoholic!" she cried tearfully, echoing the denials that her own mother had used for years. "I have a few drinks—"

"No, you drink to get drunk and you stay drunk. You wallow in self-pity and then wonder why your husband lusts after other women. Look at yourself. You're a mess. Is it any wonder that Jack has lost interest in you?"

Dorothy Rae groped for the door handle. "I don't have to sit here and listen to this."

"Yes, you do." Turning the tables on her, Avery grabbed her arm and refused to let go. "It's time somebody got tough with you, woke you up to a few facts. Your husband wasn't *stolen* from you. You drove him away."

"That's not true! He swore I wasn't the reason he left."

"Left?"

Dorothy Rae looked at her blankly. "Don't you remember, Carole? It wasn't long after you and Tate got married."

"I . . . of course I remember," Avery stammered. "He stayed gone about . . ."

"Six months," Dorothy Rae said miserably. "The longest six months of my life. I didn't know where he was, what he was doing, if he was ever coming back."

"But he did."

"He said he needed time alone to sort out a few things. He had so many pressures."

"Like what?"

She made a small, helpless gesture. "Oh, Nelson's expectations for the law firm, Tate's campaign, my drinking, Fancy."

"Fancy needs a mother, Dorothy Rae."

She laughed mirthlessly. "But not me. She hates me."

"How do you know? How do you know how she feels about anything? Do you ever talk to her?"

"I try," she whined. "She's impossible."

"She's afraid that no one loves her." Avery drew a quick breath. "And I'm afraid she might be right."

"I love her," Dorothy Rae protested adamantly. "I've given her everything she ever wanted."

"You threw her play-pretties to keep her occupied so that rearing her wouldn't interfere with your drinking. You grieve over the two children you miscarried at the expense of the one you have."

Dorothy Rae had mentioned the babies she had lost the

night Carole's abortion had come to light. Later, Avery had gleaned the details from Fancy. So much of Dorothy Rae's unhappiness was now understandable. Avery leaned across the plush car seat, appealing to Dorothy Rae to listen. "Fancy is courting disaster. She needs you. She needs her father. She needs someone to take a firm hand. If Jack weren't so worried about your drinking, maybe he would devote more time and attention to being a parent. I don't know.

"But I do know that unless you do something, and quickly, she'll keep on behaving the way she does—doing outrageous things just so she'll get noticed. One of these days, she'll go too far and harm herself."

Dorothy Rae pushed back a strand of lank hair and assumed a defensive posture. "Fancy's always been a handful—more than Jack and I could handle. She's got a willful personality. She's just being a teenager, that's all."

"Oh, really? A teenager? Did you know that she came home the other night after having taken a beating from a guy she picked up in a bar? Yes," Avery emphasized when she saw Dorothy Rae pale with disbelief.

"I'm being an armchair psychologist, but I believe Fancy thinks she deserves no better than that. She thinks she's unworthy of being loved because no one has ever loved her, though she's tried every means she knows to get your attention."

"That's not true," Dorothy Rae said, shaking her head in obstinate denial.

"I'm afraid it is. And there's more." Avery decided to throw caution to the wind. She was, after all, pleading for a young woman's life. "She's sleeping with Eddy Paschal."

"I don't believe you," Dorothy Rae wheezed. "He's old enough to be her father."

"I saw her coming out of his hotel room in Houston weeks ago."

"That doesn't mean—"

"It was dawn, Dorothy Rae. You could tell by looking at her what she'd been doing all night. I have every reason to believe the affair is still going on."

"He wouldn't."

It was a sad commentary that Dorothy Rae didn't question her daughter's morality, only that of the family friend. "He is."

Dorothy Rae took several moments to assimilate this information, then her eyes narrowed on Avery. "You're a fine one to cast stones at my daughter."

"You miss my point," Avery said. "I'm not judging Fancy's morals. I'm worried about her. Do you think a man like Eddy is interested in her except for one reason? In light of his friendship with Tate, do you think he'll continue this relationship for any length of time or let it develop into something more meaningful? No.

"What really concerns me is that Fancy considers herself in love with him. If he dumps her, the rejection would only reinforce her low opinion of herself."

Dorothy Rae laughed scornfully. "If anything, my daughter has a high opinion of herself."

"Is that why she picks up strangers and lets them work her over? Is that why she hops from man to man and lets them use her any way they like? Is that why she has set her cap for a man she can't possible have?" Avery shook her head no. "Fancy doesn't like herself at all. She's punishing herself for being unlovable."

Dorothy Rae picked at the shredding tissue. Softly, she said, "I never had much control over her."

"Because you don't have control over yourself."

"You're cruel, Carole."

Avery wanted to take the woman in her arms and hold her. She wanted to say, "No, I'm not cruel. I'm not. I'm telling you this for your own good."

Instead, she responded as Carole might. "I'm just tired of being blamed for the lousy state of your marriage. Be a wife to Jack, not a sniveler."

"What would be the use?" she sighed dejectedly. "Jack hates me."

"Why do you say that?"

"You know why. Because he thinks I tricked him into marrying me. I really did think I was pregnant. I *was* late."

"If Jack hated you," Avery argued, "would he have stayed married to you all these years? Would he have come back after a six-month separation?"

"If Nelson told him to," she said sadly.

Ah. Jack always did what his father told him to. He was bound to his wife by duty, not love. He was the workhorse; Tate was the Thoroughbred. The imbalance could breed a lot of contempt. Maybe Jack had figured out a way to get back at his brother and the parents who favored him.

Avery looked at Dorothy Rae from a different perspective and admitted that she might drink, too, if she were caught in a loveless marriage that was held together only by patriarchic decree. The situation was especially demoralizing to Dorothy Rae, who obviously loved Jack very much.

"Here," Avery said, taking a fresh tissue from her purse and passing it to Dorothy Rae, "blot your eyes. Put on fresh lipstick."

Just as she was finishing, Fancy pulled open the car door and got in. She sat on one of the fold-down stools facing them. "God, this campaigning shit really sucks. Look what that frigging wind did to my hair."

Dorothy Rae glanced at Avery with uncertainty. Avery kept her expression impassive. Dorothy Rae took courage and turned to her daughter. "You shouldn't use that kind of language, Fancy."

"How come?"

"Because it's unbecoming to a lady, that's how come."

"A lady? Right, Mom," she said with an audacious wink. "You just go on deluding yourself. Have a drink while you're at it." She unwrapped a stick of Juicy Fruit and folded it into her mouth. "How much longer is this going to take? Where's the radio in this thing?"

"I'd rather you left it off, Fancy," Avery said. "It will wake up Mandy."

She swore softly and tapped the toes of her red boots together.

"You'll need to wear something more appropriate to the rally tonight," Dorothy Rae said, glancing down at her daughter's shapely bare thighs.

Fancy stretched her arms out on the seat behind her. "Oh, yeah? Well I don't own anything *appropriate*. Thank God."

"When we get back to the hotel, I'll go through the things you brought and see—"

"Like hell, you will!" Fancy exclaimed. "I'll wear whatever I damn well please. Besides, I already told you I don't have anything—"

"How about going shopping this afternoon to buy something?" The two of them looked at Avery, clearly astonished by her sudden proposal. "I'm sure you could find a dress that is suitable but still funky. I can't go, of course, but the two of you could take a cab out to one of the malls while Tate's doing that TV interview. In fact," she added, sensing their hesitation, "I have a list of things you could pick up for me as long as you're going."

"Who said I was going?" Fancy asked crossly.

"Would you like to, Fancy?"

Fancy looked quickly at her mother, who had spoken quietly, almost shyly. She was clearly astonished. Her eyes were mistrustful, but curious as well. Avery detected a speck of vulnerability behind the worldly façade.

"Why don't we?" Dorothy Rae urged in a wavering voice. "It's been ages since we've done something like that together. I might even buy a new dress, too, if you'll help me pick it out."

Fancy's lips parted, as though she was about to nix the idea. After a moment's hesitation, however, she resumed her I-don't-give-a-damn smirk. "Sure, if you want to, I'll go along. Why not?"

She glanced out the window and spotted Eddy as he led the group back toward the waiting limousines. "There sure as hell isn't anything better to do."

FORTY

"Hello, Mr. Lovejoy."

Van was bent over, diddling with his camera. He raised

his head and shook his long hair out of his face. "Oh, hi, Av . . . uh, Mrs. Rutledge."

"It's good to see you again."

"Same here." He inserted a blank tape into his camera and hoisted it onto his shoulder. "I missed you the first week of this trip, but the family has been reunited, I see."

"Yes, Mr. Rutledge wanted us with him."

"Yeah?" Van leered with insinuation. "Ain't that sweet?"

She gave him a reproving look. Although she'd seen Van at various times during the day and they'd nodded at each other, she hadn't had an opportunity to speak with him until now. The afternoon had passed in a blur, especially after her enlightening conversation with Dorothy Rae.

"How's it going?" Van asked her.

"The campaign? It's exhausting work. I've shaken a thousand hands today, and that's a fraction of what Tate has done." It was little wonder to her that he had been so tired when she arrived in Fort Worth the evening before. Yet in front of every crowd he had to appear fresh and enthusiastic.

This was the last appearance of the day. Even though the banquet was officially over, the dais was thronged with people who had cheered his speech and now wanted to meet him personally. She commiserated with the demands being placed on him after such a long day, but she was glad for the opportunity to slip away and seek out Van.

"Heard he fired those buzzards from Wakely and Foster."

"News travels fast."

"Paschal already released a statement to that effect. If you ask me, Rutledge didn't oust them a minute too soon. They made it almost impossible to get close to him. It was like screwing with a steel belted radial on your dick instead of a regular rubber."

Avery hoped no one nearby had overheard the simile. It was one he would use with a co-worker, but hardly one suitable for the ears of a congressional candidate's wife. She hurriedly switched subjects. "The commercials you taped at the ranch are running on TV now."

"You've seen them?"

"Excellent photography, Mr. Lovejoy."

His crooked teeth showed when he smiled. "Thanks, Mrs. Rutledge."

"Have you seen anyone here that you recognize?" she asked, casually scanning the milling crowd.

"Not tonight." His emphasis on the second word brought her eyes snapping back to his. "There were some familiar faces in the crowd this afternoon."

"Oh?" She had monitored the crowds carefully, but to her vast relief, hadn't spotted Gray Hair. Obviously Van had. "Where? Here in the hotel?"

"At General Dynamics and again at Carswell Air Force Base."

"I see," she said shakily. "Is that the first time this trip?"

"Uh-huh," he said, nodding his head yes. "Well, you must excuse me, Mrs. Rutledge. Duty calls. The reporter's signaling me, so I gotta split."

"Oh, I'm sorry I detained you, Mr. Lovejoy."

"No problem. Glad to oblige." He took several steps away from her, then turned back. "Mrs. Rutledge, did you ever stop to think that someone's here to see you and not, uh, your husband?"

"Me?"

"Just a thought. But worth considering." Van's eyes telegraphed a warning. Moments later he was sucked into the ebb and flow of people.

Avery stood very still and rolled the chilling theory over and over in her mind. She was impervious to the motion of the crowd, to the noise and commotion, and oblivious to someone watching her from across the room and wondering what she and the disheveled television cameraman had found to talk about for so long.

"Jack?"

"Hmm?"

"Did you notice my new hairdo?"

Dorothy Rae was admiring her reflection for the first time in so long she couldn't even remember. In her youth, when she'd been the most popular girl at Lampasas High School, primping had been her number-one pastime. But for years there had been little to admire when she looked into a mirror.

Jack, reclining on the hotel room bed reading the newspaper, answered mechanically. "It looks nice."

"Today Fancy and I walked past this trendy beauty parlor in the mall. You know, the kind of place where all the stylists are dressed in black and have several earrings in each ear." Jack grunted. "On impulse, I said, 'Fancy, I'm gonna have a make-over.' So we went in and one of the girls did my hair and makeup and nails."

"Hmm."

She gazed into the mirror, turning her head to one side, then the other. "Fancy said that I should lighten my hair just a bit, right here around my face. She said it would give me a lift and take years off. What do you think?"

"I think I'd be wary of any advice coming from Fancy."

Dorothy Rae's reblossoming self-confidence wilted a little, but she resisted the temptation to go to the bar and pour herself a reviving drink. "I . . . I've stopped drinking, Jack," she blurted out.

He lowered the newspaper and looked at her fully for the first time that evening. The new hairdo was shorter and fluffier and flattering. The subtly applied cosmetics had moistened the dry gullies in her face eroded by rivers of vodka, and given color to the wasteland it had been.

"Since when?"

Her newfound confidence withered a little more at his skepticism, but she staunchly kept her head erect. "This morning."

Jack folded the newspapers and tossed them to the floor. Reaching for the switch of the reading lamp mounted to the headboard, he said, "Good night, Dorothy Rae."

She moved to the bed and clicked the lamp back on. He looked up at her with surprise. "I mean it this time, Jack."

"You've meant it every time you said you were going to quit."

"This time is different. I'm going to check myself into one of those hospitals you've wanted me to go to. After the election, that is. I know that now wouldn't be a convenient time to be committing a member of Tate's family into a hospital for drunks.''

''You're not a drunk.''

She smiled sadly. ''Yes, I am, Jack. Yes, I am. You should have made me admit it a long time ago.'' She put out her hand and tentatively touched his shoulder. ''I'm not blaming you. I'm the one responsible for what I've become.''

Then her fine chin, which had somehow withstood the ravages of abusive drinking and unhappiness, came up another notch. Held at that proud angle, her face bore traces of the beauty queen she had been and the vivacious coed he'd fallen in love with. ''I'm not going to be a useless drunk anymore.''

''We'll see.''

He didn't sound very optimistic, but at least she had his attention, which was something. He didn't listen to her half the time because she rarely had anything worthy of his interest.

She urged him to scoot over so she could sit at the edge of the bed beside him and primly folded her hands in her lap. ''We've got to keep closer tabs on Fancy.''

''Good luck,'' he snorted.

''I realize we can't put her on a leash. She's too old.''

''And too far gone.''

''Maybe. I hope not. I want her to know that I care what happens to her.'' Her lips parted in a small smile. ''We actually got along together this afternoon. She helped me pick out a new dress. Did you notice the one she was wearing tonight? It was still flashy, but conservative by her normal standards. Even Zee commented on it. Fancy needs a firm hand. That's the only way she'll know we love her.'' She paused, glancing at him hesitantly. ''And I want to help you.''

''Help me what?''

''Recover from your disappointments.''

''Disappointments?''

''Mostly Carole. You don't have to admit or deny anything,'' she said quickly. ''I'm stone sober now, but I know that your desire for her wasn't a drunken delusion I had. Whether or not it's been consummated doesn't matter to me.

"I couldn't blame you for being unfaithful. There were times when I loved my next drink as much as I loved you—maybe more. I know you're in love with Carole—infatuated, anyway. She's used you and hurt you. I want to help you get over her.

"And I want to help you get over other disappointments, like the one you had this morning when Tate went against your decision to keep those consultants."

Gaining courage, she touched his face this time. Her hand only shook a little. "Whether anyone else gives you credit for the fine man you are, I do. You've always been my hero, Jack."

He scoffed at that. "Some hero."

"To me you are."

"What's all this about, Dorothy Rae?"

"I want us to love each other again."

He looked at her for a long moment, more meaningfully than he had looked at her in years. "I doubt that can happen."

His futile tonality frightened her. However, she gave him a watery smile. "We'll work on it together. Good night, Jack."

She extinguished the lamp and lay down beside him. He didn't respond when she placed her arms around him, but he didn't turn away as he usually did.

Insomnia had become the norm since Carole had returned from the hospital. Indeed, these nights of wakefulness were cherished, for the night had become the best time in which to think. No one else was around; there was no motion and noise to clutter the brain. Silence bred insight.

What it obviously failed to instill was logic. Because no matter how many times the data was analyzed, the "logical" hypothesis was preposterous.

Carole wasn't Carole.

The hows, whys, and wherefores of it mattered, but not to any extent like the indubitable fact that Carole Navarro Rutledge had been replaced by someone else. Amnesia was the only other explanation for the complete reversal from her former personality. That would explain why she had fallen in love with her husband again, but still wouldn't account for the altered personality traits. Her current persona would only make sense if she were another woman entirely.

Carole wasn't Carole.

Then who was she?

The question was tormenting because so much was at risk. The plan that had taken years to orchestrate was about to come to fruition . . . unless it was thwarted by an impostor. All the elements were in motion. It was too late to turn back, even if that was desired, which it wasn't. Sweet revenge sometimes required bitter sacrifices. Vengeance was not to be denied.

Until the moment it was realized, however, this Carole, this impostor, must be watched. She seemed innocent enough, but one could never be too careful. But who she was and why she would want to assume another woman's identity, if indeed that's what had happened, was puzzling.

As soon as they returned home, answers to these questions must be sought. Perhaps one more carrot should be dangled in front of her just to see how she would respond, whom she would run to. Yes, one more message was called for. She mustn't be put on the alert that she'd been found out. The partner in this would certainly agree. Carole's every move from here on must be scrutinized. They had to know who she was.

A starting point would be to learn who had actually died in the crash of Flight 398 . . . and who had lived.

"Morning."

"Hey, Jack. Sit down." Tate motioned his brother into the chair across the breakfast table and signaled a waiter to pour him some coffee.

"You're not expecting anyone else?"

"No. Carole and Mandy slept late this morning. I got up, went out for my run, and was dressed by the time they woke up. Carole said for me not to wait on them, but to come on down. I hate eating alone, so I'm glad you're here."

"Are you?" To the waiter, he said, "The number three breakfast. Make sure the bacon's crisp and substitute hash browns for the grits, please."

"Certainly, Mr. Rutledge."

"Pays to have a famous brother," Jack commented as the waiter withdrew with his order. "Guarantees better service."

Tate was leaning back in his chair, his hands forming loose fists on either side of his plate. "Mind telling me what you meant by that crack?"

"What crack?" Jack dumped two packets of sugar into his coffee.

"Asking me if I'm really glad you're having breakfast with me."

"I just thought that after yesterday—"

"Yesterday went great."

"I'm referring to the meeting with Dirk and Ralph."

"So you're still pissed because I fired them?"

"It's your campaign," Jack said with an insolent shrug.

"It's our campaign."

"The hell it is."

Tate was about to offer a rebuttal when the waiter appeared with Jack's breakfast. He waited until they were alone again, then leaned across the table and said in a soft, peacemaking tone, "I wasn't belittling your decision, Jack."

"That's what it looked like to me. To everybody else, too."

Tate stared into the cooling remains of his waffles and sausage, but didn't pick up his fork again. "I'm sorry if you took it to heart, but their tactics just weren't working for me. I listened to you, to Eddy, to Dad, but—"

"But you went with Carole's opinion."

Tate was taken aback by Jack's viciousness. "What's she got to do with this?"

"You tell me."

"She's my wife."

"That's your problem."

Tate didn't want to get into a discussion of his marriage with his brother. He addressed the real issue. "Jack, my name is the one on the ballot. I'm ultimately accountable for how my campaign is run. I'll have to answer for my performance in Congress if I'm elected. Tate Rutledge," he stressed, "not anybody else."

"I understand that."

"Then work with me, not against me." Warmed to his topic, Tate pushed his plate aside and propped his forearms on the edge of the table. "I couldn't have done this alone. Hell, don't you think I know how dedicated you are to this?"

"More than anything in the world, I want to see you elected."

"I know that, Jack. You're my brother. I love you. I appreciate your doggedness, your self-sacrifice, and all the details you see to so I won't be bothered with them. I realize, probably more than you know, that I'm sitting on the white horse while you're down there shoveling up the shit."

"I never aspired to ride the white horse, Tate. I just want to be given credit for shoveling the shit pretty damn well."

"More than pretty damn well," Tate said. "I'm sorry we disagreed on that matter yesterday, but sometimes I have to go with my gut instinct, despite what you or anybody else is advising me.

"Would you have me any other way? Would I be a worthy candidate for public office if I could be swayed to go along with something because it would be the popular, expedient, and convenient thing to do, even though I felt strongly against it?"

"I suppose not."

Tate smiled ruefully. "In the final analysis, I'm the one baring my ass to the world, Jack."

"Just don't expect me to bend over and kiss it when I think you're wrong."

The two brothers laughed together. Jack was the first to grow serious again. He summoned the waiter to take away their plates and replenish their coffee cups. "Tate, as long as we're clearing the air . . ."

"Hmm?"

"I get the impression that things are better between you and Carole."

Tate glanced at his brother sharply, then away. "Some."

"Well, that's . . . that's good, I guess. As long as it makes you happy." He fiddled with an empty sugar packet.

"Why am I waiting for the other shoe to drop?"

Jack cleared his throat and shifted uneasily in his chair. "I don't know, there's something . . ." He ran his hand over his thinning hair. "You're going to think I'm crazy."

"Try me."

"There's something out of sync with her."

"What do you mean?"

"I don't know. Hell, you sleep with her. If you haven't noticed it, then I must be imagining it." He paused, waiting expectantly for either a confirmation or denial, neither of which he got. "Did you see her talking to that TV guy last night?"

"What TV guy?"

"The one who did the camera work for the commercial we made at the ranch."

"His name's Van Lovejoy. He's covering my campaign for KTEX."

"Yeah, I know." Jack spread his hands wide and laughed dryly. "It just seemed strange that Carole made a point to speak to him during all that hoopla last night, that's all. She made a beeline for him as soon as she left the dais. He's not exactly her type." Tate quickly averted his head. "What I mean is . . ." Jack stammered, "he's not . . . hell, you know what I mean."

"I know what you mean." Tate's voice was quiet.

"Well, I'd better get back upstairs and light a fire under Dorothy Rae and Fancy. Eddy wants everybody congregated in the lobby, packed and ready to pull out by ten-thirty." He affectionately slapped his brother's shoulder as he walked past him. "I enjoyed breakfast."

"So did I, Jack."

Tate continued to stare sightlessly out the window. Carole had been talking to Van Lovejoy again last night? Why?

He hadn't told his brother that she had had a private conversation with the video photographer once before. For all her glib explanation, their conversation on the sidewalk outside the Adolphus had appeared furtive.

She'd lied her way around it that time. He'd known she was lying, but then he'd kissed her, she'd kissed him back, and he'd forgotten what had started the argument. Things had been going so well between them. Why did this dark cloud have to show up on the horizon?

Their sex had never been as good or as satisfying. It was hot, but it had always been hot. It was dirty, but it had always been dirty. Only now it was like having dirty sex with a lady, which made it even better. She no longer rushed the foreplay. She no longer chanted gutter jargon. She didn't scream like before when she pretended to come, but took catchy little breaths that he thought were infinitely sexier. And he would swear that her orgasms were genuine. There was a newness to their lovemaking, an essence of intrigue, almost like it was illicit. He was embarrassed to even think the cliché, but each time was like the first time. He always discovered something about her that he hadn't realized before.

She'd never been modest, never given a thought to parading around unclothed. Lately, however, she artfully used lingerie rather than nudity to entice him. Yesterday morning, when they'd made love on the parlor sofa, she had insisted that he pull the drapes first. He supposed her self-consciousness stemmed from the nearly undetectable scars on her arms and hands.

The maidenly shyness excited him. She seduced by withholding. He hadn't yet seen in the light what he caressed in darkness with his hands and lips. Damned if the mystery didn't make him want her even more.

He had thought about her constantly yesterday. Prurient thoughts of her had intruded upon high-level discussions and impassioned speeches. Whenever their eyes connected, they seemed to be thinking the same thought, and that was how quickly they wanted the time to pass so they could go to bed again.

He had developed the curious habit of subconsciously knowing where she was at all times, gauging her distance from him and inventing reasons to touch her whenever she was close enough. But was she playing games with him? Was her modesty a sexual gimmick? Why did she have an unexplainable interest in this photographer?

On the one hand, Tate wanted immediate answers. But if

answers meant having to give up the peace, harmony, and sex, he was prepared to wait indefinitely for an explanation.

FORTY-ONE

Zinnia Rutledge stood gazing at the wall of framed photographs behind the credenza. She loved this office because of those photographs. She could have gazed at them for hours and never tired of it, though of course she never did. The memories they evoked were bittersweet.

At the sound of the door opening behind her, she turned. "Hello, Zee, did I startle you?"

Zee quickly blinked away the tears in her eyes and resealed her emotions in the vault of her heart. "Hello, Carole. You did take me by surprise. I was expecting Tate." They had planned to meet here at his office and go to lunch together—a special date, just the two of them.

"That's why he sent me over. I'm afraid I'm the bearer of bad news."

"He can't make it," Zee said with evident disappointment.

"I'm afraid not."

"There's nothing wrong, I hope?"

"Not exactly. There's been a labor dispute going on within the Houston Police Department."

"I'm aware of that. It's been in all the papers."

"Well, this morning things came to a head. An hour ago, Eddy decided that Tate should go down there, assess the situation, and make a statement. The latest poll shows that Tate is closing the gap. He's only five points behind Dekker now. This volatile situation in Houston presented a perfect forum for Tate to get across some of his ideas, not only on labor versus management, but law enforcement, as well.

They're flying down in a private jet and should be back in a few hours, but lunch is out of the question.''

"Tate likes to fly as much as his father," she remarked with a wistful smile. "He'll enjoy the trip."

"Will you accept a poor substitute for his company?"

The tentative invitation yanked Zee from her pensiveness. "You mean have lunch with you?"

"Would that be so terrible?"

Zee looked her daughter-in-law up and down, finding little about her appearance to criticize. Carole had refined her image considerably since her recovery. She still dressed with flair, but her emphasis was now more on style than sexiness.

Carole's flamboyance had always repelled Zee. She was glad it had been subdued. The woman inside the impeccable clothing, however, was still just as distasteful as the first time she'd met her.

"I'll pass."

"Why?"

"You never knew when to let something drop, Carole." Zee tucked her handbag beneath her arm.

"Why don't you want to have lunch with me?"

She had taken up a position in front of the door, barring Zee from making a gracious exit. "My heart was set on having lunch with Tate," she said. "I understand why he had to cancel, but I'm disappointed and see no reason to pretend that I'm not. We have so little time together these days, just he and I."

"And that's what's really bugging you, isn't it?"

Zee's small body tensed instantly. If Carole insisted on a confrontation, Zee decided to give her one. "What are you implying?"

"You can't stand that Tate is spending more time with me. You're jealous of our relationship, which is stronger every day."

Zee gave a soft, scoffing laugh. "You would love to believe that, wouldn't you, Carole? You'd prefer to think that I'm merely jealous when you know that I was opposed to your marriage to my son from the beginning."

"Oh?"

"Don't act like you didn't know. Tate does. I'm sure the two of you have discussed it."

"We have. And even if we hadn't, I'd know you dislike me intensely. You don't hide your feelings very well, Zee."

Zee smiled, but it was a sad expression. "You'd be amazed at how well I conceal what I'm thinking and feeling. I'm an expert at it." Carole's gaze sharpened quizzically, putting Zee on alert. She composed her face and said icily, "You've made an effort to patch up your deteriorating relationship with Tate. Nelson is delighted. I'm not."

"Why not? I know you want Tate to be happy."

"Exactly. And he'll never be happy as long as you've got your claws in him. See, Carole, I know that all your loving ways are machinations. They're phony, just as you are."

Zee derived petty satisfaction from watching Carole's face become pale beneath her carefully applied makeup. Her voice was faint. "Phony? What do you mean?"

"Shortly after you married Tate, when I first began to notice a rift between you, I hired a private investigator. Cheesy, yes. It was the most humiliating experience I've ever put myself through, but I did it to protect my son.

"The investigator was a repulsive individual, but he did an excellent job. As you've no doubt guessed by now, he provided me with an extensive portfolio on you before you became a legal assistant at Rutledge and Rutledge."

Zee could feel her blood pressure rising. Her compact body had become an incinerator, fueling itself on her hatred for this woman who had, with the cold calculation of a KGB infiltrator, dazzled all the Rutledge men and duped Tate into loving her.

"I don't believe I need to detail the disgusting contents of that portfolio, do I? God only knows what it omits. Only let me assure you that it encompasses your checkered stint as a topless dancer. Among your other careers," she said as an aside, giving a delicate shudder.

"Your various stage names were colorful but unimaginative, I thought. The investigator stopped digging before he discovered the name you were given at birth, which isn't important anyway."

Carole looked as though she might throw up at any

moment. Her difficult swallow could be heard in the silent office, vacant except for the two of them. Tate's secretary had gone to lunch.

"Does anyone else know about this . . . this portfolio? Does Tate?"

"No one," Zee replied, "though I've been tempted on many occasions to show it to him—most recently when I realized that he's falling in love with you again."

Carole drew a soft, whistling breath. "Is he?"

"Much to my dismay, I believe he is. In any case, he's enchanted. Probably against his better judgment. He's falling for this new Carole, who's emerged as a result of the plane crash. Maybe the next name you assume should be Phoenix, since you've risen out of the ashes."

Zee tilted her head to one side and considered her adversary for a moment. "You're an extremely clever young woman. Your transformation from skid row topless dancer into a lady charming enough to be a senator's wife was quite remarkable. It must have taken an enormous amount of planning, studying, and hard work to bring about. You even chose a surname enshrined on the walls of the Alamo—a Spanish name. Very advantageous for the wife of a political candidate in Texas.

"But this most recent change is even more incredible than the first because you seem to believe in it yourself. I could even think that you're sincere until I compare what you were like the morning of the crash to what you're like now, with Tate, with Mandy." Zee gave her head a negative shake. "No one can change that drastically, no matter how clever she is."

"How do you know I haven't changed out of love for Tate? I'm trying to be what he needs and wants."

Shooting her a look, Zee moved her aside and reached for the door. "I know as well as I know my own name that you are *not* what you want us to believe you are."

"When do you plan to expose me?"

"Never." Carole flinched with surprise. "As long as Tate is happy and content with you, I won't disillusion him. The folder will remain our secret. But start hurting him again, Carole, and I assure you I'll destroy you."

"You can't do that without destroying Tate, too."

"I don't intend to make it a public disclosure. Showing the portfolio to Tate would be sufficient. He wouldn't let a whore, even a reformed one, rear his daughter. It's intolerable to me, too, but I have no choice at this point. Rarely are we given real choices."

A look of sheer desperation came over Carole's face. She closed her hand around Zee's arm. "You can't ever tell Tate. Please, Zee, please don't. It would kill him."

"That's the only reason I've resisted so far." Zee wrested her arm free of the younger woman's touch. "But believe me, Carole, if it came to seeing him suffer through a scandal temporarily, or living in misery for the rest of his life, I would spare him the latter at any cost."

On her way out, she added, "I'm sure you'll search for this dossier I have on you. Don't bother destroying it. There's a duplicate in a private safe deposit box, which can be opened only by me, or, in the event of my death, Tate."

Avery unlocked the front door with her key and stepped inside the house. "Mona? Mandy?"

She located them in the kitchen. The cheek she pressed against Mandy's was cold. She'd driven all the way from San Antonio with the car windows down. Her face had been flaming after her unsettling encounter with Zee. The cool air had also warded off the nausea she experienced every time she thought of Carole Navarro's incriminating history.

"Is the soup good, darling?"

"Uh-huh," Mandy replied, slurping up a spoonful of chicken and noodles.

"I didn't expect anyone home for lunch, Mrs. Rutledge, but I can fix you something."

"No thanks, Mona. I'm not hungry." She shrugged out of her coat and sat down in one of the chairs at the table. "I could stand a cup of tea if it's not too much trouble, please."

She nervously wrung her hands until the housekeeper set the steaming cup of fragrant tea in front of her, then folded her bloodless fingers around the mug.

"Are you feeling all right, Mrs. Rutledge? Your cheeks are flushed."

"I'm fine. Just chilled."

"I hope you're not coming down with the flu. There's a lot of it going around."

"I'm fine," she repeated, smiling weakly. "Finish your fruit cocktail, Mandy, then I'll read you a story before your nap."

She tried to respond to Mandy's constant chatter, a sign of her continuing progress, but her mind kept wandering back to Zee and the damning information she had collected on Carole.

"All done?" She praised the two empty bowls Mandy held up for her inspection. Finishing her tea, she led Mandy to her bedroom. After helping her untie her shoes, she lifted her into bed and covered her with a quilt. She settled down beside her with a large picture book.

Her father had read to her from such a book when she was a girl. It was filled with beautiful illustrations of damsels with long, wavy golden hair being rescued from distress by handsome, brave heroes who overcame impossible odds. Her memories of lying beneath covers or sitting on her father's lap while his voice lulled her to sleep were some of her earliest and most precious memories of childhood.

Those had been coveted moments, when Daddy was home and paying attention to her. In the fairy tales he read, the princess always had a doting father. Good was always victorious over the forces of evil.

Perhaps that's why they called them fairy tales. They were a departure from reality, where fathers disappeared for months on end and all too often evil was the victor.

When Mandy fell asleep, Avery slipped from the room and quietly closed the door behind her. Mona retired to her quarters every afternoon for a couple hours of watching soap operas and resting before preparing dinner.

No one else was at home, but Avery stealthily tiptoed along the tile flooring straight from Mandy's room toward the wing of the house Zee shared with Nelson. She didn't weigh the rightness or wrongness of what she was about to do. It was a ghastly invasion of privacy and would have been unthinkable under other circumstances. The circumstances being what they were, however, made it necessary.

She located their bedroom with no problem. A very pleasant room, it was shuttered against the bright autumn sunlight. The floral fragrance she associated with Zee was redolent.

Would Zee keep such explosive documents in the dainty Queen Anne desk? Why not? It looked as innocent as a novice nun. Who would think to violate it? Nelson conducted ranching business at a massive desk in the den down the hall. He would have no reason to go through his wife's seemingly innocuous desk.

Avery took a nail file from the dressing table and applied it to the tiny gold lock on the lap drawer of the desk. She didn't even try to cover her crime. Zee expected her to check. She had said as much.

It wasn't a very sturdy lock. Within seconds, Avery pulled the desk drawer open. Inside there were several thin boxes of stationery engraved with Zee's initials, a book of stamps, an address book, two slender, black Bibles, one with Jack's name embossed in gold block letters, the other with Tate's name.

The manila folder was in the back of the drawer. Avery removed it and pried open the metal bracket.

Five minutes later, she left the room, pale and trembling. Her whole body shook as though she had palsy. Her stomach was queasy. The harmless tea had turned rancid in her stomach. She hastened to her own room and locked the door behind her. Resting against it, she drew in draughts of cleansing air.

Tate. Oh, Tate. If he ever saw the revolting contents of that folder. . . .

She needed a bath. Quickly. Immediately.

She kicked off her shoes, peeled off her sweater, and slid open her closet door.

She screamed.

Reeling away from the grotesque sight, she covered her mouth with both hands, though retching noises issued from her throat. Opening the closet door had caused the campaign poster to swing from the end of its red satin cord like a body on a gallows.

In bright red paint, a bullet hole had been painted in the center of Tate's forehead. The paint trickled down his face, hideously incongruent with his smile. Written in bold red lettering across the poster were the words, "Election Day!"

Avery bolted into the bathroom and vomited.

FORTY-TWO

"It was ghastly. So ugly."

Avery sat with her head bowed over a glass of brandy that Irish had insisted would help calm her down. The first unwanted swallow had burned a crater in her empty stomach, but she kept the glass because she needed something to hold on to.

"This whole frigging thing is ugly," her irascible host declared. "I've thought so all along. Didn't I warn you? Didn't I?"

"So you warned her. Stop harping on it."

"Who asked you?" Irish angrily rounded on Van, who was sipping at a joint that Irish had been too upset to notice wasn't an ordinary cigarette.

"Avery did. She called and told me to haul ass over here, so I hauled ass."

"I meant who asked you for your opinion?"

"Will the two of you please stop?" Avery cried raggedly. "And Van, will you please put that thing out? The smell's making me sick."

She tapped her fingertips against her lips, as though contemplating whether or not she was going to throw up again. "The poster terrified me. He really means to do it. I've known so all along, but this . . ."

She set the glass of brandy on the coffee table and stood up, chafing her arms. She had on a sweater, but nothing helped her get warm.

"Who is it, Avery?"

She shook her head hard. "I don't know. Any of them. *I don't know.*"

"Who had access to your room?"

"Earlier this morning and before I came home at noon, anybody. Mona says they should install a revolving door. Everybody's in and out constantly. As the election approaches, they come and go at all hours."

"How do you know someone didn't follow you here?"

"I kept one eye on the rearview mirror and doubled back several times. Besides, no one was home when I left."

"No clues from the folder you found in the old lady's desk?"

Avery answered Van's irreverent question with a dismal shake of her head.

"She's a strange one," he observed.

"What makes you say that?"

"I've got lots of her on tape. She's always smiling, waving at the crowds, but damned if I believe she's all that happy."

"I know what you mean. She's a very private person and says little. At least until today."

"Tell us about Carole Navarro," Irish said. "She's more to the point than Zee Rutledge."

"Carole, or whatever her original name was, was a tramp. She danced in the seediest nightclubs—"

"Tittie bars," Van supplied.

". . . Under a number of spicy and suggestive names. She was arrested once for public lewdness and once for prostitution, but both charges were dropped."

"You're sure of all this?"

"The private investigator might have been slime, but he was thorough. With the information he supplied Zee, it was easy for me to track down some of the places Carole had worked."

"When was this?" Irish wanted to know.

"Before I came here. I even talked to some people who knew her—other dancers, former employers, and such."

"Did any mistake you for her?" Van asked.

"All of them. I passed myself off as a long-lost cousin to explain the similarity."

"What did they have to say about her?"

"She had severed all ties. Nobody knew what had happened to her. One drag queen that I spoke to, in exchange for a twenty-dollar bill, said she told him she was going to give up the night life, go to business school and improve herself. That's all he remembered. He never saw her after she quit working at the club where they shared a stage.

"This is pure conjecture, but I think Carole underwent a complete transformation, finessed her way into the Rutledge law firm, then once on the inside, saw a way to take her self-improvement campaign one step further by marrying Tate. Remember the piece I did several years ago on prostitutes, Irish?" she asked suddenly.

"While you were working at that station in Detroit? Sure, I remember it. You sent me a tape. What's it got to do with this?"

"The personality profile of those women fits Carole. Most of them claim to hate men. She was probably no different."

"You don't know that."

"No? Look how she treated Jack. She flirted with him to the extent of damaging his marriage, but I get the impression she never came across. If that isn't malicious, I don't know what is. For the sake of argument, let's say she didn't view men too kindly and set out to ruin one whose future looked the very brightest, while at the same time elevating herself."

"Wasn't she scared that someone would recognize her, that her shady past would eventually catch up with her?"

Avery had thought of that herself. "Don't you see, that would have iced the cake. Tate would really be humiliated if it was revealed what his wife had been before he married her."

"He must be a real dunce," Van muttered, "to have fallen for it."

"You don't understand how calculating she was," Avery said, leaping to Tate's defense. "She became everything he could possibly want. She laid a trap, using herself as the perfect bait. She was pretty, animated, and sexy. But more than that, someone who knew Tate well coached her on the right buttons to push to elevate lust to love."

"The one who wants to kill him."

"Right," Avery said, nodding grimly at Van, who had voiced her hypothesis. "He must have sensed, as Zee did, that Carole was an opportunist."

"When he approached her, why didn't she run to Tate?"

"I'm not sure," she admitted. "My theory isn't without holes. Maybe being the bereaved widow of a public official held more allure than being a senator's wife."

"Same status, but no inconvenient husband," Irish speculated.

"Hmm. Also, she wasn't sure Tate would make it to the Senate. Or maybe her coconspirator made it financially profitable for her. In any case, once they were married, it was her responsibility to make life miserable for Tate—a job she did with relish."

"But *why* was someone out to make him miserable?" Irish asked. "It always comes back to that."

"I don't know." Avery's voice was taut with quiet desperation. "I wish to God I did."

"What do you make of the latest message?" Irish asked.

She raked a hand through her hair. "Obviously, they're going to make their move on election day. A gun of some kind will be the weapon of choice."

"That gets my vote. No pun intended," Van added drolly.

Irish shot him an irritated glance, then said to Avery, "I don't know. This time the symbolism seems a little too obvious."

"What do you mean?"

"I'm not sure," he admitted, gnawing on his lip. Absently, he picked up Avery's glass of brandy and took a hearty swig. "What happened to the subtlety of the earlier notes? Either he's testing your mettle or he's the cockiest son of a bitch I've ever run across."

"Maybe he's cocky because it can't be stopped now," Van said moodily. "It'll go down no matter what. Everything is already in place."

"Like Gray Hair?" Avery asked. Van shrugged.

"What about the footage you shot earlier today in Houston? Any more of him?" Irish asked Van.

"Nope. He hasn't turned up since Fort Worth. Not since Avery's been staying home." His eyes were mellowed by marijuana, but the look he gave her was meaningful enough for Irish to intercept.

"Okay, what don't I know, you two?"

Avery moistened her lips. "Van thinks it's possible that Gray Hair is watching me, not Tate."

Irish's head swiveled on his thick neck around to the photographer. "What makes you think that?"

"It's just an idea. A little off the wall, but—"

"In every one of the tapes he's looking at Tate," she pointed out reasonably.

"Hard to tell. You're always standing right beside him."

"Avery." Irish took her hand, pulled her back down onto the sofa, and squatted in front of her. He covered her hands with his own. "Listen to me now. You've got to notify the authorities."

"I—"

"I said to listen. Now shut up and hear me out." He reorganized his thoughts. "You're in over your head, baby. I know why you wanted to do this. It was a terrific idea—a once-in-a-lifetime chance to make a name for yourself and save lives in the meantime.

"But it's gotten out of hand. Your life is in danger. And as long as you let this continue, so is Rutledge's. So's the kid's." Since she appeared to be receptive to his argument, he eased up onto the couch beside her, but continued to press her hands beneath his. "Let's call the FBI."

"The feds?" Van squeaked.

"I have a buddy in the local bureau," Irish pressed on, ignoring Van. "He usually works undercover, looking for dope coming up from Mexico. This isn't his area of expertise, but he could tell us who to call, advise us on what to do."

Before he even finished, Avery was shaking her head no. "Irish, we can't. Don't you see, if the FBI knows, everybody'll have to know. Don't you think it would arouse suspicion if Tate were suddenly surrounded by armed bodyguards or Secret Service operatives in opaque sunglasses? Everything would have to come out in the open."

"That's it, isn't it?" he shouted angrily. "You don't want Rutledge to know! And you don't want him to know because you'd have to give up your cozy place next to him in bed."

"No, that's not it!" she shouted back. "The authorities could protect him from people outside the family circle, but they couldn't protect him from anybody within. And as we know, the person who wants him dead is someone close to him—someone who professes to love him. We can't alert Tate to the danger without alerting the enemy that we're on to him."

She took a deep breath, but it was still insufficient. "Besides, if you told government agents this tale, they'd think you were either lying or crazy. On the outside chance they believed you, think what they'd do to me."

"What would they do to you?" Van wanted to know.

"I'm not sure, but while they were figuring it out, Tate would be exposed and vulnerable."

"So, what do you plan to do?" Irish asked.

She covered her face with her hands and began to cry. "I don't know."

Van stood up and pulled on a tattered leather biker's jacket. "I've got some moonlighting to do."

"Moonlighting?"

Van responded to Irish's question with an indifferent shrug. "I've been looking through some tapes in my library."

"What for?"

"I'm working on a hunch."

Avery reached for his hand. "Thanks for everything, Van. If you see or hear—"

"I'll let you know."

"Do you still have that post office box key I gave you?" Irish asked.

"Yeah, but why would I need it? I see you every day at work when I'm in town."

"But you might need to send me something when you're out of town with Rutledge—something it wouldn't do to mail to the station."

"Gotcha. 'Bye."

As soon as the door closed behind Van, Irish said, out of the side of his mouth, "That dopehead. I wish we had a more reliable ally."

"Don't put him down. I get annoyed with him, too, but he's been invaluable. He's been a friend, and God knows I need all of them I can muster."

She checked her wristwatch—the one Tate had bought for her. Since retrieving it from Fancy, she hadn't taken it off. "I've got to go. It's getting late. Tate asks questions when I'm late, and I'm running out of plausible excuses. There's only so much shopping a woman can do, you know." Her feeble attempt at humor flew no better than a flatiron.

Irish pulled her into a hug. He clumsily smoothed his large hand over her hair while her head rested against his shoulder. "You love him." He didn't even pose it as a question. She nodded her head. "Jesus," he sighed into her hair, "why does it always have to be so goddamn complicated?"

She squeezed her eyes shut; hot tears leaked onto his shirt. "I love him so much, Irish, it hurts."

"I know what that's like."

Avery was too absorbed in her own misery to acknowledge his unrequited love for her mother. "What am I going to do? I can't tell him, but I can't protect him, either." She clung to Irish for strength. He hugged her tighter and awkwardly kissed her temple.

"Rosemary, all ninety-eight pounds of her, would fly into me if she knew I was letting you stay in a life-threatening situation."

Avery smiled against his damp shirt. "She probably would. She relied on you to watch over us."

"I'm letting her down this time." He clutched her tighter. "I'm afraid for you, Avery."

"After today, seeing that bloodcurdling poster, I'm a little afraid for myself. I'm still considered a conspirator. God help me if he ever discovers otherwise."

"You won't reconsider and let me call the authorities?"

"Not yet. Not until I can point an accusing finger and say, 'That's the one.'"

He put space between them and tilted her chin up. "By then it might be too late."

He hadn't needed to caution her of that. She already knew. It might already be too late to salvage her career as a broadcast journalist and establish a future with Tate and Mandy, but she had to *try*. She hugged Irish once more at his door before telling him good night, kissing his ruddy cheek, and stepping out into the darkness.

It was so dark that neither of them noticed the car parked midway down the block.

FORTY-THREE

The spontaneous trip to Houston to address disgruntled policemen had gone extraordinarily well for Tate and boosted him three points in the polls. Daily, he closed the gap between Senator Dekker and himself.

Dekker, feeling the pressure, began to get nasty in his speeches, painting Tate as a dangerous liberal who threatened "the traditional ideals that we as Americans and Texans hold dear."

It would have been a perfect time for him to use Carole Rutledge's abortion as ammunition. That would have blown Tate's campaign out of the water and probably cinched the race for Dekker. But whatever tactics Eddy had used on the extortionist had apparently been effective. When it became obvious that Dekker knew nothing of the incident, everyone in the Rutledge inner circle breathed a collective sigh of relief.

Dekker, however, had the endorsement of an incumbent president, who made a swing through the state in pursuit of his own reelection. Rutledge supporters feared that the president's appearance might nullify the gut-busting progress they had made.

Actually, the president was fighting for his life in Texas. The rallies where he shared the podium with Dekker had a subliminal edge of eleventh-hour desperation that was conveyed to the uncommitted voters. Tate benefitted rather than suffered from the president's vigorous campaigning. The groundswell gained even greater momentum when the opposing presidential candidate came to Texas and campaigned alongside him.

After an exhausting but exhilarating trip to seven cities in two days, everyone at Rutledge headquarters was reeling with preelection giddiness. Even though Dekker still maintained a slight margin over Tate in the official polls, the momentum seemed to have swung the other way. Word on the street was that Tate Rutledge was looking better all the time. Optimism was at its highest peak since Tate had won the primary. Everyone was buoyant.

Except Fancy.

She sauntered through the various rooms of campaign headquarters, slouching in chairs as they became available, scorning the party atmosphere, stalking Eddy's movements with sulky, resentful eyes.

They hadn't been alone together for more than a week. Every time he glanced her way, he looked straight through her. Whenever she swallowed her pride and approached him, he did nothing more than assign her some menial task. She was even put on a telephone and told to call registered voters to urge them to go to the polls and vote on election day. The only reason she consented to do the demoralizing work was because it kept Eddy in her sights. The alternative was staying at the house and not seeing Eddy at all.

He was constantly in motion, barking orders like a drill sergeant and losing his temper when they weren't carried out quickly enough to suit him. He seemed to subsist on coffee, canned sodas, and vending machine food. He was the first to arrive at headquarters in the morning and the last to leave at night, if he left at all.

On the Sunday before the election, the Rutledges moved into the Palacio Del Rio, a twenty-two-story hotel on the Riverwalk in downtown San Antonio. From there they would monitor election returns two days later.

Tate's immediate family took the Imperial Suite on the twenty-first floor. The others were assigned rooms nearby. VCRs were installed on all the television sets so newscasts and commentaries could be recorded for subsequent review and analysis. Additional telephone lines were provided. Security guards were posted at the elevators, more to safeguard the candidate's privacy than the candidate himself.

On the mezzanine level, twenty stories below, workers were draping the wall of the Corte Real Ballroom with red, white, and blue bunting. The back wall was covered with larger-than-life-size pictures of Tate. The dais was being decorated with bunting and flags, and bordered with pots of white chrysanthemums nestling in red and blue cellophane. A huge net, containing thousands of balloons, was suspended from the ceiling, to be released on cue.

Over the racket and confusion generated by obsequious hotel employees, meticulous television servicemen, and scurrying telephone installers, Eddy was attempting to make himself heard in the parlor of Tate's suite that Sunday afternoon.

"From Longview you fly to Texarkana. You spend an hour and a half there, max, then to Wichita Falls, Abilene, and home. You should arrive—"

"Daddy?"

"Tate, for crissake!" Eddy lowered the clipboard he'd been consulting and exhaled his annoyance like noxious fumes.

"Shh, Mandy." Tate held a finger to his lips. She had been sitting on his lap during the briefing session, but her attention span had been exhausted long ago.

"Are you listening, or what?"

"I'm listening, Eddy. Longview, Wichita Falls, Abilene, home."

"You forgot Texarkana."

"My apologies. I'm sure you and the pilot won't. Are there any more bananas in the fruit basket?"

"Jesus," Eddy cried. "You're two days away from an election for a Senate seat and you're thinking about bananas. You're too damn casual!"

Tate calmly accepted a banana from his wife and peeled it for Mandy. "You're too tense. Relax, Eddy. You're making everybody crazy."

"Amen," Fancy intoned glumly from where she was curled in an easy chair watching a movie on TV.

"You win the election, then I'll relax." Eddy consulted the clipboard again. "I don't even remember where I was. Oh, yeah, you arrive here in San Antonio tomorrow evening around seven-thirty. I'll make arrangements for the family to have dinner at a local restaurant. You'll retire."

"Do I get to tee-tee and brush my teeth first? I mean, between dinner and retiring?"

Everyone laughed. Eddy didn't think Tate's wisecrack was funny. "Tuesday morning, we'll travel en masse to your precinct box in Kerrville, vote, then return here to sweat it out."

Tate wrestled the banana peel away from Mandy, who was sliding her index finger down its squishy lining and collecting the gunk beneath her fingernail. "I'm going to win."

"Don't get overconfident. The polls still show you two points behind Dekker."

"Think where we started, though," Tate reminded him, his gray eyes twinkling. "I'm going to win."

On that optimistic note, the meeting concluded. Nelson and Zee went to their room to lie down and rest. Tate had to work on a speech he was delivering at a Spanish-speaking church later in the evening. Dorothy Rae had talked Jack into going with her for a stroll along the Riverwalk.

Fancy waited until everyone dispersed, then followed Eddy to his room, which was a few doors down from the command post, as she called Tate's suite. After her soft knock, he called out, "Who is it?"

"Me."

He opened the door but didn't even hold it for her. He turned his back and headed for the closet, where he took out a fresh shirt. She closed the door and flipped the dead bolt.

"Why don't you just leave your shirt off?" She leaned into him suggestively and teased one of his nipples with the tip of her tongue.

"I don't think it would be too suave to show up at campaign headquarters without a shirt on." He crammed his arms through the starched sleeves and began buttoning up.

"You're going there now?"

"That's right."

"But it's Sunday."

He cocked his eyebrow. "Don't tell me you've started observing the Lord's day."

"I was in church this morning, same as you."

"And for the same reason," he said. "Because I told everybody they had to go. Didn't you see the television cameras recording Tate's piety for their viewing voters?"

"I was praying."

"Oh, sure."

"Praying that your dick would rot and drop off," she said with fierce passion. He merely laughed. When he began stuffing his shirttail into his trousers, Fancy tried to stop him. "Eddy," she whined contritely, "I didn't come here to fight with you. I'm sorry for what I just said. I want to be with you."

"Then come to the headquarters with me. I'm sure there's plenty of work to do."

"It wasn't work I had in mind."

"Sorry, that's what's on the agenda from now till election day."

Her pride could only take so much abuse. "You've been brushing me off for weeks now," she said, her fists finding props on her hips. "What gives with you?"

"You have to ask?" He ran a brush through his pale hair. "I'm trying to get your Uncle Tate elected to the U.S. Congress."

"Screw the U.S. Congress!"

"I'm sure you would," he said wryly. "If you had a

chance, you'd give every member of the legislature blue balls. Now, Fancy, you'll have to excuse me.''

He reached for the door. She blocked his path, pleading again, ''Don't go, Eddy. Not just yet, anyway. Stay a while. We could order up some beers, have a few laughs.'' Wiggling against him, nudging his pelvis with hers, she purred, ''Let's make love.''

''Love?'' he scoffed.

She grabbed his hand and drew it beneath her skirt toward her crotch. ''I'm already wet.''

He pulled his hand away, bodily lifted her out of his path, and set her down behind him. ''You're always wet, Fancy. Peddle it somewhere else. Right now, I've got better things to do.''

Fancy gaped at the closed door, then hurled the first available thing her hand landed on, which happened to be a glass ashtray. She threw it with all her might, but it only bounced against the door without breaking and landed dully on the carpeted floor. That enraged her even more.

She'd never been so summarily rejected. Nobody, but nobody, turned down Fancy Rutledge when she was hot. She stormed out of Eddy's room, stayed in hers only long enough to change into a tight sweater and even tighter jeans, then went to the hotel garage and retrieved her Mustang.

She was damned if she was going to stop living for the sake of this confounded Senate race.

''It's me. Anything happening?''

''Hello, Irish.'' Van rubbed his bloodshot eyes while cradling the telephone receiver against his ear. ''I just got in a while ago. Rutledge spoke at a greaser church tonight.''

''I know. How'd it go?''

''They loved him better'n hot tamales.''

''Was Avery there?''

''Everybody was except the girl, Fancy, all looking as pure as Ivory soap.''

''Did Avery get to talk to you?''

''No. There was a throng of jabbering Mex'cans around them.''

''What about Gray Hair? Any sign of him?''

Van weighed the advisability of telling Irish the truth and decided in favor of it. "He was there."

Irish muttered a string of curses. "Didn't he stick out like a sore thumb in a Hispanic crowd?"

"He was outside, jockeying for position like the rest of us."

"He posed as media?"

"That's right."

"Did you get close to him?"

"Tall dude. Mean face."

"Mean?"

"Stern. No nonsense."

"A hit man's face."

"We're only guessing."

"Yeah, but I don't like it, Van. Maybe we ought to call the FBI and not tell Avery."

"She'd never forgive you."

"But she'd be alive."

The two men were quiet for a moment, lost in their private thoughts, considering possible options, and coming up with zip. "Tomorrow, you stick around here. No need to go with Rutledge."

"I figured that," Van said of his assignment when Irish finally broke the silence. "I'll be at the airport tomorrow night when he gets back. The press release said he'd be arriving at seven-thirty."

"Good. Try and make contact with Avery then. She said it's hard to phone from the hotel."

"Right."

"Election morning, come to the TV station first. Then I'm posting you at the Palacio Del Rio. I want you to stick to Avery like glue all day. If you see anything suspicious, *anything*, to hell with her arguments, you call the cops."

"I'm not stupid, Irish."

"And just because you have a free day tomorrow," Irish said in a threatening tone, "don't go out and get blitzed on something."

"I won't. I got a lot to do around here."

"Yeah, what?"

"I'm still looking at tapes."

"You mentioned that before. What are you looking for?"

"I'll let you know as soon as I find it."

They said their good-byes. Van got up long enough to relieve himself in the bathroom, then returned to the console, where he had spent nearly every free hour for the last several days. The number of tapes left to view was dwindling, but not fast enough. He had hours of them still to look at.

The wild goose he was chasing didn't even have an identity. As he had told Irish, he wouldn't know what it was till he saw it. This was probably a colossal waste of time.

He'd been dumb enough to start this harebrained project; he might just as well be dumb enough to finish it. He took a drag on his joint, chased it with a swallow of booze, and inserted another tape into his machine.

Irish made a face into the bottom of the glass of antacid he had forced himself to drink. He shivered at the wretched aftertaste. He should be used to it by now since he guzzled the stuff by the gallon. Avery didn't know. Nobody did. He didn't want anyone to know about his chronic heartburn because he didn't want to be replaced by a younger man before he could retire on a full salary.

He'd been in the business long enough to know that management-level guys were bastards. Heartlessness was a requirement for the job. They wore expensive shoes, three-piece suits, and invisible armor against humanism. They didn't give a damn about an old news horse's valuable contacts at city hall or his years of experience beating the bushes for a story or anything else except the bottom line.

They expected dramatic video at six and ten so they could sell commercial time to sponsors, but they'd never stood by and watched a house burn with people screaming inside, or sat through a stakeout while some nut wielding a .357 Magnum held people hostage in a 7-Eleven, or witnessed the unspeakable atrocities that one human being could inflict on another.

They operated in the sterile side of the business. Irish's side was the down-and-dirty one. That was fine. He wouldn't have it any other way. He just wanted to be respected for what he did.

As long as the news ratings kept KTEX number one in the market, he'd be fine. But if the ratings slipped, those bastards in the worsted wool would start sifting out the undesirables. An old man with a sour stomach and a disposition to match might be considered deadwood and be the first thing lopped off.

So he covered his belches and hid his bottles of antacid.

He switched out the light in his bathroom and shuffled into the bedroom. He sat on the edge of his double bed and set his alarm clock. That was routine. So was reaching into the nightstand drawer and taking out his rosary.

The threat of physical torture couldn't make him admit to anyone that this was a nightly ritual. He never went to confession or mass. Churches were buildings where funerals, weddings, or baptisms were solemnized.

But Irish prayed ritualistically. Tonight he prayed fervently for Tate Rutledge and his young daughter. He prayed for Avery's protection, begging God to spare her life, whatever calamity befell anyone else.

Last, as he did every night, he prayed for Rosemary Daniels's precious soul and beseeched God's forgiveness for loving her, another man's wife.

FORTY-FOUR

Tate opened the door to the suite and looked curiously at the three people standing just beyond the threshold. "What's going on?"

"Mr. Rutledge, I'm sorry to bother you," one of the uniformed policemen said. "Do you know this young woman?"

"Tate?" Avery asked, joining him at the door. "Who—? *Fancy?*"

The girl's expression was surly. One policeman had a firm grip on her upper arm, but it was difficult to tell if he were restraining or supporting her. She was leaning against him, obviously intoxicated.

"What's the matter?" Eddy approached the door and took in the scene. "Jesus," he muttered in disgust.

"Will you please tell them who I am, so they'll leave me the hell alone?" Fancy demanded belligerently.

"This is my niece," Tate stiffly informed the policemen. "Her name's Francine Rutledge."

"That's what her driver's license said, but we had to take her word for it that she was a relation of yours."

"Was it necessary to bring her here under armed escort?"

"It was either here or jail, Mr. Rutledge."

"On what charge?" Avery asked.

"Speeding, driving while intoxicated. She was doing ninety-five on the loop."

"Ninety-eight," Fancy corrected cheekily.

"Thank you, officers, for seeing her safely here. I speak for her mother and father, too."

Fancy threw off the policeman's hand. "Yeah, thanks a lot."

"How much is it going to cost us to keep this quiet?" Eddy asked the policemen.

One scowled at him disdainfully. The other ignored him completely and spoke only to Tate. "We figured you didn't need the bad publicity right now."

"I appreciate that."

"Well, after that speech you gave in Houston, taking the side of law enforcement officers and all, my partner and me figured it was the least we could do."

"Thank you very much."

"Good luck in the election, Mr. Rutledge." They doffed their caps deferentially before walking down the carpeted hallway toward the elevators and the gawking security guards.

Avery closed the door behind them. Everyone had already gone to bed except the four of them. Mandy was sleeping in

the adjoining room. An ominous silence pervaded the suite—
the calm before the storm.

"Fancy, where have you been?" Avery asked her softly.

She flung her hands far above her head and executed a
clumsy pirouette. "Dancing. I had a wonderful time," she
trilled, batting her eyelashes at Eddy. "Of course, nobody
here would think so because you're all so old. So straight.
So—"

"You stupid little cunt." Eddy backhanded her across the
mouth. The force of the blow knocked her to the floor.

"Fancy!" Avery dropped to her knees beside the stunned
girl. Blood trickled from the swelling cut on her lip.

"Eddy, what the *hell's* the matter with you?" Tate
demanded, catching his arm.

Eddy flung Tate off and loomed above Fancy. "Are you
trying to ruin everything? Do you know what could have
happened if those two cops hadn't seen fit to bring you
here? This childish stunt could have cost us the election,"
he shouted.

Tate grabbed his collar and hauled him back. "What do
you think you're doing?"

"She's got it coming."

"Not from you!" Tate roared. He gave Eddy's shoulders
a hard shove that sent him staggering backward. Eddy
regained his balance, snarled, and lunged for Tate.

"Stop it, both of you!" Avery shot to her feet and moved
between them. "You'll bring this hotel down on our heads,
and what kind of headlines will that create?"

The men stood facing each other like two bulls pawing
the ground, but at least they were no longer shouting. Avery
bent over Fancy again and helped her to her feet. The girl
was still so dazed she didn't put up any resistance, but she
whimpered with pain and remorse.

Tate touched her cheek briefly, then aimed a warning
finger at his friend. "Never, *never*, touch a member of my
family like that again."

"I'm sorry, Tate." Eddy smoothed his hands over his
ruffled hair. His voice was low, composed, cool. The iceman
was restored.

"That's one area of my life where your opinion doesn't

count," Tate said angrily, his lips barely moving to form the words.

"I said I was sorry. What else can I do?"

"You can stop sleeping with her."

All were taken by surprise. Eddy and Fancy had no idea that Tate knew. Avery had told him she suspected it, but that was before she knew it for a certainty. The women remained stunned and silent. Eddy walked to the door.

Before he went out, he said, "I think we all need time to cool off."

Avery looked at Tate with undiluted love and respect for coming so quickly to Fancy's defense, then placed her arm across the girl's shoulders. "Come on, I'll walk you to your room."

Once there, she waited while Fancy showered. Emerging from the bathroom, with her hair held away from her scrubbed face by barrettes, and wearing a long T-shirt as a nightgown, she looked young and innocent.

"I improvised on an ice pack for your lip." Avery handed her a plastic bag full of ice and led her toward the turned-down bed.

"Thanks. You're getting good at that."

Fancy propped herself against the headboard and held the ice pack to her lower lip. It had stopped bleeding, but was dark and swollen. She closed her eyes. Tears trickled through her lashes and rolled down her shiny cheeks. Avery lowered herself to the side of the bed and took her hand.

"That son of a bitch. I hate him."

"I don't think so," Avery countered softly. "I believe you thought you loved him."

Fancy looked at her. "*Thought* I loved him?"

"I think you were in love with the idea of being in love with him. How much do you really know about Eddy? You told me yourself you knew very little. I think you wanted to be in love with him because you knew deep down that the affair was inappropriate and had no chance of survival."

"What are you, an amateur shrink?"

Fancy could put a strain on anyone's patience, but Avery evenly replied, "I'm trying to be your friend."

"You're just trying to talk me out of him because you want him for yourself."

"Do you really believe that?"

The girl stared at her for a long moment, and the longer she stared, the more tears filled her eyes. Eventually, she lowered her head. "No. Anybody can see that you love Uncle Tate." She sniffed her drippy nose. "And he's ga-ga over you, too."

She pulled her lower lip through her teeth. "Oh, God," she wailed, "why can't somebody love me like that? What's wrong with me? Why does everybody treat me like shit, like I was invisible or something?"

The floodgate had been opened and all her self-doubt came pouring out. "Eddy was just using me to get his rocks off, wasn't he? I'd hoped that maybe he would love me for something more than just what I was willing to do in bed. I should have known better," she added in a bitter undertone.

Avery pulled Fancy into her arms. Fancy resisted for a second or two, then relented and let herself be comforted while she cried against Avery's shoulder. When her crying subsided, Avery eased her away.

"You know who should be in on this?"

Fancy wiped her wet face with the back of her hand. "Who?"

"Your mother."

"You're kidding, right?"

"No. You need her, Fancy. More than that," Avery said, pressing Fancy's knee for emphasis, "she needs you. She's been trying very hard to make up for past mistakes. Why not give her a chance?"

Fancy thought it over for a moment, then nodded sullenly. "Sure, why not, if it'll make the old girl feel significant."

Avery dialed the room. Jack answered sleepily. "Is Dorothy Rae already in bed? Could she come to Fancy's room?"

"What's wrong?"

Avery looked at Fancy's lip and lied, "Nothing. Just a hen party."

In under a minute Dorothy Rae knocked. She was in her nightgown. "What is it, Carole?"

"Come in."

The minute she saw Fancy's face, she stopped dead in her tracks and raised a hand to her chest. "Oh, my baby! What happened to you?"

Fancy's lower lip quivered. A fresh batch of tears filled her eyes. She stretched out her arms and, in a weak, tremulous voice said, "Mommy?"

"I left them crying in each other's arms," Avery told Tate a few minutes later. "This might have been the best thing that could have happened."

"I don't think I've ever seen Eddy so irrational." While she'd been gone, he'd stripped down to his trousers. Bare-chested, he was pacing the room, still spoiling for a fight.

"He's determined to get you elected. When something happens that could jeopardize that, his temper is explosive."

"But to strike a woman?" Tate asked incredulously, shaking his head.

"How long have you known that he was sleeping with Fancy?"

"A few weeks."

"He told you?"

"No, I picked up signals."

"Did you say anything to him about it?"

"What could I say? He's a grown-up. So is she. God knows he didn't coerce her or sweet talk his way past her virginity."

"I guess not," Avery sighed. "But for all her sexual experience, Fancy's extremely vulnerable, Tate. He's hurt her."

"Don't get me wrong. I'm not defending—"

"Listen!"

Avery held up her hand and signaled for quiet. Then, moving simultaneously, they rushed toward Mandy's bed-room and burst through the door.

She was flailing her limbs, thrashing them against the bed covers. Her small face was contorted and bathed with sweat. She was weeping copiously, her lips blubbering.

"Mommy! Mommy!" She screamed the name repeatedly.

Instinctively, Avery reached for her. Tate placed a restraining hand on her shoulder. "You can't. This might be it."

"Oh, no, Tate, please."

He shook his head stubbornly. "We have to."

So Avery sat on one side of Mandy and Tate sat on the other. Each lived through the hell the child's subconscious mind was being put through.

"No, no." She gasped for breath, holding her mouth wide. "Mommy? I can't see Mommy. I can't get out."

Avery looked across at Tate. His fingers were steepled over his nose and mouth, his eyes fixed on his tormented daughter.

Suddenly Mandy sat bolt upright, as though a spring action device had catapulted her head off the pillow. Her chest was rising and falling rapidly. Her eyes were open and unblinking, but she was still in the throes of the nightmare.

"Mommy!" she screamed. "Get me loose. I'm scared. *Get me loose!*"

Then her eyelids began to flutter and, though her respiration was still choppy, it no longer sounded as though she'd been running for miles and each breath might be her last.

"Mommy's got me," she whispered. "Mommy's got me now." She flopped back down, and when she did, she woke up.

Once her eyes had focused, she divided her bewildered gaze between Tate and Avery. It was into Avery's arms that she hurled her solid little body. "Mommy, you got me out. You got me away from the smoke."

Avery enfolded Mandy in her arms and hugged her tight. She squeezed her eyes shut and thanked God for healing this child who had become so dear to her. When she opened her eyes, they melded with Tate's. He extended his hand and stroked her cheek with his knuckle, then laid his hand on his daughter's head.

Mandy sat back on her heels and announced, "I'm hungry. Can I have some ice cream?"

Laughing with relief, Tate scooped her into his arms and swung her high over his head. She squealed. "You certainly can. What flavor?"

He ordered ice cream from room service, along with a change of linens from housekeeping to replace the damp, tangled sheets on Mandy's bed. While they waited for the deliveries, Avery changed Mandy into another nightgown and brushed her hair. Tate sat watching them.

"I had a bad dream," Mandy told them pragmatically as she used another hairbrush on Pooh Bear. "But I'm not scared anymore 'cause Mommy's there to get me away."

She'd gotten sleepy again by the time she'd finished her ice cream. They tucked her in and sat at the foot of her bed until she fell asleep, knowing that if Dr. Webster was right, her sleep would be uninterrupted from now on. As they left the room, their arms looped around each other's waists, Avery began to cry.

"It's over," Tate murmured and kissed her temple. "She's going to be okay."

"Thank God."

"Then what are you crying for?"

"I'm exhausted," she confessed with a soft laugh. "I'm going to take a long, hot bath. This day seems like it's lasted twenty years."

He had lived through Fancy's crisis and Mandy's nightmare with her. But Tate didn't know that Avery had experienced an anxiety attack at the Spanish church when she had spotted her nemesis outside the nave, surrounded by clambering media.

Once they had safely reached the limo, she had snuggled close to Tate, linking her arm through his and hugging his firm biceps to her breast. What he'd mistaken for an outpouring of affection had actually been a reaction to stark fear.

When Avery came out of the bathroom a half hour later, her skin was dewy and fragrant from soaking in bath oil. With the light behind her, she provided him with a tantalizing silhouette of her body through her nightgown.

"Still exhausted?" he asked.

The room was dim. The bed had been turned down. Avery's subconscious registered this, because she only had eyes for Tate. His hair was attractively mussed. The single light burning in the bathroom gilded his body hair. It fuzzily smattered his chest, whorled around his navel, then tapered to a satiny stripe that disappeared into the unfastened waistband of his trousers.

"Not that exhausted," she replied huskily. "Not if you have something other than sleep in mind."

"What I have in mind," he said, moving toward her, "is making love to my wife."

When he reached her, he curled one hand around the back of her neck and, without any hesitation, slid the other one inside her nightgown to cover her breast. Holding her eyes with his, he finessed the nipple.

"I don't mean just couple with the woman I happened to be married to," he whispered while his thumb continued giving her nipple glancing blows. "I mean make *love* to my *wife*."

He drew her face up close to his, paused, probed her eyes, then took her lips beneath his. There was a difference in his kiss. The difference was subtle, yet tremendous. Avery sensed it immediately. Technically it was the same, as his tongue gently but possessively mated with her mouth. But somehow it was much more personal, more intimate, more giving.

Minutes later they were in bed. Tate was naked, lying above her, his lips following down her nightgown as he lowered it inch by delicious inch.

When it was completely off, he laid his head on her belly, his shoulders between her thighs, and fervently kissed the yielding softness. "I never thought I could love you again. But after what you've done for Mandy, and for me," he added thickly, "I'll be damned if I don't love you more than ever."

He slid his hands beneath her hips and tilted them up. His parted lips whisked the smooth skin of her abdomen. He kissed the delta of dark curls, nuzzled it with his nose, feathered it with his breath.

Catching his hair with her hands, she arched up, offering her open thighs to his caressing mouth. He drew the silky, slippery, softness between his lips, imbibing her taste and scent, using his flicking, stroking, questing tongue to bring her to one crashing climax after another.

Then she inverted her body and returned the favor. Her lips covered the smooth head of his penis. She sucked it tenderly and used the tip of her tongue to cleave the groove and pick up the pearly drops of fluid already collected there.

Tate prayed to nameless gods when she took him into her mouth completely, and when he filled it with the very essence of himself, he gave hoarse, rasping cries that left them feeling perfectly marvelous and replete.

Later that night, while they lay dozing, he drew her back against his chest. He kissed her warm, soft nape. He nibbled her shoulder. He said nothing, but waited, as though asking her permission to continue.

She merely purred like a drowsy cat and responded when he eased her thigh up toward her chest, leaving her open for his smooth entry. Their bodies gently undulated against each other with no discernible motion. It was a facile, fluid fuck.

Reaching around her, he caressed her breasts, reshaping them with his hand, then fanned his fingertips across the pebbly nipples.

She pressed her buttocks into the curve of his body, and rubbed her smooth flesh against the dense hair spreading outward from the root of his sex. He groaned his approval and drew her up higher, closer.

He manipulated her from the front with breathtaking sensitivity, and sometimes replaced his rigid penis with inquisitive fingers that moved deep inside her, until immense pleasure washed over her like a warm and balmy spring rain, without thunder, without wind, without lightning— cleansing and pure and benevolent.

The rhythmic contractions of her orgasm brought on his. His body tensed. His breathing was suspended for several splendid seconds while the hot tide of his semen bathed her womb.

When it was over and their bodies were relaxed, but still emanating heat, she turned her head toward him. Their seeking mouths came together in a long, slow, wet kiss.

Then they slept.

FORTY-FIVE

Since they were scheduled to leave very early that morning, Avery got a head start by waking up before Tate. She disentangled their limbs. Getting her hair unsnarled from his fingers wasn't easy, but she finally managed.

She glanced over her shoulder at him as she left the bed. He was beautiful when he slept, one leg sticking out of the covers, his bearded jaw dark against the pillowcase. Sighing with the sheer pleasure of looking at him, and with the stirring memories of last night's lovemaking fresh in her mind, she crept into the bathroom.

The water taps screeched when she turned them on. Avery winced at the noise. Tate needed as much sleep as he could get. Today's agenda was arduous. He would spend hours in an airplane. In between, he would be delivering speeches, pressing hands, and soliciting votes.

This day before Election Day was possibly the most important one of his campaign. Today the fence-straddlers, vital to the outcome of any election, would make up their minds.

Avery stepped beneath the pounding spray. After shampooing her hair, she lathered her body. It still bore traces of Tate's fervent lovemaking. His mouth had left a faint bruise on her soft inner thigh. The hot water stung her whisker-rasped breasts. She was smiling over that when the shower curtain was suddenly whipped back.

"Tate!"

"Good morning."

"What—"

"I thought I'd shower with you," he drawled, smiling lecherously. "Save time. Save the hotel some hot water."

Avery stood quaking, as guilty in her nakedness as Eve must have been in Eden when God spotlighted her iniquity. The jets of hot water seemed to turn icy and sharp; they pricked her skin like frigid needles. Color drained from her face. Her lips turned blue. Her eyes seemed to recede into her skull, making the sockets appear huge and cavernous. She shivered.

Puzzled, Tate cocked his sleep-tousled head to one side. "You look like you've seen a ghost. Did I scare you?"

She swallowed. Her mouth opened and closed, but she couldn't form a sound.

"Carole? What's the matter?"

He looked for something amiss. His eyes scaled down her pale, trembling body, then back up. Avery's heart sank heavily in her chest as she watched his baffled gaze move down her once again. It was arrested at her breasts, belly, pubis, thighs—places only seen by a lover's eyes, a husband's eyes.

He saw the appendectomy scar, ancient and faint and almost undetectable unless bared to clinical fluorescent lighting. Avery had wondered, but now she knew. Carole had never had her appendix out.

"Carole?" His voice echoed the mystification in his eyes.

Though the protective gesture was a dead giveaway, Avery covered her lower body with one hand and extended the other toward him in appeal. "Tate, I . . ."

As sharp and deadly as swords, his eyes slashed upwards to clash with hers. "You're not Carole." He stated it softly, while his brain still sifted through conflicting facts. Then, when the impact of it hit him full force, he repeated with emphasis, "You're not Carole!"

His arm shot through the shower's spray to grab hold of her wrist and yank her from the tub. Her shins banged into the porcelain; her wet feet slipped on the tiles. She emitted a tortured cry, more of the spirit than the body.

"Tate, stop. I'll—"

He slammed her wet, naked body against the wall and pinned it there with his own. His hand closed tightly around her neck, just beneath her chin.

"Who the fuck are you? Where is my wife? *Who are you*?"

"Don't shout," she whimpered. "Mandy will hear."

"Talk, goddamn you." He lowered his voice, but his eyes were still murderous and his hand exerted more pressure against her adam's apple. "Who are you?"

Her teeth were chattering so badly she could barely speak. "Avery Daniels."

"Who?"

"Avery Daniels."

"Avery Daniels? The TV . . .?"

She bobbed her head once.

"Where's Carole? What—"

"Carole died in the plane crash, Tate," she said. "I survived. We got mixed up because we had switched seats on the plane. I was carrying Mandy when I escaped. They assumed—"

He trapped her dripping head between his hands. "Carole's *dead*?"

"Yes," she gulped. "Yes. I'm sorry."

"Since the crash? She died in the crash? You mean you've been living . . . all this time . . .?"

Again, she gave a swift, confirming nod.

Her heart broke apart like an eggshell as she watched him try to comprehend the incomprehensible. Gradually, he released his stranglehold on her cranium and backed away from her.

She snatched her robe off the hook on the back of the bathroom door and pulled it on, hurriedly knotting the tie belt. She reached into the tub and cut off the faucets, which she instantly regretted doing. The resulting silence was deafening, yet it shimmered with the brassy reverberation of disbelief and suspicion.

Into that silence he threw her one simple question. "Why?"

The day of reckoning had arrived. She'd known it would come eventually. She just hadn't counted on it being today. She wasn't prepared.

"It's complicated."

"I don't give a damn how complicated it is," he said in a voice that vibrated with wrath. "Start talking to me now before I call the police."

"I don't know how or when the initial mix-up was made," she said frantically. "I woke up in the hospital bandaged from head to foot, unable to move or to speak. Everybody was calling me Carole. At first I didn't understand. I was in such pain. I was afraid, confused, disoriented. It took several days for me to piece together what must have happened.''

"And when you realized it, you didn't say anything? Why?"

"I couldn't! Remember, I couldn't communicate." She caught his arm in appeal. He slung it off. "Tate, I tried to get the message to you before my face was restored to look like Carole's, but it was impossible. Every time I began to cry, you thought it was from fear over the upcoming surgery. It was that. But it was also because I was being robbed of my own identity and having another imposed on me. I was powerless to get that message across."

"Jesus, this is science fiction." He plowed his fingers through his hair. Realizing he was still naked, he grabbed a towel from the rack and wrapped it around his middle. "That was months ago."

"I had to remain Carole for a while."

"Why?"

She threw back her head and gazed up at the ceiling. The first explanation had been a breeze, compared to what was coming. "It's going to sound—"

"I don't give a shit how it sounds," he said menacingly. "I want to know why you've been impersonating my wife."

"Because someone wants to kill you!"

Her urgent reply took him by surprise. He was still poised to do battle, but his head snapped back like he'd taken an uppercut on the chin. *"What?"*

"When I was in the hospital," she began, clasping her hands together at waist level, "someone came to my room."

"Who?"

"I don't know who. Hear me out before asking me a lot of questions." She drew in a deep breath, but the words continued to tumble rapidly over her lips. "I was bandaged. I couldn't see well. Someone, addressing me as Carole, warned me not to make any deathbed confessions. He said that the plans were still in place and that you'd never live to take office."

He remained unmoved for a moment, then a smile tugged at the corner of his lips. Eventually, he barked a hateful laugh. "You expect me to believe that?"

"It's the truth!"

"The only truth is that you're going to jail. Now." He turned and headed for the telephone.

"Tate, no!" She caught his arm and brought him around. "I don't blame you for what you're thinking about me."

"Your worst guess couldn't even come close."

The invective smarted, but for the time being, she had to ignore it. "I'm not lying about this. I swear it. Someone plans to assassinate you before you take office."

"I'm not even elected."

"As good as, so it seems."

"You can't identify this mystery person?"

"Not yet. I'm trying."

He studied her earnest face for a moment, then sneered, "I can't believe I'm standing here listening to this shit. You've been living a lie all these months. Now you expect me to believe that a total stranger sneaked into your hospital room and put a bug in your ear that he was going to assassinate me?" He shook his head as though marveling over her audacity and his culpability.

"Not a stranger, Tate. Someone close. Someone in the family."

His jaw relaxed. He stared at her with patent incredulity. "Are you—"

"Think! Only family members are allowed into the ICU."

"You're saying a member of my family is plotting my assassination?"

"It sounds absurd, I know, but it's the truth. I didn't make it up. I didn't imagine it, either. There have been notes."

"Notes?"

"Notes left for Carole in places only she would have access to, letting her know that the plan was still in place." She rushed to the luggage rack in the closet and opened a zippered compartment of one of her suitcases. She carried the notes, including the desecrated campaign poster, back to him.

"They were typed on the typewriter at the ranch," she told him.

He studied each one at length. "You could have made these yourself just in case I caught on and you needed a scapegoat."

"I didn't," she cried. "This was Carole's partner's way of—"

"Wait a minute, wait a minute." He tossed the notes aside and held up both hands. "This is getting better all the time. Carole and this would-be assassin were in it together, right?"

"Absolutely. From the time she met you. Maybe before."

"Why would Carole want me dead? She had no political leanings whatsoever."

"This isn't political, Tate. It's personal. Carole set her sights on becoming your wife. She became exactly what you wanted, and once they teamed up she was coached on how to behave so you'd have to fall in love with her. Who introduced you?"

"Jack," he said with a small shrug. "When she came to apply for a job at the firm."

"It might not have been an accident that she sought employment in your law office."

"She had impeccable credentials."

"I'm sure she did. She would have seen to it."

"She could type," he added drolly, "which shoots your theory all to hell."

"I know I'm right."

"I guess you can prove it," he said, implying the opposite. He even folded his arms complacently across his chest.

"I don't have to. Zee can."

He reacted with visible shock. His arms dropped to his sides. "My mother?"

"She has a whole portfolio on Carole Navarro. I've seen it. Believing me to be Carole, she threatened me with exposure if I made you unhappy."

"Why would she do that?"

"She seemed to think you were falling in love with your

wife again." Avery looked at him meaningfully. "After last night, I have good reason to think that, too."

"Forget last night. As you well know, it was all a hoax." Angrily, he turned away.

Avery quietly gave first aid to the puncture wound in her heart. It would have to be thoroughly nursed later. For now, she had to deal with more critical matters.

"Even if you didn't originally see Carole for what she was, Zee did. She hired a private investigator to delve into her past."

"And what did he find?"

"I'd rather not discuss—"

"What did he find?" he asked tightly, spinning around to confront her again. "For God's sake, don't get squeamish now."

"She was a topless dancer. She'd been arrested for prostitution, among other things." At his stricken expression, she reached for his hand. He jerked it beyond her reach. "You don't have to believe me about this," she said, raising her voice in anger over his stupid, stubborn, masculine pride.

"Ask your mother to show you the data. She was saving it to use against Carole if she ever felt it was warranted. And you can't be all that surprised, Tate, because you have scorned me, as Carole, for having affairs, aborting your child, and using drugs. For months I've borne the brunt of your antipathy for this woman."

He considered her for a moment, gnawing his inner cheek. "Okay, let's say for the sake of argument that you're right about this cock-and-bull assassination plot. Do you expect me to believe that you placed yourself in harm's way out of the goodness of your heart? Why didn't you alert me to it months ago, the first chance you got?"

"Would you have believed me then, any more than you believe me now?" He had no answer, so she answered for him. "No, you wouldn't have, Tate. I was helpless. I didn't have the strength to protect myself, much less you. Besides, I couldn't afford the risk. When the person, whoever it was—*is*—found out that he'd whispered his plans to Avery

Daniels, television news reporter, how long do you think I would have lived?''

His eyes narrowed. Slowly, his head began to nod up and down. ''I think I see now why Avery Daniels, television news reporter, pulled this charade. You did it for the story, didn't you?''

She wet her lips, a signal of guilt and nervousness as good as a signed confession. ''Not entirely. I'll admit that my career factored into it initially.'' She reached for his arm again and held on this time. ''But not now, Tate. Not since I've come to love . . . Mandy. Once I got in, I couldn't get out. I couldn't just walk away and leave things unresolved.''

''So how long were you going to pretend to be my wife? Were we going to fuck with the lights out for the rest of our days? Was I never going to see you naked? How long were you going to live a lie? Forever?''

''No.'' Her hand slid off his arm and she slumped with despair. ''I don't know. I was going to tell you, only—''

''When?''

''When I knew Mandy was okay and that you were safe.''

''So we're back to the assassination plot.''

''Stop saying that so blithely,'' she exclaimed. ''The threat is real.'' She glanced at the poster. ''And imperative.''

''Then tell me who you suspect. You've been living with the same people I have been ever since you came out of the hospital.'' He shook his head again and laughed bitterly at his own stupidity. ''Jesus, this explains so much. The memory lapses. Shep. The riding horse.'' He looked over her body. ''It explains so many things,'' he said gruffly. After clearing his throat, he said, ''Why didn't I see it?''

''You weren't looking. You and Carole hadn't been intimate for a long time.''

He seemed disinclined to address that. He picked up his previous train of thought. ''Who do you suspect of wanting to kill me? My parents? My brother? My best friend? Dorothy Rae? No, wait—Fancy! That's it.'' He snapped his fingers. ''She got pissed off at me a couple years ago when I wouldn't loan her my car, so she wants me dead.''

''Don't joke about it.'' Avery shook with frustration.

''This whole thing's a joke,'' he said, lowering his face

close to hers. "A dirty rotten joke played on all of us by a conniving bitch with big ambitions. Granted, I've been a blind, deaf idiot, but now I'm seeing it all crystal clear.

"Didn't you commit a journalistic faux pas a year or so back—something about making allegations before all the facts were checked out? Yeah, I think you were the one. You devised this scheme to rectify that mistake and reinstate yourself among your colleagues. You're a reporter who needed a hot story, so, when the opportunity presented itself, you cooked this one up."

She shook her head and whispered mournfully, but without much conviction, "No."

"I'll give you credit, Avery Daniels. You go after your story no matter what it takes, don't you? This time you were even willing to whore for it. Probably not for the first time. Do you go down on all your interviewees? Is that their reward for giving you their secrets?"

She wrapped the robe around her tighter, but it did little to protect her from his chilling rebuke. "I wasn't whoring, Tate. Everything that happened between us was honest."

"Like hell."

"It was!"

"I've been fucking an impostor."

"And loving it!"

"Obviously, because you're as good at that as you are at playacting!"

Her anger had been spent with that one verbal volley. Now tears filled her imploring eyes. "You're wrong. Please believe me, Tate. You must be careful." She pointed down at the poster. "He's going to do it on Election Day. Tomorrow."

He was shaking his head adamantly. "You'll never convince me that somebody in my family is going to put a bullet through my head."

"Wait!" she cried, suddenly remembering something she had forgotten to mention. "There's a tall, gray-haired man who's been following you from city to city." She quickly enumerated the times and places she had seen Gray Hair in the crowds. "Van's got the tapes to prove it."

"Ah, the cameraman from KTEX," he said, smiling

ruefully. "So that explains him. Who else is in on your little game?"

"Irish McCabe."

"Who's he?"

She explained their relationship and how Irish had mistakenly identified Carole's body. "He has her jewelry, if you want it back."

"What about the locket?" he asked, nodding at her chest.

"A gift from my father."

"Very clever," he remarked with grudging respect. "You think on your feet and cover tracks well."

"Listen to me, Tate. If I get the tapes from Van, will you look at them to see if you recognize this man?" She told him how they had deduced that a professional assassin had been hired.

"You form quite a trio, all figuring to make big bucks at the expense of the Rutledge family."

"It's not like that."

"No?"

"No!"

The sudden knock on the door brought them both around. "Who is it?" Tate called out.

It was Eddy. "We'll meet downstairs in twenty minutes for a last-minute briefing over breakfast before leaving for the airport." Tate glanced at Avery and held her anxious gaze for several moments. "Is everything okay?" Eddy asked.

She placed her clenched hands beneath her chin and silently beseeched Tate not to say anything. "Please, Tate," she whispered. "You have no reason to, but you've got to trust me."

"Everything's fine," he reluctantly called through the door. "See you in the dining room. Twenty minutes."

Avery collapsed with relief on the nearest sofa. "You mustn't say anything, Tate. Swear to me you won't breathe a word of this to anyone. Anyone."

"Why should I trust you above my own family and confidants?"

She answered carefully. "If what I've told you is true, then your silence could save you from assassination. If it's all a wild scheme, then your silence could save you from public ridicule. Either way, you've nothing to gain right now by revealing me as an impostor. So, I'm begging you not to tell anyone.''

He gave her a long, cold stare. "You're as devious as Carole was.''

"I hate that you see it that way.''

"I should have read the signs. I should have known the changes in you, in *her*, were too good to be true. Like the way you took to Mandy when you came home.''

"She's come so far, Tate. Don't I get credit for loving her?''

"You'll get credit for breaking her heart when you leave.''

"It will break my heart, too.''

He ignored her. "Now I know why you suddenly took an interest in the election, why your opinions were more eloquently expressed, and why . . .'' He looked at her mouth. "Why so many things were different.'' For several moments, he seemed to be struggling against the pull of a powerful magnet that would draw him to her. Then, with a vicious curse, he turned away.

Avery charged after him, catching him before he could lock her out of the bathroom. "What are you going to do?''

"For the time being, not a damn thing. I've come this far. You and your nefarious scheme aren't going to deter me from winning the election for myself, and for my family, and for all the people who've placed their trust in me.''

"What about me?''

"I don't know,'' he answered honestly. "If I expose you, I would expose myself and my family as fools.'' He grabbed a handful of hair at the back of her head and pulled it back. "And if you expose us, I'll kill you.''

She believed him. "I'm not lying, Tate. Everything I've told you is the truth.''

He released her abruptly. "I'll probably divorce you, as I'd planned to divorce Carole. Your punishment will be having to remain the former Mrs. Tate Rutledge for the rest of your life.''

"You must be careful. Someone is going to try to kill you.''

"Avery Daniels has been dead and buried for months. She'll remain dead and buried."

"Watch for a tall, gray-haired man in the crowds. Stay away from him."

"There'll be no career in TV, no smashing story to make you an overnight sensation." His eyes raked over her contemptuously. "You did it all for nothing, Ms. Daniels."

"I did it because I love you."

He shut the door in her face.

FORTY-SIX

Van's search came to an end on the eve of Election Day. For several seconds, he stared at the color monitor screen, not believing that he'd finally found what he had been looking for all this time.

He had taken a catnap at daybreak, realizing when he saw light leaking around the tattered shades in his apartment windows that he had been up all night, viewing one video-tape after another. After he had slept for about an hour, he'd drunk a pot of strong, caffeine-rich coffee and returned to his console. The desk area was littered with junk food wrappers, empty soda cans, empty cigarette packs, and rank, overflowing ashtrays.

Van hadn't noticed the untidiness. He didn't care. Nor did it matter to him that he hadn't eaten a square meal or showered in over forty-eight hours. His compulsion to watch videotapes had become his obsession. His passion had grown into a mission.

He accomplished it at nine-thirty P.M. as he sat looking at a tape he had shot three years earlier while working at an NBC affiliate station in Washington state. He didn't even remember the station's call letters, but he remembered the assignment. He had used four tapes in all, each containing twenty minutes of unedited video. The reporter had compressed those eighty minutes into a five-minute special feature for the evening news during a ratings sweep week. It was the kind of piece people shuddered over and woefully shook their heads at, but consumed like popcorn.

Van watched all eighty minutes several times to make certain there was no mistake. When he was positive he was right, he flipped the necessary switches, inserted a blank tape, and began to make a duplicate of the most important, and most incriminating, one of the four.

Since it had to be duplicated at real time, that left him with twenty minutes to kill. He searched through the crumpled packets littering the console and finally produced a lone, bent cigarette, lit it, then picked up the phone and called the Palacio Del Rio.

"Yeah, I need to talk to Mrs. Rutledge. Mrs. Tate Rutledge."

"I'm sorry, sir," the switchboard operator said pleasantly, "I can't put that call through, but if you leave your name and number—"

"No, you don't understand. This is a personal message for Av...uh, Carole Rutledge."

"I'll give your message to their staff, who is screening—"

"Look, bitch, this is important, got that? An emergency."

"Regarding what, sir?"

"I can't tell you. I've got to speak to Mrs. Rutledge personally."

"I'm sorry, sir," the unflappable operator repeated. "I can't put that call through. If you leave your—"

"Shit!"

He slammed down the receiver and dialed Irish's number. He let it ring thirty times before giving up. "Where the hell is he?"

While the tape was still duplicating, Van paced, trying to figure out the best way to inform Irish and Avery of what he'd found. It was essential that he get this tape into Avery's hands, but how? If he couldn't even get the hotel operator to ring her suite, he couldn't possibly get close enough tonight to place the tape into her hands. She *had* to see it before tomorrow.

By the time the duplication was completed, Van still hadn't thought of a solution to his dilemma. The only possible course of action was to try to locate Irish. He would advise him what to do.

But after keeping the phone lines hot for half an hour between his apartment, KTEX's newsroom, and Irish's house, he still hadn't spoken to his boss. He decided to take the damn tape to Irish's house. He could wait for him there. It would mean driving clear across town, but what the hell? This was important.

It wasn't until he reached the parking lot of his apartment complex that he remembered his van was in the shop. His companion reporter had had to drive him home after they'd covered Rutledge's return to the San Antonio airport earlier that evening.

"Shit. Now what?"

The post office box. If contact couldn't be made any other way, that was the conveyance he'd been told to use. He went back inside. Among a heap of scrap papers, he found the one he'd scribbled the post office box number on. He sealed the videotape into an addressed, padded envelope, slipped on a jacket, and struck out on foot, taking his package with him.

It was only two blocks to the nearest convenience store, where there was also a mailbox, but even that represented more exercise than Van liked.

He purchased cigarettes, a six-pack of beer, and enough stamps to cover the postage—if not, Irish could make up the difference—and dropped the package into the mailbox. The schedule posted on the outside said that there was a pickup at midnight. The tape could feasibly be in Irish's hands by tomorrow morning.

In the meantime, though, Van planned to keep calling Irish every five minutes until he contacted him. Mailing the duplicate tape was only insurance.

Where could the old coot be at this hour, if not at home or the TV station? He had to show up sooner or later. Then the two of them would decide how to warn Avery of just how real the threat on Rutledge's life was.

Sipping one of the beers en route, Van sauntered back to his apartment, went in, shrugged off his jacket, and resumed his seat at the video console. He reloaded one of the tapes that had solved the mystery for him and began replaying it.

Midway through, he reached for the phone and dialed Irish's number. It rang five times before he heard the click severing the connection. He glanced quickly at his phone and saw that a gloved hand had depressed the button. His eyes followed an arm up to a pleasantly smiling face.

"Very interesting, Mr. Lovejoy," his visitor said softly, nodding at the flickering monitor. "I couldn't quite remember where I'd seen you before."

Then a pistol was raised and fired at point blank range into Van's forehead.

Irish rushed through his front door and caught his telephone on the sixth ring, just as the caller hung up. "Dammit!" He had stayed late in the newsroom in preparation for the hellish day the news team would have tomorrow.

He had checked and rechecked schedules, reviewed assignments, and consulted with the anchors to make certain everybody knew where to go and what to do when. It was this kind of news day that Irish loved. But it was also the kind that gave him heartburn as hot as smoldering brimstone in his gut. He shouldn't have stopped to wolf down that plate of enchiladas on his way home.

He drank a glass of antacid and returned to his telephone. He called Van, but hung up after the phone rang a couple dozen times. If Van was out carousing, getting hopped up on a controlled substance, he'd kill him. He needed him up bright and early in the morning.

He would dispatch Van with a reporter to record the Rutledges voting in Kerrville, then install him at the Palacio Del Rio for the rest of the day and long evening while they waited for the returns to come in.

Irish wasn't convinced that anybody would be so stupid as to attempt an assassination on Election Day, but Avery seemed to believe that's when it would happen. If seeing

Van in the crowd alleviated her anxiety, then Irish wanted him there, visible and within easy reach should she need him.

Contacting her by telephone was impossible. He had already tried to call her earlier today, but he had been told that Mrs. Rutledge wasn't feeling well. At least that's the story that had come out of the Rutledge camp when she failed to accompany Tate on his final campaign swing through North Texas.

In a later effort to speak with her, he had been told that the family was out to dinner. Still uneasy, he'd stopped by the post office on the way home and checked his box. There'd been nothing in it, which allayed his concerns somewhat. He supposed that no news was good news. If Avery needed him, she knew where to find him.

He prepared for bed. After his prayers, he tried calling Van once more. There was still no answer.

Avery spent Election Eve in tormenting worry. Tate told her peremptorily that she would not be going with him on his last campaign trip, and he stuck to it, heedless of her pleas.

When he returned safely, her relief was so profound that she was weak with it. As they convened for dinner, Jack sidled up to her and asked, "Do you still have the cramps?"

"What?"

"Tate said you weren't up to making the trip today because you got your period."

"Oh, yes," she said, backing his lie. "I didn't feel well this morning, but I'm fine now, thanks."

"Just make sure you're well in the morning." Jack wasn't the least bit interested in her health, only in how her presence or absence might effect the outcome of the election. "You've got to be at your peak tomorrow."

"I'll try."

Jack was then claimed by Dorothy Rae, who hadn't touched a drink in weeks. The changes in her were obvious. She no longer looked frightened and frail, but took pains with her appearance. More self-assertive, she rarely let Jack out of her sight, and never when Avery was around. Apparently

she still considered Carole a threat, but one she was prepared to combat for her husband's affections.

Thanks to Tate's ingrained charm, Avery didn't think
anyone noticed the schism in their relationship. The family
traveled en masse to a restaurant for dinner, where they
were seated and served in a private dining room.

For the duration of the meal, Tate treated her with utmost
politeness. She plagued him with questions about his day
and how he was received in each city. He answered courteously,
but without elaboration. The steely coldness from his eyes
chilled her to the marrow.

He played with Mandy. He related anecdotes of the trip to
his attentive mother and father. He gently teased Fancy and
engaged her in conversation. He listened to Jack's last few
words of counsel. He argued with Eddy over his Election
Day attire.

"I'm not dressing up to go vote—no more than the
average guy—and I'll change into a suit and tie only if I
have to make an acceptance speech."

"Then I'd better arrange to have the hotel valet press
your suit overnight," Avery said with conviction.

"Hear, hear!" Nelson heartily thumped his fist on the
table.

Tate looked at her sharply, as though wanting to strip
away her duplicity. If he suspected treachery of anyone in
this convivial inner circle, it was she. If he harbored any
doubts as to where his family's loyalty and devotion lay, he
masked it well. For a man whose life could be radically
altered the following day, he appeared ludicrously calm.

However, Avery guessed that his composure was a façade. He exuded confidence because he wanted everyone
else to remain at ease. That would be typical of Tate.

She longed for a private moment with him upon their
return to the hotel, and was glad when his conference with
Jack and Eddy concluded quickly.

"I'm going out for a stroll along the Riverwalk," Jack
told them as he pulled on his jacket. "Dorothy Rae and
Fancy are watching a movie on the TV in our room. It's the
kind of sentimental crap I can't stomach, so until it's over
I'm going to make myself scarce."

"I'll ride the elevator down with you," Eddy said. "I want to check the lobby newsstand for papers we might have missed."

They left. Mandy was already asleep in her room. Now, Avery thought, she would have time to plead her case before Tate. Maybe his judgment wouldn't be so harsh this time. To her dismay, however, he picked up his room key and moved toward the door.

"I'm going to visit with Mom and Dad for a while."

"Tate, did you notice Van at the airport? I tried calling him at home, but he wasn't back yet. I wanted him to bring the tapes over so—"

"You look tired. Don't wait up."

He left the suite and stayed gone a long time. Finally, because it had been such a long, dreary day, which she'd spent largely confined to the suite, she went to bed.

Tate never joined her. She woke up during the night. Missing his warmth, panicked because she didn't hear him breathing beside her, she quickly crossed the bedroom and flung open the door.

He was sleeping on the sofa in the parlor.

It broke her heart.

For months he had been lost to her because of Carole's deceit. Now he was lost to her because of her own.

FORTY-SEVEN

The bellyache Irish had when he went to bed the night before was mild in comparison to the raging one he had by seven o'clock Election Day morning.

It had dawned clear and cool. Heavy voter turnout was predicted statewide because of the perfect autumn weather.

The climate in the KTEX news department wasn't so

clement. Its chief was on the warpath. "Sorry, worthless son of a bitch," Irish mouthed as he slammed down the telephone receiver. When Van failed to show up in the newsroom at six-thirty as scheduled, Irish had started telephoning his apartment. There was still no answer. "Where could he be?"

"Maybe he's on his way," another photographer volunteered, trying to be helpful.

"Maybe," Irish grumbled as he lit a cigarette, which he'd only planned to hold between his lips. "In the meantime, I'm sending you. If you hurry, you can catch the Rutledges as they leave the hotel. If not, drive like hell to catch up with them in Kerrville. And report in every few minutes," he yelled after the cameraman who scrambled out with the reporter. Both were grateful to escape with their scalps intact.

Irish snatched up the telephone and punched out a number he had memorized by now. "Good morning," a pleasant voice answered, "Palacio Del Rio."

"I need to speak to Mrs. Rutledge."

"I'm sorry, sir. I can't put your call—"

"Yeah, I know, I know, but this is important."

"If you'll leave your name and num—"

He hung up on her saccharine spiel and immediately called Van's number. It rang incessantly while Irish paced as far as the telephone cord would reach. "When I get my hands on him, I'm gonna hammer his balls to mush."

He collared a gofer who had the misfortune to collide with him. "Hey, you, drive over there and haul his skinny ass out of bed."

"Who, sir?"

"Van Lovejoy. Who the fuck do you think?" Irish bellowed impatiently. Why had everybody chosen today to turn up either missing or stupid? He scrawled Van's address on a sheet of paper, shoved it at the terror-stricken kid, and ordered ominously, "Don't come back without him."

Avery emerged from the hotel, holding Mandy by one sweating hand. The other was tucked into the crook of

Tate's elbow. She smiled for the myriad cameras, wishing her facial muscles would stop cramping and quivering.

Tate gave the cameras his most engaging smile and a thumbs-up sign as they moved toward the waiting limousine parked in the brick paved porte cochere. Microphones were aimed toward them. Bleakly, Avery thought they resembled gun barrels. Tate's voice carried confidently across the city racket and general confusion. "Great Election Day weather. Good for the voters and for the candidates in each race."

He was bombarded with questions regarding more serious topics than the weather, but Eddy ushered them into the backseat of the limo. Avery was distressed to learn that he was riding with them to Kerrville. She wouldn't have Tate to herself, as she had hoped. They hadn't been alone all morning. He was already up and dressed by the time she woke up. He breakfasted in the dining room on the river level of the hotel while she got Mandy and herself dressed.

As the limo pulled away from the curb, she glanced through the rear window, trying to locate Van. She spotted a two-man crew from KTEX, but Van wasn't the photographer behind the Betacam. *Why not?* she wondered. *Where is he?*

He wasn't among the media waiting for them at their polling place in Kerrville, either. Her anxiety mounted, so much so that at one point, Tate leaned down at her and whispered, "Smile, for God's sake. You look like I've already lost."

"I'm afraid, Tate."

"Afraid I'll lose before the day is out?"

"No. Afraid you'll die." She held his gaze for several seconds before Jack intruded on them with a question for Tate.

The ride back to San Antonio seemed interminable. Freeway and downtown traffic was heavier than normal. As they alighted from the limo at the entrance of the hotel, Avery's eyes scanned the milling crowd again. She sighted a familiar face, but it wasn't the one she wanted to see. The gray-haired man was standing in front of the convention center across the street. Van, on the other hand, was nowhere in sight.

Irish had promised.

Something was wrong.

The moment they reached their suite, she excused herself and went into the bedroom to use the telephone. The direct line into the newsroom was answered after ten rings. "Irish McCabe, please," she said with breathless urgency.

"Irish? Okay, I'll go find him."

Having worked election days, she knew what nightmares, and yet what challenges, they presented to the media. Everybody operated on a frantic frequency.

"Come on, come on, Irish," she whispered while waiting. She kept remembering how still and intent Gray Hair had stood, as though maintaining a post.

"Hello?"

"Irish!" she exclaimed, going limp with relief.

"No. Is that who you're holding for? Just a sec."

"This is Av—" When she was abruptly put on hold again, she nearly sobbed with anxiety.

The phone was picked up a second time. "Hello?" a man asked hesitantly. "Hello?"

"Yes, who is—Eddy, is that you?"

"Yeah."

"This is, A—uh, Carole."

"Where the hell are you?"

"I'm in the bedroom. I'm using this line." Evidently, he had picked up the extension in the parlor.

"Well, make it snappy, okay? We've got to keep these lines open."

He hung up. She was still on hold. Her call to the newsroom had been ignored by people with better things to do than track down the boss on the busiest news day of the year. Distraught, she replaced the telephone and went to join the family and a few key volunteers who had assembled in the other room.

Though she smiled and conversed as it was expected of her, she tried to imagine where Van could be. She comforted herself by picturing him downstairs in the ballroom, setting up his tripod and camera to cover what would hopefully be Tate's victory celebration later in the evening.

For the time being there was nothing more she could do.

There must be a logical explanation for the switch in plans. Because she hadn't been apprised, she had let her imagination run away with her. Irish and Van knew where she was if they needed to contact her. Resolving to keep her panic at bay, she moved toward the sofa where Tate was sprawled.

True to his word, he'd gone to the polls dressed casually, wearing a leather sports jacket over his jeans. He appeared perfectly relaxed as he told Zee, who was taking orders, what he wanted for lunch.

Avery sat down on the arm of the sofa. He absently draped his arm over her thigh and caressed her knee with negligent possession. When Zee moved away, he glanced up at her and smiled. "Hi."

"Hi."

And then he remembered. She watched as memory crept back into his eyes, eating up the warm glow in his gray irises until they were cold and implacable once again. He gradually lifted his arm away from her.

"There's something I've been meaning to ask you," he said.

"Yes?"

"Did you ever take care of birth control?"

"No. And neither did you."

"Terrific."

She couldn't let his contempt intimidate her into keeping her distance. For the remainder of the day, she didn't intend to get any farther away from him than she was at the moment.

"Irish, line two's for you."

"Can't you see I'm already on the frigging phone?" he yelled across the pandemonium in the newsroom. "Put 'em on hold. Now," he said, speaking into the receiver again, "did you try knocking?"

"Till my knuckles were bloody, Mr. McCabe. He's not home."

Irish ran his hand down his florid face. The gofer was calling in with news that made absolutely no sense. "Did you look through the windows?"

"I tried. The shades are down, but I listened through the

door. I couldn't hear a single sound. I don't think anybody's
in there. Besides, his van's not here. I already checked the
parking lot. His space is empty.''

That was going to be Irish's next suggestion. ''Christ,''
he muttered. He had hoped that Van would be at home,
sleeping off a night of overindulgence, but obviously he
wasn't. If his van wasn't there, he wasn't at home, period.

Irish reasoned they might have gotten their signals crossed
and that Van had gone straight to the Palacio Del Rio, but
after checking with the crew there, they reported they hadn't
seen him either.

''Okay, thanks. Come on back in.'' He pressed the
blinking light on the telephone panel. ''McCabe,'' he said
gruffly. He got a dial tone in his ear. ''Hey, wasn't somebody holding for me on two?''

''That's right.''

''Well, they're not there now.''

''Guess they hung up.''

''Was it a guy?'' he wanted to know.

''A woman.''

''Did she say who?''

''No. Sounded kinda ragged out, though.''

Irish's blood pressure shot up. ''Why the hell didn't you
tell me?''

''I did!''

''Jesus!''

Arguing with incompetents wasn't going to help anything. He stamped back into his office, slammed the door
behind him, and lit a cigarette. He couldn't be certain it had
been Avery on the phone, but he had a gut instinct that it
had been. Maybe that's what was making his gut hurt so
bad—his rotten instincts.

He took a swig of antacid straight from the bottle and
yanked up the telephone again. He dialed the hotel and got
the same cool voice as before. When he demanded to be
connected to the Rutledge suite, the operator began her
same unruffled litany.

''Look, bitch, I don't give a fuck about your fucking
instructions or who the fucking calls are supposed to be
routed through. I want you to ring her suite now. *Now*, got

that? And if you don't do it, I'm gonna come over there and personally take your fucking head off.''

She hung up on him.

Irish paced his office, puffing smoke and chugging like a steam locomotive. Avery must be beside herself. She would think they'd deserted her.

Van, that irresponsible bastard, hadn't shown up at the hotel where he was supposed to be, where she would be watching for him, relying on him. His calls weren't being put through to her, so she had no way of knowing that he'd frantically been trying to contact her.

He stormed back into the newsroom as he pulled on his tweed blazer. "I'm going out."

"Out?"

"What, are you deaf? *Out*. If anybody calls or comes looking for me, tell 'em to stay put or leave a message. I'll be back when I can."

"Where are you . . . ?" The subordinate was left talking to wisps of cigarette smoke.

"You're sure he's not there?" Avery was struck with disbelief. "I phoned earlier and—"

"All I know is somebody said he went out, and I can't find him, so I guess he's out."

"Out where?"

"Nobody seems to know."

"Irish wouldn't go out the day of an election."

"Look, lady, it's a madhouse around here, especially since Irish decided to split, so do you want to leave a message, or what?"

"No," she said distantly. "No message."

Feeling that she'd been cut adrift, she hung up and wandered back into the main room. Her eyes automatically sought out Tate first. He was talking with Nelson. Zee was ostensibly listening to their conversation, but her eyes were fixed on Tate with that faraway absorption that often characterized her.

Jack and Eddy were downstairs seeing to the arrangements in the ballroom while carefully monitoring returns as they were reported. It was still several hours before the polls closed, but early indications were that Tate was staying abreast of Dekker. Even if he didn't pull out in front, he'd given the pompous incumbent a good scare.

Dorothy Rae had pleaded a headache earlier and gone to her room to lie down for a while. Fancy was sitting on the floor with Mandy. They were coloring together.

On a sudden inspiration, Avery called her name. "Could you come here a minute, please?"

"What for?"

"I . . . I need you to run an errand for me."

"Grandma told me to entertain the kid."

"I'll do that. Anyway, it's getting close to her nap time. Please. It's important."

Grudgingly, Fancy came to her feet and followed Avery back into the bedroom. Since the incident a few nights earlier, she had been much more pleasant to be around. Every now and then, traces of her recalcitrance asserted itself, but on the whole, she was more congenial.

As soon as she closed the door behind them, Avery pressed a small key into Fancy's hand. "I need you to do something for me."

"With this key?"

"It's a post office box key. I need you to go there and see if there's something inside. If there is, bring it back with you and hand deliver it to me—no one else."

"What the hell's going on?"

"I can't explain right now."

"I'm not gonna go chasing—"

"Please, Fancy. It's terribly important."

"Then, how come you're asking me? I usually get the shit detail."

"I thought we were friends," Avery said, turning up the heat. "Tate and I helped you out of a jam the other night. You owe us a favor."

Fancy chewed on that for a moment, then flipped the key in her palm several times. "Where's it at?" Avery provided her with the address of the post office branch. "Jeez, that's a million miles from here."

"And you said half an hour ago that you were tired of

being cooped up in this friggin' hotel suite. And I believe that's a quote. Now, will you do this for me?''

Avery's demeanor must have conveyed some measure of the urgency and importance of the errand because Fancy shrugged. ''Okay.''

''Thank you.'' Avery gave her a hard hug. At the bedroom door, she paused. ''Don't make a big deal of leaving. Just go as unobtrusively as possible. If someone asks where you are, I'll cover for you.''

''Why so hush-hush? What's the big secret? You're not screwing a postman, are you?''

''Trust me. It's very important to Tate—to all of us. And please hurry back.''

Fancy retrieved her shoulder bag from the credenza in the parlor and headed for the double door of the suite. ''I'll be back,'' she tossed over her shoulder. No one gave her a second glance.

FORTY-EIGHT

Fancy lifted her hip onto the stool and laid the small rectangular package she'd taken from the post office box on the polished wood surface of the bar. The bartender, a mustached, muscular young man, moved toward her.

The smile she blessed him with had been designed in heaven for angels to wear. ''A gin and tonic, please.''

His friendly blue eyes looked at her skeptically. ''How old are you?''

''Old enough.''

''Make that two gins and tonic.'' A man slid onto the stool beside Fancy's. ''I'm buying the lady's.''

The bartender shrugged. ''Fine with me.''

Fancy assessed her rescuer. He was a young executive

type—insurance or computers, she would guess. Possibly late twenties. Probably married. Looking for kicks away from the responsibilities he had assumed so he could afford his designer clothes and the timepiece strapped to his wrist.

This was the kind of trendy place that attracted singles or marrieds on the make. It was filled with worthless antiques and glossy, gargantuan greenery. The bar created a vortex during happy hour that sucked in yuppies from their BMWs and Porsches by the scores.

While she was analyzing him, he was analyzing her. The gleam in his eyes as they moved down her body indicated that he thought he'd scored big.

"Thanks for the drink," she said.

"You're welcome. You *are* old enough to drink, aren't you?"

"Sure. I'm old enough to drink. Just not old enough to buy." They laughed and toasted each other with the drinks that had just arrived.

"I'm John."

"Fancy."

"Fancy?"

"Francine, if you prefer."

"Fancy."

The mating ritual had begun. Fancy recognized it. She knew the rules. Hell, she'd invented most of them. In two hours—possibly less, if they got hot sooner—they'd be in bed somewhere.

Following her heartbreak over Eddy, she'd sworn off men. They were all bastards. They wanted only one thing from her, and it was the same thing they could buy from the cheapest whore.

Her mother had told her that one day she would meet a guy who truly cared for her and would treat her with kindness and respect. Fancy didn't really believe it, though. Was she supposed to sit around, bored out of her skull, letting her twat atrophy while she waited for Prince Charming to show up and bring it back to life?

Hell, no. She'd been good for three days now. She needed some laughs. This Jim, or Joe, or John, or whatever the hell his name was, was as good as any to give her some.

Like a freaking Girl Scout, she had run Carole's errand, but she wasn't ready to return to the hotel suite and sit glued to the TV set as the rest would be, watching election returns. She would get there eventually. But first, she was going to have some fun.

Finding a parking place anywhere close to the hotel was impossible. Irish finally found one in a lot several blocks away. He was heavily perspiring by the time he entered the lobby. If he had to bribe his way into the Rutledges' private suite he would do it. He had to see Avery. Together they might figure out what had become of Van.

Maybe all his worries were for nothing. Maybe they were together right now. God, he hoped so.

He waded through the members of an Asian tour group who were lined up to check in. Patience had never been one of Irish's virtues. He felt his blood pressure rising as he elbowed his way through the tourists, all chattering and fanning themselves with pamphlets about the Alamo.

From amid the chaos, someone touched his elbow. "Hi."

"Oh, hi," Irish said, recognizing the face.

"You're Irish McCabe, aren't you? Avery's friend?"

"That's right."

"She's been looking for you. Follow me."

They navigated the congested lobby. Irish was led through a set of doors toward a service elevator. They got inside; the gray doors slid closed.

"Thanks," Irish said, wiping his sweaty forehead on his sleeve. "Did Avery . . ." In the middle of his question, it occurred to him that her correct name had been used. He glanced across the large cubicle. "You know?"

A smile. "Yes. I know."

Irish saw the pistol, but he wasn't given time to register the thought that it was actually being aimed straight at him. Less than a heartbeat later, he grabbed his chest and hit the floor of the elevator like a fallen tree.

The elevator stopped on the lowest level of the hotel. The lone passenger raised the pistol and aimed it toward the opening doors, but didn't have to use it. No one was waiting.

Irish's body was dragged down a short hallway, through a set of swinging double doors, and deposited in a narrow alcove that housed vending machines for hotel employee use. The space was lit from overhead by four fluorescent tubes, which were easily smashed with the silencer attached to the barrel of the pistol.

Covered with shards of opaque glass and stygian darkness, Irish McCabe's body was left there on the floor. The assassin knew that by the time it was discovered, his death would be obscured by another.

Prime time had been given over solely to election returns. Each of the three television sets in the parlor was tuned to a different network. It had turned out to be a close presidential race—still too close to call. Several times, the network anchors cited the senatorial race in Texas between the newcomer, Tate Rutledge, and the incumbent, Rory Dekker, as one of the closest and most heated races in the nation.

When it was reported that Rutledge was showing a slight edge, a cheer went up in the parlor. Avery jumped at the sudden noise. She was frantic, walking a razor's edge, on the brink of nervous collapse.

All the excitement had made Mandy hyperactive. She'd become such a nuisance that someone from the hotel's list of baby-sitters had been hired to keep her entertained in another room so the family would be free to concentrate on the returns.

With her mind temporarily off Mandy, Avery could devote herself to worrying about Tate and wondering where Irish and Van were. Their disappearances didn't make sense. She had called the newsroom three times. Neither had been there, nor had their whereabouts been known.

"Has anyone notified the police?" she had asked during her most recent call. "Something could have happened to them."

"Listen, if you want to report them missing, fine, do it. But stop calling here bugging us. Now, I've got better things to do."

The phone had been slammed down in her ear. She wanted to drive to the station as quickly as she could get there, but she didn't want to leave Tate. As the hours of the evening stretched out, there were two certainties at play in her mind. One was that Tate was about to win the Senate seat. The other was that something dreadful had happened to her friends.

What if Gray Hair *had* been stalking her, not Tate, as Van had suggested. What if he'd noticed her interest in him? What if he'd intercepted Van this morning as he reported to work? What if he'd lured Irish away from the TV station?

It made her nauseated with fear to know that a killer was in the hotel, under the same roof as Tate and Mandy.

And where was Fancy? She had been gone for hours. Had something happened to her, too? If not, why hadn't she at least phoned to explain her delay? Even with Election Day traffic, the round trip to the post office shouldn't have taken much longer than an hour.

"Tate, one of the networks just called the thing in your favor!" Eddy announced as he came barreling through the door. "Ready to go downstairs?"

Avery whirled toward Tate, holding her breath in anticipation of his answer. "No," he said. "Not until it's beyond a shadow of a doubt. Not until Dekker calls and concedes."

"At least go change your clothes."

"What's wrong with these clothes?"

"You're going to fight me on that to the bitter end, aren't you?"

"Till the bitter end," Tate replied, laughing.

"If you win, I won't even care."

Nelson walked over to Tate and shook his hand. "You did it. You accomplished everything I expected of you."

"Thanks, Dad," Tate said a bit shakily. "But let's not count our chickens yet." Zee hugged him against her petite frame.

"Bravo, little brother," Jack said, lightly slapping Tate on the cheek. "Think we ought to try for the White House next?"

"I couldn't have done anything without you, Jack."

Dorothy Rae pulled Tate down and kissed him. "It's good of you to say that, Tate."

"I give credit where credit's due." He stared at Avery

over their heads. His expression silently declared just how wrong she had been. He was surrounded by people who loved him. She was the only deceiver.

The door opened again. She spun around, hoping to see Fancy. It was one of the volunteers. "Everything's all set in the ballroom. The crowd's chanting for Tate and the band's playing. God, it's great!"

"I say it's time to break out the champagne," Nelson said.

When the first cork was popped, Avery nearly jumped out of her skin.

John's arm grazed Fancy's breast. She moved away. His thigh rubbed hers. She recrossed her legs. His predictable passes were getting tiresome. She wasn't in the mood. The drinks no longer tasted good. This wasn't as much fun as it used to be.

I thought we were friends.

Carole's voice seemed to speak to her above Rod Stewart's overamplified, hoarse sexiness and the din the happy hour imbibers were creating.

Carole had treated her decently in the last few months—in fact, since she'd come home from the hospital. Some of the things she'd said about self-respect were beginning to make sense. How could she have any self-respect if she let guys pick her up in joints like this—this was classy compared to some of the dives she'd been in—and do anything they wanted with her, then dispose of her as easily as they threw away a used rubber?

Carole didn't seem to think she was a dimwit. She'd entrusted her to run an important errand. And what had she done in return? She'd let her down.

"Say, I gotta go," she said suddenly. John had leaned over to lick her ear. She nearly knocked him off his stool when she reached for her purse and the padded envelope still lying on the bar. "Thanks for the drinks."

"Hey, where're you going? I thought, well, you know."

"Yeah, I know," Fancy said. "Sorry."

He came off his stool, propped his hands on his hips, and

angrily demanded, "Well, what the hell am I supposed to do now?"

"Jerk off, I guess."

She drove toward the hotel with indiscriminate speed, keeping an eye out for radar traps and cruising police cars. She wasn't drunk, but alcohol would show up on a breath analyzer. Downtown traffic made the irregular maze of streets even more of a nightmare, but she finally reached the hotel garage.

The lobby was packed. Campaign posters bearing Tate Rutledge's picture bobbed above the press of people. It seemed that everyone in Bexar County who had voted for Tate Rutledge had come to celebrate his victory.

"Excuse me, excuse me." Fancy wormed her way through the crowd. "Ouch, dammit, that's my foot!" she shouted when someone backed over her. "Let me through."

"Hey, blondie, you gotta wait on the elevators same as everybody else." The complainer was a woman wearing a veritable armor of Rutledge campaign buttons on her chest.

"The hell I do," Fancy called back. "Excuse me."

After what seemed like half an hour of battling through the crowd as alive and working as a bucket of fishing bait, she stood up on tiptoe and was dismayed to find that she still wasn't anywhere close to the bank of elevators.

"Enough of this shit," she muttered. She caught the arm of the man nearest her. "If you can get me into an elevator, I'll give you a blow job you'll never forget."

A sudden hush fell over the room when the parlor telephone rang. All eyes swung toward the instrument. The mood was collectively expectant.

"Okay," Eddy said quietly, "that's him."

Tate picked up the phone. "Hello? Yes, sir, this is Tate Rutledge. It's good of you to call, Senator Dekker."

Eddy raised both fists above his head and shook them like a winning boxer after a knockout. Zee clasped her hands beneath her chin. Nelson nodded like a judge who had just been handed a fair decision from the jury. Jack and Dorothy Rae smiled at each other.

"Yes, sir. Thank you, sir. I feel the same way. Thank

you. I appreciate your call." Tate replaced the receiver. For several seconds he sat with his hands loosely clasped between his knees, then he raised his head and, with a boyish grin, said, "Guess that means I'm the new senator from Texas."

The suite was instantly plunged into chaos. Some of the aides jumped into chairs and began whooping like attacking Indians. Eddy hauled Tate to his feet and pushed him toward the bedroom. "*Now* you can go change. Somebody go catch an elevator and hold it. I'll call downstairs and tell them to give us five minutes." He yanked up the telephone.

Avery stood wringing her hands. She wanted to cheer and shout with joy over Tate's triumph. She wanted to throw her arms around him and give him a kiss befitting the victor. She wanted to share this jubilant moment with him. Instead, she shook like Jell-O, congealed with fear.

When she joined him in the bedroom, he was already stripped to his underwear and was stepping into a pair of dress slacks. "Tate, don't go."

His head snapped up. "What?"

"Don't go down there."

"I can't—"

She grabbed his arm. "The man I told you about—the gray-haired man—he's here. I saw him this morning. Tate, for God's sake don't go."

"I have to."

"Please." Tears formed in her eyes. "Please, believe what I'm telling you."

He was buttoning his pale blue shirt. His hands paused. "Why should I?"

"Because I love you. That's why I wanted to assume the role of your wife. I fell in love with you while I was still in the hospital. Before I could move or speak, I loved you.

"Everything I've told you is the truth. A threat has been made on your life. And yes, a chance for a terrific story presented itself to me and I took it, but . . ." Here she clutched his shoulders between her hands and appealed to him. "But I did what I did because I wanted to protect you. I love you and have from the beginning."

"Tate, they're—" Eddy came barging in. "What the hell

is going on in here? I thought you'd be dressed by now. They're tearing the place apart downstairs, waiting for you to put in an appearance. Everybody's gone nuts. Come on. Let's go.''

Tate looked from his friend to Avery. "Even if I believed you," he said with quiet helplessness, "I don't have a choice."

"Tate, please," she begged, her voice tearing like paper. "I don't have a choice."

He removed her hands and quickly finished dressing. Eddy coached him on whom to thank publicly. "Carole, you look like hell. Before you come downstairs, do something with your face," he ordered as he pushed Tate through the door.

Disobediently, Avery dashed after them. There were even more people in the suite now. Campaign workers had thronged the corridor and were forcing their way through the double doors to catch a glimpse of their hero. The noise was deafening. Somehow, over it, Avery heard Carole's name and turned in that direction.

Fancy squeezed through the squirming bodies. Inertia propelled her straight into Avery's arms. "Fancy! Where have you been?"

"Don't lecture me. I've been through bloody hell trying to get here. There's a guy out in the hall who's really pissed off because I welshed on a deal and another one named John who's—"

"Was there anything in the box?"

"Here." The younger woman thrust the package at Avery. "I hope to God it's worth all the hell I've been through to get it here."

"Carole! You, too, Fancy, let's go!" Eddy shouted at them, waving them toward the door above the heads of the celebrants.

Avery ripped into the envelope and saw that it contained a videotape. "Stall them if you can."

"Huh?" Stupefied, Fancy watched her slip into the bedroom and shut the door behind her. "Jesus, is it me, or has everybody else gone fuckin' nuts?" A total stranger danced by and thrust a magnum of champagne into her hand. She took a long gulp.

Inside the bedroom, Avery inserted the tape into the VCR. She backed up toward the bed until the backs of her knees made contact, then sat down on the edge of it. Using the remote control, she fast-forwarded past the color bars to the clapboard. She recognized the station's call letters. Washington state, wasn't it? The reporter's name was unfamiliar to her, but the photographer was listed as Van Lovejoy.

Excitement churned inside her. Van had sent the tape to Irish's box, so it must contain something vitally important. After watching for several minutes, however, she couldn't imagine what that something might be. Was Van playing a joke?

The subject of the piece was a white supremacist and paramilitary group that had a permanent encampment located in an undisclosed spot, deep within the forested wilderness. On weekends, members would meet to plan their annihilation of everybody who wasn't exactly like them. It was their goal to eventually take over America, making it the racially pure, undiluted nation it should be.

Van, who to Avery's knowledge, had no political predilection, must have been alarmed by the ferocity of the hatred the organization espoused, for he had documented on tape the war games they played. He featured them swapping arms and ammunition, training newcomers in guerrilla tactics, and indoctrinating their children into believing that they were superior to everyone. They preached it all in the name of Christianity.

It was captivating video and the news hound inside her regretted having to fast-forward through it. She ran it at normal speed occasionally to make sure she wasn't missing the pertinence of the tape, but she couldn't find a single clue why Van had considered it crucial enough to mail.

His camera panned across a group of men dressed in military fatigues. They were armed to the teeth. Avery backed the tape up, then slowed it down so she could study each face. The commander was screaming swill into the receptive ears of his soldiers.

Van zoomed in for a close-up of one. Avery gasped with recognition. Her head began to swim.

He looked different. His scalp shone through the buzz haircut. Camouflage makeup had been smeared on his face, but it was instantly recognizable because she'd been living with him for months.

"That all men are created equal is a bunch of crap," the instructor ranted into the hand-held microphone. "A rumor started by inferiors in the hope that somebody would believe it."

The man Avery recognized applauded. He whistled. Hatred smoldered in his eyes.

"We don't want to live alongside niggers and kikes and queers, right?"

"Right!"

"We don't want them corrupting our children with their commie propaganda, right?"

"Right!"

"So what are we going to do to anybody who tells us we have to?"

The group, as one body, rose. Van's camera stayed focused on the participant who seemed the most steeped in bigotry and hatred. "Kill the bastards!" he shouted through his mask of camouflage makeup. "Kill the bastards!"

The door suddenly swung open. Avery hastily switched off the tape and vaulted from the bed. "Jack!" She covered her lips with bloodless fingers. Her knees almost refused to support her.

"They sent me back for you. We're supposed to be downstairs now, but I'm glad we have a minute alone."

Avery propped herself up, using the TV set behind her for support. Beyond Jack's shoulder she noted that the parlor was deserted now. Everyone had left for the ballroom downstairs.

He advanced on her. "I want to know why you did it."

"Did what?"

"Came on to me like you did."

Avery's chest rose and fell on a single, life-or-death breath. "Jack—"

"No, I want to know. Dorothy Rae says you never cared

about me, that you only flirted with me to drive a wedge between Tate and me. Why, damn you? I nearly ruined my relationship with my brother. I nearly let my marriage fall apart because of you.''

"Jack, I'm sorry,'' she said earnestly. "Truly I am, but—"

"You just wanted to make me look like a buffoon, didn't you? Did it elevate your ego to humiliate Dorothy Rae?"

"Jack, listen, please.''

"No, you listen. She's twice the woman you are. Have you noticed how she's quit drinking all by herself? That takes character—something you'll never have. She still loves me, in spite of—''

"Jack, when did Eddy first come to work for Tate?''

He swore beneath his breath and shifted from one foot to the other impatiently. "I'm spilling my guts here and—"

"It's important!'' she shouted. "How did Eddy talk himself into the job of campaign manager? When did he first appear on the scene? Did anyone think to check his qualifications?''

"What the hell are you talking about? You know as well as I do that he didn't talk himself into anything. He was recruited for the job.''

"Recruited?'' she repeated thinly. "By whom, Jack? Whose idea was it? Who hired Eddy Paschal?''

Jack gave her a blank stare, then a quick shrug. "Dad.''

FORTY-NINE

The Corte Real was a lovely facility but a poor selection to host Tate Rutledge's victory celebration because it had only one entrance. Between a pair of massive Spanish doors and the ballroom itself was a short, narrow passageway. It formed an inevitable bottleneck.

The newly elected senator was propelled through that channel by a surge of family, friends, and supporters, all raucous, all jubilant over his win. Television lights created an aura around his head that shone like a celestial crown. His smile blended confidence with humility, that mix that elevated good men to greatness.

Tate's tall, gray-haired observer weaved his way toward the decorated platform at the opposite end of the room from the entrance. He elbowed aside media and Rutledge enthusiasts, somehow managing to do so without drawing attention to himself. Over the years, he'd mastered that kind of maneuver.

Recently, he had wondered if his skills weren't getting rusty. He was almost certain Mrs. Rutledge had picked him out of the crowd on more than one occasion.

Having thought of her, he suddenly realized that she wasn't among the group following Tate toward the dais. Incisive eyes swung toward the entrance. Ah, there she was, bringing up the rear, looking distraught, obviously because she'd become separated from the rest of the family.

He turned his attention back to the charismatic young man, whose appearance in the ballroom had whipped the crowd into a frenzy. As he climbed the steps of the dais, balloons were released from a net overhead. They contributed to the confusion and poor visibility.

On the stage, Rutledge paused to shake hands with some of his most influential supporters—among them, several sports heroes and a Texas-bred movie actress. He waved to his disciples and they cheered him.

Gray Hair dodged the corner of a bouncing placard that nearly caught him on the forehead and kept his eyes trained on the hero of the hour. In the midst of this orgy of celebration, his face alone was grave with resolution.

Purposefully, he continued to move steadily forward, toward the platform. The pandemonium would have intimidated most, but it didn't faze him. He considered it a nuisance, nothing more. His progress was undeterred. Nothing could stop him from reaching Tate Rutledge.

* * *

Avery arrived breathless at the door of the ballroom. The walls of her heart felt as thin as a balloon about to burst. The muscles of her legs were burning. She'd run down twenty flights of stairs.

She hadn't even attempted to take an elevator to the hotel's mezzanine level but, together with Jack, who'd only been told that his brother's life was in imminent danger, had dashed for the stairs. Somewhere in the stairwell, Jack was still trying to catch up with her.

Pausing only a fraction of a moment to draw breath and get her bearings, she madly plunged through the crowd toward the dais. Wall-to-wall bodies formed a barricade, but Avery managed to plow through it.

She saw his head rise above the throng as he took the steps leading to the platform. "Tate!"

He heard her shout and swiveled his head around, but he missed seeing her when someone on the temporary stage grabbed his arm and began pumping his hand enthusiastically.

Avery frantically sought Eddy and found him positioning Nelson, Zee, Dorothy Rae, and Fancy in a semicircle behind the podium. He then motioned Tate toward the speaker's stand, where a dozen microphones were mounted and ready to amplify his first words as a newly elected senator.

Tate moved toward the podium.

"Tate!" It was impossible for her to be heard over the blaring band. At the sight of their hero, the crowd had gone mad. "Oh, God, no. Let me through. Let me through."

A blast of adrenalin strengthened Avery's flagging energy and rubbery legs. With no regard to courtesy, she kicked and clawed her way forward, batting aside drifting balloons.

Jack finally caught up with her. "Carole," he panted, "what do you mean Tate's life is in danger?"

"Help me get to him. Jack, For God's sake, help me." He did what he could to create a furrow through the crowd. When she saw a space opening up in front of her, she jumped into the air and frantically waved her arms. "Tate! Tate!"

Gray Hair!

He was standing near the edge of the dais, partially hidden behind a Texas state flag.

"No!" she screamed. "Tate!"

Jack gave her a boost from behind. She stumbled up the steps, almost fell, caught herself. "Tate!"

Hearing her cry, he turned, wearing his glorious smile, and extended his hand. She rushed across the platform, but not toward Tate.

Her eyes were fixed on his enemy. And his were on her. And the sudden realization that she knew about him caused his eyes to crystallize.

As though in slow motion, Avery saw Eddy reach into his jacket. Her lips formed the word, but she didn't know that she actually screamed "No!" as he withdrew the pistol and took aim at the back of Tate's head.

Avery lunged for Tate and knocked him aside. A millisecond later, Eddy's bullet slammed into her, throwing her into Tate's unsuspecting arms.

She heard the screams, heard Tate's bellowing denial that this was happening, saw Jack's and Dorothy Rae's and Fancy's blank expressions of horror and incredulity.

Her eyes connected with Nelson Rutledge's the same instant Eddy's second bullet struck him in the forehead. It made a neat hole, but its rear exit was messy. Zee was showered with blood. She screamed.

Nelson's face registered surprise, then anger, then outrage. That was his death mask. He was dead before he hit the floor.

Eddy leaped from the dais into the crowd of hysterical spectators. The Lone Star flag fluttered. A man stepped from behind it and fired his previously concealed weapon. Eddy Paschal's head exploded upon impact.

It was Zee's voice that Avery heard from afar.

"Bryan! My God. *Bryan!*"

FIFTY

"I thought it would be best if we all met together like this, so I could clarify everything to everyone at once."

FBI Special Agent Bryan Tate addressed the somber group assembled in Avery Daniels's hospital room. Her bed had been elevated so that she was partially sitting up. Her eyes were red and puffy from crying. A bandage covered her left shoulder; her arm was in a sling.

The others—Jack and his family, Zee and Tate—were sitting in the available chairs or leaning against the walls and windowsills. All kept a wary distance from Avery's bed. Since Tate had disclosed her true identity to them, she had become an object of curiosity. After the tragic events of the night before, Mandy had been taken to the ranch and left in Mona's care.

"All of you experienced what happened," Bryan Tate said, "but you don't know the reasons for it. They're not easy to talk about."

"Tell them everything, Bryan," Zee said softly. "Don't leave out anything on my account. I want them, *need* them, to understand."

Tall and distinguished, he was standing beside her chair, a hand on her shoulder. "Zee and I fell in love years ago," he stated bluntly. "It was something neither of us predicted or wanted, particularly. We didn't set out to make it happen. It was wrong, but it was powerful. We eventually surrendered to it." His fingers flexed on her shoulder. "The consequences were far-reaching. They culminated in tragedy last night."

He told them how he had returned home from Korea a

few months ahead of his buddy Nelson. "At his request, I checked on Zee periodically," he said. "By the time Nelson got home, the relationship between Zee and me had grown way beyond friendship or simple mutual attraction. We knew we loved each other and would have to hurt Nelson."

"I also knew I was pregnant," Zee said, reaching up to cover Bryan's hand with her own. "Pregnant with you, Tate. I told Nelson the unvarnished truth. He remained calm, but laid down an ultimatum. If I went with my lover and his bastard child, I would never see Jack again."

Tears welled in her eyes as she smiled at her older son. "Jack, you were still a toddler. I loved you, something Nelson knew very well and used to his advantage. When I vowed never to see Bryan again, he said he forgave me and promised to rear Tate as his son."

"Which he did," Tate said.

His eyes locked with Bryan's. The man was his father, though he'd never met him before last night. And the man he had known and loved as his father had been gunned down right before his eyes.

"I didn't know about Nelson's ultimatum," Bryan said, continuing the story. "I just got a note from Zee saying that our affair—and I couldn't believe she'd given it such a shoddy name—was over and that she wished it had never happened."

Despair had prompted him to volunteer for a dangerous overseas mission. When his plane malfunctioned and began spiraling down toward the ocean, he actually welcomed death, since he'd just as soon die as have to live without Zee. Fate intervened, however, and he was rescued.

While recovering from the injuries he had sustained, the FBI approached him. He had already been trained in intelligence work. They proposed that Bryan Tate remain "dead" and start working for them undercover. That's what he'd been doing for the last thirty years.

"When I could, I came to see you, Tate," he said to his son. "From a careful distance, never getting close enough to risk running into Nelson or Zee, I watched you play football a few times. I even tracked you around the base in Nam for a week. I was at your graduation from UT and law school. I never stopped loving you or your mother."

"And Nelson never forgot or forgave me," Zee said, bowing her head and sniffing into a Kleenex.

Bryan touched her hair consolingly, then picked up the story again. His latest assignment had been to infiltrate a white supremacist group operating out of the northwestern states. At the outset, he had come across an extremely bitter Vietnam vet whom he recognized as Eddy Paschal, Tate's former college roommate.

"We already had a thick dossier on him because he had been implicated in several subversive and neo-Nazi activities, including a few ritualistic executions, although we never had enough evidence to indict him."

"Jeez, and to think I slept with him," Fancy said with a shudder.

"You couldn't have known," Dorothy Rae said kindly. "He had us all fooled."

"I would rather have kept him alive," Bryan said. "He was ruthless, but extremely intelligent. He could have been very useful to the Bureau."

Bryan looked toward Tate. "You can imagine how astonished I was when Nelson contacted him, especially since Paschal's philosophies were antithetical to yours. Nelson cleaned him up, gave him that spick-and-span image, paid for a crash course in public relations and communications, and brought him to Texas to be your campaign manager. That's when I realized that Nelson's intentions weren't what they seemed."

Tate backed into the wall and leaned his head against the pastel plaster. "So he planned to have me killed all along. It was one big setup. He groomed me for public office, instilled in me an ambition for it, hired Eddy, everything."

"I'm afraid so," Bryan said grimly.

Zee left her chair and went to Tate. "Darling, forgive me."

"Forgive you?"

"It was my sin he was punishing, not yours," she explained. "You were merely the sacrificial lamb. He wanted me to suffer and knew that the worst punishment possible for a mother would be to see her child die, especially during a moment of personal triumph."

"I can't believe it," Jack said, also coming to his feet.

"I can," Tate admitted quietly. "Now that I think back

on everything, I can believe it. You know how he preached about justice, fairness, paying for one's mistakes, retribution for transgressions? He believed you had made atonement with your life,'' he said, nodding toward Bryan, ''but mother hadn't yet paid for betraying him.''

''Nelson was very subtle, very clever,'' Zee said. ''Until last night I didn't realize just how clever or how vindictive. Tate, he manipulated you into marrying Carole, a woman he was sure would remind me of my own unfaithfulness. I had to close my eyes to her flagrant infidelity. I couldn't very well criticize her for committing the same sin I had.''

''It wasn't the same, Zee.''

''I know that, Bryan,'' she stressed, ''but Nelson didn't. Adultery was adultery in his estimation, and punishable by death.''

Jack was upset. His face was pale, ravaged from a night of mourning. ''It still doesn't make sense to me. Why, if he hated Bryan so much, did he name the baby Tate?''

''Another cruel joke on me,'' Zee said. ''It would be another constant reminder of my sin.''

Jack pondered that for a moment. ''Why did he favor Tate over me? I was his real son, but he always made me feel inferior to my younger brother.''

''He counted on human nature taking its course,'' Zee explained. ''He made it obvious that he favored Tate so that you would resent him. The friction between you would be another burden for me to bear.''

Jack stubbornly shook his head. ''I still can't believe he was so conniving. Not Dad.'' Dorothy Rae reached for his hand and pressed it between hers.

Zee turned toward Avery, who had remained silent throughout. ''He was dedicated to getting vengeance on me. He arranged for Tate to marry Carole Navarro. Even after I learned of her shady past, it never occurred to me that Nelson was responsible for her conversion from topless dancer to wife. Now I believe that he engineered that, just as he recruited Eddy. In any case, they formed an alliance at some point.

''Carole was instructed to eat away at Tate's emotions. Nelson knew that the unhappier Tate was, the unhappier I would be. She did everything she was told to do and then some. The only decision she made independently was to have an abortion. I don't think Nelson knew about that. It made him furious, but only because he was afraid it would cost Tate the election.''

Zee moved toward the bed and took Avery's hand. ''Can you forgive me for the cruel accusations I made against you?''

''You didn't know,'' she said gruffly. ''And Carole deserved your antipathy.''

''I'm sorry about your friend Mr. Lovejoy, Ms. Daniels.'' Bryan's expression was gentle—far different from when he'd taken aim on Eddy and fired. ''We had a guy watching Paschal, but he slipped past him that night.''

''Van is really the one responsible for saving Tate's life,'' Avery said emotionally. ''He must have viewed hours of video before finding the tape that explained why Eddy Paschal looked familiar to him. Eddy must have eluded your tail on several occasions, Mr. Tate, because he no doubt followed me to Irish's house. That's how he knew they were connected. It also helped him trace who Carole really was.''

''Have you heard anything about Mr. McCabe's condition?''

She smiled through her tears. ''After I insisted, they let me see him this morning. He's still in an ICU and his condition is serious, but they think he's going to pull through.''

''Ironically, McCabe's massive heart attack saved his life. It kept Paschal from shooting him. Paschal's mistake was not making certain McCabe was dead when he dragged him off that elevator.

''May I ask, Ms. Daniels,'' Bryan continued, ''what first clued you that Mr. Paschal was going to make an attempt on Tate's life?''

''She was told,'' Tate said.

Surprised reaction went through the group like an electric current. Jack was the first to speak. ''By whom? When?''

''When I was in the hospital,'' she replied, ''while I was still bandaged and being taken for Carole.'' She explained her involvement from that time up to the moment the night before when she had rushed up on the stage. When she finished, she glanced at Bryan and apologetically said, ''I thought you were a hired killer.''

"So you did notice me?"

"I have a reporter's trained eye."

"No," he said, "I was personally involved and not as careful as usual. I took tremendous chances of being recognized in order to stay close to Tate."

"I still can't distinguish the voice, but I believe it was Nelson, not Eddy, who spoke to me that night in the hospital," Avery remarked, "though I'll admit it never occurred to me that he would be the one."

On her behalf, Bryan said, "Ms. Daniels couldn't say anything to anyone at the risk of putting her own life in danger."

"And Tate's," she added, shyly casting her eyes downward when he glanced at her sharply.

Jack said, "You probably thought I was out to kill my brother. Cain and Abel."

"It did cross my mind on more than one occasion, Jack. I'm sorry." Because he and Dorothy Rae were still holding hands, she refrained from mentioning his infatuation with Carole.

"I think it's freaking wonderful how you pulled it off," Fancy declared. "Pretending to be Carole, I mean."

"It couldn't have been easy," Dorothy Rae said, slipping her arm through her husband's. "I'm sure you're glad that everything's out in the open." She gave Avery a look that conveyed a silent thank-you. It made sense to her now why her sister-in-law had been so compassionate and helpful recently. "Is that all, Mr. Tate? Are we free to go and let Avery rest?"

"Call me Bryan, and yes, that's all for now."

They filed out. Zee moved to Avery's side. "How can I ever repay you for saving my son's life?"

"I don't want any repayment. Not everything was faked." The two women exchanged a meaningful gaze. Zee patted her hand and left under Bryan's protective arm.

The silence they left behind was ponderous. Tate finally left his position against the wall and moved to the foot of her bed. "They'll probably get married," he remarked.

"How will you feel about that, Tate?"

He studied the toes of his boots for a moment before

raising his head. "Who could blame them? They've been in love with each other for longer than I've been alive."

"It's easy now to understand why Zee always seemed so sad."

"Dad kept her an emotional prisoner." He gave a dry laugh. "Guess I can't refer to him as *Dad* anymore, can I?"

"Why not? That's what Nelson was to you. Whatever his motives were, he was a good father."

"I guess so." He gave her a lengthy stare. "I should have believed you yesterday when you tried to warn me."

"It was too unbelievable for you to accept."

"But you were right."

She shook her head. "I never suspected Nelson. Eddy, yes. Even Jack. But never Nelson."

"I want to mourn his death, but when I hear how cruel he's been to my mother, and that he hired my best friend to kill me . . . Jesus.'; He exhaled loudly, raking his hand through his hair. Tears came to his eyes.

"Don't be so hard on yourself, Tate. You've got a lot to deal with all at once." She wanted to hold him and comfort him, but he hadn't asked her to and, until he did, she had no right to.

"When you do your story, I have one favor to ask."

"There won't be a story."

"There'll be a story," he argued firmly. He rounded the foot of the bed and sat down on the edge of it. "You're already being hailed as a heroine."

"You shouldn't have revealed my identity during the press conference this morning." She had watched it on the set in her hospital room while it was being broadcast live from the lobby of the Palacio Del Rio. "You could have divorced me as Carole, as you planned to."

"I can't begin my political career with a lie, Avery."

"That's the first time you've ever called me by my name," she whispered, left breathless from hearing it on his lips.

Their gazes held for a moment, then he continued. "So far, no one but the people who were in this room, and I guess a few FBI agents, know that Nelson Rutledge engineered the plot. They've surmised that it was all Eddy's doing and have attributed it to his disillusionment in America after the war. I'm asking you to keep it that way, for my family's sake. Mostly for my mother's sake.''

"If anyone asks, I will. But I won't do a story."

"Yes, you will."

Tears started in her eyes again. Fretfully, she groped for his hand. "I can't stand having you think I did this to exploit you, or that I did it for fame and glory."

"I think you did it for the reason you told me yesterday, and which I stubbornly refused to believe—because you love me."

Her heart went a little crazy. She threaded her fingers through his hair. "I do, Tate. More than my life."

He gazed at the bandage on her shoulder and, shuddering slightly, squeezed his eyes closed. When he opened them again, they were misty. "I know."

EPILOGUE

"Watching it again?"

Senator Tate Rutledge entered the living room of the comfortable Georgetown town home he shared with his wife and daughter. On this particular afternoon, he caught Avery alone in the living room, watching a tape of her documentary.

The story she had produced, at Tate's insistence, aired on PBS stations across the country six months into his term. The facts were presented fairly, concisely, and without any embellishment in spite of her personal involvement.

Tate had convinced her that the public had a right to know about the bizarre chain of events that had started with the crash of Flight 398 and culminated on election night.

He further stated that no one could report the events with more insight and sensitivity than she. His final argument was that he didn't want his first term as senator to be clouded by lies and half-truths. He would rather have the public know than speculate.

The documentary hadn't won Avery a Pulitzer prize, though it was acclaimed by viewers, critics, and colleagues. She was currently considering the offers she had received to produce documentaries on a variety of subjects.

"Still basking in the glory, huh?" Tate laid his briefcase on an end table and shrugged off his jacket.

"Don't tease." She reached behind her for his hand and kissed the back of it as she pulled him around to join her on the sofa. "Irish called today. He made me think of it."

Irish had survived the heart attack he had suffered in the elevator at the Palacio Del Rio. He claimed that he had actually died and come back to life. How else could Paschal have failed to feel a pulse? He swore that he remembered floating out of himself, looking down and seeing Paschal drag his body into the alcove.

But then, everybody who knew Irish well teased him about his Celtic superstition and closet Catholicism. All that was important to Avery was that she hadn't lost him.

At the conclusion of the piece, before the tape went to black, a message appeared in the middle of the screen. It read, "Dedicated to the memory of Van Lovejoy."

"We're too far away for me to put flowers on his grave," she said huskily. "Watching his work is how I pay tribute." She clicked off the machine and set the transmitter aside.

Nelson's machinations had impacted their lives and they would never be completely free from the memories. Jack was still grappling with his disillusionment about his father. He had chosen to stay and manage the law firm in San Antonio rather than join Tate's staff in Washington. Though they were apart geographically, the half brothers had never been closer. It was hoped that time would eventually heal the heartache they had in common.

Tate struggled daily to assimilate Nelson's grand scheme, but also mourned the loss of the man he'd always known as

Dad. He adamantly kept the two personas separate in his mind.

His emotions regarding Bryan Tate were conflicting. He liked him, respected him, and appreciated him for the happiness he'd given Zee since their marriage. Yet he wasn't quite prepared to call him father, a kinship he could never claim publicly, even if he acknowledged it privately.

During those moments of emotional warfare, his wife's love and support helped tremendously.

Thinking on it all now, Tate drew her into his arms, receiving as much comfort as he gave. He hugged her close for a long time, turning his face into her neck.

"Have I ever told you what a courageous, fascinating woman I think you are for doing what you did, even though it placed your own life in jeopardy? God, when I think back on that night, to when I felt your blood running over my hands." He pressed a kiss onto her neck. "I had fallen in love with my wife again, and I couldn't understand why. Before I really ever discovered you, I almost lost you."

"I wasn't sure it would matter," she said. He raised his head and looked at her quizzically. "I was afraid that when you found out who I really was, you wouldn't want me anymore."

He pulled her into his arms again. "I wanted you. I still want you." The way he said it left no doubt in her mind. The way he kissed her made it a covenant as binding as the marriage vows they had taken months earlier.

"I'm still finding out who you really are, even though I know you intimately," he whispered into her mouth, "more intimately than I've known any other woman, and that's the God's truth. I know what you feel like inside, and how every part of your body tastes."

He kissed her again with love and unappeasable passion.

"Tate," she sighed when they drew apart, "when you look into my face, who do you see?"

"The woman I owe my life to. The woman who saved Mandy from emotional deprivation. The woman who is carrying my child." Warmly, he caressed her swollen abdomen. "The woman I love more than breath."

"No, I mean—"

"I know what you mean." He eased her back against the sofa cushions and followed her down, cradling her face between his hands and touching her mouth with his. "I see Avery."

VISIT US ONLINE AT

WWW.HACHETTEBOOKGROUP.COM

FEATURES:

**OPENBOOK BROWSE AND
SEARCH EXCERPTS**

•

AUDIOBOOK EXCERPTS AND PODCASTS

•

AUTHOR ARTICLES AND INTERVIEWS

•

**BESTSELLER AND PUBLISHING
GROUP NEWS**

•

SIGN UP FOR E-NEWSLETTERS

•

**AUTHOR APPEARANCES AND TOUR
INFORMATION**

•

SOCIAL MEDIA FEEDS AND WIDGETS

•

DOWNLOAD FREE APPS

BOOKMARK HACHETTE BOOK GROUP
@ WWW.HACHETTEBOOKGROUP.COM